EMMY LAYBOURNE

RANSACKER

FEIWEL AND FRIENDS

NEW YORK

A Feiwel and Friends Book

An imprint of Macmillan Publishing Group, LLC

175 Fifth Avenue, New York, NY 10010

Our books may be purchased in bulk for promotional, educational, or business use. Please contact your local bookseller or the Macmillan Corporate and Premium Sales Department at (800) 221-7945 ext. 5442 or by e-mail at MacmillanSpecialMarkets@macmillan.com.

Library of Congress Cataloging-in-Publication Data

Names: Laybourne, Emmy, author.
Title: Ransacker / Emmy Laybourne.
Description: First edition. | New York : Feiwel and Friends, 2018. | Sequel to: Berserker. |
    Summary: Sixteen-year-old Sissel Hemstad and her siblings have been living
    peacefully in small-town Montana, but two men, one a mine owner and one a Pinkerton
    spy, are courting her, knowing her gift as a Ransacker could doom them all.
Identifiers: LCCN 2018003164| ISBN 978-1-250-13414-1 (hardcover) |
    ISBN 978-1-250-13415-8 (ebook)
Subjects: | CYAC: Ability—Fiction. | Supernatural—Fiction. | Brothers and sisters—
    Fiction. | Frontier and pioneer life—Montana—Fiction. | Immigrants—Fiction. |
    Norwegian Americans—Fiction. | Mythology, Norse—Fiction. | Montana—History—
    19th century—Fiction.
Classification: LCC PZ7.L4458 Ran 2018 | DDC [Fic]—dc23
LC record available at https://lccn.loc.gov/2018003164

Book design by Liz Dresner

Feiwel and Friends logo designed by Filomena Tuosto

First edition, 2019

10 9 8 7 6 5 4 3 2 1

For Rex

My dearest Stieg,

*I cannot tell you how glad I was to find your letter of June 10
waiting for me at the address of our contact in Årstad. Forgive me
if I overstep in any way, but I must tell you I am concerned—you say
the days have settled into a routine you find monotonous. You write
that life in a small town is often dull and your students have little
ambition to learn beyond the rudiments. I say thank the Gods if your
life is dull.*

    *My young friend, do not forget what your sister has done and is
capable of doing. Do not become complacent in your comfortable
small town.*

    *Since the death of his wife, the Baron Fjelstad has become
obsessed with the Nytte and those gifted with its powers. Though
Agatha could be demanding, I see now that she had a calming
influence on her husband. I serve the Baron as best I can, though his
intensity of purpose chills me at times.*

    *The Baron has assured me many times that he had no part in the
violence the Berserker Ketil brought to your family, but after all this
time, I remain uncertain.*

    *You should know that we have encountered no females with
the Nytte in the past year. This concerns the Baron. If he knew of
your sister Hanne's talents, he would come, himself, all the way to
Montana to seek her out. Of this I am certain. Though I respect him,*

I am convinced he must never learn of the powers you and your siblings possess. This is why I urge caution and restraint.

Do not think me hard-hearted. It is my love for you "Hemstads" that makes me stern.

I dearly miss our study sessions by the fire. I'm a foolish old man—here I sit, surrounded by luxury, thinking fondly of the miserable winter we all spent together huddled in that tiny homestead cabin.

I pray daily and nightly to Odin All-Father for your safekeeping and your continuing health, all of you.

Most sincerely,
Rolf Tjossem

CHAPTER ONE

JULY 1886

CARTER, MONTANA

S issel sat on a branch that swept low from an old willow, watching Stieg work his Nytte.

Her brother pressed two fingers to his temple and began, creating a little gust of wind at his feet. He made it puff, puff, puff, like a living pulse.

Then he made the gust grow and turn on itself, funneling it into a little dirt devil.

Watching it closely, Stieg made it whirl over to Sissel and pluck at her skirt.

"Don't," she said. "You'll muss my clothes, and Hanne will wring your neck."

The dancing funnel of air lay down at her feet like an obedient dog.

Stieg paused to remove his vest. He pressed his sleeve to his face to blot the sweat.

Stieg did exercises every day to improve his control over his Nytte—the ancient Viking blood-gift that ran in both sides of their family tree.

He turned his attention on the hazy mountains in the distance, shrouded in thin, peevish clouds. His tall, lanky body was drawn ramrod straight, taut with energy.

Stieg pressed his head with both hands. Sissel saw lightning dance above the closest peak.

"That's very good!" she said, clapping. "Even better than last time. There's more lightning and it's brighter."

Stieg exhaled. He made a gesture as if doffing his cap to acknowledge the compliment, then he leaned forward to put his hands on his knees and breathed deeply for a moment, catching his breath.

With his daily practice sessions, Stieg had been able to put an end to the headaches that used to plague him whenever he used his Nytte. The exercises had been prescribed to him by their wise and trusted friend Rolf Tjossem, before Rolf had returned to Norway two and a half years ago.

Now came Sissel's favorite part of the practice sessions. Stieg turned toward their sister Hanne's small garden near the side of the house, to water it. At Hanne's insistence, establishing the garden was the first thing they had done after building the house, just over two years ago. It was a magnificent garden, thanks to Stieg's Nytte, but the Hemstads never drew attention to it when they had visitors. They wanted to seem plain and commonplace, and keep their gifts a secret.

The garden was abundant and lovely—a tangle of vines splashed with colorful produce. The tomatoes were colossal—huge, beautiful fruits, skins nearly splitting apart. Snap peas and wax beans grew in a tangle over the brace Hanne's fiancé, Owen, had built. Fat purple cabbages grew in tidy rows next to giant acorn squashes with such thick rinds they had to be split with an ax.

Stieg stepped closer to the garden. He placed one fingertip on each temple and closed his eyes.

Sissel watched the air. She always tried to see it happen, but the cloud materialized in wisps so delicate the eye couldn't perceive them at first. Then they were there—white filaments drifting in the air, like tendrils of wool, fattening by the moment. Under Stieg's power, they floated together and began to swirl and dance.

A weight of gray gathered in the belly of the new cloud.

The top layer of the garden soil was bleached tan by the midsummer sun. *Splat*. Then another fat *splat*. Dots of deep brown appeared as Stieg let the raindrops fall from his cloud.

"That's the way!" Sissel called. She breathed in deeply as the sweet smell of the rain spread in the dry air.

Once the cloud was nearly spent, Stieg released a great breath. He staggered a bit, holding his hands out to steady himself.

"You're not supposed to hold your breath," Sissel reminded him. The cloud dried up in the air and was gone.

Sissel walked over to where Stieg stood. "Rolf wanted you to keep breathing."

Stieg brought his hands up to his forehead and massaged his temples.

"It's difficult," he admitted.

They walked to the house. Hanne was inside, preparing supper, and Owen and Knut would be making their way in from the fields to wash up.

"Why do you think it is so difficult to remember to breathe?" Sissel asked. "I'm truly curious."

Stieg thought for a moment, looking back at the wet, glistening garden.

"Because it sweeps me up. I feel connected to a great source of power. When I use my Nytte, I rather forget I have a body to begin with." There was a faint smile on Stieg's face, and a stab of envy pierced Sissel's chest.

Sissel's sister and two brothers each had a Nytte. Stieg was a Storm-Rend. Hanne was a Berserker, driven to kill to protect herself or anyone she loved. Knut was an Oar-Breaker. Knut had tremendous strength that would have been used in the days of the Vikings to row their massive ships.

Sissel, the youngest, had no power. This was not uncommon. The Nytte often skipped children in a family—in fact, it was unusual that three of the four Hemstad siblings had received a gift, and one of them a girl.

Still, it rankled Sissel. It was hard to forget how different she was. It did not help that her siblings were healthy and strong, while she was thin, underdeveloped, and had a limp from an old injury. Her leg ached after her daily walks to and from school with Stieg, but she would not admit it. She had spent her childhood complaining, and now, at sixteen, she had made up her mind not to bring the habit into her adulthood.

"We should write to Rolf and tell him of your progress," Sissel said. "He'd be proud of you."

"He'd be proud of you as well."

"How so?"

"Your studies. Your English is nearly better than mine."

Sissel set her foot down wrong, and a shock of pain seized her calf. She bent and took hold of it to calm the spasm.

"I wish you would let your beau drive us home from school in his wagon," Stieg said.

"No," she said through gritted teeth.

"It's cruel to him, actually. He wants to spend his every waking hour with you, but you hold him at a distance."

Sissel did not want to talk about her beau right now. And not with her brother.

"The walk is good for me. It's making me stronger."

"If you say so," Stieg said.

Sissel straightened up, and Stieg searched her face, concern etched on his features.

"Please don't worry about me," Sissel said with irritation. "It makes me tired."

"I'm sorry."

Stieg offered a smile. He exhaled, and a puff of wind toyed with the hem of her skirt.

"Don't," Sissel said. She held her skirt down with her hands.

"I will never worry about you again, I promise."

He blew the wind at her more strongly.

"Stop it!" Sissel said. She gathered her skirt away from him and walked ahead.

"I was only teasing," he said.

"I know," Sissel said, not turning back. "I'm going in. Hanne might need my help."

They came around the side of their pretty timber house. It had two rooms—a large living area with a loft above for the boys, and a small bedroom, which Sissel and Hanne shared. The living room had a cookstove in the center that served to divide the room into two halves—a kitchen, with cabinets built along the walls, and a cozy space with a table and chairs.

The brothers shared the loft with their future brother-in-law, Owen Bennett. Owen had hired on to serve as their guide when they first came to Montana. That journey had turned dangerous and deadly, when a Norwegian baron sent a bloodthirsty Berserker to track them down. Owen had learned the truth about the Hemstads and their powers. By the end of the ordeal, he and Hanne had become sweethearts.

Hanne and Owen were waiting to marry until the harvest was in, so they could afford a wedding and the addition of another bedroom onto the little house.

Their first winter in the United States had been cramped and difficult. They spent it in an abandoned homestead cabin that a friend of Owen's had told them about, provisioning themselves from a town ten miles away. During those long months Rolf had taught them everything he knew about the Nytte.

In the spring the Hemstads had traveled east to the small, burgeoning railroad town of Carter. They used the remainder of the money they had brought from Norway—some cash and two ancient Viking gold coins—to purchase the land and the building materials for the main house.

For now, the family's only income was Stieg's salary from his teaching work, but soon the wheat would be harvested and then there would be enough for lumber, and a wedding feast and a cake.

The door to their house was open, and inside, Hanne was humming to herself. She set a large loaf of brown bread on the table and a slab of her homemade cheese beside it.

"You look like a happy young wife," Sissel told her as she came limping through the door.

Hanne gave Sissel a smile. She had on a clean apron over her faded blue work dress. Hanne wore her blond hair in a plaited crown, though few young women wore their hair that way in America.

She placed a large platter of sliced tomatoes floating in a pool of fresh cream on the table.

"It was so hot in the house today," Hanne said. "I couldn't bear to cook a hot meal. I hope the boys don't mind."

Sissel sank into a chair that had been placed near the door.

"Are you all right?" Hanne asked.

"Yes," Sissel said. "Fine."

Stieg came in, followed by Knut, sweaty from his work in the wheat fields.

"Hello!" Knut said. "Is supper ready?" Knut was six foot six, a giant of a man, even though he was only seventeen, with a broad, well-muscled torso and huge, strong arms. His blond hair was plastered to his head in the shape of the crown of his wide hat.

Owen slipped in the door behind Knut. He was of medium height, with wavy brown hair and kind-looking brown eyes. He went straight to Hanne and pecked her on the cheek. Daisy, Owen's cow dog, followed him in. She paused to lap at the water bowl set inside the door.

"Did you have a good day?" Owen asked Hanne. She began to answer but Knut interrupted.

"No meat?" Knut said as he looked over the table.

Sissel felt bad for him. The food was intended to feed five, and he probably could have eaten it all himself.

"It was a very hot day," Hanne said, irritated. "I thought a cool supper would be best."

Knut shrugged. "I'm hungry."

"We've got plenty of tomatoes."

"I'm hungry for meat," he said.

"There's some roast chicken in the root cellar," Hanne said, relenting. "Go fetch it up and I'll cut some slices."

A smile broke over Knut's broad face.

"Thank you, Sister." He ambled out to fetch the chicken.

"I look forward to when the harvest comes in so we can afford some beef," Hanne said.

"The end of summer term is but a few weeks away," Stieg said.

"And the wheat is coming along real good," Owen said. "The heads are nice and fat. Everyone says we had just the right amount of rain this spring."

"Say," Stieg said, "the evening is so fine and still. Shall we bring the table outside to eat?"

"That's a lovely idea," Hanne said.

So the newly set table was un-set, and Owen and Stieg carried it outside.

Hanne lifted the platter with the tomatoes, and Sissel reached forward to take it.

"It's a bit heavy," Hanne said.

"I'm fine," Sissel answered.

"I think it's too heavy for you. But you could bring the plates."

"Please, Hanne. Don't baby me. I can carry a platter of tomatoes!"

Hanne bit the inside of her lip. "Very well." She released it into Sissel's hands, and Sissel turned for the door.

It *was* too heavy. Sissel knew it instantly.

She took two steps toward the door. Her arms began to tremble. She gritted her teeth.

Sissel lowered the platter slightly and inched out the door, as Stieg bounded back into the house, coming to fetch the chairs. Sissel shifted the platter to avoid him, but too late . . .

The edge of the platter slipped from her hands, and the beautiful red slices of fruit slid onto the ground, the cream raining down around them.

Then the platter tumbled out of her hands and fell. It broke in two pieces over a half-buried rock.

"Oh!" Sissel cried.

"Sissel!" snapped Hanne, coming to the door.

"It was my fault," Stieg said quickly. "I bumped her."

Tears welled up in Sissel's eyes.

"It wasn't your fault," she said. "It was mine!"

"Come, come. It's all right." Stieg bent over and scooped the tomatoes back onto the larger half of the broken platter. "We can eat a little dirt. It's all right."

Sissel turned back into the house, pushing past Hanne.

"Don't run off, Sissel," Hanne said. Her voice was thin and tired. "It's all right."

Sissel limped to their bedroom. She wanted to be alone.

"I'm sorry," Sissel said over her shoulder. "I should have known better."

Sissel went to splash her face with water at the washbasin, and instead she stopped, gazing into the looking glass nailed above it. She saw her thin, peaked face; her limp hair, so white blond as to be colorless; her pale eyes too large and rimmed with red. It was not a face she liked much.

She was weak, too weak to carry a platter of tomatoes. She cursed herself as she lay down on her bed—that she should be so feeble, that she should be so prideful, and that she should cry over it all.

She closed her eyes, hoping to compose herself for a moment.

When Sissel woke, it was dark. Hanne was in her own bed, across the narrow gap. Her sister's shoulders rose and fell with sound, steady sleep.

There was a slice of bread topped with cheese waiting on the crate they used as a bedside table, along with a covered dish containing a pretty slice of tomato in cream sauce.

CHAPTER TWO

The next day, Sissel thought she would help preserve the rest of the tomatoes, but Hanne wouldn't let her near the stove. Apparently Sissel's slip with the platter had been forgiven, but not forgotten.

Hanne fished the empty, sterilized jars out from the boiling water with a pair of wooden spoons and filled them with the stewed fruit. Her shirtsleeves were rolled up, and her face was flushed and sweaty.

"I don't remember last July being so hot, do you?" Hanne asked. "Owen says it's good weather for the wheat. That may be, but it's bad weather for kitchen work, and yet it must be done."

"I wish you'd let me help," Sissel said.

"Just sit, Sissel. Sit and rest and tell me about school to keep me entertained," Hanne said. "Has Howie asked Alice to the dance yet?" There was a leading, playful tone in Hanne's voice. Sissel knew where this was going.

"No," Sissel said. "*None* of the boys have asked any of the girls yet."

"What on earth are *they* waiting for?" Hanne said. "It's just a few weeks away!"

Hanne wanted her to talk about her beau, James Peavy. All her siblings seemed fascinated by him.

Maybe they were all wondering what James saw in their frail little sister. Sissel certainly wondered herself.

James and his father had moved to town two years ago and bought the general store. They had come all the way from Chicago. James was undeniably handsome, with his dark brown eyes and hair that was a deep auburn, sometimes red and sometimes chestnut. Sissel often had to fight the urge to determine the color for once and for all by grabbing a handful and holding it up to the light.

James's father, Russell Peavy, looked nothing like him, and didn't have James's nice manners, either. But Russell was proud of his son, in a gruff way. He was proud enough of James to want him to go to college. That was why James was still in school at seventeen, an age when most were already doing a man's work.

Sissel didn't like talking about James with her siblings because he made her feel a little bit woozy. Not quite herself.

It seemed strange, even to her, that James was so taken with her. Sissel was far from the prettiest girl in class. Her figure was nearly free from curves, where many of the girls were fashionably plump and round. And her limp made her seem graceless at times, Sissel knew it did. Yet James hardly looked at another girl, except to be polite.

Privately, Sissel supposed James might like her because she was smart. She knew she was smart. She was at the head of the class without really even trying.

She understood mathematics, even the more complicated algebraic formulas. Sometimes she could do them in her head, while a peer struggled to figure at the blackboard. She also enjoyed history, both American and European. She liked it when Stieg quizzed her on the lineage of the old kings of Scandinavia. As for America, it was so new you could fit all its history in your pocket.

"Abigail Masterson has a new dress," Sissel told her sister. "It's a coral-colored poplin with full hoopskirt. She looked like a great pink cloud. I suppose all the girls will now copy the fashion."

"When the wheat comes in, we could make you a dress like that," Hanne said.

"We'll make you a wedding dress when the wheat comes in. And if you wish it to have a hoopskirt, that's your own mistake!" Sissel replied. Hanne smiled at that.

"We're probably better off without them," Hanne said. "I hear they are very inconvenient."

"I hear just the opposite," Sissel said.

"Really?"

"One can hide things under them . . . like a butter churn. Or a small child."

Hanne let out a distinctly unladylike snort of laughter.

"I'd like to see that!" Hanne said.

"I bet you could fit a cannon under a full hoopskirt," Sissel said. "Only how could you hold it between your knees?"

"Sissel!" Hanne said, laughing so hard she had to dab tears from her eyes.

That made Sissel feel better. Maybe she couldn't help much with the chores, but at least she could make her sister laugh.

"You can make fun of hoopskirts all you like, little sister, however"—Hanne turned from the stove and leveled her wooden spoon at Sissel—"you need a new dress. The Ladies' Aid dance will be here soon. And James Peavy is sure to ask you."

"He hasn't asked me, though," Sissel said.

"I know. But he will," Hanne said. "He wouldn't come around visiting all the time, and bringing you candy from the store, and mooning over you—"

"Shhh!" Sissel said.

"What will you wear?" Hanne said.

"I will wear my church dress," Sissel said.

"No. It's too old."

"Then I'll wear yours."

"Sissel!"

What would it be like to dance with James? Sissel imagined his hands set down low on her back, and felt a blush spreading across her face. She picked at the fabric of the white shirt she wore. It clung to her neck with a thin layer of perspiration.

"I'll meet you in town after school on Monday. We can go to the Oswalds' shop, and Alice will help us pick out a good fabric," Hanne said.

Stieg strode in. He had four eggs in his hands.

"I found some eggs, Sister," Stieg said, holding them out to Hanne. "Some of the chickens are hiding them near the cow's bedding."

"Set them in the basket, please," Hanne said. "I'm in tomatoes up to my elbows."

Stieg put the eggs down and went to the girls' bedroom, where they kept the basin for washing hands.

"Sissel, grammar awaits us," Stieg said, returning. "I think we should review reduced relative clauses this afternoon."

"English is a horrible language," Sissel said.

"I thought you were trying not to complain anymore," Stieg reminded her.

"I'm not complaining; I'm stating a fact."

Stieg took his notebook, their grammar book, and Sissel's slate from the shelf where they sat, along with his prized volumes of Ibsen, Dickens, and Shakespeare. Sissel made her way to the table.

"Say, I heard James Peavy is renting a buggy to take you to the dance," Stieg said.

"Oh, for goodness' sake, he hasn't even asked me!" Sissel said. "And if he does, who's to say I'll say yes?"

"I believe you dislike him because he's so handsome," Stieg said. "That's not right. Even handsome men deserve to be taken seriously."

"You are an unkind person, Stieg Hemstad. I refuse to study grammar with such a bully."

Stieg was about to make a response when Hanne dropped a pot with a clatter. Tomatoes splattered onto the tidy plank floor. Sissel looked up to her sister's face and found Hanne frowning toward the door.

"There's something wrong," Hanne said. She strode over to the doorway. Distracted, she wiped her wet hands on her spattered apron, only smearing them more.

Sissel came to look out over Hanne's shoulder. To the south the sky was a strange color, as if a bright stripe of yellow and green gray had been drawn at the horizon line.

"What is that?" Sissel asked with rising alarm. Stieg hurried over.

"It's a fire," Hanne said. "Wildfire!"

Hanne ran as fast as she could toward the fields where Owen and Knut were working. "Stay inside!" she called over her shoulder.

"Dear God, no," Stieg said. He pushed past Sissel and strode out into the yard.

"What do we do?" Sissel asked.

Hanne raced out of sight, over a rise on their land toward Owen and Knut. They were out in the beautiful, nearly ripe wheat fields, directly between the fire and the house.

Stieg began to pace in the yard.

"If we're lucky, it won't come this way," Stieg said.

He pressed his fingers to his temples.

"What are you doing?" Sissel asked.

"I'm going to blow it away. It will take our wheat!"

"But if you blow it away from us, it will go toward the town!" Sissel cried.

"Damn it all," Stieg yelled.

He pressed his head again and began to concentrate.

"What should I do?" Sissel cried.

"Quiet, now!" Stieg snapped. "I'm making it rain."

Sissel watched him for a moment. The air to the south was thickening with sick green smoke. She turned around, feeling terribly helpless.

"I'll go for water," Sissel said to no answer.

The sky was darkening at an alarming rate. Now Sissel could smell the fire, not a smell like wood smoke from a stove, but the smell of green things burning.

Sissel took the buckets and ran to the gully near their house as fast as her leg would allow. She pushed through the scrub oak and dropped the tin buckets into the stream with a clatter. Bits of ash were landing in the water like snowflakes.

Sissel lifted the heavy buckets. The water sloshed in the pails as she limped back toward the farm. Much of the water spilled, and she cursed her lame leg.

As she neared the house, she felt rain on her face.

Stieg stood in their yard, hands pressed to his temples. The rain fell in a circle around the house and the barn as he tried to wet down the structures so the fire would go around them.

"Stieg, is Hanne back? The boys?" Sissel tried to shout. Her words were strangled as she choked on the dense smoke now rolling over them.

Sissel turned to the fields. She could see the fire itself now, a terrible orange-and-yellow streak, racing toward their farm. It was moving faster than she could believe, faster than a horse or a train. It was like someone was drawing a blanket of fire up across the prairie.

She started toward the rise with her half-full buckets as Hanne, Owen, and Knut came stumbling to the house.

Hanne had her shoulder under Owen's and was half dragging him as he coughed and struggled to breathe. Daisy ran with them, barking at the fire and the smoke.

The heat was rising. It made everything in Sissel's vision shimmer and boil.

Hanne dropped Owen at the house.

"Sissel!" Hanne shouted.

"I brought water," Sissel said. She blinked, her eyes stinging from the smoke, and in that one blink Hanne was at her side. Hanne picked up the buckets, one at a time, and dumped the water over Sissel herself.

Sissel sputtered, shocked.

Hanne slung Sissel over her shoulder, like a shepherd would a lamb, and ran for the house. Sissel gasped for breath. Her belly and rib cage jounced against her sister's shoulder.

Rain pelted the house and the barn. Stieg was clutching his head with both hands. He fell to his knees as Hanne knelt and deposited Sissel on the ground.

"Are you all right?" Hanne asked Sissel.

Sissel could only cough, nodding her head. Her eyes streamed with tears, some from the smoke and some from her anger at being so useless. Daisy came to lick at Sissel's face, and she pushed the dog away.

"It's coming closer!" Knut cried. He was pacing within the circle of rain Stieg was holding.

The smoke and heat assaulted them.

Owen appeared from inside the house. He had their good wool blankets, which had been stored for the winter.

"We can beat it back with these!" he shouted.

"Come, Knut!" Hanne yelled. She grabbed a blanket and threw one to Knut.

The fire was upon them. It ran at the house, crackling and streaming in flaming runners around Stieg's circle.

Hanne, Knut, and Owen beat at the flames, trying to defend the edge of the circle. Daisy barked at the fire, as if she could chase it away.

Sissel lay there, good for nothing. Struggling just to breathe.

Stieg let out a cry of effort. The rain was evaporating in the terrible heat of the fire. Steam rose in great clouds.

"The house!" Owen shouted.

Fire licked at the house, sending black lines of scorch up the planks. Soon flames surrounded the two front windows, beautiful glass windows Owen had set with pride. They exploded outward in a shower of shards that caught orange and yellow.

Hanne shouted, "Into the barn!" Hanne tried to lift Sissel again, and she pulled away. Sissel struggled to her feet, holding her arm across her mouth, trying to breathe through the wet fabric. They all hurried to the barn. Owen dragged Daisy by the collar. She continued to bark at the fire, fiercely trying to scare it away.

Inside, the usual smells of hay, manure, and sod mingled with the terrible smoke.

Only a half dozen of their chickens were inside, the rest gone. Their cow, Buttermilk, was out to pasture! She was lost. And what of Owen's horse, Pal? Pal would have been yoked to the harrow . . .

"Owen!" Sissel said, her voice croaky. "Is Pal all right?"

But Owen was on his hands and knees, coughing, coughing until he vomited up black, tarry bile. He did not hear her.

Knut shut the great wooden door to the barn, dragging it along the rut in the earth.

Outside there was a roar and a crash from their house.

Hanne knelt next to Stieg, who was also on his knees. His eyes were fixed toward the ceiling, commanding the elements outside.

The temperature in the barn kept climbing. It was like being in an oven. Sissel sank down near the cow's stall. She struggled to breathe, drawing in painful gasps of the scorching air.

There were two narrow, empty slots high in the walls—glassless windows near the roof, set there to let in fresh air. Sissel saw flames licking at them.

Yellow light also shone through the cracks and chinks between the sod bricks. It looked like a scene from hell, all of them smeared with char, the harsh light from the dancing flames making their faces into hideous masks of shadow and light.

They did not have long now.

"*Ásáheill*," Hanne began to pray in Norwegian. "Hear me, Odin; hear me, Freya. Strengthen our brother! Great Thor, lend us your strength."

She knelt next to Stieg. Knut came, too, putting his large meaty hands on his older brother's thin shoulders.

"*Ásáheill!*" Knut said. "Father Odin, help my brother!"

Stieg began to tremble. He gave a great roar, as if spending all his remaining strength at once.

Sissel felt something hit her neck. Like pebbles. She looked over her shoulder, and there, coming through the high window in the wall—hail!

"You're doing it, Stieg!" Sissel cried. "It's working!"

The heat was still fierce, but the crackle of flames receded. The sound of the fire moved past them, racing north.

Then the yellow glare through the cracks went dark.

"Praise the Gods!" Hanne cried.

The fire had passed them by.

Stieg fell back into Knut's arms. Hanne collapsed onto them, weeping, embracing them both. Owen staggered to them and threw his arms around them all.

Sissel could not rise to join the huddle of bodies. She could not get her breath. More hail spattered through the window. One bit landed near her face, and she looked at it.

Ice. Ice in a wildfire.

Her brother had magic. Powerful magic. His gift had saved them— the Nytte had saved them.

And she had helped not one bit.

22

CHAPTER THREE

James Peavy rode fast, grimly assessing the possibility the Hemstads had survived the wildfire.

The fire had cut a swath miles wide across the prairie. Every bit of brush and low-lying plant life in its path had been incinerated. A few broken black trees jutted here and there, forsaken scarecrows protecting nothing at all.

There were houses beyond the charred fields, James knew that. He knew the Hemstads' neighbors: the Hensleys, the Wicks, and the Baylors. He had taken pains to introduce himself, to spread goodwill. He had delivered groceries and other supplies from the store to these neighbors, sweating and straining to unload their purchases from the wagon. Country folk took their time to come to trust city folk.

It had been dull, slow work, earning their trust. It had taken months. And it had taken far longer to get the Hemstads themselves to trust him. They were wary and skittish.

From what James had read in the files pertaining to the case, they had every right to be.

The Pinkertons had been briefed by their client, a Norwegian baron named Fjelstad. There had been a big mix-up several years ago. Sissel's brother Knut had been falsely accused of a series of gristly murders in Norway. Months later, in America, a dead man had been identified as Knut, and the reward claimed.

Coming to America, Knut and his siblings had all changed their last name to Hemstad. But even though the warrant had been canceled and their last name didn't match, Knut still looked everything like the man on the wanted poster. It would be easy for a bounty hunter with the outdated poster to try to bring him in or take a shot at him. The Pinkertons were there to prevent that.

The Baron not only wanted the Hemstads protected, he wanted them observed. He seemed, to James's mind, a bit obsessed with them. James's boss and make-believe father, Russell Peavy, had to file weekly reports on all the Hemstads' doings, no matter how routine.

That was fine with James. The Baron was rich, the Pinkertons paid well, and this was the easiest job he'd ever worked. Much easier than his last job as a bellboy at the Palmer House back in Chicago.

When one of the guests at the hotel had noticed James flirting with an older woman, the wife of a prominent businessman, James was sure he'd be sacked. Instead, he was offered a job. The guest was a Pinkerton agent, and if he hadn't had the badge, James wouldn't have believed him about the job. New clothes, a train ticket west, a chance to go to school, and all he had to do was keep tabs on a schoolgirl?

He'd signed up on the spot.

Now the job was over, James thought bitterly. It had to be.

James had no hope for the Hemstads as his horse galloped past the blackened fields. Who could survive this?

He thought of Sissel and felt his chest tighten up with emotion. He liked her more than he'd ever thought he would. Sissel was thin and sickly, but never complained about it. Instead, she was funny. She told the truth. It was so unusual. Other girls her age were busy giggling and patting the lace around their necklines, hoping he'd notice their developing bustlines. James'd known plenty of bustlines. Honesty was something else.

He liked all the Hemstads. Stieg was an excellent teacher. Sissel's older sister, Hanne, and her beau, Owen, were so transparently, deeply kind, one couldn't help but enjoy them. Then there was slow, smiling Knut, always amiable and amusing in his own way.

James had come to enjoy his moments in their small, clean house, posing as Sissel's suitor.

He kicked the horse to go faster, though the animal was already pouring sweat and its eyes rolled with fear.

James focused on identifying the road that led between two hills to the seventy-five acres the Hemstads owned. He recognized the shape of the turn and the dip in the elbow of the turn. It was a rut he'd had to watch out for when he brought a carriage to take Sissel driving.

Now he came over the hill, around the bend, and the farm was in sight, what was left of it.

The house was a smoking shell. His heart sank.

James steeled himself to what he might find . . . but as he came closer he saw, somehow, the barn was standing, its roof intact.

He felt a jagged burst of hope and then saw two figures standing near the house! Sissel and Knut!

"Dear God, you made it!" James said as he slid off his horse. Sissel and her giant brother looked dazed and exhausted. Sissel's face was stained with soot, streaked with tears. He clasped her hands in his.

"I thought . . . I worried you'd all been lost."

"We are all right," she said, her voice a hoarse whisper.

Owen came from behind the house. He looked grieved and somber, as he set down blackened parts of stovepipe near a pile of their belongings. Clearly he was rummaging for anything that might be saved from the smoking husk of their home.

James shook his hand. "Did the fire reach town?" Owen asked.

"No, no. The river stopped it."

Owen motioned to Knut, and the two went to the back of the house, to leave James and Sissel alone for a moment.

James cast his eyes around the farm. "Hanne and Stieg?" he asked Sissel.

"Alive. Safe," Sissel said. Using her voice clearly pained her.

"I can't believe you are all right." He felt foolish. After the mad rush to get there, he hardly knew what to do with himself.

"Do you have any fresh water?" Sissel asked.

James shook his head.

"How stupid of me!" he said. "I was worried. I didn't know what I'd find."

Sissel coughed again. James walked toward the small pile of possessions that Owen and Knut had gathered and saw a bucket there.

"I'm going to go refill this bucket," he told her. "And then I'll go to town and bring back supplies—"

James was interrupted by the jangling of a wagon. It carried what must be a crew of volunteers and was driven by Isaiah McKray,

Isaiah was the son of the famous gold miner Jerome McKray. Isaiah was a stout, muscly fellow with sandy-brown hair and a beard, only twenty years old but already given charge of a hotel in town and several mining outfits in the hills nearby.

He was thick in body, built like a barrel. He was notably blunt, always spoke his mind, and was uncannily shrewd in business. James didn't like how smart he was, or how successful.

Now McKray hailed them from the wagon, as did the other volunteers. There was Mr. Campbell, from the mill, and Mr. Trowley, one of the carpenters who was building the new town hall, along with some other workers from that site.

Hanne came out from the stable, and Owen and Knut walked out from the smoking shell of the house. The volunteers began exclaiming and thanking the heavens when they saw the Hemstads were alive.

McKray climbed down, his fine suit straining at the seams to accommodate his powerful build. He was what they'd call in Chicago a bruiser. No fine suit could hide it.

McKray shook Owen's hand. "We've been making a circuit of the area, looking for survivors."

"Is the teacher all right?" Mr. Campbell said, craning his neck to search for Stieg.

"He's resting in the barn," Hanne said.

"Thank God!"

"We've got fresh water and some blankets," Mr. Trowley said.

"We have food as well," McKray added.

Mr. Trowley started unloading supplies from the wagon.

"Are the Hensleys all right?" Hanne asked McKray. "Did you come that way?"

McKray shook his head. "Mrs. Hensley was in town, selling eggs, but Mr. Hensley . . ."

"No!" Hanne said.

Owen pulled her into a hug.

"What of the Baylors?" Hanne asked, her face anxious.

"We'll visit them next," McKray answered.

Hanne rested her forehead against Owen's chest.

One of the workers had a flour sack bulging with food. He reached in and handed Knut a red apple and a sandwich wrapped in waxed paper. Knut took a bite of the apple, and the crunch of it made everyone look at him. He didn't seem to notice.

"What a blessing it is you all made it safely," Mr. Campbell said. "How did you survive? Did you hide in the stream?"

"We took to the barn," Owen said. "Being sod, it didn't burn."

"You got lucky," Mr. Campbell said. "The Hensleys' house and barn burned, and they were both sod."

"Listen," Mr. Trowley said. "I think we should take you back to town. We need to stock up on more supplies, anyway, and folks will be so glad to know you all are safe."

Owen scratched his head, looking around the ruined farm. "Hanne, maybe we should—" he began.

"I don't think so," Hanne said. "Stieg shouldn't be moved."

"You can have room and board at my hotel," McKray offered.

"You're also welcome to stay at the store," James said. He was irritated with himself for not offering it first. He didn't want to be outdone in hospitality by the jackass McKray.

"I don't want to go anywhere," Hanne said abruptly. Owen put a hand on her arm to steady her. "But if you have it, we would take some coffee. Oh, and you don't have any headache powders, do you?"

"We have them at the store," James said. "I can ride back to town and get them for you."

"That would be very helpful," Hanne said.

"What else needs doing?" Mr. Campbell asked.

"We are just tired. Thank you so much for your help," Hanne said. "We just need to rest now."

"We'll let people in town know you're all right," McKray said. "And do let me know if you want to come to the hotel. I would never turn away a neighbor in need."

James wanted to snort at that. So McKray wanted to be seen as a model citizen, did he? What a clod.

After another round of hand shaking and promises to return in the morning, the men climbed back onto the wagon and rode off.

James watched them go. He decided to mention McKray in his report. Maybe the boys back east could dig up something on the ambitious young man and his infamous father.

Then James set about making a list of provisions to gather from the store. Owen worried aloud about the cost. Of course he'd worry, James realized—they'd just lost their whole crop.

James assured Owen that they could have an unlimited extension on their line of credit.

The siblings were grateful. He looked around at their grim, tired faces and suddenly wished he could tell them, *You have a secret bene-factor. The Baron Fjelstad is looking out for you. He's the one who owns the store. You can have anything you want.*

But he would never do such a thing. He'd be fired, and Peavy would surely beat the pulp out of him.

CHAPTER FOUR

Twilight settled over the blackened fields. Lingering smoke magnified the sunset—the sky was shot through with dusty apricot and brilliant orange, the colors so intense they seemed nearly lewd to Hanne.

Their supper was bread and cured sausage that the men from town had left. Hanne had also built a fire—a fire, of all things, in order to make coffee for Stieg.

Hanne crouched next to the small blaze, feeding it just enough so that she could boil water. Their coffeepot survived the wildfire, though the wooden handle had burned away. Hanne settled it into the embers, using the iron poker that Owen had also plucked from the wreckage.

Sissel was in the barn with Stieg now. She had the assignment to force him to drink water every time he woke.

It was too early to know if Stieg's vision was intact. The headaches

Stieg suffered when he used his Nytte would someday take his sight, or at least this is what their aunty Aud had told them to expect.

Aud was a Storm-Rend, like Stieg. Before they had met Rolf, their aunt had been the source of almost all their knowledge about the Nytte. The little else they had learned had come from their bitter drunkard of a father.

Each Nytte had a curse that accompanied it. Storm-Rends would eventually go blind; Oar-Breakers would grow so large their hearts would give out. Shipwrights, which is what their father had been, gradually lost their fingers and toes, like lepers. Berserkers, when they killed to protect their loved ones or themselves, became intensely hungry and would die if they did not eat. There were other types of Nytte mentioned in the ancient poems, Shield-Skinneds and Ransackers, but there had been no sign of them in generations.

Hanne had eaten more than her share of the goods left behind by the volunteers, but then, the hunger had not been too powerful today. She had not killed anyone.

"I found another cup," Owen said, approaching. He sat down, collapsing onto the bare earth. He reached forward and set a dented tin cup on a rock near the fire. He had scrubbed it in the stream, and it was nearly clean.

"I'm so sorry about Pal—" Hanne began.

"We can't stay here—" Owen said at the same time.

They stopped speaking. Hanne reached out her hand, and Owen took it in his. She noticed there was char under his nails and embedded in the lines of his knuckles.

His hand, no matter how grimy, was so dear to her.

"It's hard to say what we should do," Hanne said.

"We can stay here until Stieg recovers, but then . . . I don't know."

Daisy padded out from the barn and flopped herself down at Owen's side. She offered up her belly for scratching.

"At least Daisy is all right," Owen said.

Hanne burst into tears, her first of the long, awful day.

"Oh, Owen, I'm so sorry for Pal. You never wanted to farm, anyway. If you had been off on Pal, doing the work of a cowboy or training cow dogs the way you wanted to—"

"Shhh," Owen said, drawing her close.

"This was never your idea to farm, and now all your work was for nothing!" She choked on a sob. "And poor Pal!"

Hanne pressed her head against Owen's chest. His shirt reeked of sweat and smoke.

"Shhh," Owen said. "Hanne, animals die. That's a fact of working on a ranch or a farm. We made it, and it's a miracle we did. We're all safe and alive, and that's what matters."

Daisy, not liking to be left out, came over and nosed into their embrace, licking faces.

"Off," Owen told her, not unkindly. "Down stay." Daisy sank immediately to her haunches and set her face on her paws. "Good girl."

"Do you wish you had never met us?" Hanne said quietly.

"Hanne, meeting you and your brothers and sister is the best thing that ever happened to me. Please don't doubt that even for a second."

Hanne closed her eyes and allowed herself to be truly comforted, body and heart, by the solidity of the man she loved.

There was a sound behind them, and they turned to see Stieg emerging from the barn, leaning on Sissel.

Hanne wiped her face and rose quickly to help them. Anxiety

flared up—Sissel was too weak for him to lean on, and Hanne didn't want either of them to fall.

"Why are you up?" Hanne said. "You should be resting. Both of you."

"Not so loud," Stieg said, his eyes squinting against the small brightness of the fire. "I smelled coffee."

Owen had retrieved their single surviving chair from over by the house and offered it to Stieg. Hanne and Sissel helped ease him down onto it.

"How is your vision, Brother?" Hanne asked in a low voice.

Stieg shrugged. "It's a bit blurry, but I can make out the fire. And the sunset. And your face. It's scowling at me."

Owen chuckled.

"I'll be all right," Stieg said.

Hanne put her hand on her brother's shoulder.

"You saved us all today," she said.

Stieg squinted into the fire. He was shivering a bit.

"The Gods saved us," he said. "Once again, we must be thankful for the Nytte."

Hanne saw Sissel look away. She knew Sissel wished she had a Nytte. Hanne saw it on her sister's face sometimes.

Hanne wished she could tell Sissel how lucky she was to be free of it. It was hard on one's body and one's mind, and Sissel was frail to begin with.

She could escape their history altogether, Hanne thought. She could marry James Peavy, take his name, and move back to Chicago with him.

James planned to go to college and become a lawyer. Sissel could make a new life with him, free forever from the fear that the Baron

Fjelstad would one day track down her family and send more Berserkers after them.

There came a sudden crash from the back of the house, where Knut was still working at extracting items that might be of use.

Though Hanne felt no inner alarm, she crossed anyway, to make sure Knut was all right.

He came around the side of the house just as she approached. In his hands he held the straw tick from her bed. The fire had not taken the small bedroom she and Sissel had shared. Their precious trunk had survived, and so, it seemed, had this straw tick.

"Look what I got for Stieg!" Knut said. "It smells smoky, but it's still better than sleeping on the ground, don't you think?"

"Yes," Hanne said. A smile came to her lips. Her strong brother, holding up a mattress, and grinning as if he'd just caught a fat fish.

As bad as the fire had been, Owen was right. They survived, each of them—a miracle of their own contrivance.

CHAPTER FIVE

C hurch service in town that Sunday was crowded. Every family from miles around wanted to give thanks for their deliverance from the fire, and to mourn neighbors and acquaintances who had not been spared.

Sissel had walked to town for the service with Hanne and Owen while Knut looked after Stieg back on their farm. The Hemstads attended services, but they were barely Christian. They had been baptized Lutherans, back in Norway, but the presence of the Old Gods in their lives made worship of Christ feel false and disloyal. Nevertheless, the church was the town's social and moral center. Their absence would certainly have been noted by the townsfolk, so they attended services regularly.

The service was somber, a fitting memorial to the seven souls the town had lost in the fire. The minister himself seemed deeply humbled by the magnitude of the disaster.

"In the face of such destruction, we see signs of God's great mercy everywhere," Reverend Neville preached to the congregation.

Sissel sighed. She wished her friend Alice Oswald could sit with her, but Alice was with her parents, toward the back of the church. Sissel was, in fact, wearing one of Alice's dresses. She and her mother had brought clothes out to the farm on Saturday, the day before.

It was a lovely dress of tan-colored calico patterned with little white bouquets. It had a row of mother-of-pearl buttons all the way up the front and a ruffled collar. Alice's parents operated the Dry Goods Emporium. This meant Alice had her pick of fabrics and lace. She gave the dress to Sissel, claiming she'd made a mistake with the pattern and it didn't fit her well. This couldn't be true, not only because Alice was a talented seamstress but because the girls' figures were nothing alike. Though of the same height, Alice was fashionably plump—Sissel was a string bean compared to her.

Alice and her mother had also brought a dress for Hanne, and new shifts, corsets, and undergarments for them both. Hanne's dress was a hand-me-down from Alice's mother, a striking blue color, not as fancy a fabric as Sissel's or as well-decorated, but still beautifully made.

When they arrived at the church, many townspeople wished them well; and Sissel, Hanne, and Owen had many thanks to give to them. In the days since the fire, the Ladies' Aid Society had sprung into ferocious activity. Wagons arrived to the Hemstads' farm morning and noon with food—fresh-baked bread, fried chicken dinners, jars of pickles and preserves, even a whole new set of dishware, much finer than the dishes that had shattered in the fire.

The minister gave the final benediction, and the service was, at last, over. It was hot in the church, and Sissel was ready to be out of the crowded, mournful congregation.

The weight of the lives lost was settling on her. Real people had died—people she knew.

Her mind kept circling to their neighbors' possessions. She thought of their wooden spoons, their Sunday clothes, their butter churns. All burned to ash now, along with their owners.

Hanne turned and peered into Sissel's eyes, frowning. She put her hand on Sissel's forehead.

Sissel batted it away.

"Honestly, Hanne," Sissel said.

"You don't look well."

"I'm not a child," Sissel replied, keeping her voice low. "Don't handle me like one."

"Good morning, ladies," James said. He leaned into the pew toward the sisters.

"Let's go outside," Sissel said, and she rose.

"All right," James said. He took her hand as she stepped into the aisle.

Sissel knew she'd probably hurt Hanne's feelings by leaving so abruptly, but Sissel felt she'd go mad if she had to tolerate any more of Hanne's hovering.

They walked up the aisle, greeting schoolmates and their families.

"Sad stuff," James said to her.

Sissel gave a sigh of agreement. He took her arm, and the thrill it gave her made her feel remorseful. How could her body respond in such a way when the circumstances were so sad?

Outside, the air was still warm, but not nearly as stifling as inside. Alice came over to them.

"Sissel!" she said. "You look lovely!"

"I'm so glad to see you!" Sissel said. And she was. Alice was smiling, as always. Her brown curls were heaped on her head, and she wore a new dress of polished green poplin. Alice had snappy brown eyes and perfect dimples that made her seem pleased at everything.

"I'm so glad I made a mistake cutting that dress," Alice said. "It's perfect for you, and I think the color would be horrid on me, now that I see how well it looks on you."

"You know, the fiction that you of all people made a mistake will not stand up to much scrutiny," Sissel said. "Perhaps we'd better just call the dress a gift and have it out with."

Alice's cheeks glowed rosy.

"See," Sissel said to James, "she's blushing."

"Nevertheless," James said, "Alice has the right of it. The color is very becoming on you."

Now it was Sissel's turn to blush.

"I am usually right," Alice said. Sissel laughed.

It felt comforting to have things be normal and light for a moment. Family was most important, of course, but it was good to have friends.

Reverend Neville came out and started walking around the back to the graveyard. Everyone followed in little clusters.

The graveyard was just a cleared field, bordered at the back by the hill that ran along the north side of the town. Several boulders protruded from the earth, promising difficult digging for graves.

At the center of the yard a long trench had been dug for the seven caskets. This seemed peculiar, but Sissel supposed that it had made more sense to build one wide grave rather than seven individual ones.

The plain-hewn wooden caskets were already laid within the

hole, a respectable distance between them. There were several great mounds of earth and stone waiting to be shoveled on top.

The crowd fell silent and still in the presence of the caskets.

"Come," James said, "there's shade this way," leading her and Alice under one of the trees. It was cooler under the deep shade of the canopy of the tree. The green shadows felt like a balm on her strained nerves.

Reverend Neville began a benediction. They were a bit far off to hear his words, but Sissel didn't want to move from the tree. She saw Hanne and Owen standing to the side. From her sister's posture alone, Sissel could tell she was upset.

Sissel took in as deep a breath as the corset Alice had given her would allow. She willed herself to relax and think of nothing for a moment.

She heard a humming. A strong, low vibration nearby. She dismissed it as a bumblebee. But then her fingers began to tingle and her hands twitched.

She wanted to roll her eyes at her body's exasperating weakness. Likely this tingling and twitching was some new, terrible symptom of some new, terrible sickness. Was she going to faint or swoon or embarrass herself somehow?

Suddenly there was a lurch of movement in her heart. Sissel put a hand beneath her collarbone.

A feeling opened in her chest, a great, warm sensation.

The feeling was a yearning. Sissel's breath caught.

The hum grew very, very loud.

Sissel glanced to Alice, then to James. Neither of them seemed to be noticing anything. Both were focused on Reverend Neville.

James must have felt her glance, because his eyes sought hers, asking was she all right. She gave a weak nod, then closed her eyes, willing the strange feeling to be gone.

Instead, the yearning called her forward. The sound grew more resonant. No longer a buzzing but a gonging.

Sissel took a step forward, then two.

"Sissel?" Alice whispered. "Don't you want to stay in the shade?" Alice's words seemed muted.

Sissel looked at Alice and nodded. She *did* want to stay in the shade. She grasped at her friend's hand. But then the feeling in her chest pulled her again and she stumbled into the sunlight. Her hands were now crawling with the prickles.

The minister had finished blessing the first of the caskets.

The grave. The grave was calling her. There was a warm, golden force calling to her heart from that pit of earth. It was singing, ringing for her. It was lighting up her hands, the shared light beckoning to them.

"Oh," she moaned. She shut her eyes, trying not to move forward, but walking forward nonetheless.

"I think she's not well," she heard James say to Alice, his voice muffled oddly. She felt his hands on her arm. But she stepped toward the call. She was pushing through the mourners now, stepping on toes, surprising them all by stalking forward.

Her hands reached out, as if she could touch it, whatever it was that wanted her so badly.

She felt James's strong grip on her forearms. "This way, Miss Hemstad," he said. He made apologies to the people she was pushing past. "I think it's the heat." His voice came as if from a great distance inside her head.

Then her sister was beside her.

"Sissel!" Hanne hissed. "What are you doing?"

Sissel saw Hanne's mouth moving, but could not hear well.

"Let me go," Sissel said.

She reached for the open grave. The minister stumbled in his prayer. James's arms encircled her, restraining her. Villagers withdrew, gasping and whispering.

Under the dark, sandy loam inside the graves, the force sung, beckoned, insisted Sissel come.

"Let me go," Sissel told James.

She couldn't hear her own voice over the resonant gonging from the grave.

She must have it. She reached forward. She would find it, she would hold it.

Sissel broke free at the edge of the grave, and she bent her knees to jump.

James hauled her away.

"No!" she cried. "Please!"

Mercifully, the force overpowered her and the world went dark.

CHAPTER SIX

James stalked into Peavy's Mercantile and General Stores, letting the screen door slam behind him.

The bang made elderly Mrs. Denmead jump. "Heavens!" she shrieked.

"James! What on earth?" said Peavy.

James wheeled around.

"Apologize!" he commanded.

"I'm sorry."

"I'm sorry?"

"I'm sorry, sir," James amended. Then, "Father."

"Not to me! To Mrs. Denmead."

James took a breath. "I am very sorry, Mrs. Denmead."

Mrs. Denmead, usually crabby and demanding, thought about this for a moment. "It's a difficult day, James. I could slam a few doors myself."

She gathered her parcels, stopping to give him a little pat on the arm as she passed. "It's a strain on the nerves. The business with the fires and the church this morning," she said. "It's just a strain on the nerves, son."

James nodded. "I shouldn't have slammed the door. I'm truly sorry."

She gave him another pat on the arm.

Peavy waited until she had tottered down the porch stairs before laying into James.

"Jesus, boy. Get ahold of yourself," he said.

Russell Peavy was a man of considerable bulk, most of it belly. He had pudgy features, shaggy hair, and bushy eyebrows that allowed him to seem soft. He was genial and pleasant for the customers, but once they were gone, the smiles dropped and Peavy looked shrewd, cold, and sharp. James had seen the transformation hundreds of times, but it always made him feel wary.

"What's eating you?" Peavy asked, leaning on the counter with his arms spread wide.

James shrugged. He turned his back to Peavy, fiddling with some sacks of beans that had shifted sideways on a shelf. He was worried about Sissel. Sincerely worried.

After her strange spell, James carried Sissel to the doctor's offices, Owen and Hanne hurrying next to him. Sissel weighed nearly nothing in his arms. It was like carrying an armload of laundry.

Dr. Buell pronounced Sissel's episode a clear-cut case of nervous exhaustion. Sissel's health had not been good before the fire, and the shock of it was traumatic to her nervous system. She simply needed to rest, he had assured them. She would be just fine. Buell dosed Sissel with laudanum to sedate her, as Hanne paced in the small space and Owen stood twisting his cap.

James had then driven them home in the store's delivery wagon. Hanne sat in the bed of the wagon, near Sissel, who slept the loose-limbed sleep of the drugged the whole way home.

Now James walked through the store into the back room. Peavy followed.

James shucked his jacket and hung it on one of the nails driven into the wall for this purpose.

"It's damn hot," James said. "How's Rollie? Any word?"

"How do you think? He's flat on his belly in a burned-out field, watching the Hemstad farm through his goddamn field glass. He doesn't get to dress up and nance about, pretending to be some well-off schoolboy."

Peavy poured himself a cup of cold coffee from the pot on the stove.

"I hear your girl tried to throw herself into a grave," Peavy said. "You gonna get around to telling me about it, or do I have to get my news from old Mrs. Goddamn Denmead?"

"It was during the funeral. She started acting funny. Dr. Buell says it was nervous exhaustion. I'm sure he's right, after all that's happened." James didn't want to tell Peavy how strange and alarming Sissel's behavior had been, didn't want to hear the nasty things he'd doubtless say about her.

Peavy walked to the door and hooked his thumbs into the waistband of his pants, rocking on his heels. This action always precipitated a long, nostalgic lecture.

"I was one of the first detectives Mr. Pinkerton hired—"

"Yes, I know," James said. "You were there to guard President Lincoln during the war. That's where you got that scar on your back. We've all heard it—"

"Grisly work. Years and years of dark dealings. Only a few jobs that didn't end with me sticking someone in the ribs or pulling a trigger."

James sighed and rested his head back against the plank wall.

"Here's the surprise of it all. After all my deeds and misdeeds, I find I truly enjoy playing shopkeeper."

Peavy chuckled, looking out into the shop at the well-stocked shelves.

"We're lucky our Baron's got such deep pockets. Money no object and all that. Look at what we get to work with. This might be the best assignment I've ever had."

Bankrolled by the Baron, Peavy had bought the store fully stocked from the previous owner, a rheumy fellow named Zagaruyka. The building had sleeping quarters upstairs and a cookstove in the back room, with access to a community well right out the back door. Not only this, but the store served as the town's post office, which made monitoring the Hemstads' mail easy.

In addition to Peavy and James, there were only two more men on payroll. Rollie, a Pinkerton from Chicago, was on surveillance. He had bought an abandoned mining claim on a tract of land only a mile and a half away from the Hemstad farm, and posed as a prospector.

Rollie had weathered the fire deep in the belly of the defunct mine. He monitored the farm with binoculars, and mostly reported being extremely bored.

The other man on the job was an old friend of Peavy's, Tyrone Clements. Clements was a tall, slovenly man whose face rested perpetually in an expression of dull malice. He lived at the boardinghouse, pretending to be a day laborer, and served as Peavy's eyes and ears about town.

Rollie and Clements were supposed to remain unnoticeable to

the Hemstads. It was Peavy and James who were allowed contact, hired to play their parts carefully and well.

"You know I love this damn store now," Peavy said. "We have three kinds of suspenders, James. I've just signed up a new line of farm equipment. I may have you and Clements build a lean-to to display it."

Peavy removed a tin of chewing tobacco from a pocket in his vest and stuffed a pinch into the pouch of his cheek.

"What are you saying, sir?"

Peavy turned and fixed James with his bright, dark eyes.

"My point is that it's easy to fall in love, son. It's easy to dream of going straight and joining the community, as it were.

"But remember, the James Peavy your Sissel knows is a sham and a lie. She don't know you're just a bellboy. And before that you were just tenement scum, doing all sorts of filthy business to get by."

He laughed.

"She thinks you're going to college! To be a lawyer!"

James looked past Peavy, out the door. Here in the West, it seemed a new world. It was easy to forget the dark and the stench of the slums of Chicago. His handsome, lying father, Conway Collins, cheating immigrants from their coins at the train station. His mother and aunt Elena, doing dirty, low work and drinking the money away. Always drunk, always crying on him, begging for him to help.

The job at the Palmer House had been his first step out. It had been so hard to get clean enough so his neck wouldn't get the stiff white collar of his uniform dirty. He'd bathed, scrubbing himself down in the alley next to the building where he and his parents lived. Buckets of cold water and a whole bar of store-bought soap. Limp laundry on lines above blocking the sunlight.

James looked at his fingernails. They were clean. He meant to keep them that way.

His head snapped up as Peavy set his coffee cup on the table and leaned in close.

"Look here, I'm determined to train you to be a fine detective," Peavy said. "I know you come highly recommended from Chicago, et cetera, et cetera, but I'm telling you—you've got a lot to learn. Your heart's in the wrong place, son. Hell, your heart has no place in this business whatsoever.

"Now, I'd like to hear your full account of what transpired this morning at the cemetery, and don't leave a detail out, not a fart, not a sneeze, not a fly landing on a clod of horseshit."

CHAPTER SEVEN

S issel lay outside, near the barn, on their one straw tick. She was wrapped in a wool blanket given to them by the Ladies' Aid Society. It was checkered red and black and had come, she had been told, from the Hudson's Bay trading company, all the way in Canada.

Her family was talking, gathered around the small campfire a few paces away.

She woke to residual calmness from the laudanum. Even when she remembered the call of the grave, she was able to consider the issue with detachment.

What had happened to her? Was it hysteria? She had felt a power beckoning her. She had been compelled by some force outside her.

Could it be madness? Was she losing her mind now, after a lifetime of physical weakness and debility? No one else had heard the strange call. Madness seemed the only logical explanation.

Sissel tried to close her eyes and go back to sleep. She wanted to return to the blissful haze of the medicine Dr. Buell had given her, but the conversation among her siblings and Owen wouldn't let her rest. They were talking about her.

"I'm inclined to believe the doctor. Dr. Buell is a good physician, and he knows Sissel's case well," Stieg said.

"You weren't there, Stieg," Hanne said.

"It must be nervous exhaustion."

"No," Hanne said. "I told you. She tried to jump into the grave."

"Could it be she had a fainting spell?" Stieg asked.

"I don't know what it was! I've never seen anything like it," Hanne said.

Stieg spoke carefully, after a long moment.

"In that case, Hanne, we must trust the doctor."

Hanne sighed. "I suppose you're right."

"She will be fine," Knut said. "She just needs some sleep and good food."

"Well, I don't think living here, out of a barn, is doing her much good," Hanne said. "We must figure out what to do next, and where we go."

"We should move her to town," Stieg said. "I would like for her to be close to Dr. Buell."

"We could look for a place to rent, perhaps," Hanne said. "How much money do we have?"

"Not much," Stieg said.

"How much?"

"Three dollars and some change."

"Three dollars?" Hanne said. "But how can that be?"

"I've been paying down our debts," Stieg said. "I am to be paid soon, and we had run up some costs at the store."

"How much do we owe? I thought we were doing all right," Owen said.

"Altogether," Stieg said, "we owe two hundred and forty-two dollars."

Owen whistled.

"Over two hundred dollars!" Hanne exclaimed. "Stieg, we can't owe that much."

"I took out a small loan from the store," he said. "I hadn't meant to tell you. I thought I would just repay it when I got a bigger school."

"What was it for?" Hanne said.

"It was for the medicine for Sissel, from when she was so ill last spring. The medicine from London," Stieg said, keeping his voice low. "The iron bitters and the lung tonic, they were more expensive than I told you. But it did do some good—"

"Oh, Stieg," Hanne said, her voice strangled and tight. "How could you?"

"I would do anything to help our sister, Hanne. You know that."

"And so would I. But to do it without asking us was not right."

Sissel remembered the vials of bitters, each one glass, sealed with wax. One hundred of them packed in cotton wool. They had looked plenty expensive, though Stieg had played the cost down at the time.

Tears came to the back of Sissel's eyes. She had griped and complained endlessly to Stieg about how bitter the medicine was and how it burned her stomach. How ungrateful she'd been!

"You should have told us," Knut weighed in. He was seated near the fire, stroking Daisy's back.

"I know," Stieg said. "I'm sorry."

Hanne began to portion out beans onto their new, donated china bowls. The bowls were painted with a pattern of dainty blue roses around the edge and looked extremely out of place at their scorched campsite.

Her silence spoke of how angry she was.

"I felt bad, Hanne, for how little I was able to get for the last of the gold our aunt gave us," Stieg said. "I should have traveled to get a better price. To San Francisco, if need be. If I had gotten a better price for the gold, we could have afforded the medicines easily. I'm not excusing what I did, only trying to let you see the emotion that influenced me."

"It's bad news, Stieg. We've lost our home and the crop. Pal is gone. And Sissel is sick. Very sick! Now you tell us not only are we out of money, but we are in debt!"

The siblings fell to silence. Hanne passed the bowls around. Sissel wiped away the tears from her eyes, careful to remain unnoticed.

"Well, I have an idea how to make some money," Owen offered. "About two weeks ago I had a letter from my friend Hoakes. He said he'd backed out of a job. He was headed to Texas, but he wanted me to know he'd recommended me for the job, in case I wanted it. A ranch not too far from here, the Bar S, is gearing up to drive around fifteen hundred beefs down to Helena. It'd be nearly two months' work."

"Why didn't you tell us before?" Hanne asked.

Owen stretched his neck side to side and blew out a deep breath. "Guess I knew I couldn't go," he said. "So I didn't want to make a fuss."

"Do you think they still need you?" Stieg asked. "Are you thinking you could go?"

"They'd pay at least thirty or forty a month for me," Owen said.

"But you'd be gone for two months," Hanne said, then quickly added, "Of course, we could manage."

"Well, Hanne . . . you could come along," Owen said. "Sometimes they like to hire wives on to help with the cooking. Keeps the cowboys a bit settled down to have a lady around."

"Hanne's not a lady," Knut said with a laugh. "She's just Hanne."

"I'm not a wife," Hanne said. "That's the real problem."

"Let's get married, then!" Owen said. "We could get married tonight!"

Sissel imagined her sister's tense posture. Owen had wanted to marry for a long time, but Hanne wanted to wait until they could afford a wedding.

"You don't need to get married to go," Stieg said. "You only need to *pretend* to be married."

There was silence as everyone mulled this over.

"What if they didn't want to hire me on? What if they don't want me there at all?"

"Then you can come back," Owen said. "Not like you'll be in danger."

"I don't know. There's Sissel to think of. I worry for her health," Hanne said.

"Sissel, Knut, and I could move into town," Stieg said. "We could take Isaiah McKray up on his offer and stay in his hotel. I have the remainder of my salary coming to me, only twenty dollars, but it will be plenty until you get back."

"It *would* be good for Sissel to be in town," Hanne said.

"And Alice is such a cheerful and lively girl," Stieg added. "She's good for Sissel."

Sissel lay perfectly still, anger and shame fighting for control of her emotions. Her siblings were deciding her fate without even asking her, because she was just a child to them. A child and a burden.

"I'm not sure that works," Owen said. "Knut, would you like living in town?"

"Yes, what about you?" Hanne said, turning to their brother. "Would you be all right? You'd have to be very careful about what you tell people. You can't talk about where we're from. If someone recognized you, things could get ugly again."

It was a risk with Knut. He frequently slipped up, mentioning their hometown of Øystese, or their father's name, Thorson. There was still a risk that someone would connect him to the murders in Norway that had caused the Hemstads to come to America back in 1883. They all worried that someone might see an old wanted poster and come for their brother, even though the warrant had been canceled.

Sissel couldn't make out Knut's face. His back was to her. But she knew his brow would be furrowed, and he'd be thinking hard.

"I will hire out as a farmhand," Knut said. "The farms that did not get burned away, they will be needing help. Many times, the Lilliedahls have asked me to come work for them, and I always say no. But I can tell them yes."

Hanne and Stieg exchanged a look of surprise.

Sissel herself was surprised. This was the first time Knut had ever ventured an idea about his own life or future.

The Lilliedahls were an older couple whose son had gone east to find work. They usually kept several laborers with them all summer long and well into the fall.

"That sounds like a good plan, Knut," Stieg said.

A huge grin had spread over her brother Knut's face. She could see the lift of Knut's shoulders. He sat up tall and proud.

"They'd pay you a fair wage, plus room and board," Stieg went on.

"And, as you say, you like them. That's important. And Sissel and I can come visit you, to make sure you are happy."

Knut nodded. He returned his attention to his bowl of beans.

"It is decided, then," Stieg said. His voice was loosened by a clear note of relief. "Owen and Hanne will go see if they can find a place on the cattle drive. Knut will hire on to help the Lilliedahls with their harvest, and Sissel and I will move to town."

The talk grew animated and hopeful as they began to discuss packing their few belongings and planning what would need to be purchased in town.

Sissel lay on her back, looking up at the endless stars in the broad Montana sky. She was inconsequential, it turned out. They didn't need or care to hear her opinions on the future of the family. They hadn't even asked her if she'd mind moving to town.

Worse than that, she couldn't help. She was too thin and weak to hold a real job, not to mention too young. All her cleverness in school counted for nothing—she could not help her family when they most needed it.

Sissel turned her back on them and tried to get to sleep without crying.

CHAPTER EIGHT

In the dark barn early the next morning, Hanne dressed in the work clothes the Ladies' Aid had provided—a used white blouse and plain gray skirt, cut wide enough to ride in easily. Then she dragged the saddlebags outside so she could pack them in the dawning light.

She put the rest of her clothing into one saddlebag, including some of her smoke-tainted skirts. She imagined that a sour smell wouldn't matter too much on the trail. Into the other saddlebag she packed Owen's clothing. He had even less than she did. In the remaining space she packed their coffeepot and stuffed it with some venison jerky, a paper knot of coffee, and the remnants of a small sack of cornmeal. She added in a heel of brown bread, and some thick-rinded sheep's milk cheese Mrs. Baylor had sent over. They needed to head through town to procure a horse, and she could pick up more food for the trail then.

Owen said they'd be at the Bar S Ranch in a day and a half, stopping in a town called Fitch on the way.

"Almost ready?" Knut said from the door.

"Yes," Hanne said. "You should gather up the chickens."

"All right." Knut sighed. "Easy to say. Hard to do."

Owen hauled his rig off the hook on the wall where they'd had it stored. Daisy trotted into the barn. Excited by the mere sight of Owen handling his cowboy gear, she went to Owen, then to Hanne, then back to Owen, nearly dancing with joy.

"I see Daisy is happy about our trip," Hanne said. She stopped to scratch behind Daisy's ears. The dog's tongue lolled out as she grinned at Hanne.

"I have my clothes in one side, and yours on the other," Hanne said, indicating the saddlebag. "What else will we need?"

"We'll each need an oilskin slicker for the rain, and a couple bandannas for the dust and the smell. It gets pretty ripe out there, I have to warn you."

"So you've said. What else will we need? Bedrolls, I suppose?"

"Mmmm," Owen said. He stood scratching his head for a moment. "About the bedrolls . . . We can get singles. But . . ."

"What?" Hanne said.

"If we're to appear to be married . . ."

"I hadn't thought of that," she said.

Hanne felt a ferocious blush creep up her neck.

"Of course," Owen rushed on, "we won't . . . act married . . . in the bedroll." He looked mortified, and Hanne burst out laughing.

"It's a good idea, Owen, and I know you will behave in a respectful way."

"I will," he said, gruff with embarrassment.

Hanne kissed him lightly.

"Are you going to call me 'missus'?" she asked.

"I am. But mostly I'll just holler, 'Wife!'"

They laughed. It felt so good to laugh with him.

"Are you ready?" Sissel said from the door. "Stieg is eager to leave."

OUTSIDE THE BARN, Knut stood looking over the ruins of their home. There was a dejected slump to his broad shoulders. Hanne felt for him.

"See how things are starting to grow already," Stieg said to Knut, pointing to some green shoots that were peeking through the charred soil. "Fire is good for the land. The grass will come back as thick as it was, or better, this time next year."

"I don't care about the grass. We needed the wheat crop. And now we must leave," Knut said.

Stieg clapped a hand on his brother's arm.

"We'll be back," Stieg said. "We'll build it up again, don't worry."

"I know. But I'm just sad for a moment."

"I suppose that's the right way to feel," Stieg said. "I won't try to cheer you out of it."

"Everyone ready?" Owen asked. Daisy was certainly ready. She kept running a few paces down the road, then turning and panting at them with a plaintive look in her eyes, then circling back.

Sissel's expression was sullen. She listened when Stieg had told her the plan with pursed lips and said nothing.

Sissel was exhausted, it was clear to see. Hanne prayed that a few weeks living in town would do her good.

"Are you sure you feel well enough to walk?" Hanne asked Sissel. "We could go ahead and ask James to come for you."

"I'm fine," Sissel said. "Let's go, for heaven's sake."

Hanne was stung, but tried to hide it. Maybe some distance between her and her sister would be for the best, after all.

Knut hoisted the beautiful old trunk to his shoulder without the least bit of strain. In it was packed Stieg's and Sissel's clothing and a few small personal items they might be able to use at the hotel, along with the family Bible and the girls' hand-embroidered traditional clothes from Norway.

Owen carried his rig and the saddlebags; Stieg carried a bag with Knut's clothing in it; and Hanne carried the surviving hens, all quieted down, in a gunnysack.

The chickens were to go with Knut—a gift to the Lilliedahls. The hens would not survive long left alone at the farm. A fox, a weasel, or a raccoon would come for them if they slept in the barn with the door open.

Sissel had expected to carry something as well, so Hanne gave her their water pail, in which she had stored some leftover pie for Knut's lunch, as it would take him until the afternoon to walk to the Lilliedahl farm.

Sissel swung the pail as she limped along behind them. Hanne couldn't pinpoint what was bothering her sister, but knew that asking would not help. They walked in stubborn silence.

The boys ambled along ahead, trading remembrances about the last time they were all together on a journey, the winter before last.

"I only knew Daisy was fighting the mountain lion because of the colors and the sounds," Owen said. "I could hardly tell one animal from the other."

Daisy looked up at her master, happy to hear her name mentioned.

"I remember the scream of the cat," Stieg said. "Sissel on the ground, and Daisy between them."

"I thought Daisy was a goner and then Hanne ran at 'em." Owen shook his head in wonder. "I never saw a person move so fast. She was down the hill and on that animal like lightning."

Hanne looked sidelong at her sister. Sissel had her head down, limping along, miserable.

"Hanne saved your life, Daisy," Owen said to the dog, who wagged her tail in response.

"She saved Sissel's life, too, don't forget," Stieg added. "And that was not the first time, either."

Hanne saw Sissel sigh. She must be tired of hearing these stories, Hanne thought.

"Will you miss us, do you think?" Hanne asked Sissel. "I know that I will miss you. But you'll have Alice to keep you company, and I imagine Mrs. Oswald will invite you and Stieg to supper as often as you'll accept—"

"I'm not worried about being lonesome."

"What is it, then?" Hanne asked.

Sissel's mouth was pursed tight.

Hanne suddenly made a decision.

"I won't go. I shouldn't," Hanne said. "I don't know what I was thinking to even consider it. You're not well and you need me here—"

"Stop," Sissel said.

"No. I'll tell Owen. I'm sorry, Sister. It was a bad plan. I'll be happy to stay here and take care of you—"

"No!" Sissel said, her voice raised. She stopped walking and stood, landing a furious gaze on Hanne.

"I'm not upset that you're going. I'm upset that I wasn't asked," Sissel said. Her eyes were bright and focused. "You all decided what I would do without asking me, without even thinking I had an opinion."

Hanne stepped back. "We thought—"

"I know what you *thought*. You *thought* that I am sick and weak and must be protected," Sissel said. Hanne was horrified to see tears jump from Sissel's eyes. "And I don't blame you. That's what I am. Only . . . only I'm so tired of it!"

The boys had stopped and were watching. Stieg took a few steps toward them, but Hanne waved him off.

Sissel rubbed away her tears.

"What would you have said, if we had asked you?" Hanne said. "Are you unhappy with the plan?"

Sissel resumed walking. Hanne hauled the heavy bag over her shoulder again and moved to keep up.

"It's a good plan," Sissel allowed stiffly. "I would have said so."

Hanne sighed.

She walked alongside her sister, but then allowed her natural pace to take her ahead. If Sissel didn't appreciate it, didn't even want her there, then Hanne would not suffer herself to linger behind.

Walking, catching up with the boys, Hanne wished she could teach her sister that life was easier when you wanted what you had.

But, Hanne thought, perhaps if she had as little as Sissel had, she would also feel bitter.

CHAPTER NINE

t wasn't yet eight, so Russell Peavy was in the store tidying up and doing some bookkeeping before opening for the day. James sat in the back room, writing his report of the events of the day before.

He drank his coffee heavily sweetened with condensed milk—a perk from operating a general store that James enjoyed daily.

Peavy would include the document James was writing in the sheaf of papers he sent every week to Chicago. From there, a report would be typed and sent to the Baron Fjelstad in Bergen, Norway.

James had spent some time thinking about this Baron. To his mind, the most obvious reason for the man keeping such close watch on the Hemstads was that they were family. Distant family, perhaps. Maybe Stieg was his heir.

He liked that thought. Stieg Hemstad was a fine teacher and a pleasant fellow. As a teacher, he was encouraging, yet strict, and always fair. James had enjoyed school for the first time in his life. Back in Chicago, he had attended a cramped, boisterous school with teachers who hit hard. Reading and arithmetic had come easy, but he got in trouble for flirting with the girls and dropped out when he hit fourteen.

After James finished the report, he planned to put together some foodstuffs for the Hemstads and ride out, as he'd taken to doing since the fire. Many of the townsfolk kept asking him if he knew when school was starting up again. They had only three weeks left before the term must end—the harvest wouldn't wait for them to wrap up their studies. Then school would be dismissed until early December, when the three-month winter school term would begin.

James jumped as the back screen door was jerked open and shut with a bang. It was Rollie, and James could see his horse outside, lathered up.

"Where's Peavy?" Rollie said.

"In front," James said. "What happened?"

"The Hemstads broke camp this morning. They're on foot, headed to town," Rollie said. "They're carrying just about everything they own."

Peavy strode in from the front room.

"They see you?" Peavy asked.

Rollie nodded. "I passed them on the road. Just tilted my hat at 'em and came on. Thought you should know right away."

"Well, hopefully they'll come in here for supplies. You should take some grub and some hardtack. Make quick about it. Then lie low out of town a bit and watch for 'em."

Rollie began taking food off the shelf, and James helped wrap up a great bunch of hardtack. Rollie loaded the items into his rucksack.

"If I were you, Peavy, I'd telegram the offices—" Rollie said.

"You ain't me," Peavy said.

He hit the return on the cash register, and it sprang open with a heavy clang. He gave Rollie twenty dollars from the till.

"We're gonna need more men if they split up—" Rollie said.

"We haven't needed more men until this very instant," Peavy said. He threw a new canteen at Rollie's head. Rollie caught it neatly.

"James," Peavy said. "Go get your horse from the livery, just in case they do split up."

"Me?" James sputtered. "But I don't know the first thing about surveillance."

"Keep your drawers dry. It's just in case. You ride behind them, well behind, and wait to see where they go. Come report back when it gets dark."

"When it gets dark?"

"God, but you're greener than a hickory switch." Peavy pushed him toward the door. "Get on and go."

IT TOOK MR. HENNINGS, the livery master, an age and a half to get his horse saddled. James would have done it himself, only he hadn't quite gotten the trick of it.

By the time Mr. Hennings brought the gelding out and tethered him to a stable hook, James could see Sissel, Stieg, and Knut walking down the street right toward the livery.

He hung back in the shadows.

"You riding out or not?" Hennings asked.

James held up his hand.

"Not just yet," he said. "I forgot something at the store."

Hennings grumped off to tend to the other animals in his care.

James watched Sissel, Stieg, and Knut approach the Royal Hotel. It was a stately wood building, two stories high with ornate gingerbread cornices.

Knut had their antique trunk hoisted up on his shoulder as if it were no heavier than a basket of apples. Hanne and Owen were nowhere to be seen.

They set their burdens down. Stieg and Sissel hugged Knut in turn. He took the bucket Sissel had been carrying and the sack Stieg was holding. He shook Stieg's hand again and got one more embrace from Sissel, and then Knut headed off down the road.

James looked down the street. Where was Rollie? What should James do?

Sissel and Stieg dusted themselves off as best they could and walked into the elegant lobby of the Royal.

So Sissel and Stieg were moving into the hotel. But where was Knut headed?

James waited until Knut was a speck on the road, then he mounted his horse and followed.

CHAPTER TEN

Stieg flashed Sissel an encouraging smile, then pushed open the door to the Royal Hotel. Inside, the lobby was busy, with a couple speaking to the manager while a porter in a blue uniform saw to their bags.

The walls were papered a floral print, pink roses over a cream-colored background. Every surface, with the exception of the gleaming front counter, was topped with a crocheted doily or a piece of lacework. Two wingback chairs upholstered in worked satin stood in the corner, a table with spindled legs and a lamp with a fringed silk shade eavesdropping between them. An oriental carpet lay on the floor near the front counter. Sissel and Stieg stood on it, waiting behind the young couple. Sissel noticed how plush the carpet was under the shoe, especially after their long walk.

Two closed glass doors with lace curtains led to the hotel's dining room, but it was too expensive for them to eat there for everyday meals. Stieg had decided they would eat breakfast and supper at Mrs. Boyce's boardinghouse across the street. They'd also buy sandwich stuffs at the general store to make sack lunches to bring to school.

Sissel discreetly tugged down the waist of her tan dress. The dress badly needed laundering. It was difficult to keep clothes clean living at a campsite covered in ash. The walk from their farm had made her overwarm, so not only was her clothing dirty and rumpled, but her hair was limp with sweat and her cheeks flushed. She knew she must look as out of place as she felt.

Finally the couple was ushered upstairs by the porter, and Stieg and Sissel stepped up to the counter.

They knew the man who ran the hotel, Timothy Collier. Everyone in town knew Mr. Collier because he had an unforgettable mustache. It was dark brown, highly dense, and twisted up at the corners to two precise curls. His personality seemed to match his whiskers—fussy and immovable.

He had little hair on his head, as if the mustache had used all of it up. The wisps of hair he had were kept pomaded slick across his scalp from left to right.

"Ah," he said, as if he hadn't seen them waiting, "the young Hemstads. Good day."

"Yes, good day, Mr. Collier. We hoped to speak to Mr. McKray."

"Pertaining to?"

"An offer he made to us," Stieg said.

"And that offer would be?"

Stieg cleared his throat, thinking for a moment. It was clear to Sissel that her brother did not want to talk about their business with Mr. McKray in public. A housemaid entered the lobby, curtsied to Mr. Collier, and began to dust.

"I'd rather not say," Stieg said.

Mr. Collier gave an impatient harrumph. "If it is in regards to an offer of free housing he may or may not have made, I'm afraid we do not have any vacancies."

"I see," said Stieg stiffly.

Sissel felt a blush of shame spread over her cheeks.

"We are hosting three displaced families already. Three! There is hardly room for paying patrons!"

A door behind Collier swung open on well-oiled hinges. The room beyond it was darkened, an office. Collier didn't seem to hear the door open, because he continued in an officious, obnoxious tone. "See if they can't take you in at the boardinghouse across the street. Mrs. Boyce hasn't done nearly her share, in my opinion. And she is used to a rougher sort."

Stieg's posture was drawn ramrod straight. Sissel knew he was as offended as she was.

"Collier!" came a voice from the shadowed doorway.

Mr. Collier jumped. He turned to see the young Mr. McKray stride from the office.

"You can't possibly be turning the Hemstads away, can you?"

Collier's mustache twitched.

"I told you I offered rooms to all the locals who lost homes in the fire."

"Yes, sir, only I thought that they might inquire across the street—"

"Nonsense."

"Might I ask, sir, how you think your father would approve of giving all these rooms for free?"

McKray raised an eyebrow at Collier and went completely still. They were an oddly matched pair for employer and employee: McKray, short, young, and dressed every inch the wealthy businessman; and

Collier, tall, lean, balding, and old enough to be McKray's uncle at least.

"Are we to have this discussion again, Collier, in front of customers?" McKray said.

"They're not customers if they are not paying."

"Never mind," Stieg said quietly. "We can make inquiries elsewhere."

"Please, Mr. Hemstad, I beg your pardon," McKray said to Stieg. "Mr. Collier is a longtime employee of my father's, and he isn't quite used to the way *I* run things here in *my* hotel, that *I* purchased and maintain with *my own damn money*."

McKray's voice had deepened with intensity.

Collier gave a dramatic sigh. "I apologize, Mr. McKray," he said. "The problem is that we only have two rooms left—" Collier gestured to the ledger, that he might see for himself.

"Perfect," McKray said, reading out of the book. "Give Mr. Hemstad the single and put Miss Hemstad in the bridal suite."

"The bridal suite?" Collier squeaked.

"My brother and I can share a room," Sissel suggested.

McKray waved her offer away. "That wouldn't be seemly, a young lady like you, sharing a room with her brother."

Sissel felt herself blush.

Stieg cleared his throat. "We are thankful for your generosity. And of course we will pay you back for the rooms." Stieg directed this at Collier, who was scowling at them across the counter. "The bridal suite might prove to be a bit out of our reach, however."

"We'll only charge you for the single," McKray said. "The balance is on me."

Collier sputtered, but McKray silenced him with a look.

"Let me remind you that plenty in these parts have lost everything," he told Collier. "We're not going to profit from their misfortune."

Sissel studied McKray. What a strange, gruff fellow he was. He had hazel eyes and a nose that turned up a bit, a boyish nose, though he was built so thick and strong, it was clear he was a man grown. McKray had rather a lot of sandy, nut-brown hair that didn't seem to obey very well. It was tufty, and cut shorter than was fashionable. He had bushy eyebrows and kept his beard trimmed close and neat. The beard was dense and probably would have loved to grow wild.

Well, Sissel thought, he was certainly acting like a gentleman, if he didn't quite look the part.

Stieg seemed to be wrestling with the offer. Sissel extended her hand to McKray to shake.

"Thank you," Sissel said. "Your offer is very kind and we accept it."

McKray took her small, pale hand. For a moment, it seemed he wasn't sure whether to squeeze it or kiss it. He did a combination of both, compressing it and bowing his head to let his lips graze on the back of her hand.

Sissel was embarrassed by this. In fact, all of them seemed a bit embarrassed—including Stieg and Collier and McKray himself.

"Enzo, get their bags!" McKray called to the porter.

Mr. Collier frowned as he wrote *Hemstad* into the ledger in two places. He slid two keys across the counter. Each had a brass plate affixed. Stieg's read *#5*. Sissel's said *Bridal Suite* in an elegant script.

The key and the tag were heavy and cool in her hand. Sissel smiled. Holding a key to her very own room—there was power in it.

CHAPTER ELEVEN

After saying good-bye to her siblings at the edge of town, Hanne and Owen stopped at the general store and stocked up on food for the trail. Mr. Peavy had already opened for the day, a lucky accident. They had expected to have to wait for him to open.

Peavy had a lot of questions, and showed an interest in the cattle drive. He was generous with the prices and even made Hanne a gift of a cowboy hat for her adventure. It was a pretty dove gray, with a braided leather band. He said he'd hold their mail and wished them safe travels.

Hanne hadn't warmed to Peavy before. She never understood how Peavy, who was crass and excessive, had raised smart, socially graceful James. But she couldn't deny that he was being kind and solicitous now. And it was such a nice hat.

After they left the general store, they went to the livery where Owen had rented a horse, which was a thing Hanne hadn't known was possible. They were to deliver her back in six weeks, but Mr. Hennings said eight would be fine, if it came to that. The creature was a tall chestnut mare named Brandy.

Owen fit the saddlebags and the double bedroll on her back. Hanne was to ride in front of him for the journey to the ranch. Brandy looked like she had opinions about the saddlebags; she kept swinging her head around to take a look at them.

"Don't mind her. She'll learn who's boss soon enough," Owen said, extending his hand to Hanne. She was swinging herself up when Brandy turned her head and tried to take a bite out of Hanne's shoulder. Hanne's danger sense flared up, and before she knew what she was doing, she'd punched the horse in the throat with her free hand.

The horse let out an undignified gulping snort and sidestepped. Hanne let go of Owen's hand and dropped to the ground. Daisy barked at Brandy, scolding.

A passing stranger with a beery complexion let out a long whistle.

"Better watch out for that one," he said to Owen.

Hanne frowned as he walked off unsteadily.

Owen led the horse in a circle back to Hanne.

"Maybe we should rent a different horse," Hanne said. Owen shook his head.

"She's the biggest, strongest horse available. Don't worry. A few hours on the trail with the two of us on her back will settle her down. I've ridden ornery horses before. I know how to handle them."

Hanne eyed the mare and Brandy eyed her back. Daisy sank to her belly in the dust, waiting for the standoff to end.

"She won't try to nip you again, I don't think. Horses don't like being punched in the neck, any more than you or I," Owen said, trying to hide a smile.

When he reached out his arm again, Hanne took hold, and Owen lifted her up onto the horse. Sometimes she forgot how strong he was.

With some shifting, she got her body centered on the saddle in front of him.

"Hold on to her mane," Owen instructed. Hanne dug her fingers into the coarse hair, gritty with dust. Then Owen gave the horse his heels and they set off.

It took them all of a minute to canter out of town, away from the life they'd built over a course of years.

Hanne was surprised to find it felt good to leave it all behind—the responsibilities, the constant worry. She leaned back onto Owen's chest, enjoying the feeling of him behind her and his ropy, tanned forearms snug around her sides.

Owen edged Brandy into a gallop. Hanne drew in a great breath as the warm air rushed by. Owen leaned forward, pressing Hanne down, the reins in one hand and the other holding tight on to Hanne's waist. Faster and faster, they flew along the road.

Owen let out a long, loud cowboy whoop. Hanne laughed and hollered, too.

"Feels good to ride!" Owen said. Then, after he caught his breath, "That wasn't too fast for you, was it?"

"That was wonderful. Let's do it again."

Hanne turned enough to see the side of Owen's face and his grin.

"Better not," he said. "We got a long day ahead. But it does feel good to ride hard, if only for a minute."

They fell silent. The slowed gait of the horse made their bodies come together and apart. Hanne's shoulders leaning away, then back to Owen's chest, away, then back. It made her flustered, and she liked the feeling.

Riding with Owen, her body pressed to his, made her think of their wedding night. She could feel her cheeks flushing, and she felt like she ought to be ashamed of the way her body was feeling. But there was no one to see her, no one to judge, so Hanne let herself savor the sensations that were coming.

"DO YOU THINK they'll give me a job?" Hanne asked after a while.

"Fifty-fifty they'll offer you one out straightaways. But once they see how handy you are, and a good cook, I think they'll hire you."

"And how much could I make?"

"Maybe twenty dollars?"

Hanne thought about this. To return with sixty dollars—that was something.

Perhaps enough, once some of their debts were paid, to marry. She wanted a new dress, and to have a cake and a party for the neighbors. Of course they would have to pay Reverend Neville. Perhaps there would be enough to pay a fiddler to walk her to the church.

Hanne enjoyed daydreaming about it. It was so peaceful to be off, away from all their troubles in Carter. Her siblings were taken care of. Knut would reach the Lilliedahls in the evening. She knew they would be glad for his help.

Stieg would take care of their little sister, and Sissel would enjoy living at the Royal.

She closed her eyes and settled back against Owen's warm chest. Hanne allowed herself to feel happy and safe, riding double with her betrothed, in the sunshine.

CHAPTER TWELVE

Sissel gasped awake in the darkened hotel room. Moonlight played through the lace curtains at the window. All was still in the room except for her, shaken by her dream.

She had dreamed of a great eye hung in the sky, clouds streaming away on either side of it. She had been resting in the selfsame bed she lay on now, and the eye had come closer and closer, peering into her head, it seemed. She could not move, as if some great centrifugal force had held her down. As the eye had blinked, she felt a contraction in the core of her chest and then a dilation, a release of warmth, a huge intake of breath.

She had heard a booming voice say, "Awaken," in an old language she had understood easily.

She rose and kicked her feet free of the lace-trimmed bedsheets. She walked to the washstand and poured herself a glass of water from the pitcher.

She heard a thrumming. A low, warm vibration. Gooseflesh crept over her arms. The sound was coming from outside.

It was the call of the graveyard.

Sissel's body began to quake.

"Not again," she said aloud. "Please."

The vibration grew louder. She crumpled to the floor. What was she to do? She clamped her hands over her ears.

The sound was in her chest and it glowed, twinkling to her, beckoning.

Her fingers began to tingle.

She stood and grabbed her dressing robe and left the room.

The hallway was sleeping quiet.

She should wake Stieg, she knew, but how would she explain it to him? He would think she was going mad—having a spell.

Instead she decided to leave the hotel. A fine oriental carpet covered the stairs, held in place with brass rods. Sissel stole down the stairs on bare feet without a creak.

The lobby was dark and still.

Sissel unlocked the front door slowly. On the street the call was even stronger. Her fingers began to tingle, as if they'd been asleep and were now coming back to life, all prickles. She clutched them together.

She walked quickly down the boardwalk past the storefronts, away from the church and the graveyard.

The town was so strange and empty in the night.

Sissel limped along as fast as she could. Gone was the exhaustion she had felt earlier in the day.

The boardwalk was coarse and dry under her bare feet. She moved down Main Street. The farther she got from the graveyard, the less she felt the strange thrum. The throbbing in her chest let up; the prickling in her fingers faded.

Sissel stopped to breathe. Now she felt something else playing at the edge of her consciousness. It was a light tinkling. Another call, this one more playful and musical.

"Oh!" she said softly. "Why won't you leave me alone?"

But the strange sensation glimmered and called to her, like a half-remembered song she recognized, with a melody she could not place.

"All right!" she said crossly. "I surrender!" She followed the new sound.

She left the walkway and trod on the street, thankful for the full moon, wishing she had brought her boots. The skin on the soles of her feet was thin and soft because she'd worn shoes almost every day for most of the summer.

Sissel came to understand it—the shape of the forces calling her were fluid—it was the stream calling her! The pretty little stream that came out of the hills behind the town. It ran east of town, and into the river. The schoolchildren fished there, and James had taken her and Alice there on a picnic one time.

She left the road and began to walk through the tall summer grasses toward the thick cottonwoods and brush that banked the stream.

She found an old, worn path, her feet padding on smooth dirt between clumps of grass. The closer she got, the denser the bushes on the banks grew. It was dark under the shadows of the trees. Gnarled scrub oak brushes with their scabby branches blocked her way and plucked at her hair, her shift, her arms and legs. Out alone in the woods, she began to feel afraid and frantic. Her hands were tingling like before, and there was a pulling sensation in her chest. She must reach the water.

Finally plunging through the brush, she came to the edge of the stream. The bank dropped several feet down to the water rushing by. Sissel took a false step with her bad leg, and suddenly it went out from under her.

She fell down into the stream, banging her knees on the slippery rocks. The icy water made her gasp. She might have cut the palm of one of her hands, but she couldn't tell. It was cold, but at the same time she felt a buzzing, joyous kind of warmth in the water. The glittering sound was so loud now, it was crashing down around her.

Suddenly Sissel became conscious of the strangeness of what she was doing. She became sensible to the fact that she was wearing only a linen shift and robe, both now wet. She was on her hands and knees in a moonlit stream, nearly naked and just outside town.

She sat back onto her heels. She looked around at the muddy banks of the stream, at the dark shapes of the scrub oak on the banks. She rubbed her arms with shaking hands.

"I've gone mad," she said aloud, her voice so small she could not even hear it.

Sissel put her hands into the water again. They immediately began to thrum with her quickening pulse. She tried moving her fingers in time with her heartbeat, flaring them out, then pulling in. It was so absurd she laughed.

"What is it?" she said. "What am I supposed to do?"

The water ran over her icy hands. In the moonlight, her fingers were pearly white and pale. Numb from cold.

Sissel closed her eyes. *Come, then*, she thought. *Whatever you are. Come.*

She felt her hands begin to heat up. Prickles of fire on the tips of her fingers. Pinpricks, coming so fast they hurt.

She snatched her hands out of the water.

They were shining, not the shine of moon on wet skin, but shining with gold. She turned them back and forth.

Her hands were covered in gold flake.

She brought her palms together. She could feel the flakes and tiny gold crystals rubbing against her skin. The gold held, as if magnetized to her skin.

My Nytte is born, she thought. Gooseflesh rippled along her arms and legs. She found her body shaking now, quaking not with cold but with awe.

She knew what she was, even though Rolf said there had not been one of this type of Nytteson for hundreds of years.

Sissel was a Ransacker.

She thought, *I must give thanks.*

"*Ásáheill*," she prayed. "Thank you, great Odin." But she could not hear her own voice. All sound had been leached from the world. Not even the water dared to trickle.

It frightened her, the silence.

"Hello," she said. Nothing. And she let out a frightened cry that she could not hear. It was an eerie, awful sensation.

Her Nytte had stolen her hearing.

Sissel heaved her shaking body back toward the rocks on the banks of the stream. Her shift was dripping wet, her limbs numb with the frigid water. She climbed out of the stream, grabbing on to branches to help her. She wondered if the gold would rub off on the branches, but she also knew she had to get out of the stream. Her health demanded it.

She was terribly tired now. Tired and cold. Only her hands were warm. She made it to the footpath and lay down to catch her breath.

Sissel held her hands up, turned them back and forth.

The gold was still there, warming her skin.

She had the strange feeling the gold was smiling at her. It liked her.

No, the little gold flakes loved her, wanted to be with her, and all she had to do was pull them to her. Gold, it seemed, had a personality.

She laid her two hands over her chest, to warm it.

Sissel thought about the graveyard. There had to be gold there, in the rocks near where the caskets were laid. Perhaps her Nytte had been trying to be born in that moment during the funeral.

Sissel found she was grinning.

She pressed her hands to her face, and the gold flakes vibrated between the two surfaces of her skin, warming her cheeks. She laughed.

Her pale, thin hands looked like they were covered in gloves made of golden lace.

Sissel sat up. She needed to get back to the hotel. She needed to dry off and figure out how to transfer the gold on her hands to a plate or a dish or a cloth. She couldn't wait to show Stieg!

It was difficult to rise. Her leg ached, and she shook with exhaustion. She was thankful for how soft the bent and trodden grasses were underfoot. No longer driven by the rush that had possessed her, she felt the scrapes and cuts on her feet and legs.

She limped to town. The street was still. It was the same as when she'd left it. Everything was different for her, but the town was the same as she'd left it.

A fleck of gold went floating past her vision in the air. She brought her right hand to her face, and a few more flecks of gold fell away.

"No," she said.

She tried to call the gold to her, but she had lost the rhythm from the creek.

Sissel closed her eyes, searching for her pulse, for that strange thrum she had felt, but she was too agitated.

"Wait," she said. More of the gold was falling away now. *Come back*, she willed.

Fat, heavy flakes fell from her fingertips, drifting away like apple blossoms on a warm spring breeze.

Sissel scraped at the gold on her left hand, trying to collect it in the palm of her right. She had only a small amount, maybe a teaspoonful, but she clutched it and hobbled back to town.

Sissel sneaked up the front stairs to the hotel. She sent a silent prayer to the Gods of the Æsir and turned the knob. Her prayer was answered—there was no one in the lobby.

The stairs seemed much steeper on the way back up. She saw she had left the door to her suite open! Wide-open! She entered her room and locked it behind her. Exhaustion was overtaking her now.

Sissel caught a glimpse of herself in the mirror. She looked wild, her shift grass stained and mud splattered; tendrils of her thin white-blond hair wisping out in all directions.

On the bedside table, there was a little painted china dish, left there to hold jewelry or hairpins or other delicate items. Sissel scraped the contents of her palm out into the dish with her fingernails—gold dust mixed with dirt, sticky with her sweat. She grinned at the sparkling mess of treasure.

She fell into bed.

I have a Nytte, she thought to herself one last time. She thought of what it would be like to tell Hanne when she returned. Sissel imagined the look of surprise on Hanne's face—and what shock and joy Hanne would feel when Sissel showed her what she could do!

CHAPTER THIRTEEN

Hanne and Owen made camp on a rise overlooking a pretty little brook. There was a thatch of green chokecherry that grew up and over the hill, and the bushes were full of red fruits and songbirds. The birds flew away with a great beating of wings when Hanne and Owen rode up on Brandy, but they soon fluttered back down to their feast.

Owen led the horse down to the stream, and Hanne followed behind with the canteens and the coffeepot.

There wasn't any dinner to cook—they hadn't brought the cast-iron spider or any other pots or pans. They would have cold chicken to eat, and some slices of brown bread slathered with sweet-cream butter and sandwiched together.

Owen made a fire, and Hanne set the kettle on. She kept sneaking looks across the fire and finding him grinning.

"What's got you so happy?" she asked. It was foolish to ask, because she knew the answer—they were in the beautiful Montana country-side and they were alone.

"It's a pretty good life. Riding in fine weather with my girl and my dog."

Daisy was rooting around in the bushes. She stuck her head out of the brush as if to check on them, then resumed her foraging.

"What about you?" he asked. "Do you miss your sister and brothers?"

"No!" she said, so resolute that Owen laughed.

"Well, that's all right," he said.

"It's nice to be alone, isn't it?" Hanne asked.

"I could get used to it."

Hanne went to the saddlebags and got out the food for supper, wrapped carefully in waxed paper.

She wouldn't blame Owen if he might actually prefer to live apart from Hanne's siblings. This was as close as he'd ever come to saying it outright. It had to be trying to him, to have become, all of a sudden, a member of their small and close-knit family.

They didn't often discuss it, but she knew that Owen under-stood Hanne felt compelled to remain as close as she could to her kin. Her Nytte made it uncomfortable to be away from them, or maybe it was her own anxious nature.

She set out the two tin plates and began dividing up the chicken. Hanne worried: Did her attachment to her siblings bother Owen? He had been so good about it, putting no pressure on her to marry, agree-ing that when they married, they'd just add on to the small house. It was the only practical thing to do—Sissel wasn't strong enough to keep house for Stieg and Knut. Hanne must do it for all of them.

Owen whistled as he curried Brandy. The horse turned her head from him as if she were a great noble and couldn't be bothered to notice the work of a mere human. But as he continued, working patiently and methodically, her eyelids began to droop and she let out a snort of pleasure.

"I know," Owen said to the horse. "Feels good, don't it?"

When they'd finished their supper, and the sun began to set behind the hills in a showy display of peach and vermillion, Hanne laid out the new double bedroll they'd purchased. The wide canvas cover enveloped two warm woolen blankets.

Owen stood, hat in hand, studying the dwindling fire. Was he blushing as much as Hanne? It was hard to say in the glow of the fire.

"I'll sleep on this side of the fire, don't you think?" he finally said. "I don't need a bedroll."

"Yes," Hanne agreed. "If you don't mind. And . . . we'll marry soon—"

"I could marry you right here on this hilltop," he said. "Not tonight, I mean, of course. I just mean when we do marry. There couldn't be a prettier place to marry in the world. No church could match it."

Hanne crossed to him and took his hand. They stood that way looking out over the valley as the flames of the dying sun washed the trees and the brush in red and orange.

THEY HAD NOTHING but cornbread and hot coffee for breakfast, but Owen said they'd pass through the town of Fitch around midday on their way to the Bar S Ranch.

Fitch was an old town, and fairly small. Owen told her it was a fur trading post that had become a town. The railroad had passed it by, and that meant the town might not grow much more. The livery in town had some small reputation as a center for horse trading.

The streets of town were laid out in a contrary tangle; none ran straight. The center of town was a three-way intersection. Prominent in the cradle of this Y shape was a small, triangular building—a general store.

Across the street on one angle there was a large livery stable, with several big pens behind. There were horses milling about, at least twenty of them.

Across the other street from the store was a dingy, low building with a sign on the wall that read SALOON. The sign looked like it had been rained on, though the morning was dry. Hanne got a whiff and realized—it wasn't rain spattered on the sign but urine. Though it was early in the day, the sounds of men laughing and arguing came from the building. Some high-pitched women's voices came through as well.

"We'll not stop here long," Owen said.

"Good," Hanne agreed.

He took her elbow and escorted her into the store. Then he left to take Brandy over to the livery. He wanted some oats for her.

The shopkeeper was happy to help Hanne, though he had none of the stores of baked goods, butter, or cheese that Hanne had hoped for. It made her realize how good the Peavys' store was—they had so many fresh foods from the farmers nearby.

This store had some cans of condensed milk, some canned peaches, a lone battered tin of sardines, and several swollen cans of pickled pigs' feet. There were barrels of beans, and sacks of flour and oats on the shelves, and a rather extensive assortment of used and new saddles, bits, and bridles hanging on the wall.

Hanne selected two cans of peaches, and was inspecting the can of sardines to make sure it was whole and sealed when she heard the door open and close behind her.

A young, gaunt cowboy had entered. Though he had the tan face of a cowboy, and wore a hat and the long duster favored by men who worked with cattle, he had a look of wealth about him. He wore a polished silver belt buckle, and Hanne saw his hat had a braided leather band, ends tipped with more silver. The trappings of wealth could not disguise how poorly the man looked. He leaned against the counter as if he needed help to remain on his feet.

She nodded to him, and he tipped his hat to her.

"I'm looking for a man named Will Pernice," he said to the shopkeeper.

"You'll find him in the saloon, most likely."

Then the door opened and Owen came in. She flashed him a smile, put the cans she'd selected on the counter, and was shocked to hear him cuss.

"Matthew!"

"Owen," said the cowboy.

Owen looked odd to Hanne, deeply discomfited.

"Hanne, this is my brother Matthew," Owen said. "Matthew, I present to you . . . my wife."

Matthew flashed his eyes over to Hanne again. He reached up to touch the brim of his hat, and Hanne thought she read a dark look on his face. But why?

"Are you all right, Matthew?"

"What are you doing in Fitch of all places?" Matthew asked at the same time.

"We're passing through. Heard about a drive out of the Bar S," Owen said.

Matthew nodded. "I hear they started out last week."

"I expect we can catch up with them," Owen said. "What about you? I saw Double B horses in the livery."

"I've come to sell them."

"Selling the horses?" Owen said in surprise. "I saw Jigsaw out there!"

Matthew began to cough. He held up his hand and withdrew a handkerchief from within his jacket. The linen dearly needed laundering. It was stained with gobs of dark yellow phlegm, and Hanne saw several spots of blood.

"We been sick, at the ranch. Whole place took with the ague."

"I'm sorry to hear that," Owen said.

"Mother's very ill. Doctor says she doesn't have long."

Hanne put her hand to her heart.

Strong emotions passed over Owen's face, and Hanne saw him try to master it.

"I'm very sorry, Matthew—"

"Everyone's got it," Matthew said. "I'm only getting over it now. Father's sick with it. Paul's sick. Anyway, we can't afford the horses."

"Harvey?"

Matthew just shook his head no.

"What about the cattle?" Owen said. "Who's minding the cattle?"

"Hired some men to drive them to Helena two months ago."

"*All* of them?"

Matthew nodded.

Hanne didn't understand this, but it was clear from Owen's posture of shock and the disbelief in his voice that this was enormous.

Matthew began to cough again. Hanne went to Owen's side.

"We should go to them, Owen," Hanne said quietly. "If things are so bad. We should help."

Matthew took a flask out of his pocket and took a nip. It seemed to help quiet the hacking.

"Matthew, do you want us to come?" Owen asked. "We could help out."

"There's nothing for you there," Matthew said, his voice low and bitter. "We've been selling it all, piece by piece."

"I don't want anything," Owen said, taking offense. "We're offering to help!"

"We don't need it!" Matthew snapped.

"Say, now, fellas, if you're going to fight, please step outside," the shopkeeper said with some anxiety.

"How can you sell Jigsaw?" Owen asked.

"Father's got it bad, Owen." Matthew put his hand up to his eyes. All the tension had gone out of his body. He looked very old all of a sudden. "I don't know if he's getting up again."

"Well, then . . . ," Owen said. After a long moment he reached up to his face and brushed the back of his hand along his eyes. "Tell him . . . tell him . . ."

Matthew put his hand out and landed it with a thump on Owen's shoulder.

"I'll tell him I saw you and that you found yourself a wife, and he'll be very pleased."

Owen nodded. He didn't seem to trust himself to speak.

Matthew hacked again into the handkerchief.

Hanne tentatively put her hand on Owen's back. He let out a deep breath.

"Take Jigsaw," Matthew said. "Father would want it that way."

Owen began to protest.

"You know he would," Matthew said. "You were always his favorite, damn you."

"That's hardly true," Owen said.

"Take Jigsaw, anyway," Matthew said. "I can't stand to sell him."

"I will, then."

"Good."

Owen headed for the door. Hanne followed. She had not bought the peaches. The cans stood on the counter, but she did not want to make a fuss.

"Matthew, tell everyone I send my regards," Owen said. "Tell Father I'm doing fine. Tell Lucy, too. Will you do that?"

Matthew nodded his head. He was leaning now on the counter.

"You should go," Matthew said. Hanne heard his voice was thick with emotion.

THEY WALKED TO the livery in silence. The paddock behind the stable was packed with horses, all of them bearing the same brand, two *B*s.

Owen climbed over the fence. Hanne followed. Several of the horses turned to sniff at him. Perhaps they remembered him.

He put his hand on the rump of a bay horse, running his hand over the darkened brand.

"The Double B, that's our ranch," he said.

"I'm so sorry, Owen, about your parents. I think we should go and see your father. Even if Matthew doesn't want us to—"

"No," Owen said. "They don't want me there, and I don't want to risk it. It's catching, the ague. I can't let it get you. I won't."

Owen spotted the horse he was looking for. Jigsaw was a beautiful paint—white, with dark brown patches scattered over his coat.

Jigsaw gave a nicker when he saw Owen and bobbed his head, as if nodding hello.

"Hello, old boy," Owen said. He leaned his forehead against the horse's massive head and closed his eyes.

Hanne felt that perhaps she should leave the paddock, give Owen a moment to himself, when she heard a voice calling her.

"Ma'am. Oh, ma'am!" It was the shopkeeper. He was lugging a saddle. It was a lovely saddle, sized for a lady, with a pommel inlaid with mother-of-pearl.

"The gentleman wants you to have this for a wedding present."

CHAPTER FOURTEEN

Sissel awoke to an insistent knocking on the door.

"Sissel!" came Stieg's voice from the hall. "Are you ready?"

Sissel sat up with a start. From the angle of the sun coming in her gauzy window curtains, she could tell she had overslept.

Then she was awake in an instant—the night! The gold! It all came back to her. She threw away the sheet and thin summer blanket and gasped.

There was dried mud in the bed. Her shift was stained, and mud still clung to her feet. But there, in the dish, was the precious thimble-ful of gold flake.

"Are you well, Sister?" came her brother's voice. Sissel slid out of bed and limped to the door. The soles of her feet were tender. She unlocked the door and threw it open.

"What on earth!" Stieg gasped as he took in the sight of her muddy shift, dirty feet, and general disarray.

Sissel grabbed him by the arm and pulled him inside.

"Stieg!" A fierce, sudden joy swept into her. Sissel embraced him. "You won't believe it! Oh, Stieg!"

"Why are you covered in mud? Are those scratches on your legs? Were you outside in your nightclothes?"

Sissel had to laugh at his expression of utter bafflement.

"Brother, I have a Nytte!"

"What?" His eyes widened in disbelief.

"Look!" She picked up the little dish of gold flake mixed with dirt. He sat, abruptly, on the bed.

"I had a dream. I think it was Odin—he said, *Awaken*. And then I followed this call from the little stream outside town. I can hear . . . no, not hear, but sense, gold calling to me, Brother!"

"But, Sissel, this is amazing! There hasn't been a Ransacker in five generations. Or more. Rolf thought they might only be a myth."

They traded places—Sissel sat on the bed and Stieg began to pace.

"The calling you felt," Stieg said, interrupting her thoughts. "The way the gold was pulling you to it, do you feel it now? Can you sense it?"

"No," Sissel said.

"What about the other metals in this room?" He strode to the door. "The doorknob, it's iron. Can you feel it?"

Sissel closed her eyes. She had trouble focusing; there was too much excitement in her. Her face was screwed up in concentration. She jumped when Stieg put his hand on her shoulder.

"Easy, Sister," he said. "Try to reach more lightly for it."

Sissel released a great breath. She imagined a flower opening in her mind, and there, she could feel it—the iron doorknob. Iron was heavy and phlegmatic. It had a low, unpleasant vibration, almost crass.

She tried to turn the knob with her mind. No, it was too heavy to turn. Just handling it made her a bit nauseous.

Sissel cast her eyes around the room. There was the gold in the dish, twinkling and twittering. There was the brass tag on her room key. Brass was lovely, not as warm as gold, but friendly still, and pliant somehow.

Other bits of metals called for her attention. The iron nails. The metal pulls on the bureau. Her head began to spin with the sudden cacophony of noise. She lay down on the bed, holding her stomach.

Stieg put a comforting hand on her shoulder. His cool fingers pressed her forehead, testing for a fever. She hadn't realized how tired she was. Now, closing her mind to the Nytte, she felt so tired she slipped into sleep.

When she awoke, there was a note from Stieg saying he had left to teach school and that she should rest.

She was happy to have the day off from school. She spent some time shaking out her sheets and trying to get as much dirt off her night-gown as she could. Then she passed the rest of the afternoon getting to know the metals in her room.

CHAPTER FIFTEEN

James watched for Stieg and Sissel out of the schoolhouse window. Sissel had not come to school the day before. When James had inquired about her health, Stieg said she wasn't feeling quite herself, but when he said it, there was a little smile he was suppressing. Odd. Now they were late, and Stieg was never late.

In the yard, small boys squatted in the dirt, playing a throwing game with pebbles as markers. The little girls were dancing in a ring, chanting about London Bridge.

James had a bag of licorice allsorts for Sissel in his pocket, and another bag with identical contents for Alice. There were three other girls the age of Sissel and Alice at the school, but they didn't seem to like Sissel much. It never failed to surprise him, how mean-spirited girls of this age could be. But he was also surprised by Sissel's reaction to it—she didn't seem to care one bit.

Nate McKinnon ambled into the classroom and greeted James, then Howie Ackerman came in and asked a question about what kind of nails they had at the store. The older students continued to trickle in. Finally Sissel and her brother arrived, discussing something in hushed, happy tones.

"Good morning, Mr. Hemstad, Miss Hemstad," James said, making his way to them.

"Yes, good morning, James," Stieg said. He crossed to his desk and began to prepare his papers for the day.

"I hope you're feeling better," James said.

"Yes, thank you," Sissel said. There was a faraway look in her eyes. She was smiling with some private happiness.

"How is the bridal suite?" James asked.

"Quite lovely," Sissel said.

"Any word from your sister?"

Sissel refocused her gaze, coming back to him as if from a distance.

"No. I'm not sure she'll be able to write at all, assuming they are hired on for the drive."

Sissel was removing items from her school satchel and setting them inside the desk. She lifted her pencil case and regarded it for a moment.

What was going on with her?

James put his hand onto hers. That got her attention.

"We've got peaches into the store," James said. "May I bring one to you later today?" He'd been telling Sissel all about the curious fruits—she'd never tasted one.

"That would be lovely," she said. Then she seemed to wake up a bit. "Only, Stieg has asked me to go on a walk with him later."

"A walk?"

Sissel nodded. Her cheeks colored a bit as she removed her reader from her satchel.

"Very well," James said. She was hiding something, but what? "Perhaps tomorrow."

It made him feel a bit edgy, to be dismissed in this way. He sought for another topic of conversation to pursue, but thankfully Alice came swirling in.

"Good morning, you two!" Alice said.

"Good morning," James said.

Alice kissed Sissel on the cheek. "We've got the most wonderful fabrics in. Crepe de Chine. There's a Napoleon blue you must see and a light pink, soft like a cherry blossom. That one's taffeta, but taffeta wears better than people say."

"Taffeta? I'd never," Sissel said.

"What do you think about taffeta, James?" Alice turned to him, her eyes playful and bright.

Sissel laughed. "Yes, do you find it wears well?"

"It depends on who's wearing it," James said.

"What about Sissel here?" Alice said.

"She's lovely in anything she wears," James said, glad for a chance to regain his footing. Flattery was familiar territory. "If you made her a dress out of a flour sack, she'd be radiant."

"Please," Sissel said. "Don't be silly."

Did she look pleased or irritated? He couldn't quite tell.

"Sissel," Alice said, loud enough for everyone to hear, "Howie asked me to the Ladies' Aid dance yesterday." Alice gave a wave to Howie, who blushed beet red and scratched behind his ear.

"How nice," Sissel said.

Alice turned to James, her eyes sparkling.

"Are *you* going to the Ladies' Aid dance, James?" Alice asked.

"Alice . . . ," Sissel said in a warning tone.

"I think it's time we know our friend's plans, don't you?"

Of course, James meant to ask Sissel, but had been waiting for her to settle in to life in town. He didn't want to seem callous by asking too soon after the loss of their farm.

It seemed like now was to be the time.

Alice stood looking at him with an expectant arch to her eyebrows. Sissel was flushed and scowling at Alice comically.

"I have a mind to, if I can find the right partner," James said with a bit of swagger. "But I haven't got up my courage to ask anyone yet."

"James Peavy!" Alice cried.

"Don't ask Millicent Crawford," Sissel interjected. "She's only seven."

James turned to Sissel.

"Miss Hemstad," he said, drawing out a pause dramatically, "who do *you* think I should ask?"

Sissel laughed. So did Alice.

"I'm sure I don't care," Sissel said. "I'm planning to ask Mr. Collier, the manager at the Royal."

Now everyone laughed; the older students had all started listening in.

"No, no, don't do that," James said. "He'll hook you like a fish with that mustache of his. Go with me, instead."

Sissel rolled her eyes with a melodramatic flair. "If I must," she said.

James patted her hand. "I'm glad." He felt himself smiling sincerely.

"Thank goodness that's settled," Alice said. "Now we can get to work on your dress!"

Stieg rose from his desk. "Let's get the school day started as well. James, would you be so kind as to ring the bell?"

AT THE END of the day, Sissel bid Alice and James a hasty good-bye, then rushed over to Stieg.

"Aren't you coming to the shop?" Alice asked.

"Sissel and I have plans, I'm afraid," Stieg said.

"But we need to get started on our dresses—"

"All in good time," Stieg had said. He'd taken Sissel's arm and they'd gone straight out.

The Hemstads had an air of conspiracy about them, to be sure.

James followed them, at a safe distance, but as he was passing the store, Mrs. Denmead came out.

"Come help me with my parcels, James," she said.

"I would . . . only—"

"Only nothing! I've spent nearly eight dollars here today, and I expect your complete and utter devotion."

James sighed. "Yes, ma'am, of course." He couldn't refuse her, not without being rude.

James caught one last glimpse of his mark walking off down the road arm in arm with her big brother, then he gathered Mrs. Denmead's parcels from the front porch of the store and helped her home with them.

He was confident he'd find out what was happening in due time.

CHAPTER SIXTEEN

"All right, you can turn around," Stieg said. Sissel spun, squinting into the golden afternoon sun. Stieg was about twenty feet away. They stood in a grassy field outside town that was dotted with thick clusters of yellow larkspur. It was railroad land, uninhabited and unused, except for the tracks cutting through.

Above the meadow, the enormous Montana sky was a deep, friendly blue. Shadows floated along the green meadow, cast by the tall puffed clouds above.

Stieg had carefully washed and strained Sissel's muddy pinch of gold flake, then transferred it to the center of a handkerchief and knotted it tight.

"I've hidden three metals for you to find," Stieg said. "Good luck!" He smiled, the corners of his eyes crinkling with happiness for her. She squeezed his hand.

Sissel took a deep breath, released it slowly, and opened her senses to the Nytte.

She rotated her head back and forth. There were multiple vibrations, each rather faint. First, she picked out the warm, resonant call of the gold. She walked over to a stand of grass and plucked the little cloth bundle from scrub.

Sissel handed Stieg the gold. He winked at her.

She listened for the other metals, but the gold was so close. It was difficult to sense past it.

"The gold is very loud," she said. She stepped a few paces away from Stieg, and then a few more. Again, she opened her mind to her Nytte.

Sissel allowed herself to concentrate on the peculiar sensation she was experiencing, which was much less upsetting now that she knew she was a Ransacker. What she sensed from the metals was not a sound, but she experienced it like one, because she felt a vibration within her body. She felt the reverberations within her core, and each metal had a different song. She could differentiate between them the way an ear could differentiate between musical instruments.

She scanned the field and caught a pure but faint sound. She swiveled her head until she was locked into the vibration and started toward a small clump of chokecherry brush some distance across the field. The feeling from this metal was different from the gold. This was a haughtier, more restrained metal. Powerful but aloof.

Stieg watched her weaving around the bush.

The vibration got louder as Sissel drew near, so she knew she was close. She bent and ruffled the grasses near the base of the chokecherry bush with her fingers.

Instead of searching with her eyes, she held out her hands. Could she draw it to her, as she had with the gold in the stream?

There was a flash of movement in the bush as a white bundled cloth fell from its hiding place between two branches.

This wasn't actually a handkerchief but a napkin pinched from the dining room at the Royal, and inside were two silver spoons.

Sissel couldn't believe the nerve of her brother! They were from the Royal. She looked over and saw him laughing silently. She shook her head at him, pretending to be scandalized.

Sissel cast out with her senses again, and a faint, grating sound opened in her mind. Like the buzzing of an overlarge housefly. As she approached another clump of grass, she grew queasy.

She picked up the third bundle with two fingers. She turned her head away from it as if it stunk.

Stieg walked over and took it from her. Opening it, he showed her the contents—three dark lead bullets.

"They make me feel sick," she said. Her voice sounded distant.

Stieg said something to her, and she asked, "Pardon?"

He brought his fingers up to her ear and snapped them.

At first, Sissel thought he was pretending. Then she realized suddenly that she could barely hear the snapping.

"I can't hear," she said.

She found her legs failing her, and so she sat abruptly in the sedge grass. Stieg lowered down to his haunches beside her. She could see that he was talking. He took out his pocket watch and marked the time as he spoke.

"I can't hear you," she said, probably too loudly. She could hear her voice, but so faintly. Stieg nodded and kept talking.

After a few moments, with Sissel looking around her at the mute world, his voice began to come back.

"... of all the Norwegian playwrights, Ibsen is the most innovative, and has such insights into the lives not of men, Sissel, but of women ..."

On and on he went, talking about his favorite playwright.

"I can hear you now," Sissel said. "Why are you bothering with talk of Ibsen?"

Stieg noted the time on his watch. "I just wanted to keep up a steady stream of conversation so I would be able to see when your hearing came back."

"And?" she asked.

"Around three minutes, I'd say."

He stood and offered a hand to hoist her up.

"What do you make of it?" Sissel asked.

"We've found the curse that accompanies the Nytte of being a Ransacker. Hearing loss."

Sissel felt a jolt of fear.

"Will I someday go deaf, Stieg?"

"It's possible," he said. "Just as there is a possibility I will lose my eyesight. Or that the hunger that accompanies Hanne's gift will take her life if she fails to eat. Each Nytte has such a curse."

Sissel felt her heart sink. She wouldn't be able to hear voices, or music!

"Still, I'm pleased," Stieg said.

"How can you say that?"

"It could have been something much worse, such as going mad, or being struck dead without warning, as happens to Oar-Breakers."

Sissel nodded solemnly. She often thought with dread of the terrible price Knut would pay for his Nytte.

"All I mean to say is that we don't know much about Ransackers," Stieg said. "But this we can work with."

Sissel nodded.

"I think that's enough for one day," Stieg said. "We don't want to overtax you."

"THERE IS AN assayer at the bank," Sissel said later as they walked back to town. "Two of the boys at school were talking about it. He would tell us if the gold is of any quality and how much it's worth."

"We're not selling the gold."

"Why ever not?"

"What if people ask questions about where we got it? What about mineral rights? It might be illegal for you to have taken gold from the stream, which runs on railroad property."

"We need money to tide us over until you get paid," Sissel said. "We owe all over town—Mrs. Boyce, the Oswalds' Dry Goods Emporium, the general store. We're taking advantage of our friends."

"Everyone understands what we've been through," Stieg said.

"Are you telling me it wouldn't feel good to put a dollar or two in Mr. Collier's hand?"

Stieg walked ahead for a moment. He tended to let his stride get long when he was deeply occupied in thought. Sissel had to walk double time to keep up. Her bad leg began to complain, but she said nothing about it.

"Very well," he said. "But let me do the talking."

"All right," Sissel answered.

THE BANK WAS the only brick building in town. It was square with white stone cornices and window ledges.

Inside, a long wall with three barred windows ran the length of the room. Tellers worked behind two of the barred windows, and customers lined up three or four deep in front of them.

It turned out that Isaiah McKray was one of the customers waiting. Stieg nearly turned and left, but Sissel clamped down her hand on his arm.

McKray looked impatient to be kept waiting. There were two tall farmers in the queue with him, one in front and one behind. He had to rise up on his tiptoes to look over the shoulder of the farmer in front of him. It made him look even shorter and younger. Sissel felt a sudden pang of sympathy for him.

Apparently McKray had never gone to school. He'd been raised up on his father's prospecting claims, and later near the large mine that his father had established high in the mountains in the southwest of Colorado. This Sissel had learned from Bridget, the maid who cleaned her room. Bridget had it from the cook, who took coffee to Mr. Collier in the afternoons. Collier apparently became chatty when he drank his coffee, so that much of McKray's life history was known to the employees at the hotel. Bridget had told Sissel that McKray had been forced to work in the mines as a boy, learning every job from drilling to smelting. And that McKray Sr. had staked McKray Jr. in the hotel business, but was charging interest on the investment.

McKray caught her looking at him and doffed his hat in greeting. She was embarrassed to be caught looking, and a flush spread on her cheeks.

Then Sissel remembered the silverware Stieg had pilfered from the hotel. Her eyes flitted to his pocket. How humiliating it would be if he was somehow caught with it before he could return it!

The line wasn't moving because there was a dispute of some kind with one of the tellers, and Sissel began to feel weary. Her bad leg was aching now from the long walk to and from their practice field. But she could not tell Stieg she wanted to leave, not after she had worked so hard to get him to agree to sell the gold dust.

Behind the tellers, Sissel could see a large safe. As an experiment, just to pass the time, Sissel opened her mind to the metal. The iron hit her as loud as a gong. She staggered back, and Stieg gripped her arm to keep her from stumbling.

"Sissel?"

Sissel focused on shutting her mind to the metal. She gritted her teeth and imagined herself pushing the sound away. That didn't seem to work.

Instead she thought about pulling tight on a drawstring. That was the image. She imagined the booming vibration of the iron getting smaller and smaller, a circle closing tight.

A strong hand took her arm.

"Are you well, Miss Hemstad?" It was McKray. His face was close, sincere concern written on it.

He pressed a handkerchief into her hand. She used it to dab at her damp forehead.

"She's fine," Stieg said. "It's the heat. Let's go, Sissel. I'll take you back to the hotel."

"I'm all right," Sissel protested.

She shifted her body, shaking off the steadying hands of both her brother and McKray.

"Truly, I'm fine," Sissel said. She gave McKray back his handkerchief, and he resumed his place with the teller next to them.

"Our business can wait," Stieg said. "Let's *go*."

But the man ahead of them kindly bowed out of line and gestured for them to go ahead.

"We'll come back later," Stieg told him.

"Nonsense. I'm happy to wait," the man said.

"Thank you," Sissel said firmly. Stieg stepped up to the teller, resigned.

"We have some gold dust to be assayed, if possible," Stieg said, making his voice quiet as to not be overheard. "I have been dabbling on the weekends, and I found a bit of flake."

Sissel saw McKray stand up tall, interest piqued.

"I see," the teller said. "Please step to the far window." The teller stepped away from the bars and nodded to the teller at the other window, who closed his station.

Now all eyes were on Stieg and Sissel as they peeled away from the line and headed to the empty window, a paper shade pulled down tight.

A moment later the paper shade retracted and there stood the teller from the first window, a rumpled man with spectacles and a walrus-like mustache.

"I am Fejdor Rusk, an assayer for Chouteau County. How may I serve?" he asked in a thick Slavic accent.

"You're an assayer as well as a bank teller?"

The man shrugged. "That's how it works. I repeat, how may I serve?"

"I was lucky enough to find some gold flake," Stieg said. He held out the knotted handkerchief.

All the customers drew close behind Sissel and Stieg, their business put aside. One of them was a man she'd seen helping Mr. Peavy with odd jobs around the store, Tyrone Clements. Another was Frank Ebbott, a hunched-over man with long, yellowing whiskers whom Sissel recognized from church, where he sat at the back and scowled.

He was an old trapper, and now that the area had been hunted out, he'd turned to selling shingles.

McKray came up to stand next to Sissel.

"Exciting stuff," he said.

She heard Stieg sigh. This was exactly the kind of attention he had hoped to avoid.

"Please move away," Rusk said. He made a flicking gesture with his hand, and Sissel and Stieg, as well as everyone else, took a step back. "Not you two," he said to Stieg and Sissel.

Rusk brought out a wooden tray lined with black velvet. He untied the handkerchief and tipped the contents out onto the tray.

He produced a jeweler's eyepiece from a drawer and commenced to study the gold.

Sissel felt a fondness for it, the gleaming gold. There wasn't much, but she still felt proud of it.

The bank customers had edged close again. Sissel cast her eyes sideways to gauge McKray's expression. He was studying the flake intently.

"Hmm," Rusk said. Then, "Amateur?"

"Pardon?" Stieg asked.

"You're an amateur? Prospector?"

"Yes, sir," Stieg said.

"Many a prospector go out with a burro, work for a year, not find so much." Rusk looked at Stieg with undisguised appraisal. "Congratulations. You are very lucky."

"Congratulations, indeed," McKray said.

"Rest assured, part of it will go to you, Mr. McKray," Stieg said.

McKray waved his hand as if their debt to him meant nothing.

"Must have taken you some time to collect," the old trapper said.

"You know, I almost bought that land you're on. Over by the Baylors, ain't you?"

"Shut your mouth, Ebbott!" Rusk snapped. Then he pointed at Stieg. "Many in town will try to get this information of where you find the gold. My advice, don't tell nobody, unless they bring the law on you."

"Yes, sir," Stieg responded.

"I was just curious," Ebbott said.

"Back away from my desk," the assayer said.

The trapper shook his head in disgust and headed off. The other teller, who had stepped over to see the gold, returned to his window, and the other customers got back to business.

Rusk began to inspect the gold, poking at it with a pair of tweezers. Next he carefully scraped the flake into the bowl of a set of scales. After weighing it, he scribbled some figures on a scrap of paper.

"I put this gold at eighty-seven to ninety percent pure. Pretty good. You have a bit over point eight ounces here. I can offer you fifteen dollars and fifty-five cents for it if you wish to sell. Prices are high. I recommend you sell."

"Thank you. Yes. We'll be delighted to sell," Stieg said.

Sissel watched the assayer count out one ten-dollar bill, five singles, and fifty-five cents. She felt herself swelling with contentment. She had found that money! She had drawn it to her from a stream, and now they were fifteen dollars richer.

Her joy was soon deflated. Leaving the bank, Stieg held her elbow tight as a vise.

"I knew it was a mistake," he said through clenched teeth.

"Why?"

"Now it's a story. Word will get out. You heard McKray—we may have prospectors crawling over our land."

"There's nothing there for them to steal," Sissel said. "At least, I don't think there is. Oh, Stieg, we should go out there! Who knows what I might find!"

"It's attention on us, and we don't want it. Do you have any idea what the Baron would do to get his hands on you if he knew what you are?"

Stieg was hustling her back to the hotel, where she was sure he would give her a less restrained scolding.

Sissel pulled her arm away from him.

"Goodness, Stieg, look around," she hissed. "We are in a safe town, surrounded by friends. Something good has happened to me, finally something good! Give me one moment to enjoy it!"

Stieg stood there, dumbfounded. Sissel walked ahead. Though it pained her bad leg, she strode quickly and with confidence. She could rub down her leg later if it ached. Right now, she was walking straight and tall.

CHAPTER SEVENTEEN

Jigsaw was a delight to ride. Hanne hadn't known a horse could have so much personality. He was content to have Hanne as a rider, or so it seemed, because he rode so easy, and never tried to snatch a mouthful of grass from the path, and because he frequently turned his head to look at her and made a happy snuffling sound.

Owen, on the other hand, had become a dour companion. He wouldn't talk to Hanne about his parents, not even after they'd left Fitch and were well on their way to intersect the Bar S drive.

"It was lovely of Matthew to give us this saddle," she said.

He said, "Yup," and gave Brandy his spurs.

"I'm so sorry about your parents, Owen. I know you weren't close, but this terrible news must come as a shock," she tried when they stopped to water the horses. He said nothing, only nodded and chucked a rock into the muddy stream.

"You must be upset," she pushed.

"I know it's hard to understand, but not all families are close like yours," he snapped.

Then she realized he needed to be left alone.

Owen had rarely spoken of his family. Every once in a while, he'd speak with some admiration for his father—the way he ran the ranch, or how he taught Owen to tie knots. But of his mother Owen said little. Hanne formed the impression that she was a cold and formal lady. Highborn and difficult to please.

When they camped for the night near a small pond, Owen set off grimly with his shotgun. There was only a heel of bread left of their provisions. Hanne found some hen of the woods mushrooms growing at the base of an oak tree and collected them. Some mallows grew near the water's edge, but she couldn't remember how to cook the tubers, so she left them be. Hanne made a fire and got coffee brewing. That was the one thing they had plenty of.

Owen returned an hour later, with two fat hares, gutted and skinned. Hanne could see his expression was still grim. She decided to push on, to act as if everything was all right.

"These will be lovely roasted over the fire," she said. "If you can find two notched sticks, we can make a spit."

Owen nodded, grateful to be given a chore to do.

Hanne gathered some leaves from a sagebrush and stuffed them inside the hares, along with the mushrooms. Then she stitched the hares up with a bit of string from her sewing kit, hoping the mushrooms wouldn't fall out.

She roasted the hares over the spit Owen had fashioned, and it made for a delicious meal. Daisy sat rather close to the fire, as if hoping a morsel would spill for her to gobble up.

After they ate, and Daisy happily devoured the scraps, and once the sun set, so that the flickering, popping campfire was the only light, Owen spoke.

"I can only imagine what you must think of me," he said. "To hear my brothers and parents are in trouble and not rush to their sides."

Hanne waited; surely he'd say more. He'd explain. But he did not speak, and the silence became oppressive. By not answering, it now seemed that she did think poorly of him.

She chose her words carefully.

"I wish I knew more about your life with your family," she said at last. She looked at his face across the fire. He was cradling his forehead in his hand, rubbing his brow.

"You've said very little about them. And now I suppose . . . I suppose I wonder how they could have mistreated you so badly that you wouldn't want to go."

"I know it begs an explanation." Owen stood up abruptly, removing his face from the circle of firelight, hiding it from view. "Only please don't ask me for it."

"Owen!" Hanne said. "I am yours, always. Nothing you could tell me would change that. Do you know that?"

He nodded.

She went to him and kissed him, and hoped it would reassure him, get him to talk, to tell her what was wrong. But he stayed mute, and shortly thereafter, they went to bed on opposite sides of the fire.

CHAPTER EIGHTEEN

"I wish we could at least tell Knut," Sissel said.

They were trudging out of town, headed for the rugged, rocky hills that bordered the town to the north.

"You know he is not good with secrets," Stieg said.

"I know," Sissel said. "But it feels wrong that Knut and Hanne and Owen don't know."

"Yes, but think of the great surprise they'll have when they all come back."

Sissel breathed in deeply and looked around with satisfaction. Several hours of sun were left in the day, but the color of the light was mellowing. There had been rain, and the slope they were climbing was dotted with fresh wildflowers.

It had taken her several days to persuade Stieg to let them work outside again. After the fuss at the bank, Stieg was sure that if they went wandering together, someone would follow them.

All Sissel wanted to do was work on her powers, but Stieg insisted they follow a normal routine. After school, Sissel had spent her time in the Oswalds' shop. The girls were working on their dresses together. Then Sissel would visit with James for a few minutes in the general store, then go back to the hotel to study.

Only after her lessons were completed to Stieg's satisfaction would he work with her on her Nytte.

Stieg had used their windfall from the gold flake to pay down their debts all over town, but he had reserved a bit to buy materials for her training. He'd raided the general store, buying steel nails, brass screws, bits of nickel-plated hardware used for bridles. He'd even purchased a small silver locket.

Then, in her room, he had given her exercises. At first, it was identifying the metals by their vibration. Then finding them when hidden. At last they had moved on to her pulling them to her.

The first time she had pulled a brass tack, rolling, then tumbling end over end across her desk into her outstretched hand, Stieg whooped so loudly that Mr. Collier came up to complain.

But there was only so much they could practice in the bridal suite, and so this afternoon Stieg said they might work outside again.

"It will be a surprise," Sissel said. "And you know, I'm convinced there is gold in the graveyard, I know there is! I can get it. Wouldn't that be a great surprise, Stieg? What if I could find enough to pay off our debts?"

"You are not going to go prospecting in the graveyard! People will take you for a grave robber!"

Sissel laughed. "I hadn't thought of that. What if I just worked in the stream . . . Perhaps at night."

"We must be careful, Sissel. I've written to Rolf. He'll have the letter soon. We must wait for a reply. He'll tell us what to do."

"It will be weeks before he even receives the letter. Months even."

"Rolf would say to be patient and careful. You know he would."

Stieg stopped so Sissel could catch her breath. It was difficult to climb in a skirt, but her leg was holding up well. She found she wasn't as out of breath as she would have expected.

"You know," she said. "I think my Nytte has made me stronger."

Stieg turned to look at her.

"Yes, I've been thinking the same thing. Your color is better, you have more energy. You're eating."

He resumed the walk.

"Maybe it's as simple as that," he said. "Using your Nytte makes you hungry, and so you're finally eating, and your body is building strength."

"I could not have made this climb a month ago," Sissel said.

"I agree."

They crested the hill. On the other side, where they could no longer be spotted from the road, Stieg spread his arms wide. "This is our classroom today."

The down slope of the hill was dotted with more boulders. Growing between them were sedge grass and clumps of wildflowers.

"I have brought some coins to work with," he told her.

Then began the fun. He explained her assignment straightaway, as he knew her hearing would diminish once they started. Then he walked ten feet away.

One by one he held up the coins, and one by one Sissel snapped them out of his fingers and caught them in her palm, held as if by a magnet.

He offered up several pennies, which emitted a mild vibration that felt sweet and tannic. The copper in the penny was sweet like honey, but there was some tin in there, which gave it some bitterness and bite.

Reaching for a copper penny felt to Sissel like inhaling the scent of a cup of tea with honey in it.

Silver dimes winked at her in a bright, confident way. Then Stieg held up some nickels. She disliked the feel of them. They contained a good bit of copper, but the sweetness of it could not mask the cold, sharp nickel itself. It felt to her as if nickel did not want to be handled.

After she'd called them all to her, she handed them back. Then Stieg paced ten more footsteps away and they repeated the exercise.

Perspiration gathered on Sissel's forehead; her heart thumped in her chest. It was fun to whip coins from her brother's hand. Using her Nytte made her feel warm and powerful and alive.

The sun beamed down from a bright blue sky. She shouted to her brother, but she couldn't make out her voice or his response. Her hearing was gone but she didn't panic. She knew it would return a few minutes after they were done.

After Stieg had stepped back another ten paces, and they had run the drill again, Sissel realized she could hear something else. A new vibration. An uncomfortable one.

She held up her hand for Stieg to stop and breathed in long and slow. She passed her mind's eye over the land, searching.

She took a few steps to the east. She felt Stieg approach and touch her arm, a question in his eyes.

"There," she said, waving her hand in a loose circle. "There's something out there."

She strode toward it, the hem of her skirt gathering dirt.

Yes, there. On the ground near a sagebrush.

Sissel felt prickles go up the back of her neck. The feeling was cold and oily.

"I don't like it," she said. "Whatever it is."

Stieg put a hand on her arm to restrain her, but Sissel pushed it away.

Louder and louder, the sound crashed in her head, a twister of noise.

There, half buried in the dirt, lay a ruined and discarded shotgun, the barrels bent.

Gunmetal and steel.

This was the first rifle she had come across when using her Nytte, and there was something abominable about the touch of it on her senses. Gunmetal was a fusion of metals that felt all wrong. Steel, too, was a mixture. Heavy, sluggish iron was there, but burned together with something charred and noxious.

Sissel's knees gave out. The world spun, and the grassy prairie rushed up to meet her.

SISSEL WOKE UP to Stieg's anxious face hovering near hers. He was shading her from the last of the afternoon sun with his hat.

Sissel glanced toward the sagebrush where she'd located the shotgun. It was gone. Stieg must have taken it and thrown it over the hill.

Stieg gently helped her to sit up. He gave her a sip of water from his canteen.

"Can you hear me?" he asked.

"Yes," she said. "I don't know what happened."

Unsteadily she got to her feet. Stieg brushed dirt and twigs off her clothing, and they made their way back down to the road.

"How is your head? How is your body? Any aches and pains?"

"I feel all right," she said. "A bit embarrassed. To faint over an old gun."

Stieg pressed her to explain what had happened, and she told him about how wrong the metal had felt to her.

"I believe steel and gunmetal are both alloys," Stieg said. "I know that steel is different from other metals. I will look into it, and try to find out why it would have this effect on you."

"Never mind," she said. "Perhaps we could work with a small amount, and I could learn to close my mind to it—"

Her leg ached now, and she remembered her boasting earlier that she was so much stronger.

"Sissel," Stieg said. "I'm afraid we must be more careful from now on. Your powers are coming in, they are stronger than we know, we don't understand what they do . . . or how dear a price you will pay for using them. I think it would be best if we stopped your lessons for a while."

"What? No!" Sissel protested. "We've only just begun!"

"You have your whole life to master your Nytte," Stieg said. "But there are forces at work here we do not understand. Why would steel affect you this way? Perhaps it is poisonous to you!"

"We'll go slow, then," she said. "We'll be careful."

"And there is the matter of your hearing. What if you unwittingly pull on a metal too hard and damage your hearing for life? No." Stieg had his eyes fixed ahead on the road. He spoke carefully and slowly, the way he did when he was teaching. "Best to wait for Rolf to tell us what he knows. We never discussed the powers of a Ransacker. Not in any detail. Maybe he can recommend exercises, like the ones he gave me—"

"No!" Sissel said. "I like using my Nytte. It makes me feel alive, Stieg. I don't want to stop."

"Come now, Sissel. Show some restraint. I'm only asking you to hold off for a month or two."

"It's improving my health, you know it is!"

"You just went deaf and blacked out for a half hour," Stieg said. His eyes were snapping now; he was angry.

Sissel had her arms crossed over her chest, and Stieg had his hands on his hips. Suddenly he took a deep breath and let it out slowly.

"Let's take a few days for the effects of this great exertion to wear off. Then we can discuss it again."

"Very well," she said.

But he can't keep me from my gift, she thought. She could practice on her own. She didn't need his approval, and she didn't need his help.

CHAPTER NINETEEN

Peavy was not pleased with James. He showed this in a hundred irritating ways. He made only enough coffee for one in the morning. He used more water than necessary when shaving so James would have to go to the well twice in the morning instead of once. He even set James's composition on the Magna Carta too close to the cookstove on purpose. It was singed, and James had had to stay up into the night to recopy it.

They fought over it, as James placed the new copy carefully into his satchel the next day. He looked over at Peavy, who had his feet up on their rough wooden table. He was reading a month-old issue of the *Bozeman Weekly Herald* and eating his way through a plate of fried back bacon, washing it down with whiskeyed coffee.

"Don't glare at me, Casanova. You're not on the payroll to be an A student," Peavy said. "You're on the payroll to know what the girl and her brother are up to."

"If I pester her with too many questions, she gets irritated," James said. His voice sounded too close to a whine. He tried to beef it up. "I have to remain somewhat aloof."

"You're busy being aloof while they go off panning for gold?" Peavy ranted. "You think I like to hear of these things from Clements? Clements is supposed to be my last line of defense!"

"Perhaps I'm not as good at surveillance as the others, but I'm—"

"You're nothing at surveillance!"

"I'm learning best I can."

James took a fork and reached for a couple of pieces of bacon to make a sandwich for his lunch. Peavy moved the plate out of his reach.

"What kind of training they give you in Chicago, anyway?" Peavy groused.

"Why don't you call for more men, if you don't like the way I'm doing it?"

This was a dangerous subject to broach, as James suspected Peavy had not asked for backup because he didn't want to lose authority over the job.

Peavy leaned over and grabbed James's wrist. James dropped the fork. Peavy tightened his grip as James tried to pull away.

"How about you romance the girl and leave the strategy to me?" Peavy said.

He released James, and James stumbled back, rubbing his wrist.

"Go on along now, afore the school bell rings," Peavy said, returning to his paper.

NOW JAMES CUSSED SILENTLY. He was trailing Sissel and Stieg, walking a good, long distance behind them.

He'd spent the afternoon flat on his belly on the top of a hill looking down over a frustratingly strange scene. How the hell was he going to write this up? *"Sissel and her brother spent an hour walking to an empty field, traipsed around a bit; then Sissel found an old gun and fainted dead away."*

How else to describe what he'd seen?

James had trailed Sissel and Stieg on a couple of their apparent artistic outings. The siblings carried an easel and a painting board, but they never used them. At first, he thought they were secretly tracking game. It might explain why Stieg stood back, watching Sissel as she scouted over the terrain. Perhaps they'd felt it was unladylike for Sissel to hunt?

That theory, however, was now smashed to bits.

What was this with the gun?

Why had she fallen that way?

He must report these strange goings-on, but he knew Peavy would rip into him for being uncertain about what he'd seen. He could hear Peavy mocking him already. How could he describe this? None of it made any sense!

James strode toward town. He kicked a small rock, startling a hare from the grasses. It bounded away, off toward the hills.

It wouldn't hurt to wait a day or two to make the report, he decided. He needed more information. Whatever it was they were doing, it was the reason Sissel had seemed so changed recently.

She was happier, that was easy to see, and her limp didn't seem to be bothering her as much. But how and why was she improving so? Surely it wasn't just from taking rambling walks with her brother in the countryside.

CHAPTER TWENTY

Hanne and Owen had no trouble finding the Bar S drive the next day. The trail was trampled and littered with dung for miles behind. They smelled and heard the cattle well before they saw them. Daisy ran back and forth, sniffing the trail, then racing back to Owen with such joy it made Hanne feel bad Daisy had been kept from her true vocation for so long. She was a cattle dog through and through.

Coming over the hill and gazing down onto the massive spread of longhorns on the valley floor beneath, Hanne couldn't believe how vast the herd was.

"They've stopped to let the cattle graze," Owen explained.

Owen was more like himself again. Hanne had decided to let the matter of his family go. When he was ready, she reasoned, he'd tell her about it.

For now, he talked about longhorns, how both steers and cows had the long, sharp horns. How they were good foragers, and could eat more kinds of grasses than Angus or Herefords or other types of cattle, but that their horns meant more danger to the cowboys.

He pointed out the cowboys riding at intervals around the edges of the herd. He also showed Hanne the remuda—the small herd of extra horses that the cowboys needed. He said a cowboy might change mounts as many as three times in a day, depending on how difficult the terrain was and what their tasks were.

"See that?" Owen asked, pointing out a short, stout covered wagon with a team of four horses riding out a distance to the left of the herd and somewhat faster.

"That's the chuck wagon. The man driving it is the cook. He's sort of like the second boss of the drive. It's him we need to convince."

OWEN LED HANNE in a wide circle around the grazing cattle, downwind of the chuck wagon. He told Daisy to stay near and she did, trotting nearly parallel to Brandy in a perfect heel.

They came upon the chuck wagon and its driver, a fat fellow with a clean-shaven face. His cheeks were terribly sunburned, as was the top of his mostly bald head.

"Howdy!" he said. "I don't guess you folks happened to see my hat, did you?"

"No, sir," Owen said.

"I got rope. I got bandages. I have a sewing kit. I have a keg of pickles and two tins of cinnamon, but I didn't bring an extra hat!"

"If we had one, we'd give it to you," Owen said.

"What's a handsome young couple like the two of you doing out riding along the pastureland?"

"Well, sir, I'm Owen Bennett, Howard Bennett's son, from over in Bullhook Bottoms. I'm looking to hire on as a hand, if you need one. My wife, Hanne, is an excellent cook and a hard worker."

"My name's Witri," said the man. "We are a bit shorthanded, I guess someone told you. A bunch of our cowhands took off down to Texas."

"I had a letter from a friend a way back, telling me he'd had to leave the drive and did I want his space."

"Which one?"

"Oliver Hoakes, sir."

"He was the best one we lost. Has a voice like an angel! I used to love to hear him singing to the beefs. You a good singer?" he asked Owen. Witri had a smile on his face. It was clear he was ribbing Owen.

"No, sir. I'm afraid not."

"What about you, young lady, you a good singer?"

"No, sir. But I'm good at making pies," she answered.

He gave a laugh. "Well, the boys like pie and I got two sacks of dried apples."

He clucked at the horses and snapped the reins to keep them moving. They rode for a few moments while the man considered it.

"I'm a bit concerned over your gal's pretty face. Don't mind me saying, missus. Sometimes a pretty gal will get the boys to fighting."

Hanne was going to speak up, but Witri continued on, "Then again, sometimes having a lady in the camp gentles the men. They tend to get a bit more respectful."

He seemed to have talked himself into it.

"All right! I'm for it if the boss signs on. You should ride on up and tell him so. His name's Lorry Tincher. Negotiate your pay, and don't let him skimp you, either."

Owen rode ahead to speak with the trail boss, and Hanne stayed behind, walking Jigsaw next to the wagon.

Witri began to ask her about her family, about Norway, about her horse. He was starved for conversation, it seemed, and Hanne wondered if he'd hired them on for company as much as for the help.

HANNE HAD NOT seen Owen again that day. Witri assured her that this meant that they'd been hired on.

With the team of four horses, the chuck wagon easily got ahead of the drive. It seemed Witri and the trail boss had already agreed where Witri should make the evening camp. He identified the place and pulled the wagon off until it was close to a stand of ponderosa pines.

Then he heaved himself up and started showing Hanne around the chuck wagon.

The wagon held everything the cowboys might need on the drive, from blacksmithing equipment to spare parts for the wagon to doctoring supplies. Toward the driver, the personal gear of the cowboys was stored—bedrolls and toiletry items. In the bed of the wagon were two giant barrels of water, to be refilled at any convenient watering hole. A buffalo hide was stretched under the wagon, making a pouch for firewood. Several times during the day, cowboys had ridden up with bits of wood collected along the trail and chucked them under the wagon. Witri said this was called a *possum belly*.

One man had been so surprised to see Hanne riding along with Witri he'd dropped the branches he carried. Witri had teased him, and the poor young man went away red behind the ears.

The back of the chuck wagon was ingeniously devised. It folded down and a wooden leg supported it, making a table. Once the table was stowed away, Hanne was presented with a cabinet, better stocked than most pantries. Wooden drawers offered flour, cornmeal, oats, spices, coffee, and three types of beans: pinto, red, and black.

When Hanne marveled—everything was right at hand—Witri grinned. He was clearly proud of his chuck wagon.

Witri showed Hanne the coffeepot, claiming it was the most important piece of equipment on the whole drive.

"Cowboys run on coffee," he told her, "the thicker and blacker the better."

He showed her how to make it—to toss generous handfuls of the roasted, hand-milled beans into boiling water in the pot. When they wanted to serve it, he told her, they'd throw some cold water to bring the grounds down to the bottom and that was that.

Witri said to celebrate her and Owen's joining the team, they'd have a pie. He let her prepare the filling and the dough for the crust, watching her, commenting on her work. He liked it. When she asked for pie tins, he laughed.

They cooked the pie in a Dutch oven, nestling it into the coals, then shoveling hot coals onto the iron lid. Then they set to preparing the evening's meal. It was bean stew. Witri told her to get used to beans. They were the main staple. He took a piece of bacon from a drawer and hacked off a good hunk.

"Little bacon in the beans and the boys are happy," he said.

He set her to dicing the bacon into small pieces and got to work himself on making bread. His prize possession was a jar of sourdough starter he said he'd kept alive for twenty-three years. He'd named it Alice.

This got Hanne chatting about the Alice she knew, Alice Oswald, back in Carter. Together, the two passed the afternoon happily, trading stories and preparing the evening meal.

The cowboys rode in, keeping upwind of the camp so as not to send dust into the food. Most of them were quite young, some as young as fourteen or fifteen. All of them were covered in dust.

They all came, rowdy and joking, into the camp, and when they saw her, they stopped. It was comical, the way they swept off their hats. They looked as surprised to see her at the chuck wagon as they would have if a snowman were there, serving beans.

All the men stood back a bit, shy to come forward. Owen came riding in, Daisy at a heel.

"Fellas, this is young Mrs. Bennett," Witri said. Hanne was surprised to hear herself called so. "We hired her on, along with her husband, Owen, who was riding drag today, I believe. Don't worry. Young Mrs. Bennett is nice, and she makes a good pie. You all treat her like your own grandma, you hear."

There was a chorus of "Yes, sirs." The cowboys ambled up and took shallow, dented tin bowls out of a box that got stored under the wagon.

Owen took his place in line, and the cowboys processed in an orderly fashion, holding out their bowls. Hanne gave each a dollop of beans.

"You can give them a bit more," Witri said, overseeing. "We got plenty."

Hanne began to dish out more vigorous portions. Owen winked at her as she served him. Then she heard a voice, "Son of a bitch. Don't that look like Bennett's dog?"

Owen had been eating, sitting on a tree stump.

Now he stood as two older cowboys swaggered into camp.

"Whistler, Mandry, you missed my announcement. Owen Bennett

and his wife have joined our company. I take it you're formerly acquainted?" Witri asked.

Hanne felt her Nytte awaken. There was malice coming from these men toward her beloved.

"Come, Freya," she prayed. "Be with me. Make me wise. Stay my hand."

She knew the name Mandry. He had been the trail boss on Owen's last cattle drive—Mandry had gotten Owen drunk at the end of the trail and was possibly the person who'd robbed him as well.

Mandry was strong and stout, an old, experienced hand with a deeply lined face and a sneer at his mouth. Whistler was the same age, but looked weaker. He had eyes that bugged out and yellow teeth.

Mandry didn't answer Witri, just kept his eyes trained on Owen.

"I'll be," Mandry said. "It *is* Bennett's dog. What the hell are you doing here, Owen Bennett?"

"Watch your language, Mandry," Witri said. "We got a lady in camp now."

"That right?" Mandry said. He took a long look at Hanne. She fought her urge to move into the stance of a warrior. Her knuckles turned white on the handle of the wooden spoon she held.

"That's my wife, Mandry," Owen said. "You'll treat her with respect."

Mandry held his hands up.

Whistler shook his head. "Owen Bennett gets a pretty wife and he brings her to trail? Lord, if she was mine I'd not bring her anywhere near this ugly business."

The other cowboys, scattered around the chuck wagon, sitting on rocks or saddles or grass, watched this exchange tensely.

"We've come to work," Owen said, his words measured. "Anything else on your mind, we can settle it away from the herd."

"Now, now, fellas, you know I don't put up with any nonsense," Witri said.

Mandry said, "Yes, sir," acting innocent, and took a plate.

When he approached Hanne for the beans, she prayed to Freya for calmness. She felt like whacking the man across the face. She was proud her hand was steady as she scooped the beans out.

"Mmm," Whistler said, slightly inclining his head toward Hanne's body. "Smells good."

Owen came over to stand at Hanne's side.

Whistler laughed, and took his plate away to eat.

"You fellas won't get pie if you keep that sort of behavior up," Witri said. "You all right, Mrs. Bennett?"

"Yes, sir," Hanne said.

"Well, you take a plate and go off and sit with your husband."

Hanne was grateful to be away from the eyes of the many men. She sat next to Owen. Daisy came to sit near Hanne, as if to protect her.

"Hanne, those men—" Owen said. He looked worried.

"I'm not afraid of them," she said.

"Of course not," Owen said. "But . . . they're ugly men. They're nasty inside. They'll . . . they might say ugly things."

"I've heard ugly things, Owen. My ears aren't so delicate they will break if I hear bad language."

"I suppose not," Owen said. He was silent as he finished his food. Hanne pondered her husband-to-be. He was a quiet man, that was true. But there was something else at work here besides his usual reserve. He was keeping something from her.

CHAPTER TWENTY-ONE

Sissel felt bad about tricking Stieg, but she could not bear to sit another day in school. Not when she felt so good, so vital, and not after Mrs. Boyce had made another pointed request that they pay the rest of their bill. They needed money, and Sissel was determined to see if there was any gold on their land.

When Stieg had knocked that morning, she came to the door and told him she needed to rest in bed. He looked so truly concerned for her she felt bad. She assured him it was just a summer cold and asked for tea and toast to be brought up.

He had said he would look in on her after he dismissed school. That meant Sissel had seven hours, seven hours of freedom, before she must again appear at her door, looking bedraggled and under the weather.

She knew James would wonder where she was. He would likely beat Stieg to her door. He'd bring her some treat from the store or a posy of wildflowers. Of course, he could not think she would admit him to her room, but she was sure if she let him, he would come in and sit and talk to her all day, asking her questions.

It was peculiar—it seemed the more she withdrew from him, the harder he tried to gain her attention.

Sissel had started to think she might break things off with him. After the dance, of course. It would be cruel to do it before then. When he touched her, she still felt the wild quickening of her pulse, and she still marveled at his good looks, but he seemed almost desperate to know her mind. It made her anxious, especially because she had such a big secret to keep from him.

Sissel was glad she had broken away from him today.

Sissel pocketed a sandwich and an apple for her lunch and left her room.

She silently crept down the stairs, waiting until Mr. Collier was called away by one of the porters so she could slip out the door unobserved.

She crossed Main Street and then took the alley that ran along the backs of the buildings on the train side of the town. The noises of town life were a chorus of ordinariness all around, and as she went sneaking along, Sissel found herself smiling. She had to keep herself from laughing outright—how good it felt to have somewhere to go and something exciting to do.

IT HAD RAINED several times in the weeks since she and Stieg had moved to town. There was a thin green blanket of new growth over the fields around their old house. Thicker, mottled patches of grass were growing in spots. The burned land reminded her of the coat of a stray cat with a case of mange.

The day was hot and dry—late July blending into August. She heard birds calling. Summer insects whirring down low.

Seeing the burned-out husk of their once-cozy little timber house, Sissel felt a terrible ache in her throat. She wished they could have drawn a great sheet over it, as one might do for a corpse.

Worse of all was Hanne's kitchen garden. What hadn't burned had now rotted. The garden had crumpled in on itself, blackened stalks covered with mold.

Sissel peered into the barn. There was a flash of movement, and her heart leaped in her chest. It was a hen. One lonesome, fat buff hen sitting on a nesting box.

"Oh, you poor thing," Sissel said to it. "All your sisters have gone."

The hen fluttered gracelessly to the ground and pecked hopefully near Sissel's feet. She looked fat enough—was probably eating the new grass as quick as it was coming in and had all the yard's share of bugs and worms to herself.

Sissel used her teeth to take a chunk out of her apple and threw it to the bird. She saw there were eggs in the nesting box—about a dozen of them.

She took another bite of the apple and chewed it herself, thinking about bringing the eggs to town. Only then, of course, she realized she could not. Stieg could not know she'd been to the farm. She would have to invent some reason for them to come visit.

Sissel pushed that from her mind. She had work to do.

Was there any gold on their land? She meant to find out.

There was a small pile of their possessions in the corner—things for the house that they'd stored in the barn until they could rebuild. Sissel saw several tin pie pans that had survived the fire. She picked them up. If she did find gold flake, she could use the pans. Releasing the gold into some clean water in the pan would be a better way to collect the flake than scraping it off.

Sissel threw down the rest of her apple for the hen, tucked the pie tins under her arm, and went outside. She took a deep breath, planted her feet, and called on her Nytte.

Of course, the first thing she felt was the bright, bitter jangle of tin. She set the pie tins down on a stump.

Then came a dull, deep throb from the barn behind her that immediately flooded her senses. Iron. It was the stove. Owen had moved it there to save it from rusting out in the weather. There were other sources of iron, too. Knut and Owen had rakes, shovels, hoes, and the like. Sissel could feel the clover-shaped spade head, the tines of the rake.

Sissel gave an involuntary shudder. Iron was heavy and sluggish. She did not enjoy touching it with her mind.

She concentrated on closing her mind to the tin and the iron. This was something she and Stieg had worked on; she needed to be able to shut out one type of metal in order to find the more precious ones.

She reached out again with her senses. It was quiet. There was no glimmer of gold. That was no great surprise. There would not likely be gold on the good, flat farmlands—if there was anything to be found on their property, it would be in the little gully or up in the rocky hills that bordered their parcel of land on the west.

She reached farther, trying to feel along the bed of the little stream in the gully near the farm. Nothing, nothing . . . Her eyes were closed, but on some instinct she opened them and saw movement coming from the direction of the gully, through the brush.

Sissel turned, breathless, and slipped back into the barn.

She would be found out! Whoever was out there would tell Stieg, and he would know she had disobeyed him. That was her first thought. Then she got angry. Who was it, out walking on their land?

She came close to the door and listened, waiting for her hearing to return. She had not used her Nytte for long, but sound was muffled. What would she do if they came into the barn! Were they there to rob her family? Should she be afraid?

The hen came to peck at Sissel's feet. Sissel willed herself to hold still, even as the bird pecked at her boots.

Finally she could make out the voices.

"It stands to reason that there wouldn't be any flake, not if they've been panning for it."

"Not necessarily," came a low, deep voice. "I'd expect to see some sign, if they got an ounce out like they said. If I were you'd I'd steer clear of this land. I don't think there's anything here."

"But then, where did they get the flake from?" she heard the first man say. His tone was gruff, but his voice was young—she knew him!

She knew the voice! It was none other than Isaiah McKray!

Sissel's hands became tight fists. The nerve of the man! He had brought an assessor to their land!

"But where did they do the panning? I see no evidence of it."

Sissel stormed out of the barn. McKray had his back to her. He was talking to a potbellied man in miner's clothes.

"If I had a shotgun I'd shoot you both for trespassing!" she declared.

McKray jumped and cussed, language more foul than Sissel had heard before. The miner took a step back. McKray spun around, his mouth gaping with surprise. Seeing her, he had the decency to blush beet red. He swiped off his hat and gave a bow.

"Miss Hemstad!" he said. "What a surprise."

"What are you doing on my family's land?"

McKray held his hands up.

"I brought a friend to see if there's any gold here," he said plainly. "Herb Nowak is one of my best surveyors."

"Miss," Mr. Nowak said, doffing his cap. He, too, looked abashed.

Sissel continued. "And if you found gold, or thought there was the promise of gold, you'd have offered to buy us out? For some pittance, I'm sure—"

"No, no. I was going to offer we partner up, that's all—"

"I may be young, but I'm not a fool, Mr. McKray—"

"I know it," he said.

Herb Nowak was watching their exchange. He seemed to be hiding a smile, which only made Sissel angrier.

"Herb, would you mind fetching the horses," McKray said.

"Sure thing, boss."

He tipped his hat again to Sissel and walked off. Sissel supposed they had tied their horses upstream somewhere.

Sissel turned back to McKray to find he had been watching her.

"It's a dirty trick you were trying to pull, coming out here, trespassing on our land—"

McKray held his hand up.

"I've told you my business here. I've nothing to hide. I wanted to see if there's gold here so I can make your family an offer, fair and square.

"You know," he continued. "I think the matter at hand is the question of why you're skipping school to come wander around your family's deserted farm."

Sissel nearly spluttered with surprise.

"Mr. McKray, that is none of your business."

McKray studied her, his arms crossed. The way he was looking, she ought to feel her privacy violated—it was so honest and appraising. But instead of turning away, she answered his glare with one of her own.

She saw, in the sunlight, that his beard had more red in it than sandy brown. The beard gave him a bearish quality and made him look older. No doubt that's why he wore it.

She wondered for a moment what he would look like if he shaved his beard.

"You're the one who found the gold flake, aren't you?" he asked.

Sissel stepped back, aghast. Her words caught in her throat. "Pardon?"

"That's how you found the gold flake. That's what you are doing here."

"What are you talking about?"

He stalked toward her, coming quite close, then picked up the pie tins she'd left on the stump behind her.

"You found it with these!" he said.

"That's none—"

"I know, I know. None of my concern," McKray said.

The chicken picked this moment to come clucking out of the barn.

McKray watched it distractedly. Sissel could tell he was thinking.

"There's something about you that I recognize, Miss Hemstad. I have from the beginning."

Sissel was so flustered she didn't know what to say.

"My father is . . ." He scrubbed his hand over his face. "My father is a great many things. But above 'em all he's a gold man. He's obsessed with it, sure, but it's more than that. He understands it. He has a natural feeling for how it accumulates and where to find it."

McKray put his hat back on. He wasn't looking at her now, but staring off toward the hills in the west.

"He's not alone being this way. I've met others with the same kind of gold sense. Men who can tell where gold is. I remember one fellow said his knee would ache when he was near gold. Another who swore he could smell it."

"I think you should be on your way, Mr. McKray," Sissel said. She did not want him to continue talking about this.

"You have it," he said. "Gold sense."

Sissel turned away from him. Her pulse was racing and she needed to think.

He didn't know about the Nytte. He wasn't accusing her of being a Ransacker. But he knew, somehow, he knew about her affinity for gold. How could this be?

Deny, deny, deny, Sissel told herself. Deny and attack. She spun around.

"You say your father is obsessed with gold," she said. "But I think you're the one obsessed. How much land have you bought around town, for all your qualms about it being Blackfoot land? How many mines have you opened? All to no success, and now you're accusing a schoolgirl of having a magical 'gold sense'?"

McKray's face had gone stormy. He frowned.

"Maybe you should focus your efforts on running your hotel," Sissel said. She knew she was baiting him, but she wanted to get him off balance and away from the truth.

Herb Nowak approached, riding one horse and leading another. He waited a respectful distance.

"You can put me off all you want," McKray said. "And you can insult me. You're not the first. But I know what I feel, and you do have gold sense—"

Sissel leveled a hard glare at him.

"I was lucky, Mr. McKray. I'm just a schoolgirl, an amateur, and I got lucky panning for gold. I'm sorry if that stings your pride, but that's the truth of it."

McKray tipped his hat. "Good day, Miss Hemstad."

As he walked toward Nowak, Sissel heard him mutter, "Just a schoolgirl, my foot."

ONCE THEY'D GONE, Sissel picked up the pie tins and threw them at the side of the barn. She resigned herself to going back to her room. She could study and complete her written assignment on the Bill of Rights. She started walking back to town.

Nothing had gone the way she'd planned it! She had only wanted to practice her powers, and now McKray was suspicious of her. What was this gold sense? Was it a real power, one like hers, or was it just legend and superstition?

And she couldn't discuss it with Stieg and get his advice because she'd lied to Stieg about being sick and needing to rest. She couldn't even tell her brother that she'd caught McKray sneaking around on their land.

Now she had to try to get back to the hotel without being noticed. Why had she taken such a stupid risk? And for naught!

She had to make a better plan for the next time she was to go

Ransacking. The only comfort she had, during the long walk to town, was plotting and scheming her next adventure—she'd return to the first stream where she'd summoned the flake. There had to be more.

LATER IN THE AFTERNOON, after school had been dismissed, she went to meet Alice at her family's shop. Sissel had told her brother she felt better, and Stieg let her go, especially when she explained that she and Alice couldn't waste a day—the dance was drawing nearer.

Sissel stood in the fitting room in the corner of the Oswalds' shop. She had her arms out, and Alice was trying to bring the unfinished seams of the dress together in the back.

The dress wouldn't close. Too small at the waist and the bust.

"What in heaven's name?" Alice muttered.

"Is it the corset?" Sissel asked.

"No, it's laced tightly. I suppose we might be able to draw it a tiny bit more."

Alice came around to the front and peered at Sissel with an appraising eye.

"Either you've grown or I've cut the waist too small," Alice said.

"I may have gained some weight," Sissel said. She thought of the stacks of steaming flapjacks at Mrs. Boyce's boardinghouse, smothered in molasses; and the platters of fried ham and summer sausage; and the baked beans she served at supper, with plenty of bits of fried bacon. She swallowed.

"I'm glad for it," Alice said. "Your health is much improved these past few weeks. I'm happy to let out the seams for such a good reason."

"I'm sorry," Sissel said. "Do you want me to help?"

Alice waved her offer away.

"You'd only slow me down," she said.

Both girls laughed.

Alice helped Sissel to step out of the dress.

After Alice had eagerly shown Sissel nearly every bolt of fabric in the store, they had settled on a polished poplin that was a light shade of greenish blue. It reminded Sissel of the fjords—it was just the color of the crest of a wave.

"Are you quite sure about the keyhole neckline?" Sissel asked. Alice settled the dress back onto her dressmaking mannequin as Sissel dressed.

"Mmm-hmm," Alice said. "Especially now that you're filling out so nicely."

"Alice!" Sissel exclaimed. She batted her friend on the arm. "It seems like such a grown-up kind of cut. You don't think people will think I'm putting on airs?"

"Oh, Sissel . . . You're much lovelier than you think you are."

Alice handed Sissel a hand mirror with an ivory handle from the table next to her.

"Look at yourself, for gosh sakes."

Sissel brought up the mirror. She tried to look at herself as a stranger would.

White-blond hair in a meager bun at the nape of her neck. Her blue eyes on a pale, oval face. There was so little color on her face, even her eyebrows and eyelashes were almost invisible because of her coloring.

But there were some improvements.

She found her cheeks more full than she remembered, and her skin rosy on the cheeks. Her eyes, though still pale, had sparkle.

"There! You see it," Alice said. "I can tell you do because you're smiling!"

Sissel handed back the mirror.

"Are you in love?" Alice asked quietly.

"Goodness . . . what a question," Sissel said. Alice shrugged.

"You've got your head in the clouds all the time. Your appetite is better. You seem happy, and I thought it might be James . . ."

Sissel flushed. She concentrated on buttoning up her boots.

How she wished she could tell Alice about her Nytte! In the weeks since it had announced itself, she felt better every day. She was sleeping deeply and could feel herself stronger each morning when she awoke. Before they sold the gold flake, Sissel had kept it with her as she slept, and she felt somehow it had made her more healthy. Her bad leg did not ache anymore. It was only now that the pain had vanished that Sissel realized what a constant grief it had been.

"I'm such a nosy Nellie. I'm sorry," Alice said. She put her hand on Sissel's arm. "I say too much. Forgive me!"

There was genuine concern on Alice's face.

"Nonsense," Sissel said. "You're perfect the way you are."

Sissel gave her friend a hug.

"I'm not in love," Sissel said. "I just feel better. Maybe it's living in town. Or maybe it's the food at the boardinghouse. Mrs. Boyce is truly an excellent cook."

Sissel hated to lie to Alice. Her stomach felt heavy and leaden.

"To tell the truth, I find James a bit tiresome these days." This felt better—she could tell her friend *a* secret, just not *the* secret.

"Really?" Alice asked.

"He's become, not possessive, but just . . . persistent. He's always around, always asking, 'A penny for your thoughts?' I want to say, 'Keep your pocket change and give me some peace!'"

Alice laughed.

"Well, if you throw him back, only every single girl at school will be delighted."

There was a knock on the door of the fitting room.

"Girls, James is here," Alice's mother called in. "He wants to know if you two are in the mood for a picnic."

Sissel and Alice looked at each other and started laughing.

"What's so funny?" Mrs. Oswald said.

This made the two girls laugh all the more.

"What should I tell him?" Mrs. Oswald said, irritation rising in her voice.

"Tell him we'd be delighted," Alice finally choked out.

"Thank you, Mrs. Oswald!" Sissel called.

"Honestly," they heard Alice's mother mutter as she returned to the front of the store to give James the news.

CHAPTER TWENTY-TWO

The days found their pattern, each filled with work so that at night Hanne and Owen fell into their bedroll exhausted.

Hanne's knuckles chapped, then bled, then toughened, until she could scour the cooking pots with sand and feel no ill effect.

The camp was kept as quiet as possible so as not to startle the longhorns. Any loud sound, even sounds from nature like thunder or branches breaking, could spook a herd. It made for a pleasant camp. Hanne liked the calm of it.

The cook served not only as the provider of food for the small company but also, Hanne learned, as the doctor, the tailor, and occasionally the arbiter of minor disagreements.

Her skills as seamstress were in high demand. One cowboy had asked her if she could help him sew on a button. He had said he couldn't sew on buttons to save his life, and it was true—every one of his buttons was hanging on by tangled, gnarled threads. She'd taken them all off and returned the shirt to him tidy and neat.

After that, many of the men came and asked her to sew this or that. She didn't mind—it passed the time when they were riding in the wagon, and the cowboys were so appreciative of her good, careful stitches.

The cowboys returned her kindness in many small ways. They helped haul water or scrub pans without being asked, and they all said "Please" and "Thank you, ma'am."

Witri liked to see the cowboys pitching in; and Owen was proud of her, she could tell it. Hanne found she liked the work very much.

Mandry and Whistler were the only problem, each trying to outdo the other in provoking Owen. Half the time, Hanne didn't even understand their barbs, but she could see how they bothered Owen.

"I wonder, are these beans a mix?" Mandry asked loudly one evening over supper.

"Mixed beans?" Whistler said.

"Half Irish, half English."

Whistler guffawed at that, while the rest of the men looked puzzled. Owen ate, head down.

"These beans is beans, you dummies," Witri snapped. "Keep your jokes to yourselves if they're not gonna make sense."

One morning at breakfast, Mandry sidled up to Owen in the line. "Say, Bennett, don't you find it ironic that you married a little cook? A foreigner?"

Owen's back went straight, but instead of telling Mandry to leave him alone, he tried to deflect the comment. "She's not a cook. She's just helping out. Earning a wage."

"All the same, though," Mandry said, in a voice soft enough only Hanne and Owen could hear. "What would your papa and mama say? You and a pretty little foreigner cook . . ."

Owen flushed. Hanne saw his hands were trembling holding his bowl. She ladled a heavy portion of oatmeal into it. He nearly dropped the bowl, so focused was he on Mandry's oily sneer.

"Mr. Mandry," Hanne said loudly. "If you have a problem with my cooking, please direct it to Mr. Witri."

Mandry looked taken aback. He'd not mentioned her cooking, but Hanne knew Witri would come in a flash if he felt she'd been slighted.

"What's this now, Mandry?" Witri said, edging Owen aside. Hanne was set to dollop his oatmeal into Mandry's bowl, but Witri stopped her arm.

"If you don't like Mrs. Bennett's fine oat porridge, then you can well go without."

Mandry looked from Hanne to Witri, who towered over both of them.

"There's no problem, sir," he said. "She's a delicious little cook. I was merely making conversation."

"Well, maybe by the time you catch up with us for supper, you'll be a little more focused on your food, and a little less focused on chatting."

With that, Witri took back Mandry's bowl and he was pushed out of line, no breakfast. He went off scowling.

A FEW DAYS LATER, they set up camp near the river. It was a nice change, having water on hand.

In the early morning, all the cowboys had gone off to bathe. Hanne kept close to the chuck wagon, of course.

Owen had asked her if she wanted to bathe, but she decided against it. She was getting some lovelorn gazes from a couple of the younger cowboys. She didn't want to risk any of them trying to peek at her and making trouble. Nor, for that matter, did she want Owen guarding her modesty. She wasn't ready for him to see her bathing, either. Not until they were truly married.

Being so near to water, though, she and Witri decided to wash the pots and pans out properly, instead of scrubbing them with dry grass and sand, as they usually did.

She and Witri were at the banks of the river. The water had been churned up earlier by the cowboys, and from the cattle that had drunk upstream, but now that the herd was on the move, the water was flowing clear and calm again.

Hanne scrubbed one of their three large cast-iron Dutch ovens with a brush. Witri swished out their coffee kettle and set it to dry upside down on a rock. "Say, would you mind if I went off a ways and had a bath myself?" he asked her.

She was amused to see him blushing.

"Of course not," she said. "I'll finish up with these and then bring them to the wagon."

"Much obliged," he said. "You know . . . I think I'll even use soap!" Hanne laughed.

Witri walked off to get his soap and his spare shirt from the wagon.

Hanne bent over the pot. There was a ring of dried stew clinging to the top that she couldn't get off. She set the worn brush aside and gathered a handful of river pebbles. Maybe they would work better.

She made a mental note to tell Witri they needed a new brush. They'd be passing within five miles of a town in the next day or so, and he was going to have a cowboy make a run into town for supplies. There would be mail, too. Anyone who wanted to send a letter to one of the cowboys had been told to send their letters to Albee, which was about halfway along the drive.

Hanne knew Witri meant to get more dried apples, and they were low on precious coffee. He'd kept her laughing the day before, telling her about the many hats he planned to buy himself. He'd taken to wearing a flour-sack towel tied on his head to keep his scalp from sunburn.

All at once Hanne's whole body prickled awake and alert. Her Nytte came pounding into her mind and body.

There was a man sneaking up on her.

She didn't even need to turn her head to find him. The sounds gave him away. Fifteen feet downstream, hidden behind an old ponderosa pine.

It was the worm Mandry.

He was breathing heavily. She could smell the lust on him.

Hanne reached for prayer. She did not want to kill this man. She needed to get control of her Nytte.

"*Ásáheill*," she murmured. She withdrew her hands from the pot and crossed them over her chest. With her fingers she traced *Uraz*— strength, and *Algiz*—protection, on her forearms.

"Hey there, little filly," she heard him whisper.

He stepped out into the water, letting it run over his boots. He came up toward her.

"You need some help?" he asked, pretending to be relaxed, but the way he held his arms gave him away. They were out, his shoulders leaning forward. He was ready to pounce.

The Nytte was raging in her body. She trembled to hold it in. "Gods, to me!" she prayed.

If they did not come, she would kill this man. She could not hold out against the Nytte much longer. Not when she was in danger this way. Her Nytte would force her to protect herself, or anyone she loved, this she knew.

"Don't be scared, little missus. I just thought I'd help you, is all," he lied.

She brushed her hands on her shirt and slowly stood.

He was but two paces away now.

She raised her eyes to his, saw the malice glittering there. There was a telling bulge at the front of his trousers.

He lunged forward, thinking to lay her flat on her back.

Damn the Gods—they had not arrived in time. Hanne let the Nytte possess her, and her mind went blank with the joy of it.

She brought her knee up and drove it into the attacker's groin. She slipped her hand up, knocking his hat into the water and grabbed him by the hair. As he screamed in pain, contracting to protect his privates, she wrenched his head back.

He swung wildly and his fist connected with her eye. She saw stars and laughed at them.

"Mandry!" she heard a man shout.

Hanne saw a narrow rock cleaved in two on the ground. It was shaped like a spear point. She reached for it, dragging the man down by his hair so she could reach it. She'd poke it through his temple.

"What the hell is going on?" She was being hauled off her prey. She fell down onto her seat.

The newcomer was someone she did not want to kill. A fat man with a shining head. Part of her tribe. He had separated them.

"You son of a bitch!" the tall, fat one yelled at the man on the ground. "Did he hurt you?" He turned to Hanne.

There was a barking and here rushed her dog. It came leaping at her, licking her hands and her face.

She knew the dog. It was beloved to her. It licked her and wriggled all over her lap so that she did not immediately get up.

THE RAGE DRAINED AWAY. Hanne came jerking back into her body.

"Are you all right, Hanne?" Witri asked.

Hanne could not speak a word. She was too shaken. She dropped the rock she found in her hand. She had clutched it so hard it caused a shallow cut.

She rose and walked away. She walked briskly, Daisy at her heel watching her anxiously.

Hanne went to the chuck wagon and began to eat a loaf of the sourdough bread for dinner without realizing it.

Owen came up, riding hard. Hanne turned her back to him. She could feel the blow Mandry had dealt her rising around her eye. Her heart beat a wild rhythm. What would Owen do once he knew what had happened?

"Everything all right?" he called.

Hanne nodded.

Owen slid off his horse and came over. He reached down and scratched Daisy behind the ears.

"Daisy ran off and I got worried," he said.

Witri came into the campsite, Mandry limping behind him, head downcast.

Owen put his fingers on Hanne's chin and raised her face. He saw the rising black eye, and she saw understanding crash over his features like waves on a cliff.

"You son of a bitch!" Owen roared. He crossed the campsite and had Mandry by the collar. Before Witri could wrench him off, Owen got one, two, three solid punches in. Mandry fell to the ground, bringing his hands up to shield his face from further abuse.

"I didn't do nothing," the man spat.

"You hit her!" Owen shouted.

Owen aimed for a kick, but Witri pulled him away.

"All right, all right," Witri said. "Hanne's all right. She held her own and then some."

Owen's eyes flashed for the first time to check Hanne's expression. Only at that moment did he seem to realize what might have happened.

"We'll take it up with Tincher at the end of the day," Witri said.

"It's all a misunderstanding," Mandry said. "I was offering to help her!"

Hanne put her hand on Witri's arm. "I don't want to tell Tincher," she said. "I just want to forget about it."

"You gotta tell him," Witri said. "He should know what kind of scum he has working for him."

"No, no," Hanne said. "I don't want to make a fuss."

"I don't understand. Are you afraid of Mandry?" Witri said.

"Please," she said. "I don't want to make trouble. It's better if we all get along."

She sent a pleading look to Owen. He must understand that it would be bad for her if Mandry started talking about how strong she was. How she'd nearly killed him.

"I suppose . . . it's up to my wife," Owen said. "She's the one who got attacked."

Witri looked all three of them over. Owen had his arm around Hanne. Mandry sat on the floor where he'd fallen. He was poking at a broken tooth, spitting out strings of bloody drool.

"Sorry," he said. "I gotta tell Tincher. He's gonna know there was a fight. Look at Mandry's face, for God's sake . . ."

"Could you tell him that Mandry and I had a fight?" Owen said. "Leave Hanne out of it."

Witri sighed and spat. "I guess so. If that's really how you want it." Hanne nodded.

"You'll keep your fool mouth shut about this?" Witri asked Mandry. Mandry cussed and spat out more bits of tooth.

"Yeah, sure," Mandry said. "No helping."

"You pull anything like that again and I'll fix you myself," Witri said. "Now, God's sakes, let's get back to work."

CHAPTER TWENTY-THREE

Sissel's chance to revisit the stream came two nights later, when Stieg was asked to dinner by two men on the school board in Helena. He'd fussed about her, and asked her if she'd mind terribly taking supper alone, or if she'd like to go to the Oswalds', perhaps. She had shooed away his concern—telling him she'd be fine.

Sissel took a pail with her, lined with a piece of homespun. If stopped, she was going to say that she was looking for blueberries. There were bushes by the stream—the berries were mostly gone, but that didn't matter.

She thought she'd use the pail to dip her hands into once she'd pulled the gold to her. Then she could release it into the water and strain it through the cloth. She was pleased with the plan.

Sissel nearly held her breath as she crossed through the lobby. Just behind the glass doors, Stieg was supping with the men from Helena. With Stieg out of the way, she had only to avoid James. He would no doubt insist on accompanying her if they crossed paths. Lately he was everywhere.

OUT IN THE STREET, she went quickly. She didn't see James straightaway, and that was a good sign. Usually he popped out from one of the stores nearby, as if he'd been shopping.

The work of the day was coming to an end, and the afternoon sun cast a golden glow over the young town. She saw workmen, shirts stained with sweat and sprinkled with sawdust, breaking their work on the town hall. She passed a mother scolding an errant child as she carried him toward home and the supper table. Reverend Neville nodded to her as they passed. She dipped her head in return and hoped she looked innocent.

Finally clear of the main street, Sissel headed toward the thatch of scrub oak that bordered the stream. There was such freedom to be away from prying eyes, she felt like skipping.

She pressed through the scrub on the grassy footpath. When she came to the stream, she looked on it with affection. Here she had learned what she was!

First she made her preparations. She tucked the square of cloth into the pocket of her dress, that she might have it at hand. Then she dipped the pail into the stream, filling it halfway with water.

Sissel looked around to make sure no one was near; then, drawing in a great breath of air, she opened her mind to her Nytte. She felt so strong today. Strong and robust. There was a thick, pleasurable feeling in her legs, almost as if she could draw power from the very minerals of the soil itself. Her Nytte was getting stronger.

Sissel was beaming as she knelt to place the fingertips of her right hand in the water.

She sensed gold in the waters, buzzing both upstream and downstream. Her heart flooded with the warmth of it. She knew she must stay alert and watch in case someone came, but, oh, it did feel good to use her gift.

Sissel pulled, and the tiny bits of gold came tumbling through the water, responding to her call with soft, friendly resonance.

It felt like minnows were nibbling her fingers. She pressed her entire hand down into the water, palm flat, providing more surface area for the gold to cling to.

She called, called some more, but it seemed she had gotten all within the expanse of her reach, because the sensation of gold coming to her palm slowed, then stopped.

While maintaining her pull on the gold, Sissel withdrew her hand—it gleamed and glowed in the fading light of day. Sissel laughed.

She looked around sharply, remembering she would not be able to hear if someone came upon her. There was no one there.

Now Sissel lowered her hand into the pail. The gold still clung to her, but she used her power to push it off her skin, just slightly. It released in a glimmering flurry, settling to the bottom. There was at least as much as before.

Sissel couldn't keep from grinning. She had done it again! Gold, real gold, and she'd just skimmed it out of the stream! She had the feeling that if she came again, she wouldn't be so lucky. She had likely pulled all the flake out of the waters, and it would take more time for it to flush down out of the mountains to the north of town.

Sissel carefully poured off the water, and then, when there was just a bit left, she made a little bag of the rough cloth and strained the water through it.

The brush moved nearby, and Sissel's heart lurched.

But it was a small movement, just from a chipmunk or such creature passing through. Sissel put a hand to her chest. She could not hear her heart in her ears, but she felt it thumping.

Now feeling some urgency, Sissel squeezed out the bundle over the water, getting it as dry as possible. The gold felt warm in her hand, even though the cloth was wet.

Then she folded the handkerchief in quarters, then in eighths, and tucked the little wet linen packet within the bosom of her corset. She knew the heat of her body would dry the cloth, and in the meantime, having the gold next to her heart felt good.

The light was failing now, and she knew Stieg would be finishing his dinner at the hotel at any time. Sissel walked back along the footpath to the main road.

The town glowed before her, candles and oil lamps alit in the windows of the buildings. Above Carter, the broad sky was shot through with a band of sunset. Sissel hurried onto the board walkway on the southern side of the street, the same side as the boardinghouse. As she walked, sound returned to the world. She nodded to people she passed on the street, all of them hurrying home as she was.

Sissel was passing two dark buildings, the Oswalds' store and the bank beside it, when her head was abruptly jerked back. Someone had her by the hair! She was dragged off her feet, hauled into the alley.

The man pulled her roughly into his body so that her back was to him.

She felt a knife jab her in the hip.

Sissel cried out.

"Quiet!" he said, spitting the word into her ear. The stench of whiskey hit her. She felt long whiskers and a raspy growl to his voice. She knew who it was. Ebbott, the trapper. Her flesh crawled. "Now, where is it?"

"What do you want?" Sissel asked.

"I seen you come from the stream." He gave her a shake. "I know you been prospecting. Where's your gold?"

He started to pat down her body with the hand not holding her hair. He pushed a grimy hand down her neckline.

"Let me go!" Sissel cried out.

Then James was there, stepping into the alleyway.

"Sissel?" he said.

Ebbott cursed and pushed her hard toward James. He caught her, but James lost his footing and they both went over, limbs tangled.

"Stop!" James shouted. Sissel turned to look, but Ebbott had run down the alley toward the back street. James pushed free of Sissel and scrambled down the alley, but Sissel heard the sound of hooves retreating.

A moment later, James rushed back toward her, into the space between the buildings and to her side.

"Are you all right?" he asked. He lifted Sissel to her feet.

The fright of it had taken Sissel's breath away. She gasped for air, as if she'd just run for miles.

"Shhh," James said. "There, there."

He fumbled into his vest pocket for a handkerchief and gave it to her. Sissel wiped her eyes. She could not get her heart to slow. She felt panicked and sick.

"Was that Frank Ebbott?" James asked.

"Yes, it was."

"What on earth did he want?"

Sissel saw that the corner of the cloth with the gold was sticking up out of her neckline. She tucked it in, in the guise of straightening her dress. James began to brush the dirt off her skirts.

"I suppose the usual thing a man wants when he drags a girl down an alley," she said.

"Did he hurt you?"

She shook her head.

"I'm angry, but not hurt," she said.

"I'll take you back to the hotel," James said.

Out in the street, where there was more light, Sissel found her sleeve was torn and there were stains on the front of her dress from Ebbott's grimy fingers. Worse were the scratches on her chest from where his filthy hands had raked her skin.

James put a protective arm around her and walked her to the hotel.

As they neared the hotel, several carpenters Sissel knew from meals at the boardinghouse stopped.

"Miss! Are you all right?" one asked.

"Frank Ebbott attacked her," James said.

"I'm all right," Sissel said.

"Sissel!" came Stieg's voice. He had seen them through the windows and had rushed out to them. "What happened?"

"This young lady was mauled!" a farmer told him.

"Who was it?" asked Mrs. Denmead, pushing through the growing crowd.

"That old scoundrel Ebbott!" one of the carpenters said.

"I'm fine," Sissel said. "He was drunk and he grabbed me, but he's gone away and I'm fine."

"Nonsense, we can't let that kind of lawlessness stand. Not here in Carter!" Mrs. Denmead said. "We will wire Fort Benton and tell the sheriff to come!"

"We can't wait for the sheriff," the farmer said. "I know where Ebbott lives!"

"Let's go get him!" one of the carpenters shouted. "We'll keep him prisoner till the law can get here."

Shouts of agreement went out. Sissel and Stieg shared a look—they didn't want a posse formed, nor did they want the attention of the sheriff.

A crash of summer thunder resounded overhead. Startled, the townspeople looked up. Sissel sneaked a look at her brother, who had a finger to his temple.

A warm and thickly humid wind tunneled down the street, whipping up skirts and dirt. Horses whinnied. More thunder boomed overhead, and a sheet of rain overcame the street. As it neared, the small crowd dispersed.

James led Sissel to the hotel and stood there holding the door, getting soaking wet, as she and Stieg passed inside.

"Thank you," she said as the door closed. Through the rain-splattered glass, she saw James watching her, concerned. She put her hand to the glass and mouthed the words *Thank you* again.

"YOU WENT RANSACKING," Stieg said once they were safe in the privacy of Sissel's room. Their wet clothes were making a dark patch on the carpet beneath their feet.

Sissel handed him one of her two towels and used the other to blot her face and neck.

"Yes," she said. "But just back to the stream—"

"And Ebbott saw you?"

"I was so careful!"

"He saw you!"

Sissel pressed the cloth to her face. She did not want her brother to see her cry.

"Sissel, how can I press upon you the need to be careful?"

Sissel said nothing, only hid her face in the towel and waited until she felt calmer.

"So he followed you, and then he cornered you?" Stieg asked, his voice more gentle. "Are you all right?"

Sissel set the towel into her lap. She found Stieg had poured her a glass of water and was holding it out to her. She took a sip.

"He dragged me into the alley between the bank and the Oswalds' store. He tried to find where I had hidden the gold. But James came and scared him off."

Stieg's mouth was drawn tight. "I expressly asked you not to go Ransacking!"

"You did not ask me, you told me. You decreed it, as if I were your royal subject."

"Yes, fine." He threw up his hands. "I *decreed* it for our safety. What if Ebbott tells someone?"

"I'm sorry," Sissel said.

"You should be."

"Not sorry that I went, but that I was discovered!" Sissel said. She reached into her corset.

"Sissel!" Stieg said, shocked.

She drew out the cloth packet with the gold.

"Look!" she said. She opened it. "I think it's double what I got last time."

Stieg looked at the flat little disk of gold, pressed together by the warmth of her chest.

"We can't cash it in," Stieg said softly. "We'll draw too much attention."

Sissel set down the cloth and rubbed a finger over the gold flakes.

"Did you hear me? We can't draw attention to ourselves, Sissel."

"Yes," she said. "I heard you."

Stieg exhaled heavily. "Please do not go out Ransacking again," he said. "I should have asked, instead of ordered. I'm asking now. Your safety demands it and also the safety of our family. We cannot forget about the Baron. He is surely looking for us still."

"I know," Sissel said.

"I will hide that in my room," Stieg said, holding his hand out for the gold. "After a few weeks, we can exchange it at the bank."

"May I keep it?" Sissel said. "I like to hold it. I know it's odd, but I do think it makes me stronger."

Stieg sighed. He rubbed his head with one hand.

"Oh, how I wish Rolf were here," Stieg said. "There is so much about your gift we do not understand."

"Yes," Sissel said, moving the gold this way and that to admire the glow from the lamp on the surface of the disk. "But we are learning about it, bit by bit."

"Perhaps we should try to reach Hanne," he said.

Sissel tore her gaze away from the gold. "Why?"

"Because you don't seem willing to understand—you are putting yourself in danger."

Sissel frowned. If Hanne came back, Sissel's freedom would end. Hanne would mother-hen her to death.

"Don't call for Hanne," she said. "She'll smother me with worries."

"Then can you promise me you won't use your power without me?"

Sissel nodded yes, miserable to have made a promise she did not want to keep.

CHAPTER TWENTY-FOUR

The roof of Ebbott's cabin was bowed and mossy. Several deer skins stretched on frames rested against the exterior walls. The trapper sat hunched in front of a small, smoky fire out front, muttering to himself.

James felt his pulse pounding. He, Clements, and Peavy had come up on foot, following the rutted tracks by the light of the moon. Now they were spread out around the camp, hidden in the shadows.

It seemed a pretty small life, James thought, watching the man eat some kind of gruel out of an old, dented pan. James wished he, Peavy, and Clements could just turn around and go back to town.

Ebbott wiped his mouth on his sleeve.

Peavy stepped out of the darkness into the circle of light.

"Hey," he said.

Ebbott got up to run, but Clements was right behind him. He grabbed the trapper by the collar of his coat.

"Easy, there, Ebbott," Peavy said. "We just want to ask you some questions."

James stepped forward to show he was there. His heart was hammering so fast he felt like a rabbit.

"I didn't do nothin'!" Ebbott said. He had stepped in his pan of mush accidentally, and now slipped, trying to keep upright. Clements got hold of his arms from behind and hauled him up.

"That's the one lie you get, you old badger," Peavy said. "You tell me another and Clements there will start removing your teeth for you."

Ebbott's eyes darted from Peavy to James and back.

"This ain't right," he said to James, a tone of pleading in his voice. "This is my land you're on. Y'all are trespassing."

Peavy slugged Ebbott in the gut.

"Why were you watching the girl?"

Ebbott heaved, trying to get his breath.

"Gold," he gasped. "Gold, I reckon."

"How so?" Peavy asked.

"She and her brother have been panning, and I thought she'd lead me to their spot. Don't hit me again. I'm an old man."

"What did you see?" Peavy asked.

Ebbott shook his head.

"She took something out of the water. I think it was a nugget. I was too far away to see."

"You think she fished a nugget of gold out of the stream that runs near our town."

"She had something and put it in a cloth. That much I saw for sure."

Peavy shrugged. "So then you tried to drag her into an alley, huh."

"Look, I drink too much. I do stupid stuff."

"James, see if Ebbott's got himself a gun, would you?"

He indicated the cabin with his head.

"Now, look here," Ebbott said. "I didn't hurt her or nothin'. I didn't even break a law, I don't think."

James stuck his head into the dank shelter. It reeked of mold and urine. Several empty bottles clattered on the dirt floor when he accidentally kicked them. There were no windows, only a rectangle of moonlight to see by.

He didn't want to touch the old man's bed—just a heap of furs and blankets on the floor. He turned and scanned the room. There was the gun, hung on two wooden pegs over the door. The oiled barrels gleamed.

James took it down and brought it outside.

Ebbott shrunk back against Clements when he saw the gun.

"Fellas, come on. Let me buy you a drink. I got a good bottle inside."

Peavy turned to James. "Is it loaded?"

James struggled to open the heavy stock. Two bullets were loaded into the chambers. Say one thing for Ebbott, James thought, he kept his rifle clean. He closed the gun again.

"It's loaded."

"Good," Peavy said. "When Clements lets Ebbott go, you're gonna shoot him."

"What?" James said.

"No!" Ebbott shouted. "For God's sake!"

"You killed a man before?" he asked James, though he knew James had done no such thing.

"Wait, Peavy. I don't want to do this," James said. "It's not right."

"He assaulted one of our clients. We're paid to protect her. It's every bit of right."

"No!" James said.

"You want to be a real Pinkerton, don't you?"

James felt sick with the pressure of it. He knew he was being goaded, but at the same time, he did want to prove himself to Peavy.

But to take a man's life? James found his hands were trembling badly.

"Let me free," Ebbott squealed.

Peavy nodded to Clements.

Clements let the old man go, and Ebbott staggered forward.

"Shoot him, James," Peavy said.

"No," James said. "I won't."

Clements started to laugh, and Ebbott started to run.

Tripping and sliding on the grass and leaves, the old man went careening off into the woods.

"Shoot him!" Peavy shouted.

James raised the gun. His arms were shaking so hard he couldn't even get a sight. Ebbott was crashing through the brush. Getting away.

Then *BANG*. The brush went still.

Peavy lowered his pistol.

"Lord," he said, exhaling, disappointed. "I'm trying to make you a Pinkerton, son. You ain't making it easy."

CHAPTER TWENTY-FIVE

Sissel couldn't get over how good Knut looked. He had come to town with the Lilliedahls for supplies, and they had given him the afternoon off to visit with his siblings.

Mrs. Lilliedahl had cut Knut's blond hair quite short. Hanne had always left it longer when she cut it. But the shorter cut favored Knut's square jaw. He looked cheerful and well fed and had kept up a steady patter of the events at the farm, most of which featured the antics of a goat named One-Eye.

Knut had, with great pride, handed over twelve dollars, the bulk of his pay these past two weeks. Stieg had asked if Knut needed any of the money to buy things for himself, but Knut said he did not. Stieg had paid down most of their hotel bill with the money from the first gold Sissel found. With this money, he brought their bill up to date. Then, to celebrate Knut's visit, they decided to dine at the Royal, instead of the boardinghouse.

Sissel changed into her best dress, the tan one Alice had given her, and Stieg put on his Sunday suit, but they couldn't do much for Knut, except let him wash up in Stieg's room and brush off his work clothes as best he could.

Knut stepped into the dining room as if entering church, meek and awestruck.

A young waiter wearing a black vest over a crisp white shirt with a long canvas apron tied around his waist greeted them at the door.

"Good evening," he said. "Will you be joining us for dinner tonight?"

"Yes," Stieg said. "Three, please."

Nodding, he led them to a pleasant table near the window.

Sissel had to admit, it was a lovely restaurant. Each table was set with white linens, silver cutlery, a covered glass dish with sugar, and a small silver pitcher of cream. Another waiter swooped in and offered them menus, Sissel first.

"This place is too fancy for me," Knut said in Norwegian. He cast a shy glance at the table next to them, where two wealthy-looking men in dark suits seemed to be discussing business.

"Nonsense," Stieg said. "After all, it's your good work that's paid for us to be here!"

Sissel leaned over and whispered to him, "Just watch your elbows and we'll be fine."

He rewarded her with a grin.

The menus were printed on cream-colored card stock. Sissel traced the items with her finger as she read. There was such a range of foods! Two soups, chicken broth and fish chowder. There were more than ten choices of entrée from mutton with caper sauce to roast chine of pork to Irish stew with dumplings. One section listed all sorts of mayonnaise salads: potato, chicken, even steelhead trout.

As they read over the choices, Knut's stomach let out an audible rumble.

The two men in suits looked over with displeasure. Sissel stifled a laugh.

Knut set his menu down. "Will you order for me, Brother?"

"I will," Stieg said.

Then he set his menu down, too.

"I can't hold in my good news for one moment longer," Stieg said. "I've been offered a class in Helena! Eighty dollars a term, with three terms a year!"

He sat back to take in the delight that dawned on his siblings' faces. Two hundred and forty dollars a year? It was a tremendous amount!

"What wonderful news!" Sissel said.

"Very good, Brother!" Knut said. "Is it better than the one here?"

"Quite so," Stieg said. "It's no one-room schoolhouse. It's a two-story brick building with four classrooms. I've been offered the youngest pupils, from age five to eight."

Sissel saw how her brother's eyes were shining and knew how happy this made him. He liked teaching the youngest classes best.

The waiter arrived, and Stieg ordered for himself and Knut—venison steaks with red currant jelly. Sissel chose something called Duffield's Sugar Cured Ham with champagne sauce, though she had no idea where Duffield was. The waiter asked if they would like wine, and Stieg said yes—so it was a celebration, indeed. They never had wine at home or anywhere. It was water or coffee.

"What does your job mean for the family?" Sissel asked once the waiter had left. "Would we all move?"

She had heard much about Helena from Alice, who went there with her parents to shop for goods every so often.

"I'm not sure," Stieg said. "We have the land here. It might make more sense for me to go to Helena and teach for a year. We'll have to see what Hanne and Owen want to do."

"I don't want to live in a city," Knut said.

"It's not such a big city as all that," Stieg said.

A waiter came with three glasses of red wine.

"Let's toast to Stieg's fine job offer," Sissel proposed.

They clinked their glasses and drank. Stieg sipped his wine as if measuring the bouquet and Knut just drained the glass. It tasted fine to Sissel—she didn't know enough about wine to have an opinion. Then the plates came, all three plates at once, delivered by the two waiters and a cook's aide.

Stieg's and Knut's venison steaks came slathered in a thick, creamy gravy. Each got his own little crystal bowl heaped with quivering red currant jelly on the side. Sissel's ham steak smelled wonderful. Cloves studded the edge, crusted over with browned sugar.

Next, one of the waiters set down three small side dishes on the table—candied carrots, fried green squash, and thick-cut slices of potatoes cooked in cream.

"I could get used to this!" Stieg said, tucking his napkin into his collar. He cut into his steak and popped a gleaming bite into his mouth. "Mmmm . . ."

"With eighty dollars a term, you may as well get used to it," Sissel quipped. She took another sip of her wine.

Her own ham was delicious, and soon the conversation faded away, replaced with happy sounds of the table.

With her brothers engrossed in their plates, Sissel took a moment to look around the fine room. It seemed a terrible shame that she couldn't tell Knut her own big news, but he was no good at keeping a secret. He might very well tell the Lilliedahls about Sissel's Nytte. She and Stieg had decided together to wait until the family was reunited to announce her gift.

She wondered what would happen if she opened her mind to her Nytte right now. What would the collection of silver cutlery sound like? What about the gold edging the plates? Could she draw it all to her if she pulled?

Sissel was quite absorbed in her own thoughts and did not see McKray approach until he was at their table.

"How's dinner?" he asked.

Sissel jumped. She choked on a bite of ham, and Knut gave her a wallop on the back. She took a sip of her wine to clear her throat.

"Didn't mean to startle you," McKray said. "I apologize."

Sissel gave him a brisk nod.

"The food is delicious," Stieg said. "Everything is perfectly prepared."

"Yes," Knut said. "Very good."

"Yes," Sissel said, lamely echoing her brother. She hadn't spoken to McKray since their frustrating exchange. They had passed several times, both in the hotel and in the street. Each time, Sissel had tried to pretend she didn't see him tipping his hat to her.

She'd been cutting him, on purpose, and now he was barreling on as if nothing had happened.

"Robert," McKray said, stopping one of the waiters. "Their meals are on the house tonight."

"Yes, sir," Robert answered.

"That's not necessary!" Sissel protested.

"We are happy to pay," Stieg said. McKray waved their protests away.

"I consider this a business expense," he said.

"How so?" Stieg asked. "We are not in business with you."

"Well, that's the thing. I'd like to make you an offer on your land," he said. "May I join you for a moment?"

Stieg welcomed him to do so. McKray grabbed an empty chair and dragged it over to their table.

Sissel's heart began to thump. If he mentioned seeing her on the land, Stieg would know she had lied to him. What could she do? How to get McKray to stop?

"As Sissel likely told you—"

Sissel shook her head. Just a small, subtle shake. Stieg and Knut had their eyes on McKray and didn't see it.

McKray cleared his throat. "As she likely told you . . . she and I ran into each other in the street the other day."

Sissel let out her breath.

"I don't believe she mentioned it," Stieg said, unsuspicious. He put another bite of venison into his mouth and chewed.

"Here's the thing," McKray continued on. "I saw the state of your lands back after the fire. I know they're not going to produce anything for you, not until next season, anyway. I think it should be mined for ore. I like the look of the hill there, on the west of the property. I'd like to sink an exploratory shaft into it. I've been doing this in several places around the town. I believe there's gold in the hills around Carter."

The two men dining at the table next to them looked over. McKray gave them no notice.

Sissel was perplexed. She studied McKray. Did he believe there was gold on their land? He shouldn't. She had heard his surveyor tell him there was nothing there.

McKray wouldn't quite meet her eye. He seemed, in fact, to be studiously ignoring her. She should find his face disagreeable, but she had to admit the symmetry of his thick, rugged features was pleasing to the eye. He was no fine-chiseled beauty, like James—James and McKray side by side were a thoroughbred and a quarterhorse.

McKray caught her looking at him. She ducked her eyes, picked up her wineglass, and studied the contents instead.

"Have you gotten any gold out of your existing mines?" Stieg asked.

Sissel saw that the two gentlemen were still eavesdropping.

McKray cracked his neck. "No, but they're promising."

"Yet you want to buy our land?" Stieg asked.

"I'll offer you what you paid for the land, plus five percent. That's a good offer—a very good one!"

"Not so good if you truly think there's gold there," Stieg said.

"An exploratory shaft can cost thousands," McKray said. "It's a big gamble I'm willing to take. My gamble, my profit."

"I'll relay the offer to the rest of the family," Stieg said. It was all very providential—Stieg getting a job offer and then McKray saying he'd buy their land. But Stieg wouldn't make such an important decision without consulting Hanne and Owen.

McKray didn't seem too pleased with Stieg's moderated response. He gave a dissatisfied grunt and then rose. Stieg stood as well, so Sissel and Knut also rose to their feet.

The two men shook hands, Stieg tall and lean, McKray short and square.

McKray turned to Sissel, and she offered him her hand. With more confidence than he'd displayed weeks ago in the lobby, he kissed the back of it. His lips were warm and his grip strong.

She watched him walk his short-legged stride out of the dining room. The waiters gave him a slight bow. He ran an excellent hotel, that was indisputable.

"Eat, you two, your food is getting cold," Stieg said.

Sissel sat and returned her attention to her plate. She speared a carrot and put it into her mouth, chewing thoughtfully.

"This is so good," Knut said. "McKray wants to buy our land. You have a new job. Could we get a new farm down there?" He forked a big bite of venison into his mouth.

"I'm sure we could," Stieg said. "But we must consider the needs of everyone in the family. Sissel has a beau. She might be unhappy to move away from Carter."

Both Stieg and Knut looked up at her.

She hadn't thought of James Peavy in hours.

"It's all very sudden," she said. She ducked her head and turned her attention to her plate.

"I wonder why he thinks there's gold on our land, though," Knut said. "That's silly. I don't think there's any gold there."

Nor do I, Sissel thought.

"Sissel," Stieg said, changing the subject. "Tell Knut about the upcoming dance. I know he'd love to hear about the preparations."

Knut nodded, and Sissel was glad to move on to safer territory.

"Alice's dress is a dotted swiss pink chenille. It's so lovely. And Mrs. Oswald is letting Alice wear her golden dove hair combs."

Sissel let herself get carried away, telling her brothers all about the dresses and the slippers and who was planning to go with whom. This kind of gossip wasn't her usual choice of topic, but she embraced the role of giddy schoolgirl. Anything to avoid talking of gold or Isaiah McKray.

CHAPTER TWENTY-SIX

James had indeed rented a buggy to take Sissel to the dance.

The buggy was small, built for two. It had a fringed canopy and padded leather seats. The wheel spokes were painted yellow. George, the Peavys' piebald gelding, kept looking nervously over his shoulder at the wheels, as if he expected them to swarm up and sting him.

James stood at the horse's neck, calming him, as Sissel stepped out of the hotel.

Sissel smoothed the front of her dress. It was by far the fanciest garment she had ever worn, and she was nervous about it. James turned and saw her.

His face was wide-open, expression unguarded.

"Goodness, Sissel, you keep getting prettier," he said with a startled honesty."

Sissel was flustered by this. The dress *was* beautiful, with tight sleeves giving way to fullness at the shoulder. The waist was small; the housemaid Bridget had helped Sissel to tighten her corset to a wasp-like width. Below her waist generous skirts swelled from the hip down. The gentle blue of the fabric gave her eyes some color. Alice had even persuaded Stieg to give Sissel money for dancing slippers. The delicate shoes peeped out from beneath the skirts. Sissel's feet felt almost barefoot in them, they were so thin and light.

"What a lovely dress," James said as Stieg came out of the hotel. He had tempered his tone a bit.

"I agree," Stieg said, stepping forward to shake James's hand. Stieg looked over Sissel's outfit with pride. "You look regal, my sister."

"All right, enough, you two," she said.

"And I like the way you've done your hair," Stieg added.

Bridget had helped Sissel with her hair, brushing it until it shone, then pulling it into a low bun at the nape of her neck. No plaits tonight. Sissel meant to look thoroughly modern and American. Sissel had tipped Bridget ten cents for her help, then when she'd learned Bridget was planning to go to the dance herself, Sissel helped Bridget with her own hair.

"I do as well. Sissel, you look like a fashion plate," James said.

"Enough!" Sissel protested. She could feel her blush spreading from her face to her neck.

"Time to go," Stieg said. "Shall we?" And he moved as if to climb into the buggy. James looked stricken for a moment.

"He's joking," Sissel explained. She elbowed Stieg in the side.

"No room?" Stieg sighed. "Well, I can see where I'm not welcome."

"No, no, we can squeeze you in," James offered, smiling back.

"I'm walking," Stieg said. "It'll warm up my legs for dancing. I'll see you there." Stieg waved and headed off on the road.

"Don't mind him," Sissel said. "On festive occasions, he thinks it's his duty to tease everyone."

"Shall we go?" James asked. Sissel nodded.

James held the horse's reins with one hand and helped Sissel climb up into the rig with the other. Then he climbed in beside Sissel. Their legs were pushed against each other's by the snug fit of the carriage.

Across the street, she saw Minnie from school being helped into a wagon by Nate. Though Minnie wasn't friendly to Sissel at school unless Alice was nearby, now she waved. Sissel waved back. James gave George a tap with the lines, and they were off.

THE FAHAYS' BARN was lit from within. The sound of chatting and laughter spilled into the night through the great, open doors. It was easy to see why the Ladies' Aid Society had asked the Fahays if their barn could be used—it was enormous, a two-story structure with a large gabled roof. Mr. Fahay raised prize heifers, and their dairy was known statewide.

Members of the Ladies' Aid Society stood at the door, taking the admission fee. It was a quarter for each person. James handed over two coins to Mrs. Denmead, who gave him a friendly nod.

"Be sure to try the pecan pie with the cutout of an eagle on top," she told them. "That one's mine."

She nodded to two long plank tables laden with pies and sweets that stood against one of the side walls. There was a large tub at one end, filled with lemonade, and another at the end with plain water. A collection of tin cups to be shared stood near each.

The Ladies' Aid Society had outdone themselves with the space. The barn was thoroughly swept out. Streamers of crepe paper looped between the railings of the hayloft. The hayloft itself had been cleared and swept. Tables and chairs had been set up there so people could enjoy the scene from above.

Below, the support beams were wrapped in crepe paper streamers. Wildflower bouquets were affixed to them, one on each side. The place smelled nice, too. Pine needles had been scattered on the floor to mask the scent of the animals who usually lived there.

"Oh, look at the band," Sissel said. She gave James's arm a squeeze.

Musicians were tuning up in the corner. Sissel counted two fiddlers, a mandolin player, and a fellow with a washboard and some spoons. There was a very short man who looked to be in his fifties, wearing a red vest, with a brown shirt underneath and trousers in an even brighter shade of red. He seemed to be gargling.

"That's the caller," Sissel said. "He called the dance in Fort Benton last summer."

"That pipsqueak?" James asked.

"Wait until you hear his voice!"

Everywhere, the young and old of the town were milling about, all dressed in their finest. Sissel even saw Mr. Collier there, chatting with some employees from the hotel. There was Bridget, on the arm of one of the porters.

Alice came pushing through the throngs of people, Howie in tow. She glowed in her dotted swiss pink chenille. She had risked rather more than Sissel in the décolletage area.

Alice's hair was piled on her head in an elaborate style. Sissel saw Alice's mother's gold hair combs fetchingly arranged at the back—the two golden doves that seemed to nest in the brown curls.

"Oh, Alice!" Sissel exclaimed. "You look splendid!"

"As do you!" Alice said. "Turn for me."

Sissel might have balked for shyness, but she swirled and even gave Alice a curtsy.

Both James and Howie applauded.

"I take all the credit," Alice joked. "It's all in the dress!"

James said something, doubtlessly charming, but the music began and it was lost.

Some couples rushed forward to the clearing in the center of the barn; others quit it, heading for the sides.

"Shall we?" James asked.

"Let's shall!" Sissel answered. She knew the American contra and square dances. In the time since they'd come to Carter, there had been several other dances like this one, though none quite so grand. Stieg insisted they all learn the steps, and they worked on them over the long winters, clapping a rhythm and calling the figures.

It was much more fun with music.

"Line 'em up now. Make four rows. Ladies on the left, take hands with your beaus."

The caller's voice was deep and loud. Sissel looked at James, and they both laughed. They hurried to join one of the lines of dancers.

She saw Stieg and Mrs. Denmead take positions a bit down the row.

Stieg winked at Sissel.

The fiddles were merry, the spoon man set a rollicking rhythm, and the caller hollered out strong and fine—it was the most fun Sissel had ever had. Her bad leg hurt only a little. With all the lilting of bodies and the jolting when they collided, which happened frequently, Sissel didn't think anyone could even see she had a limp.

Though all the girls looked their finest, and became even prettier as the evening progressed, their cheeks rosy from the warmth in the barn, James kept his eyes on her.

Every time the reel came around and she found herself back in his hands, she got a private thrill. The dances had them part and return to each other a hundred times, and each time she felt his hands on her she felt touched by fire.

She began to perspire and could see him sweating, too.

In spite of her recent irritation with James, she found she very much wanted to kiss him. Every time they came close together again, before he'd spin her this way or that, Sissel imagined herself pressing her lips to his.

Toward the end of a set, he swung her around and her feet nearly left the floor. She landed, careening into an older couple. She and James laughed, but the elders were not impressed.

"Let's have some lemonade," he said.

"Yes, please," Sissel said.

They broke from the dance, and James led her by the hand toward the tables.

There was a bit of a crowd next to the tub. The lemonade was an unusual treat, and everyone wanted to have a cup.

"Wait here a moment. I'll be back," James said, and pushed into the throng.

Sissel saw Stieg, dancing with one of the littlest girls from school. The girl was grinning ear to ear, her braids flying as Stieg led her through the steps. The girl's eyes were shining with admiration for Stieg. He did cut a fine figure in his best suit.

Sissel saw McKray coming through the throngs of people toward her. She gave him a polite nod of the head, assuming he'd pass by. To her surprise, he stopped and planted his feet right in front of her.

"Would you care to dance, Miss Hemstad?" he asked.

"Me?"

"Yes, you. With me."

Sissel's eyes flashed toward the queue for the lemonade, but James wasn't in sight. She wasn't quite sure what to do, so she shrugged and said yes.

He led her toward the floor, then took her hand tightly in his big mitt, as if he were afraid he'd lose hold of it otherwise.

Isaiah McKray wanted to dance with her. Her mind couldn't quite catch up to this fact. He was at least five years older than she. Surely it wasn't romantic . . .

Was it possible she was the only young lady he knew well enough to ask? That did seem quite possible.

The previous dance came to an end, and cheers of applause went up. Without missing a count, the band launched into a new song. This one a contra dance, a slightly slower tune.

Stieg was exiting the floor. She caught his eye and saw him raise an eyebrow at her dancing partner. She gave him a slight shrug.

"Are you enjoying your stay at the hotel?" McKray asked as they pulled side by side to promenade.

"Very much so," Sissel said. They dipped away and circled around the couple to their right. Each time they came back, McKray pulled her in strongly.

"Do you fancy the decor?" McKray asked.

"I do."

"I don't know the first thing about it, to tell the truth."

His expression was earnest. He seemed to be making a sincere attempt at polite conversation.

"Collier picked it all out."

Sissel smiled at that. When they came around again, she added, "It does seem rather more his style than yours," she said.

McKray smiled.

Then the dance quickened, and he left off the small talk to focus on the steps.

He was not the dancer James was, not nearly so, but was he ever strong! He went bashing into the other couples without even noticing, keeping his attention either on Sissel or on his feet. James had held her lightly, but McKray grabbed on in a way that was rough but nevertheless pleasing.

At the end of the dance, he mopped his brow with his handkerchief. Sissel found she was also out of breath.

"Thanks," he said. "That was more fun than I thought it was gonna be."

Sissel put her hands on her hips.

"Really, Mr. McKray, what a thing to say!"

"I meant to say—"

James appeared, coming to push between Sissel and McKray. He looked irritated.

"Come, Sissel, I have lemonade for you," James said.

"Good evening, Mr. Peavy," McKray said.

James nodded. McKray turned, with a little smile on his face, and went back into the crowd.

"Not very polite of him, to steal a fellow's girl," James said. "Did he stomp on your feet?"

"No," Sissel said. "Not too much."

"I suspect he practiced with a chambermaid," James said in a voice that was somewhat unkind.

Then, suddenly, Alice was at Hanne's elbow. She was crying.

"Alice! What is it?" Sissel asked.

Alice pulled her away from the dancers. James followed. Sissel wondered for a moment if Howie had done something untoward, but he was there behind Alice, looking concerned.

Alice led them all to the corner near the door, where it was quieter.

"My mother's combs!" Alice cried. "Someone's taken them!"

Sissel checked. Sure enough, the pretty gold combs were gone.

"Did you feel them take the combs?"

"No, we were dancing and then we stopped and when I felt for them, they were gone!"

"Let me check for you, darling," Sissel said. "Maybe they've just gotten stuck."

She patted her fingers in Alice's hair, to be sure the combs hadn't just become tangled in the dark tresses.

"I don't find them," Sissel said.

"Oh! They are my mother's greatest treasure!" Alice cried. Tears shone in her eyes. "What am I to do? She'll be heartbroken."

"We have to tell someone!" Howie said. "We'll . . . we'll search everyone."

"No," James said. "That's not the way. If it's a thief, then he will still be at work. We can catch him."

Alice clung to Sissel's arms, crying into her shoulder.

"I was a fool to wear them," she said. "My mother told me to be careful! I never thought someone would take them!"

"It's not your fault," Sissel said, patting her on the back.

"I never thought we'd have crime like this here in Carter!" Howie said.

"There's bad men everywhere," James said.

Sissel looked out over the dancers. She saw Stieg do-si-do-ing with Mrs. Denmead now.

What would he say? He would forbid her from using her Nytte. There was no doubt, that's what he'd do. He might even make her leave.

Best not to tell him, then.

"I say we tell the sheriff!" Howie said stoutly.

"No," James said. "Give me a half hour and I'll find your thief."

"How?" Alice asked.

"I just will," James said. His eyes were already roaming the crowd.

"Let's do as James suggests," Sissel told Alice. "If we can catch the thief ourselves we won't have to break up the party."

Alice nodded, sniffling.

Sissel turned to Howie. "Howie, why don't you get Alice a cup of lemonade, then take her outside for some air. James and I will search for the thief."

James flashed a look of surprise at Sissel, as if he hadn't expected her to help.

Howie groused, "We're wasting time here." He didn't like it, but did as he was told.

"Let me look on my own," James said. "I can't explain, but I know something about crooks like this one. I'll find him."

Sissel nodded. That was fine with her.

SISSEL WALKED TO the table with desserts and picked up a pecan tart. Squares of waxed butcher's paper were laid out for people to use to put their food on. She nibbled on the crust. She needed something to appear to do while she opened her mind to her Nytte.

"What a party!" said Mrs. Trowley to her. Sissel nodded politely. She slipped away, taking her food toward the wall. Some chairs had been set there for spectators. She sidled in and stood behind them, her back to the wall.

"Where's your beau?" Mr. Campbell asked. He was one of the people seated.

"I told him I needed to rest for a moment."

"Here, then, you'd better take my chair," he offered. She didn't see the point in refusing, so she sat.

Sissel held the tart on the paper in her lap. She relaxed her body, hoping she would look like she was resting. What if she looked odd when she started searching? She had never used her Nytte in front of anyone but Stieg. Why hadn't she thought to ask him how she looked?

She took a deep breath and called on her gift. Immediately, the colors and sounds of the dance dimmed. It was as if half the lamps had been extinguished. Rushing in came silver. There was so much of it in the room, all of it in tiny amounts. A glittery, confusing sensation, like watching a star shower.

She tried to push the silver aside, but the forms called to her, brooches, buttons, bar pins, and hair combs. There was brass there, too. On belt buckles and vest buttons. And tiny flashes of gold. Earrings, maybe. A few rings. Nothing of the right size or shape.

She began to sense the coins the Ladies' Aid members had collected. Coin boxes set on the food table. One coin box, brimming with quarters, was hidden under a hat. That didn't seem smart.

Sissel frowned, concentrating. Where were the gold hair combs?

Mr. Campbell was at her shoulder, a kindly look on his face. He had a tin cup full of water, and he held it to her, his face drawn with concern.

Sissel rose, pushing away the cup. The tin, shrill, weak, and needy, was too loud to be borne.

"Thank you," she said, not knowing if she was speaking loud enough to be heard. "I'm better now."

She stepped away from the chairs.

Gold, she directed her gift. *Find me the gold.*

She walked a few steps toward the dancers.

"Gold," she said aloud. A cowboy looked at her funny.

Then she felt them. Two pieces of gold, their vibration fluttering up above, like moths against a light, almost out of perception. She turned and walked in the direction the gold was calling from. To the left, to the left and up. Up somehow.

The hayloft. A good number of people were up there, leaning over the railing, enjoying a view of the dancing below. One of those people had Alice's combs. Might it be the cretin Ebbott himself? Sissel steeled herself to face him. She would not let him go this time.

The stairs to the hayloft were more like a ladder—narrow slats climbing steeply at an angle. A boy from school was coming down; she had to wait for him to reach the bottom before she could start to climb.

He asked her something, no doubt a pleasantry. She couldn't hear for the cacophony of metal noises in her mind. They were swarming her like a flock of sparrows, chittering, swooping, too fast to follow.

She smiled, said yes to whatever it was he had asked, and pushed past him.

The gold combs were so close now. And the thief wouldn't get past her. He couldn't—not on the narrow ladder.

Sissel poked her head up. She was at shoe level. Her mind seized on the incongruence of some of the footwear. Folks had worn their best outfits, but many made do with their sole pair of footwear.

Never mind the shoes, she told herself. Where was the gold?

She kept climbing, and as her body emerged from the square hole in the floor of the hayloft, a handsome young man she didn't recognize held out his hand to help her up.

Was it him? She listened for the metals on him. No, silver and nickel in his pocket. A brass belt buckle. She ducked her head, embarrassed to be sending out her senses in that direction.

He spoke to her, but she did not reply. The gold was close now, and the strain of doing this much looking—holding her Nytte so strongly over such a busy scene, was starting to tell. The back of her head was throbbing, and her ears ached. She had her hands out now, she needed them out, no matter how strange she might look. Her fingers were burning for the gold.

She walked along the line of partygoers looking down at the dance below. Ebbott was not among them. She staggered once, nearly losing her footing.

She closed her eyes and cast out strongly. There. Behind her.

She turned and saw a figure pressed in the corner of the loft, where the lamplight did not reach.

They were there, Alice's combs. The figure started as Sissel approached. Sissel looked around, realizing she should have someone strong with her. What if the thief attacked her? She knew she should call for help, but now all the world was silent for her. How would she explain?

Then the figure lurched forward, as if to escape. Sissel reached out and grabbed. It was a girl! Sissel held tight to a thin arm. It was Bridget, from the hotel.

Sissel was shocked. Bridget, a thief? The girl was sobbing; tears had already stained the front of her plain gingham dress. She was explaining something, making some kind of excuse to Sissel, God knows what it could have been.

Bridget pressed the gold combs into Sissel's hand and squirmed away. The gold expanded in Sissel's touch, sending a release of warmth through her body.

Sissel turned, knowing she should stop the girl. That's when she saw McKray.

He was standing right behind her, and he was grinning ear to ear.

She was not a lip reader, but she could make out his words just fine, "I knew it."

Gods, it was a trap.

She pushed past him, and he made no move to stop her.

She climbed as carefully down the ladder as she could, given her shaking hands and her tired limbs.

She saw Alice by the food tables, looking around, but Sissel ducked out, weaving through the dancers, until she came to the door on the other side. She couldn't face Alice now, not as she was—trembling all over and deaf as a stone.

She slipped outside and set off to find a dark, quiet place where she could shut off her Nytte, wait for her hearing to return, and make her pulse steady.

"WHERE WERE YOU?" James asked when she returned. It sounded as if he were talking from a great distance away, but she could make out the words. He looked flustered and agitated. He had been searching

187

that whole time for the thief, and then must have started searching for Sissel.

It was now stiflingly hot in the barn, with all the bodies dancing.

"I had the idea they might have fallen outside," she said to James. He didn't believe her. She opened her hand, revealing the two doves within it.

"Outside? Really?" he said.

Sissel walked past him. He put his hand on her wrist, some question in his eye. Sissel wriggled away; she couldn't let his eyes search her face too long—she wasn't a good enough liar.

Stieg reached them. "Is everything all right?" he said. "I lost you in the dancing, then James said—"

"I'm fine," she said. Stieg had hold of her arm now.

"What did you do?" he asked, low.

"Alice needed my help," she said.

"What?" he asked. Sissel realized she hadn't spoken loudly enough to be heard.

"Alice needed my help," she repeated. This time someone nearby looked around. Too loud.

Sissel saw Alice sitting down with Howie in the collection of chairs near the door. She was staring at the floor, and Howie was talking to her, trying to cheer her up.

Sissel swept over and took Alice's hand in hers. She pressed the gold doves into it. Alice's brown eyes widened with joy.

She let out a happy squeal and jumped up, nearly knocking Sissel back. She hugged Sissel.

"Where did you find them?" she asked.

"Outside. On the ground," Sissel said.

"Outside! But how on earth did they get outside?" Howie said.

"Oh, Sissel, you have saved me!" Alice said, hugging her again.

It was a relief, at least, to have made her friend so happy, even if she had fallen into McKray's trap.

Alice folded the combs into a handkerchief and then made Howie tuck the handkerchief deep inside the interior pocket of his suit vest.

Stieg stood behind Sissel, frowning, no doubt. Worried, no doubt. Sissel felt drained and wobbly. She wanted to go home, but she felt bad to cut the evening short for James.

He had looked on as Alice thanked Sissel. She couldn't quite read his expression, and she worried he was trying too hard to read hers. His eyes kept flitting between her and Stieg, noting her brother's tension and disquiet.

"Come," Alice said gamely. "You've all spent too much time helping me. I'll have wasted the whole evening for us all. We must dance again before the night ends!"

She took Sissel's hand and led her toward the floor. Stieg, James, and Howie followed.

Sissel dodged Stieg's glare the rest of the night. She tried to enjoy the music, but she couldn't get her mind off McKray.

He had set her up. Bridget had probably stolen Alice's combs while he was dancing with her! Sissel remembered Bridget saying something about McKray forgiving past mistakes. Was the girl a pickpocket? A professional thief?

Bridget had been crying, though, upset. He had forced her to do it. That was plain to see. What a cad! Sissel was furious.

And now McKray knew she could find gold. He didn't have the full measure of her powers, but he knew her secret. What would he do with the information?

Sissel kept stepping on James's feet as they danced. She could tell he was upset with her, irritated she was so distracted. She tried to focus on the touch of James's hand at her waist, which had so enthralled her before. But it could not compete with the worries that pressed down on her now.

CHAPTER TWENTY-SEVEN

Stieg paced Sissel's room, glowering at the Persian carpet. It was Sunday, in the quiet hours after church and before dinner.

"You risked a great deal—"

"Alice needed me. Those combs are her mother's best pieces!"

"You've never used the Nytte in a space like that—so full of people. A million things could have gone wrong!"

Sissel chewed on her lip.

"Why didn't you come to me?" he asked.

"I knew you'd tell me not to interfere!"

Stieg considered that for a moment, then shot back, "You're right! I would have! It was reckless, what you did! You could have truly hurt yourself."

"I feel better than I have in my whole life, Stieg. Every time I use it I get stronger."

"You use it often, then?"

Sissel's face flushed red.

"It is mine to use," she said. "It is my gift."

They were surprised by a knock on the door.

Sissel opened it to find one of the porters there. He held out a small cream-colored envelope to Sissel.

"I gotta wait for a reply," he said. He seemed embarrassed.

She said her thanks and shut the door.

"What is it?" Stieg asked.

Sissel opened the envelope and read the note within, printed in a blocky, graceless script.

"A social card?" Stieg asked.

"Mr. McKray requests the pleasure of my company on a carriage ride," she said. She looked up at Stieg, her surprise written so baldly on her face that Stieg laughed. He shook his head.

"I think you've got another beau," he said.

Sissel looked back down at the note. Her heart was pounding. This was about last night.

"So it seems," she said.

Stieg was watching her closely. "You don't think he's trying to influence you to get us to sell our land, do you?"

"No," she said. "I don't think it has anything to do with our land."

"Well," Stieg said, his eyes twinkling, "you need not go if you don't want to, but I'm not entirely surprised. I saw the way he was looking at you when you danced. Do you think he's too old for you?"

"I don't know," Sissel said.

"Five years seems like a great distance now, but the difference between a man of thirty-five and a woman of thirty seems like nothing."

Sissel simply shrugged. She wasn't thinking about the age difference one bit. She was thinking about what McKray knew about her, and how to get him to keep it a secret.

"Do you want me to tell the porter you aren't feeling well?" Stieg asked.

She shook her head, and hoped her voice sounded casual. "No, no. I suppose I could go out for a ride."

Stieg smiled in an indulgent way that made her feel terrible. Another lie told to her brother—that she would consider Isaiah McKray as a beau.

Sissel opened the door. "Tell Mr. McKray I will be down presently," she said. Relief dawned over the porter's face. Obviously he knew the nature of his errand.

"I'll tell him, miss," he said, and scurried off down the hall.

Stieg let himself out, telling Sissel to report in when she returned, reminding her their discussion wasn't finished. But in general, he seemed amused.

Good, Sissel thought, let him be amused and not suspect the trouble I'm in.

She tucked her white blouse into her skirt. She had changed into these more casual clothes after church, not expecting to be going anywhere. She knew anyone would think she was preening for McKray, making herself look pretty. That was not it at all. She wanted to look capable and grown-up.

Her hair was forever escaping the bun. It was too thin. Sissel didn't have time to take it down and repin it. She patted it into place and found her hands were shaking.

She placed her hands on the cool, lacquered top of the bureau and leaned toward her reflection.

"Steady," she told herself.

MCKRAY WAS WAITING in the lobby, talking to Collier.

Sissel stopped on the stairs. They were discussing a shortage of mutton for the restaurant. Such a mundane, adult conversation. Suddenly she felt like a small child, playing at being grown-up. She wanted to turn back, but lifted her chin and marched bravely down.

McKray turned. When their eyes met he ducked his head.

Good, she thought. He should look away, ashamed.

"Miss Hemstad," he said, tipping his hat.

"Good afternoon," Sissel replied.

"I hope it's not too presumptuous of me to ask you to take a ride with me?"

"Not at all," she said.

As far as Sissel was concerned, all this dialogue was for the benefit of the gossip hound Collier, who stood behind the counter, officiously polishing his glasses.

Collier nodded to Sissel as she passed. She dipped her head back.

McKray led her out the door to the carriage waiting outside.

This was a finer buggy than James had procured for the dance the night before, richly appointed, with a leather cover lined with red silk. Joshua, one of the hotel porters, stood holding the reins. The leather was fastened with brass rivets. Sissel stepped up into it as Joshua held the horses. They were a pair of matched palominos. Showy horses, very pretty. Their tails were braided with red ribbons to match the cushions of the surrey.

McKray held her hand as she climbed inside.

Minnie and Abigail were walking by, and their eyes nearly popped from their skulls, seeing Sissel being courted by Isaiah McKray.

Sissel wasn't happy about being summoned by McKray this way, but at least she got to enjoy the amazement on her schoolmates' faces.

McKray followed Sissel's gaze to the girls and tipped his hat to them.

"Ladies," he said.

Then he gave the horses a touch of the reins and they drove forward. Sissel was sure the two girls' mouths hung agape as they passed.

"I guess we're an unlikely pair," McKray said.

"Maybe we are," Sissel said.

The horses trotted and swiftly put the town behind them.

"The town's booming," McKray said, just as Sissel said, "That was some trick you pulled last night."

He cleared his throat.

"I'm sorry about that. I didn't mean to give your friend such a scare. But I had a mind to know the truth about you, and now I know it."

"You used poor Bridget terribly!" Sissel said. "To make her steal?!"

"She owed me a favor," McKray said, frowning.

"For what?" Sissel asked.

"I bought out her contract from a Telluride cathouse, if you really want to know."

Sissel snapped her mouth shut.

"Perhaps you'd better take me back," Sissel said.

"Now, now. I didn't mean to offend. She approached me and asked for my help, and I gave it to her. She's working off her debt to me."

"Well . . . after what you made her do last night, I should think her obligation to you is over. What a risk! What if someone else had caught her?"

"No one would have," he said. "Little towns like this, people want to believe everything's safe and sound. They should be on guard, but they want to trust and for life to be easy."

Sissel had to admit he had a point. She and her siblings had lived in Carter for nearly three years. Her sister was a murderer—had killed six men—and no one suspected a thing.

"We've got more important things to talk about," McKray said.

Sissel sat back, arms crossed.

"I was right about you, but I've not come here to gloat about it. I want your help. You know I'm developing several mines around the area. I want to hire you to help me. I'll pay you as much as I pay my top assessor. That's ten dollars a day, fifty a week."

Now clear of town, he gave a snap of the reins and the horses began to trot.

"Is that where we are going now?" Sissel asked. "To one of your mines?"

He made a gruff noise of assent.

"Do you truly think I will help you, after the nasty trick you pulled on me last night?" Sissel said.

"Don't you need the money?" he asked.

"You made my friend Alice cry," she said. "Not to mention poor Bridget. No kind of gentleman would do such a thing."

"I never claimed to be a gentleman."

"No? Then why do you wear those fancy suits? Why do you drive such a lovely surrey?"

McKray turned and glared at her.

"You're awful forward," he said.

"Perhaps I am."

McKray frowned at the reins in his hand and kept driving straight.

"Let me try again," he said. "I'm not much good at this . . . Miss

Hemstad, you can tell where gold is, and I own several mines. That seems a promising situation."

Sissel thought about this, watching the birds dart and hide in the prairie grass.

"I know I tricked you, and I do apologize. But look, I have teams of miners. You could just waltz into one of my mines and tell us where to dig. Why, imagine their faces, all lit up with wonder! Imagine them breaking great hunks of ore riddled with gold out of the ground."

Or silver or nickel or platinum, Sissel thought to herself.

"Picture yourself buying a new dress for your sister. Or a silver-backed brush and mirror set. Imagine having so much money none of you Hemstads have to work another day. All just from walking into a mine and pointing."

Sissel cast her eyes up into the endless blue sky above. She could see it all.

Then she sighed, letting go of the fantasy.

The word would get out. The miners would talk. The Baron would find them, bringing more Berserkers, or worse, the law would catch up with them and they'd hang her sister.

"Thank you for your offer, but my answer is no," she said.

A wagon was drawing near on the road. The driver, a farmer, raised his hat in salutation; McKray gave him a terse nod back.

"What if I offer you fifteen percent? Fifteen percent of gold from *my* land, dug up and processed by *my* miners. It could be thousands of dollars, Miss Hemstad. Tens of thousands. My father took two hundred seventy thousand in gold out of his mine in Ouray, Colorado, last year alone."

Sissel tried to grasp that.

"I can't, Mr. McKray. I appreciate your offer. I do." She laid her fingers on one of his big meaty hands. He turned to look at her. "It's a good offer. I see that. But I have to keep what I can do a secret. And I need to ask you, to beg you, if I must, to help me keep it a secret."

"Oh," he said. "I can keep a secret."

McKray directed the team of horses onto a thin side road, little more than wagon wheel ruts through the grass. He drove on until they reached a bit of shade from a couple of forlorn willows.

McKray shifted in his seat so he was facing in her direction. He removed a folded piece of heavy stock paper from the inside pocket of his jacket and handed it to her.

She opened it.

There was her brother Knut's face, staring up at her from the wanted poster.

Sissel looked to McKray, then back to the poster, and to McKray again.

He wasn't smiling now, but looking grim and resigned.

"This is over two years old," she said. "This man, this poster, it's not correct—"

She was stumbling over the words, realizing, as she spoke, that she should pretend not to know anything about the poster or the boy pictured on it. Only now it was too late.

"That's a drawing of your brother," McKray said.

"No," she said. "This warrant is no good. They found this boy. Someone turned in his body for the reward. Don't you see?"

McKray sighed.

"It doesn't matter what I see. What matters is what everyone else sees. If this poster were to find its way to the hands of the locals . . . For five hundred dollars? Lots of men would try for that bounty."

Tears sprang to Sissel's eyes.

"I'm not saying I'm going to do anything with this," he said, then he fumbled for his handkerchief. "I didn't mean to upset you. I just saw that poster when I was visiting my father in Colorado last spring. I've held it ever since."

"You mustn't tell anyone!" She took the handkerchief and dabbed it to her eyes.

"I won't! I haven't! All this time, I've kept this secret. And I'll keep on keeping it, too. In fact, if you would help me, I'd do everything in my power to protect him. Protect all of you."

Sissel was cold. Her belly felt like it was being filled with lead. "This is blackmail. You're blackmailing me?"

"No, no," he said. "That's not what I'm about. Work for me, Miss Hemstad. Let me hire you to do what you're so good at. You'll get rich and keep your family safe."

"Safe from you!" she blurted out. "Don't pretend *you* are not the threat."

"Listen, Miss Hemstad, I'm just after money. That's all. I promise. Take that poster. Keep it safe or burn it up."

Sissel looked to his face, to be sure he meant it. He held his hands up.

"I'm not here to ruin your life," he said. "I just . . . when I see an opportunity, I seize it."

Sissel clutched the poster. She leaned against the leather backrest. She felt alone and scared and exhausted all at once.

McKray whisked the reins at the horses and brought them around in a large circle. He set them back toward the main road.

For a while, the only noise was the horses' hooves hitting the road and the squeaking of the fancy leather upholstery.

"If you change your mind about visiting my mines, do let me know," McKray said.

"I suppose I should thank you for finding this poster and keeping it safe," Sissel said.

"Only if you feel like it," McKray said, in a voice so low she pretended not to hear.

CHAPTER TWENTY-EIGHT

Things weren't as easy as they'd been before Mandry assaulted her, but Hanne tried to make sure Owen and Witri and all the cowboys knew she was all right.

Tincher had been informed of a scrap between Owen and Mandry. He might have figured out what had really happened, between Hanne's black eye and Mandry's bruised and battered face, but no one had felt the need to comment on it and bring it into the open.

Hanne presented a cheerful face to the company and tried to let them see she wasn't worried or afraid.

In stolen moments late at night, she reassured Owen—it could have been so much worse. She could have killed Mandry. It was only Witri's intervention and Daisy's appearance that had kept her from it. But Owen was upset about the whole thing and there wasn't any time for them to talk it out. He was away riding all day and sometimes had night guard as well.

That morning Hanne had moved to embrace Owen before he

mounted his horse, and Owen hadn't seen her stepping forward. He swung up, just past her reach, and given the horse his heels, riding off.

She turned and caught Witri watching this small and likely accidental snub.

An hour or so later, he presented her with a little bundle, made of a flour sack.

"You go on and take your husband some dinner today," he told her. "You deserve an afternoon off, and anyway, it's Son of a Gun stew tonight, and I want to save you the horrors of preparing that dish."

Son of a Gun stew, Hanne knew, was made from a freshly butchered calf, every last bit of it, from tail to horns.

"Are you sure?" she asked.

Witri nodded, his kind green eyes twinkling at her from beneath his towel headdress.

"Lovely young bride like you can't be keeping company with an old dried-up cow pie like me day and night," he said gruffly. "Go on. I put some molasses cookies in there, too."

DAISY WAS VERY happy to see Hanne. Hanne could tell the dog didn't like it that her two masters spent so much time apart during the day. Since Mandry's attack, Daisy seemed particularly anxious.

Nevertheless, Daisy had a job to do. She needed to be with Owen, helping bring the cattle into line. But each evening she came racing into camp, body squirming with joy to be reunited with her mistress.

Now she played in the flowers, while Owen and Hanne sat on a large rock, enjoying the sun and the last bites of their picnic. Scattered around them were the grazing longhorns. They were near the front of the drive. Tincher had switched around the positions after the fight, moving Owen up toward the front and assigning Mandry to ride drag. It was a hard place to ride, at the back of the herd, where the dust and the smell was the worst. Hanne knew Tincher did it to punish Mandry.

Jigsaw and the horse Owen was riding for the morning, a mature chestnut gelding named Brutus, had their heads together as they cropped the grass, as if gossiping.

But on the rock, Hanne and Owen said little. It seemed they could not get a conversation started past a few mundane sentences.

"We should have mail tomorrow," he said.

"Mmm-hmm. Not from home, though. They wouldn't know where to send it."

"I suppose not."

Then, a few moments later, she said, "These cookies are a bit hard, aren't they?"

"They're fine. Better than what the men are used to, I figure."

"Yes."

Fat fluffy clouds drifted overhead. Flowers dotted the field, yellow owl's clover and asters in pink and white. Hanne knew she should feel happy, overjoyed to be in such a beautiful place, doing work she enjoyed alongside the man she loved. But she could not help but feel sad at the distance between her and Owen.

Owen lay on his side, propped up on his elbow.

He sighed. "It's a pretty sight."

"Yes," Hanne said. Then she exhaled suddenly. "For heaven's sake, I wish you'd tell me what's wrong."

"What do you mean?"

"Ever since we saw your brother, you've been closed off to me."

"I don't know what you're talking about," he said. He sat up, turning slightly away from her.

Hanne sighed. "Are we going to be married?" she asked.

"Well, yes, of course." Owen said.

"Then you must tell me when something troubles you. Otherwise, it's . . . It hurts me."

"You gotta know everything?" he asked with a tinge of meanness. "Every little thing about me, for us to love each other?"

"It's not like you to be cruel, Owen Bennett."

"That's just it!" he said, and he cussed.

Daisy whined. She had come back to the rock, and now she nosed her muzzle into Owen's hand. He crossed his arms over his chest, denying Daisy's offer of affection. "Owen Bennett. It's hardly my name. My name is a godforsaken punishment!"

She reached for him. "Owen—"

"I'm a bastard, Hanne."

Hanne drew back.

"I didn't want you to know. I don't know why."

Owen rubbed his temples as if he had a headache.

"My mother was an Irish girl. My father found her in Chicago on one of his trips to the slaughterhouses, and he brought her back to the ranch, to give his wife some company and to cook . . ."

"Oh, Owen," Hanne said.

"And then he got her with child. Me. She died giving birth to me.

"I guess they could have sent me back to her folks, or given me to an orphanage, but instead I was raised there, along with the natural sons of my father. It was a kind of punishment for him, you see?"

There was pain and bitterness in his voice. Hanne moved forward to him over the stone. She took his hands into her own. He allowed her to do this, but he wouldn't meet her eyes.

"That's why Mandry and Whistler make all those jokes about

Irish cooks, you see? They learned about me. I never told you, and I'm ashamed of that, too," he said.

Hanne thought how to best answer this confession.

She put her hands on either side of his face and drew him toward her, kissing him deeply. When she sat back, he finally met her gaze.

"I'm so glad you told me," she said. "It doesn't matter one bit to me that your parents weren't married to each other when you were born. What does matter is how you were treated. And for that I am so sorry. I'm angry at them, and I'm sorry for you."

"They never wanted me around," Owen said.

"They're fools."

"That's why Matthew acted the way he did when we saw him in Fitch," Owen said.

"It all makes sense to me now," Hanne said. "And now I see, of course, why you never wanted to take me there to meet them."

"I hope it didn't hurt your feelings."

"It doesn't matter," she said. "Because now I know the truth and I wouldn't care to meet them."

They sat there, watching the cattle. Daisy settled down at the edge of the rock. A butterfly fluttered too close to it, and she snapped at it, sitting up to snap again when it drifted just out of reach.

Hanne snuggled into Owen's arms.

"Secrets weigh heavy, don't they?" Owen said. He gave a laugh. "I feel like I just lost about eighty pounds."

"Yes," Hanne said. "I know."

"Well," Owen said after a moment. "Do you think we'd better get you back to Witri?"

Daisy sprang up and barked.

"Oh, heaven's sake, Daisy," Owen said.

Then Hanne heard it, felt it—a rumble.

She and Owen sat up at the same time. He put his hat on.

There was dust coming from the drive behind, and a sound that grew by the second. The cattle near to Owen and Hanne began to mill. They bawled and snorted.

"Stampede," Owen said, jumping down from the rock. "Dear God! Get on Jigsaw! You've got to ride!"

Tons of bellowing cattle—meat and muscle and horn—thundered toward them like a tidal wave.

Owen made a snatch for Jigsaw's bridle, but she was panicking along with the cattle. The two horses ran and the cattle nearby went with them.

The force of the stampede was headed right for them.

"*Ásáheill!*" Hanne shouted. "Odin! Hear me!" Then she felt a tremendous gathering within her body, and a burst of light. The Gods and the Nytte possessed Hanne entirely.

Owen took off his hat and began to wave it at the cattle. "Hey! Hey!" he yelled.

Hanne looked around with new eyes. There was the dog, standing on the rock, barking. There was her mate, standing in front of her, waving his hat at the cattle.

She grabbed her mate by the back of the shirt and hauled him up onto the rock.

"Hold the dog!" she commanded. The dog was beloved to her and must be protected, as well as the man.

Then she stood in front of that rock and waited for the herd to crash down.

The cattle tossed their heads in terror, clashing horns. Running all as one. The ground shook with their hooves.

Time slowed for Hanne, every detail clear to her eye.

A great source of illumination shone from her own heart, making all movements clear to see.

She had no worry or care. She felt the terror of the poor dumb beasts and pitied them, but that would not keep her from slaying every last one if need be.

A huge black steer came at them. A dun brown heifer at his left. Hanne launched herself into the air. She gripped the heifer's shaggy ears and jerked its head sharply to the right, using its long, sharp horn to slice through the cordage of the black steer's throat.

Dark red blood sprayed, the drops slow to Hanne's all-seeing eye.

Hanne had snapped the heifer's neck. The beast fell. The steer crashed into it. The bulk of cow flesh slid up the rock toward her man and his dog. Gravity slowed it.

The man stood at the top of the rock, holding the dog.

Hanne climbed up onto the beast's heaving sides. She stood in a crouch, waiting.

Blood from the steer sprayed down the rock. The longhorns veered, eyes rolling, snorting with terror, around the gruesome island made of rock and fallen cattle.

She and her man stood watching as the stampede flowed around them. The dust was blinding. The hooves deafening. But the cattle veered around the rock and they were safe.

A great light was behind her, illuminating the cattle. Split into two streams by the obstruction in their path, the animals eddied into slower, churning masses.

She looked down and saw the light was emanating from her own body. Her limbs, her chest, her skin—glowing like a lantern.

"Dear God, you're shining," her beloved said.

Some cattle broke out from the milling masses. As more followed, they gradually stopped running. Some ran on but many stood, sides heaving.

As this happened, Hanne's breathing sped up. The scene before her sped up. Hanne felt herself released by the Gods and stumbled forward. She landed on her hands and knees, onto the back of the giant steer.

"You did it, didn't you?" Owen said. "Like back in Wolf Creek? The Gods were in you. What did Rolf call it—divine possession?"

Hanne couldn't quite speak. She could only beam at him. Such a beauty of a man.

"Look at yourself, Hanne."

She looked down. As had happened at Wolf Creek, she was clean. Her dress, her skin, all blown free of any dirt or debris or blood.

Owen, on the other hand, had blood plastered to his face and neck and hands. Daisy, too, was spattered with it.

Owen took his hat off and rubbed his hand through his hair.

"I'm not hungry," Hanne said.

"You gotta write to Rolf. Tell him what happened," Owen said.

"What now?" she asked. "What about the herd?"

"It'll be bad," Owen said. They looked out at the flattened meadow. The two dead cattle lay at the base of the rock. There were other fallen beefs here and there. Some bawled pitifully.

Owen exhaled.

"We make our way back to the chuck wagon. See who made it. Hopefully Lester kept the remuda together. I'll get another horse and go looking for Jigsaw and Brutus. Then we start gathering the herd back up.

"It's bad, a stampede." Owen glanced at her. "But it's not as bad as it could have been."

He extended an arm to her, and she slid under it. Blood and dust from his wet shirt made a streak along her shoulder.

That's fine, she thought. She'd have to dirty her dress and face and hair, anyway. There was no way to explain her appearance otherwise.

There was no way to explain it at all.

But she was glad for it, her Nytte, her magic. Perhaps for the first time, Hanne was truly glad to be a Nyttesdotter.

CHAPTER TWENTY-NINE

Hanne and Owen walked on foot back to the chuck wagon. Daisy followed close by. It was spooky terrain, the ground pounded flat.

The cattle hadn't come near the camp. The chuck wagon had made it through completely unscathed. In fact, there was still a swath of green grass surrounding it. Witri stood there directing the cowboys as they staggered in from one place or another. Three men were seated at the campfire, drinking coffee. Others were preparing to go out.

"Thank God you two are all right," Witri said, as Hanne and Owen approached. "I kept thinking if only I hadn't sent you on a danged picnic you'd be safe!"

He pulled Hanne into a dusty embrace.

"We got up on a rock," Owen said. "The cattle broke around us."

"So far, we've got no casualties," Witri said. "We got lucky. Riley there has a broken arm, but I think that's the worst of it far as I know."

The cowboy named Riley was off sitting near a cottonwood. He was one of the older cowboys, face tanned and lined from years out in the sun. He sat cradling his arm and pulling slugs off a bottle of whiskey. There was a terrible lump halfway up his forearm—a break.

"Will you help me set his arm?" Witri asked Owen, nodding toward the cowboy.

"Let me," Hanne said. "It is something I'm good at."

"You sure? Takes a lot of strength."

"She's got a knack for it," Owen said. "I'll help her. We've done it before."

Hanne knew he was remembering the man they'd met on the trail, who'd been crushed under a wagon. They'd set his leg.

"All right," Witri said. "If you're good at it."

"We are," Owen said.

Witri moved off to bandage a young cowboy bleeding from a wicked gash on his forehead.

Owen sat down on the ground and scooted up behind Riley. He held him tight around the torso and pinned down the upper part of the injured arm.

"That right?" Owen asked.

Hanne nodded. "I'll pull hard so be ready," she said.

Riley sought her eyes as she crouched in front of him.

"Be as still as you can," she said.

He nodded somberly and took one last swig of whiskey.

Hanne took hold of the cowboy's arm just above his wrist, under the break.

Then Hanne dug her feet in and pulled. Her sense of anatomy was keen; she supposed it was a benefit of being a Berserker. Even without her Nytte flooding through her, she had a sense of the bones and the shape of the break. The bones came apart. Riley gasped. Then she moved the bones back into place.

She released her hands, and the tall, tough cowboy fainted dead away into Owen's arms.

Owen gently edged back until the cowboy was flat on his back. He took Riley's coat, which lay curled in the dirt, and wadded it into a pillow that he placed carefully under Riley's head.

"Clean break?" Owen asked.

"Yes, I think it will heal well," Hanne said.

"Want my help bandaging it?" he asked.

"No, thank you."

"I'm needed out there," Owen said.

"Yes, you should go."

Owen drew her close and planted a kiss on her forehead, a rare public display.

"I'm sorry," he said. "For ever keeping anything from you. You're . . . you're a wonder and I love you."

Hanne let go and allowed herself to be comforted by his embrace.

At this moment, Whistler rode up. His face was white with fury.

"Whistler, glad to see you," Witri called.

Whistler bounded off his horse and stomped toward Hanne and Owen.

The Nytte flickered suddenly in Hanne's chest, mild, but strong enough to heighten her sense and make her stand tall. Get ready.

Whistler's eyes were red and crazed. He grabbed Owen by the shirt and shook him.

"You shot Mandry," he said. "You son of a bitch, you shot him right through the heart!"

Owen pushed Whistler off. "Are you crazy?" Owen said. "I wasn't anywhere near Mandry! Mandry was at the back, riding drag. I was up front."

Hanne soothed the Nytte away with slow breaths.

Whistler extended a hand that was shaking, pointing back from where the stampede had started.

"I found his body, shot through the heart!" he said, talking to Witri and the wounded men. "I found him back there. Someone tried to make it look like an accident, but he was shot before the stampede even started.

"Hell," Whistler continued, "I bet that shot is what started the stampede in the first place!"

There was sharp interest around the camp now.

Hanne saw a few of the faces look at her and toward Owen with something like suspicion. After all, she realized, everyone knew about the fight between Mandry and Owen. Everyone knew something had happened, but no one knew exactly what.

She could almost see them thinking it—Mandry had done something to Hanne that got him shot. It wouldn't be hard to imagine what it was.

"Bennett started the whole stampede!" Whistler shouted.

"Now, now," said Witri. "You're way ahead of yourself there, Whistler. No way to know how a stampede got started."

"Mandry's shot dead! What else could it have been?!" Whistler's voice was strained to breaking.

He wiped at his mouth, and Hanne could see he was truly upset, truly believed that Owen had shot his friend.

Now Tincher came riding back shouting orders. He hadn't heard a bit of it.

"What are you all doing lazing around? Everyone get on a horse. I don't care if you got a busted head!" he said.

Tincher swung off his horse and headed for the coffeepot. "The cattle are spread out for miles! Get off your asses and go get 'em!"

The cowboys near the fire set down their coffee cups and wearily rose to their feet.

Whistler strode over to the trail boss.

"If you're looking for the person who started the stampede," he said, pointing at Owen, "there's your man."

Tincher looked at Owen, then looked back at Whistler. "Are you kidding me?" he said. "We've got enough things to worry about without the petty feud you got with Bennett. That nonsense is over. Where's Mandry?"

"Dead! Shot dead!"

Witri walked over to stand between Whistler and Tincher.

"Whistler here says he found Mandry's body, and he's been shot," Witri said.

"Owen Bennett shot him," Whistler said.

"For God's sake, I was up at the front," Owen said.

"Mandry's been shot? You sure?" Tincher said.

"A hole in the center of his chest."

Tincher turned to Owen. "And where were you?"

"I was having dinner, sir. Hanne was with me," Owen said.

Tincher leveled a flat look at Hanne. "That true, missus?"

"Yes, sir. Witri told me I could take a lunch to him, and that is what I did."

"All true," Witri confirmed.

"You gotta send for the sheriff!" Whistler said.

Tincher rubbed at his eyes. "Look, I got fifteen hundred headaches right now. They are beefs. They are the profit from this drive, spread all across this damned valley."

"I demand justice for the murdered body of Harold Mandry!" Whistler spat.

"Go haul in that body, and we'll take a look. Everyone else, back to work."

CHAPTER THIRTY

James stared at the history book, but there was nothing in the War of 1812 that could catch his attention. At the blackboard, the youngest students were writing out sentences about pigs, wigs, and jigs.

Sissel sat one row ahead of him, on the girls' side of the classroom. The back of her head revealed no answers to any of the mysteries that surrounded her.

Something had happened to Sissel at the dance, James was sure of it. The music and the dancing had worked beautifully on her. She'd been ready to trust him, or at least to kiss him. Things had been about to progress, in one way or another, and then Alice's combs disappeared and it all went to hell.

One minute she had been warmed up and laughing, growing careless as the reels gained speed, and then for the rest of the night she was a different girl. Closed off and distant.

He'd gained footing and lost it. That was all right. He could stomach that. It had happened before. But when he had gone to call on her Sunday afternoon he was informed that she was out riding with Isaiah McKray. Collier gave him a patronizing, self-satisfied little smirk when he told the news, too.

Isaiah McKray? Isaiah McKray courting Sissel? It was suspicious. It was preposterous.

He included it in his report, dutifully logging in: *Miss Hemstad went driving with I. McKray, local hotelier and mine owner.* The only benefit to reporting on it was that he could now justify writing back to Chicago, asking them to look into McKray's interests.

Mr. Hemstad complimented the children on their work and sent them back to the front seats.

"We'll have lunch and recess now," Mr. Hemstad said.

As if in agreement, the stomach of a ten-year-old boy named Finn Coffey rumbled loudly. Finn didn't move, but his face shot red with a fierce blush.

"Just in the nick of time, I suppose," Mr. Hemstad said with a wink to Finn. "Off you go."

Then there was some laughing and ribbing, and the sounds of chairs being pushed back. James fished his lunch out of his desk. It was the custom of the younger children to eat outside, and the older students to eat inside, the girls in one cluster and the boys in another.

Sissel shared a desk with Alice, and both girls now took out their lunches. Alice spoke in a low voice to Sissel, but one James could overhear.

"I can't believe you didn't tell me, is all," she whispered.

"There was nothing to tell; we just went for a ride."

Alice gave a small, hurt sniff. She laid back the tea towel covering the top of her lunch bucket.

"I just would have thought you would tell me," she repeated.

Then Abigail went over to them, a sandwich in hand. Minnie followed.

"I can't believe the dance is over," Abigail sighed. "Your dress was divine, Alice."

"Everyone looked so pretty," Minnie said.

"I didn't get home until past eleven!" Abigail said.

On the boys' side, there were often awkward pauses in the lunchtime conversation. Mostly, like now, they listened to the girls chattering. Sometimes they talked about the weather or farming.

"Did you enjoy yourself at the dance?" one of the boys asked.

It was a polite question, made mostly to pass the time, but it galled James. The whole thing did. Sitting there, pretending not to listen to the girls, pretending to be someone he wasn't.

He sprang out of his seat.

"Sissel," he burst out. He took a steadying breath. "Would you care to take your lunch with me outside?"

Around her, the girls' eyes went wide with the forwardness of it. Some of them looked to one another, titillated smiles on their faces.

Sissel avoided looking at him.

"Outside?" she asked.

"Yes," James said. "I'd like the chance to speak with you. That's all."

He tried to project an earnest and lovelorn air. Sissel let out a small breath of resignation.

"All right," she said. She packed up her sandwich, back into the waxed paper it had been wrapped in, and allowed him to lead her from the room.

"Alice, whaddya say?" he heard Howie say. "Shall we eat outside as well?"

Look there, he'd started a new fashion.

Now that they were out, James wasn't sure where to go. He indicated two boulders that sat at the edge of the schoolyard. "How about over there?" he asked.

"Good."

They walked over to the rocks, past the younger children, who were sprawled on the long grass near a couple of old, gnarled cottonwoods.

She took a seat on the boulder and he leaned on it next to her.

"Something happened Saturday night, and I wish you'd tell me what it was," he said.

Sissel took a bite of her sandwich. She chewed thoughtfully.

"I had a very nice time," she said. "I'm sorry if I seemed removed. I guess it's my health. I'm not used to dances, even though I have been feeling better lately."

She wouldn't meet his eye.

"That's all?" James asked. "Really?"

"I think I was tired, from all that excitement with Alice's combs."

Her eyes were cast to the ground, then to the trees. Anywhere but to his face. She fidgeted with her sandwich, pressing the cheese back between the bread. She was lying.

She took another bite of her sandwich. He did the same. The chunks of ham and bread were distracting. He swallowed them down.

"I wish you trusted me," he said. God, what was he doing? Was he going to come at her with no art whatsoever? Just say whatever came into his head?

Sissel wasn't eating now, or answering. She was staring off toward the children, looking miserable. In fact, tears came up in her eyes as he was studying her. He rushed to find his handkerchief and pressed it into her hand.

"What's wrong, Sissel? Tell me. Does it have to do with Isaiah McKray?"

Sissel shook her head. Tears came on even harder.

"I'm so sorry," he said. "I'm a heel. Please forgive me."

"No, you must excuse me. I'm just tired," she said. "You did nothing wrong."

"Can I get you something? A drink of water?"

Sissel nodded.

James balanced his lunch bag on the rock and hurried to the classroom to get her a dipper full of water. He carried it back, trying to keep it steady. Big drops splashed over the rim despite his best efforts, splashing onto his shoes and the dirt.

"Here you are," he said, and he gave her the dipper. She had stopped her tears, though she still looked upset.

She took the dipper and sipped from it.

Her eyes flitted up to his face. Sissel's face was so open in that moment, James felt he could finally read her—she felt confused and alone. She was burdened by a secret and wanted to share it with someone.

He did not blurt anything out this time. He waited until she drained the dipper and offered it back to him.

He placed his hand over hers, on the handle, and held it firmly. With confidence.

"I want you to know you *can* trust me," he said. "If there is something you need to say. Or some way I can help."

She turned her head away.

"Are you sure that Isaiah McKray isn't bothering you?" he asked.

She shook her head and gathered her lunch items into her bag again.

"I'm not feeling well. I think I should go back to my room and rest."

"Don't go, Sissel. Talk to me."

She shook her head.

"Can I walk you? Let me walk you."

"I can walk down the street by myself!"

The small children turned to look, surprised by her raised voice.

"I'm sorry," she said. "Of course you may walk me, if you wish."

So they went inside and she told her brother she did not feel well. Stieg dismissed her and seemed glad when James said he would see her safely to the hotel.

HE TOOK HER arm as they walked down the board walkway that fronted the shops. She was quiet and clearly troubled. James had a feeling if he could just keep her walking, she'd come out with the truth.

He feared she was going to tell him she was breaking it off with him. What would that mean for his job? Peavy might send him back to Chicago if he was no longer Sissel's beau. He'd do it just for spite.

Mr. Campbell came out of the boardinghouse as they passed and nearly crashed into Sissel.

"Pardon me, Miss Hemstad," said Mr. Campbell. He snatched his hat off. "Good day! Good day!"

"Good day," James said.

"Have you heard the news? McKray struck gold!"

"What?" Sissel said. "Where?"

"He won't say! He's got five mines, you know, scattered in the hills. It's anyone's guess."

"A large strike?" James asked.

"Trowley saw it. He said there's rocks shot through with ore. And one nugget big as a plum!"

James kept his eyes on Sissel. Fireworks of emotion were cast across her face. He read hope, relief, anxiety, then hope, again. Dear God, she did fancy McKray over him! How was it possible?

Sissel stepped out into the street, heading for the hotel, having forgotten him entirely.

"May I visit you later?" James said.

Sissel stopped and seemed to remember her manners. She turned to face him.

"Campbell has brought in his root beer," James rushed on. "It's very good. I'd love to bring you a bottle. Perhaps we could go for a walk?"

"I'm not sure," Sissel said. "I may go visit Alice. Or go painting with my brother."

"Of course," he said. "I understand."

Sissel bid him a polite farewell before she turned and pushed open the door to the hotel.

James stood helplessly. Her limp, he noticed, was much less noticeable. She was changing, right before his eyes.

He kicked at a small rock and cussed under his breath. He needed some new tactics if he was going to remain her beau, and keep his job.

CHAPTER THIRTY-ONE

Sissel stood at the front desk. There were more people in the lobby than usual. Three men in suits and big-city-style bowlers stood talking near the entrance to the restaurant. Collier came out from McKray's office, closing the door behind him. Seeing her, an odd little smirk came on his face.

"May I help you, Miss Hemstad?"

"Yes, thank you. I wanted a word with Mr. McKray, if he's in."

"These men are also waiting to speak with him." He gestured to the businessmen. "But I will let him know you are here, shall I?"

Sissel fought the urge to roll her eyes—Collier so enjoyed these little displays of self-importance.

"Please do," Sissel said.

Collier knocked on the office door and stuck his head in, then went inside.

Was it true? Had McKray really found gold?

Just as an experiment, just to see if she could, Sissel opened her senses to her Nytte.

Immediately she felt a great fist of gold on the other side of the wall. She took a step back, staggered by the intensity she felt. Flecks of gold were massed in a small area, like fireflies in a jar. And next to that was a knotted clump of ore. The size of a plum? Yes, that was about right. Maybe even bigger. It was intermingled with granite or some other cold, dead-feeling rock.

The gold had such personality and presence. Casting more deeply, she felt silver intermingled with it, like two forms dancing. It was a glorious little knot of gold. She was warmed head to toe.

She felt a hand at her elbow.

It was one of the businessmen, doubtlessly asking if she was well, though his words were muffled. His clothes smelled of old tobacco smoke, and his eyes were bloodshot, but kind enough. It must have seemed as if she was swooning.

"I'm fine, thank you," she said. And she forced herself to close her mind to the gold. She found she regretted leaving its presence.

Collier came back. "Here's the catalog you wanted," he said, slightly overloud.

He handed her a catalog for fine furnishings. He pursed his lips, mustache twitching, indicating she should look in the brochure.

"Thank you," she said.

The man who had come to help Sissel leaned over the counter.

"See here," he said. "We've come a long way to speak to Mr. McKray. It's not fair to keep us waiting."

Sissel took the brochure and stepped away from the counter.

She walked over to the window and opened it. On the front

page, written in McKray's blockish hand, was a message: *Meet me in the livery in fifteen minutes.*

Sissel looked toward the men congregating at the counter, growing vociferous in their demands to see McKray.

What on earth had McKray dragged her into?

"CAN I HELP YOU, young miss?" Mr. Hennings asked.

"I'm waiting on a friend," she said, feeling a bit silly.

"A lady friend?"

"A gentleman. Mr. McKray," she said.

"Ah," Mr. Hennings said, with a lecherous wink. He went off toward the back. What a scoundrel, to wink at her that way. Sissel knew she ought to feel offended, but it struck her more as comical.

Soon McKray came in through the large doors open at the back of the stable.

"Tell me about the gold," Sissel said.

"Shhh!" he said, looking around. "Those were reporters waiting for me. The longer I keep the story quiet, the better."

"Why's that?" she asked.

McKray looked off toward the door. "Well, for one thing, I don't know what's in the mine yet. Could be a big strike. If it is, there's a lot of preparations to be made. Don't want the town crawling with prospectors."

"If you found gold, you don't need me—"

"I do, though. I need you more than ever," he said. He stepped closer and Sissel's heartbeat quickened. He was so intense, it was unsettling. "I'll pay you twenty dollars to go with me and have a look around one of my mines."

He reached into his vest pocket and removed a thin, fine leather billfold. He took out two ten-dollar bills.

"We go to a mine. You tell me what you sense—how much gold, where it is—that's it. I'll never tell a soul. You know I'm good at keeping secrets."

Sissel chewed on the side of her lower lip. Twenty dollars! That was half Stieg's salary for teaching a three-month school session!

"All right," Sissel said. "But you must swear never to tell."

McKray held out the two bills. Sissel took them. She very much liked the feeling of having money of her own. She didn't have time to ponder how she would tell Stieg she got the money, or even if she should tell him at all, because Mr. Hennings came with McKray's two fine, gleaming horses saddled.

Sissel went to the left side of the horse to mount, and as she did so, she tucked the ten-dollar bills safely into her décolletage.

Hennings held the horse while she mounted.

McKray pressed a bill into the livery master's hand.

"For your silence," he said.

"Yes, sir," Henning said. He didn't wink now, Sissel noted.

THE MINE WAS about a half hour's ride out of town. McKray kept looking over his shoulder as they left Carter. Sissel wondered if he wasn't a bit paranoid—no one was following them, that she could see.

For a while, they followed the road that led to the Hemstad farm, into the area savaged by the fire. After twenty minutes, McKray led them off the road, up into the singed forests at the base of the hills.

The fire had consumed the branches of the pine trees, but left the charred trunks standing. On the ground there were rocks coated black, but between them the brown soil peeked through, and with it, shoots of grass and some tiny green saplings. Each sapling sent three or four small, tender leaves up to the sky, as if in prayer.

"Quiet, ain't it?" McKray asked.

"Yes," Sissel answered.

"It's a little spooky."

Soon the sounds of voices reached them, and some sounds of tools clanking and banging. The trees thinned, and they came to a clearing. There was a great heap of jagged stones at the base of a tree. She saw tents and a campfire and a squared-off hole in the side of the hill. It was shored up by wooden support beams. Miniature train tracks came out of the hole and ran to the pile of rocks.

A dirt-faced miner came out of the hole, pushing a cart laden with rock. He was coated in rock dust. He stood up and stretched, coming out of the low shaft, squinting against the light of day. Then he saw the horses and their riders.

"Howdy, boss," he said to McKray. "Young lady." He politely touched his hat. It was a large, flat-brimmed hat with a candle affixed to the front. Rivulets of wax crusted the brim. Sissel wondered how much the whole thing weighed.

"Good afternoon," McKray said.

"Well, we're still clearing—" the miner began, but McKray held his hand up to cut him off.

"Get the others out. We're going to have a look around," McKray said.

McKray jumped off his horse, then held the bridle of Sissel's horse so she could dismount.

The miner disappeared inside. A moment later three more men followed him out, stooping. Each carried a pick and wore a hat with a candle. The last one out had a lantern.

"My friend would like to go into a mine," McKray explained to the squinting, confused men. He seemed a bit nonplussed, unsure if he needed to explain himself at all.

"Be careful, boss," said the first miner they'd encountered. "Tracks only go a few feet in. Ground's bumpy."

"Pretty dark in there," one of the others said. He held out the lit lantern.

Sissel felt the eyes of the miners on her. They seemed to be waiting for some confirmation from her.

"She's not scared," McKray said. "Are you?"

Sissel shook her head. She took the lantern and turned to the mine.

"There aren't bats, are there?"

"No, ma'am," one of them replied earnestly. Sissel realized what a stupid question it was as she walked away. Never mind. She bent her knees and ducked her head and crept into the mine with as much dignity as she could muster.

THE MINERS HAD not exaggerated: It was dark in the mine. Ten paces in and the tracks and the level ground they required ended. The ground was a mess of rock and dust. Big jutting pieces of rock made it treacherous to walk. The lantern shed a weak and wavering arc of light maybe three feet wide, and she stumbled several times. Putting aside her pride, she took ahold of McKray's extended hand.

It was tricky business, making it through a mine in progress. Her skirts didn't help.

"Let me go first," McKray said eventually. "You put your feet where I do."

The jagged walls of the mine closed in, getting more and more narrow. Sissel could make out the divots from the pick blows when she held the lantern up.

"Well?" McKray asked. "Any gold?"

"Let's go a bit farther in."

McKray placed each footfall carefully. Sissel followed.

His large, paw-like hand was reassuring to hold. She didn't get the electric thrill she felt when holding James's hand, but she did feel something. It was grounding, holding his hand.

Soon they couldn't go farther. McKray stood, one foot up on a ledge of rock. Sissel was close behind him, both of them stooping low.

"All right," she said.

"Well?"

Sissel held her hand up for him to be quiet.

"It will take me a few minutes," she said. "And I should tell you . . . there's an odd thing that happens when I look for gold—my hearing goes out. It lasts longer or shorter depending on . . . different things."

She handed him the lamp. In the light, McKray's face was rapt and eager.

"I may need as much as fifteen minutes or so before I can hear again. I will be able to speak to you, but you will have to communicate with your hands during that time."

It was odd, to lay out the conditions so plainly. It made Sissel feel peculiar—as if she were performing some professional service, like a doctor or a lawyer. Then again, she did have his twenty dollars, so she supposed she was in his service.

"All right," McKray said. "Whatever you say."

Sissel turned away from him, facing the wall, mostly so she didn't have to be distracted by him staring at her.

She focused and calmed herself, tuning in to the sensations around her. The cold, damp air of the mine. Her own breathing, and that of McKray.

She cast her Nytte out. The rock was dense, and for a moment there was a rebound effect, all her calling echoing around her. The four brass buttons on the front of McKray's vest clanged like gongs, and thirty cents in dimes in his pocket shone out strongly. Even the tiny brass grommets on her own boots were loud in so small a space.

She shifted her feet on the floor, letting go of her effort for a moment.

Sissel felt McKray's hand on her arm. His hand was cupping her elbow, offering support.

"It's a bit echoey," she said.

McKray nodded as if that made perfect sense.

Sissel closed her eyes and tried to work the energy in a different way. She sent it out slowly, in soft waves, trying to permeate the stone.

There was a feeling of heaviness, all around. So much stone pressing down on them, it was smothering. Sissel sought along the rocks near the walls of the cave. Surely the deposit of gold McKray's miners had found continued on into the bedrock.

She raised her hands, sending her fingers out, feeling along the rocks. She visualized a mist, a seeking mist that could penetrate every nook and crevice, and she sent it from her hands.

There, in a thin trail through rock off to the left of her, downward, was some silver. A spattering of silver.

She was aware of sweat on the small of her back and at her hairline. She ground her teeth together and cast more strongly.

There were faint vibrations. She sensed nickel wafting around, cold and sharp. And it was married to some other vibration. Another mineral she'd not yet encountered. It had a pine-like greenish quality to it. There was a lot of that around, whatever it was, but gold? Nowhere.

Sissel lowered her hands and opened her eyes.

She found McKray had drawn closer to her and was holding the lamp up to study her face.

She shielded her eyes from the light.

His mouth moved, and she knew what he was asking. "Gold?"

"No," she said. "None."

She watched him cussing.

SISSEL DID NOT know what else, if anything, McKray was saying as they made their way, painstakingly, to the surface. She did not even care to know—she was furious.

Tricked again by the cagey miner. The gold she had sensed in his office hadn't come from this mine, but one of his others. He had just wanted to know if there was gold in this stupid, pointless mine.

He was keeping the location of the gold mine a secret, even from her!

She was thankful for the enforced silence between her and McKray. It gave her time to think and prepare some cutting remarks.

So it was a nasty surprise she had when they reached the mouth of the cave and she found the three men from the hotel there waiting for them. Two of them had notebooks out, and a third was setting up a camera on a tripod.

They peppered McKray with questions, and she was helpless—she couldn't hear what they were saying. One of them was asking her questions and pointing to the mine.

McKray started yelling. The men wrote in their little notebooks. The miners stood by, enjoying the spectacle. Then a flash went off.

Sissel felt cold to the bone. A photograph of her, in a newspaper?

McKray stormed over to the man, grabbed the legs of the camera, and smashed it to the ground.

She could not hear the shouting that ensued, coming from both sides, but when McKray gestured for her to get on her horse, she did so in a hurry, not waiting for anyone to hold the bridle of the horse this time.

SISSEL RODE IN angry silence until she finally heard her own constricted breathing, then the clip-clopping of the horses' hooves, then the birds in the meadows.

The sun was high in the sky. Stieg would dismiss school soon, and probably hurry home to make sure she was all right.

"What did they say?" Sissel asked. "What did you tell them about me?"

McKray turned to her, coming out of his own worried reverie.

"Got your ears back?"

"What did you tell the newspapermen about me?"

"Nothing. I told them you wanted to see a mine, just like I told the other fellows."

"Did they believe you?"

"I don't know what they believe. But I expect to find all my holdings flooded with gold-crazy claim jumpers within a week."

"Here's the headline I'd write: *Deceitful Miner Tricks Young Lady into Helping Him Find Out There Is No Gold Whatsoever in His Mine.*"

McKray shot her a sideways look.

"None at all, eh?"

"That big knot you have in your office certainly didn't come from that mine," she said.

McKray didn't meet her eye, but looked straight ahead down the road toward town.

"I wanted to know if there was anything in there," he said. "I was told it was promising."

"If your land surveyor told you it was promising, then you were lied to. And you lied to me in return," Sissel said. "Don't you remember you said you'd help me keep my family's secret? Those newspapermen took my photograph!"

"I smashed the plate."

"Still!"

"Come along, we'd better get you back before school gets out." McKray kicked his horse into a canter.

"If you'd taken me to the mine with the gold, I could have told you exactly where it lay in the stone. I could have drawn you a map, and I would have."

"I paid you twenty dollars for a service I needed performed. And if you'll come to my other mines, I'll pay you more to do the same again!"

"You tricked me. You can't be trusted. I won't go riding with you again."

"I never said the gold was from that mine, not explicitly."

"What you said was purposefully misleading," Sissel said. "Don't

233

try to argue it with me. I won't be convinced. And what about your offer to buy my family's land? Was that part of some hoax as well?"

"I was told the area in the hills on your land is promising."

"Well, it's not. Your surveyor is up to no good."

A few minutes later, McKray broke the silence.

"I'll make sure the newspapermen don't put your name in the paper," he said.

"How will you do that?"

"I'll give them an exclusive about the gold I found," he said begrudgingly.

They rode along for a moment.

"Thank you, Mr. McKray."

"You're welcome, Miss Hemstad."

CHAPTER THIRTY-TWO

The atmosphere around the camp was grim that night. A cowboy had been sent to butcher one of the fallen beefs, and they had steaks, but the good meat did nothing to lighten the mood.

As directed, Whistler had brought the body of Harold Mandry to the camp, strapped facedown across the back of a horse. Now Mandry's corpse lay wrapped in his bedroll off a good distance from the fire.

When Tincher had arrived for supper, he went over and pulled back the canvas. Everyone gathered around behind, looking down at Mandry's body.

There was no question about it, he had been shot through the chest. It looked like it had been done with a rifle—there was a small, neat puncture in the man's chest. His shirt was dark with dried blood, the blood clogged with dust. Mandry's body looked small and shriveled in death. Hanne gave a shudder.

Tincher threw the canvas back over him and straightened up, a look of extreme disappointment on his face. He turned around.

"This is ugly business," he said. "A man shot on one of my drives? This is ugly, ugly business. And furthermore, what I just don't understand, cannot understand, is how a cowhand hired onto this drive would go and shoot somebody at the back of the herd! That just don't make sense to me."

He kept his voice low, but no one doubted how absolutely furious the man was.

"None of you could possibly be that stupid, could you?"

Everyone looked over to Owen, some covertly, some making it obvious.

"I see you all looking at me," Owen said, "but I promise you I did not shoot this man. We'd already settled things between us—you all saw that written on his face after we fought."

"Well, who did, then?" said Whistler. "Who shot my friend?" His voice seized up with emotion.

"I'll get the local sheriff out," Tincher said. He assigned a young cowboy to ride for town in the early morning. "Bring the sheriff back and fetch our mail while you're at it. We'll spend the day here tomorrow, see if we can't round up more steer. Wolves will be out there, so make sure you keep on the lookout."

Tincher walked off alone.

Talks started up around the fire.

"Whistler, I'm sorry to say it, but Mandry wasn't the nicest fellow in the world," someone said.

"He was a right son of a bitch," another added. Then, "Sorry to cuss, missus."

"It stands to reason someone could have sneaked up on us and shot him. Maybe someone from town, someone he'd wronged?" the second one said.

Whistler said nothing, only nursed a tin mug of black coffee and sat muttering toward the fire.

The cowhands began to argue, to discuss it, to turn it over and worry at the problem. Hanne passed among them, refilling coffee cups.

Then she took the pot, still heavy with the coffee grounds at the bottom, back over to the chuck wagon to make another pot.

She dumped the grounds out and poured a ladleful of water from the barrel in the wagon into the large pot. She swirled it around and emptied the last grounds onto the earth.

Owen came to stand beside her. When she went to do it, he took the coffeepot and filled it with water from the barrel for her.

"Owen," she said. "Who did it?"

"I don't know," he said. "Someone who wanted to start a stampede, maybe."

"Yes," Hanne said. "Or someone who doesn't know a thing about cattle."

Her Nytte was still and silent. She and Owen and Daisy were not in immediate, physical danger, but something was wrong. There was trouble following them.

Hanne went to bed early. Owen did not join her in the bedroll. Tincher wanted extra men watching the cattle.

THE NEXT MORNING, the rider Tincher had sent to town came back with the sheriff right as breakfast was ending.

The sheriff was an imposing figure, a tall man in his fifties with a close-cropped silver beard. After grimly inspecting Mandry's body, he told everyone to stay in camp until he released them.

Then he rode off with Tincher and Whistler to examine the spot where the body had been found.

It didn't seem like anyone was unhappy to be told to wait in camp. Men had more thick black coffee and then eagerly gathered around Witri as he handed out the mail.

Hanne and Owen unloaded the supplies the rider had gotten from the general store. He had taken an extra horse with him, and laden the poor beast down with sacks like a pack mule.

Witri read off the names from the letters, and the cowboys took their mail almost reverently, then headed off to read in private. Letters from home were rare and treasured on the trail.

"Owen Bennett, one for you," Witri said.

Hanne and Owen looked at each other in surprise.

Owen set down a sack of coffee and walked to Witri.

Hanne rushed to his side.

"How did they find us?" she asked.

But Owen shook his head.

"It's not from home," he said. "It's from a lawyer."

Hanne followed him as they headed away from the press of men surrounding Witri.

"'Dear Mr. Owen Bennett,'" he read. "'It is with the greatest sadness that I write to inform you of the deaths of your parents, Howard and Lavinia Bennett.'"

Owen fell silent, reading ahead. He handed her the letter. It was written on fine, cream-colored stock in an elegant, spidery hand.

"Why, Owen," Hanne said. "This says the ranch is yours."

"Yes," he said.

"Your brothers . . ."

"Dead," Owen said.

They looked at each other, eyes wide.

"I never wanted it," he said. He looked white and shocked. "The ranch."

"I know you didn't," Hanne said.

THE SHOCK HAD not passed much by the time the sheriff came back with Tincher and Whistler. Owen moved as if in a dream. Hanne knew it must be hard to take it all in—the deaths of his family, all wiped out by the fever and ague, and the ranch now his.

"Gather up," Tincher hollered. Their small party had been joined by another man, a young man riding a piebald gelding. He appeared to be a deputy, as he wore a brass star on his vest.

The men dismounted and approached the campfire. Witri offered them some coffee, which they took.

"There's a bit of a complication," the sheriff said, scratching his head. "My deputy here tells me that our Harold Mandry was a wanted man. Convicted of theft. Both horse theft and property."

Murmurs of surprise and a good bit of cussing went up around the camp.

"There was a hundred-dollar bounty on his head."

He spoke these words to a general air of bafflement in the camp. "Any of you want to claim it?" he asked. There was only more confused grumbling from the men.

Whistler spat tobacco juice out onto the ground. He had his shoulders up and his arms crossed.

"I didn't expect so," the sheriff said. "So I'll be hauling the body to town and we'll deal with it from there." He drained his coffee cup and handed it back to Witri.

He tipped his hat toward Hanne. "Ma'am," he said politely. "Gentlemen," he said to the rest, "I hope the remainder of your drive goes peaceful."

"You heard him," Tincher addressed the camp. "This case of Mandry's death is closed, and we got fifteen hundred cattle to move to Helena, so let's get back to work, gentlemen."

CHAPTER THIRTY-THREE

When Sissel returned to the hotel, she found that Stieg had not come to check on her. In fact, she had to track him down. He was at school, with papers spread on his desk. It was nearing seven o'clock, and he had lit a lantern to read by.

"Hello, Brother?" Sissel called.

"Yes, Sissel. Are you feeling better?" he asked without looking up.

"Aren't you coming back to the hotel?" she asked.

Stieg sighed. He patted a stack of compositions.

"I'm afraid I left myself a bit more grading than I should have. Would you forgive me if I work through supper?"

Sissel shrugged. She half wished Stieg would confront her about leaving school early. Carrying such secrets was beginning to wear on her. But he was fully immersed in his work.

Sissel wondered at the distance she felt between them. She knew she bore the responsibility for the divide. The secrets she kept had pushed them apart.

"Go on up to Alice's house," he urged her. "They're always saying we're welcome for dinner. Go take them up on it."

"All right."

"Don't forget to study for your oral examination," Stieg reminded her.

"I won't."

The Boston Tea Party. No taxation without representation. Sissel had all the facts memorized.

THE OSWALDS LIVED on Elm Street, two streets up from the hotel and one street over. The house was a timber house, two floors, neat and cozy. Lamplight poured out of the first floor windows. Two potted nasturtiums stood on either side of the front door, which made the house seem all the more inviting, but Sissel found herself feeling shy. It felt awfully forward to just up and knock on the door.

Sissel was halfway up the walkway to the front door, but now she stopped. Maybe she should sneak away and just do as Stieg was going to do, eat in the room. She was very hungry, and tired, too.

Perhaps the bakery was still open. She didn't want to go to the general store, not after the scene earlier with James.

She turned to leave just as the door opened and there stood Alice.

"Sissel," Alice said. "What a surprise. Are you feeling better?"

There was a funny set to Alice's mouth.

"Yes, thank you."

Alice ought to have asked her in, but instead she slipped outside, closing the door behind her.

"Did you have a good rest?"

"Yes," Sissel said.

"Sissel! How can you lie to me?" Alice said. Tears sprang to her eyes. "I had to run an errand at the livery, and Mr. Hennings told me you went riding with Mr. McKray!"

"I'm sorry," Sissel said. "It's . . . I can't explain it. I'm sorry."

Alice led Sissel away from the house. She brushed at her tears with the sleeve of her shirt.

"That's not all, Sissel!" Alice wrung her hands. "One of the housemaids from the Royal came in to the shop this afternoon. She burst into tears and begged my pardon, for stealing my combs. You can imagine my shock! I didn't know what to say!

"This girl stole from me, and you didn't tell me. I don't understand. Please, explain to me what is happening."

"Oh, Alice," Sissel said. "I can't. I can't tell you."

"Of course you can! Aren't we friends?"

"We are. We are! You are my very best friend, Alice."

Alice's mother opened the door to their home. She waved at Sissel.

"Sissel! How lovely to see you! May I set a place for you at the table?"

"Oh no, thank you, ma'am, I just came by to say hello."

"Are you sure? We've plenty."

"Yes, ma'am, thank you so much."

"Anytime!" Mrs. Oswald closed the door.

Alice clutched at Sissel's hands. She spoke very quietly. "Please, Sissel. I just don't understand why you're lying to me. Has McKray done something to you? Does Stieg know about this all?"

"Please don't tell my brother," Sissel said.

"Just tell me why you lied to me about finding my mother's combs. That much you owe me."

"If you love me, you won't ask," Sissel said.

"If you loved me, you'd tell me!" Alice said.

Sissel turned abruptly and walked away.

SISSEL FORCED HERSELF to calm down as she walked back to the hotel. She had no right to feel angry, but that was how she felt. Cornered, defensive, and angry.

She had found the combs! Why wasn't that enough?

And did Alice have to know absolutely everything about her life?

Then there was McKray, tricking her into using her Nytte. It was a nightmare that he knew so much about her.

Now it was getting dark and people were going home for a nice hot supper. The bell rang from the boardinghouse. If she hurried, she could make it in time for the seating. But she couldn't stand the thought of sitting with all those dull workmen, alone.

The anger was burning in her, and she got an idea—the gold in the graveyard.

She walked toward the church, looked up and down the street to make sure no one was watching, and then ducked around behind the building.

In the graveyard she opened her senses to the Nytte.

Gold. There it was, warm, sensual, insistent. She was not sensing gold jewelry that the poor buried souls were wearing, but a large deposit of natural gold, lying in the rocks to the left of the grave.

It felt so good to flood her senses with it, to give in to her power. She paced over to the mounded earth above the long grave. There had been a bit of rain since the burial. Some weeds and grass had taken purchase on the soil.

Sissel walked a few paces in a circle, keeping her hands open to the spot, as if it were a campfire and she were warming them.

She cast her eyes over the backs of the nearby buildings. There was no motion.

She focused on the ground. There was a ledge over the gold. An outcropping of rock. The gold was deposited under this ledge. The vibration of the gold was coming sideways, as if it were spilling out from under something heavy and cold; that's how she knew there was rock over it.

She felt a few trinkets nearby. A silver square, maybe a belt buckle. Surely this was from one of the bodies buried nearby. Would she disturb the coffins if she went for the gold?

Could she even pull it up? It seemed fused to the rock.

She wanted to pull it all together. To let out a giant shout of effort and rip it from the earth—let the town see her. Let them all know what she was!

She was breathless now.

She cast her hands down at the gold and began to pull.

Suddenly two hands seized her by the arms. She jumped, her heart jolted terribly.

James stood there, his mouth forming her name. Asking what she was doing here.

The gold was so clear in her mind, the connection so strong. She had to close it off, and she didn't want to. She wrestled with the power.

The Nytte surged up, and she pushed it away, straining to close her senses to it. James still had a hold on her.

His hands held her up, as the gold in the earth pulled her down.

She felt dizzy, sick. Her stomach was roiling. All the blood rushed from her head, and she felt herself collapsing into James's arms.

THE SMELL OF coffee woke her. She was in a room she didn't know.

She had been laid on a bench next to a table and covered with a woolen blanket. Sissel sat up, pushing the blanket aside.

James's back was to her. He was standing at a wood-burning cookstove, boiling coffee. The room was darkened, the only light coming from a lamp and the grates and cracks on the woodstove where firelight shone through.

There were some rough shelves with food staples on them. A few cups and mugs. On the walls were nails with invoices and receipts stuck onto them.

Sissel realized she was in the back room of the store.

James had set some bread, butter, and honey on the table, near the lamp. He turned and saw she was awake.

"Sissel," he said. He came over to her. "Are you all right?"

"Yes," she said. What could she tell him? How could she possibly explain what she was doing in the graveyard?

"Here's coffee," he said, putting a steaming tin mug down in front of her. "Do you like it sweet?"

She nodded.

He took a can of condensed milk down from the shelf and poured a thick swirl into the dark coffee.

Sissel sipped it. It was sweet and good.

"Thank you," she said.

She drank for a moment, shifting the mug between her hands when the handle got too hot.

James spread a piece of bread with butter and honey.

"That's Mrs. Trowley's bread and Mr. Fahay's butter. And this is heather honey imported from England. Mrs. Denmead kept going on and on about it, and the Ladies' Aid Society requested we order it. Have you ever tried it?"

"No," Sissel said.

"I thought all honey would be the same, but it does taste different."

She took the bread and bit into it. The combination of crusty bread, salted butter, and fragrant honey was distinctly delicious.

"This might be the best thing I've ever eaten in my whole life," she said.

James laughed. He was smiling at her in the lamplight. She was glad not to see a concerned frown on his face or a dozen unanswered questions in his eyes.

If only she could sit here and eat and not have to talk. Not have to explain what had happened.

"I missed my supper," she said.

"Do you want more?"

"If it's not too much trouble."

James studied her, then clapped his hands.

"I have a better idea," he said. He rose from the bench and crossed to the door that led into the store. "Come on. Bring the lamp."

The store in the nighttime seemed bigger somehow. Maybe it was that the packed shelves seemed to reach up forever, since the light didn't reach to the top shelf.

The barrels of sugar and wheat, the rows of cans gleaming softly in the lamplight, bottled medicines and tins of tablets, polished boots lined up on lower shelves, along with small farm equipment—all of it seemed magical in the warm light.

"Let's have a feast!" James said.

Sissel looked at the loaded shelves.

"Really?"

"We've got pickles, soda crackers, salted peanuts in the shell." He started taking down jars and tins, holding them in his arms.

"Sardines! Do you like them? What about smoked ham?"

Sissel laughed.

"Won't your father be angry?" she answered. "Where is he?"

"He's off playing cards at the boardinghouse. I don't expect him home until late. And I'll work off the costs of our feast. Don't worry. Have a seat," he said, waving to the checkerboard table near the woodstove.

"We need biscuits. These are good. They're from St. Louis. Do you fancy a cup of hot chocolate?" He reached toward a tin of cocoa powder. She shook her head.

"Good," he said. He set down the items he had gathered in front of Sissel. "Too much fuss, anyway. But we do need sweets. Candy! We must have candy."

James walked to the lidded jars of sweets set at the end of the counter.

"Horehound, peppermints, fruit drops, licorice whips, ribbon candy, peppermint humbugs. Have you had nectar drops?"

"No, I haven't, but come, James, you're turning out the whole store for me! This is enough."

He waved away her concern. He scooped out candy into a little waxed paper bag and presented it to her with a flourish. Then said, "Wait, we need pickles."

Sissel tried to stop him, but he couldn't be deterred. Soon they had over a dozen different foods on the table. Sissel began opening and sampling the items.

"Ooh, these little crackers are good," she said.

"Oyster crackers. To lay on top of your soup. We've got smoked oysters. Want to try them?"

"Cold? No!" Sissel laughed. "Anyway, how will we ever finish what we've got here?"

James chomped down on a pickle. His face screwed up.

"Gah, these are sour!" He took another bite.

Sissel laughed. She felt better, so much better with the food in her, and with James clowning around.

"So . . . ," he said after a few minutes of their happy eating.

"Is there any way . . . is there any way you could not ask me about the graveyard?" Sissel said.

James bit off a piece of licorice whip and chewed on it, thinking.

"You can see how I'd worry about you, can't you? First something upsets you at the dance, but you won't say. Then I find you out at night, standing at the graveside, staring down into it."

Sissel stood up. She paced to the counter, brushing the crumbs off her fingers.

"I have to worry, you see that," he said.

Sissel's heart was pounding. What could she tell him? Anything but the truth. McKray knew the truth, and that was a disaster!

"I feel I must talk to your brother about it," James said.

"No!" she said, whipping around. "Please don't."

"Shouldn't I, though? Sissel, why the graveyard? Please. Tell me— what fascination does it hold for you." James was standing now.

"My brother is overprotective as it is," Sissel said. "If you tell him I was there . . . he'll worry. He'll watch me closer. And oh, James, I've so been enjoying my freedom. Can't you see that?"

"I just want . . . I want you to trust me. To tell me what's happening. Please. Did you . . . were you grieving for your neighbors who died in the fire?"

Sissel shook her head.

"What is in the graveyard?" he asked.

Sissel looked into his eyes. They were pleading. But if she hadn't told Alice, her best friend, how could she tell James, who was not nearly as trustworthy, nor as dear to her.

"I am sorry, James," she said. "I can tell you this—I don't need protecting. I am fine and I can take care of myself."

"But the way I found you—"

"I would have been fine," she said. "If you hadn't come along, I would have been just fine—"

"Sissel—"

She held her hands up.

"Thank you again for this feast. Should I go out the front door or the back—"

James grabbed her arm.

"Come, Sissel! All the time we've spend together. The places we've gone, the fun we've had. Can't you trust me?"

"Let go of my arm."

There was a glint in his eye. A look of desperation.

James released her. He walked away, to the far side of the store, and stood looking out the window.

"I don't understand," he said, drawing his hand through his hair. It made him look wild and worked up with passion.

"I'm sorry, James. I'm truly thankful for all your kindnesses to me. And I know that I seem terribly ungrateful. If you don't want to . . . take me to dances anymore, or to come visiting, I'll understand."

"I don't blame you. I know what I seem to be. A vain, shallow kind of man."

"No," Sissel protested. "You've been very kind—"

"I'm nothing to you, and why should I be? I'm not bright like your brother Stieg, or hardworking, like Knut. I'm not rich like McKray, that's for sure. I must seem like a child compared to a man like that."

James turned around to face her.

"Can I tell you something?" he asked.

CHAPTER THIRTY-FOUR

James could see Sissel's reflection behind him, soft from the lamplight, wavy from the glass, but there was nothing soft or diffuse about Sissel Hemstad. She was hard as steel.

He had envisioned the moment of her confession so many times—Sissel clinging to his chest, tears rolling down her face, the secret spilling out of her. Somewhere in her story she would reveal there was a warrant for Knut's arrest. She'd tell about the murders that had been committed back in Norway. Then somewhere in the story James might learn who the Baron was to them and why he had come to protect them.

He had seen the scene in his imagination, but Sissel held out and held out and held out. But no longer. He hardened himself to the task—tonight he would have her story from her, whatever the cost.

"You remind me of my sister Clara; did I ever tell you that? She was slight, like you. And did not suffer fools. If I tried to get away with something, she put a stop to it."

"James," Sissel said, stepping toward him, her voice overflowing with sympathy.

Tears came up in his eyes, and he let them come.

"The reason we left Chicago . . . It wasn't to follow opportunity. I lied to you. I'm sorry. We came to get little Clara here, to the clean air."

"You never mentioned—"

"She died one week before we were to move. She just . . . she got weaker and weaker. In the end, she was coughing blood.

"Father insisted we go through with the move. We had our passage booked, had already bought this place. I didn't want to leave. Our rooms, they weren't much, but she had lived there. Laughed there."

James was laying down story as fast as he could, and she was drinking it in.

"She wasn't tough, like you. I think it's why I was drawn to you: You never let your sickness bother you. I never saw anything like it. And look, now you're better. You made yourself get better, somehow. I wish Clara had been more like you."

Sissel put her hand on his arm. James half turned his torso from her. He swiped at his watering eyes with the back of his hand. "I'm sorry. I don't know what's come over me."

"I'm so sorry, James," she said. "I didn't know."

He waved it away.

"I didn't tell you because it's too hard to talk about her. Ah, forgive me."

He shook himself and straightened his posture.

"Listen, Sissel, if you don't want me to call on you, I understand. But I want you to know that I do care for you. That I truly admire you."

Sissel placed her arms around his shoulders and hugged him. James thrust his head forward gently, bringing it next to her ear.

He breathed onto her pale neck, let his lips rasp against it as he said, "Oh, Sissel. I know I am going to lose you."

She pulled away, just a fraction, and he slid his arms under hers, to encircle her waist. She leaned back, unsure, and he tilted his face to look her in the eye.

"I don't blame you for not wanting to tell me your secrets, but I promise, I would have kept them for you."

He had his hands at her hips, and he brought her in closer to his body. Her slender, corseted form pressed into him.

"James," she said. "If you promise not to tell . . . ," she began.

He had her.

He did not say a word, just let out a long breath against her neck.

"There is gold in the grave," she said. "There is a deposit in the ground, maybe ten feet down. That's why I was there . . ."

She bit her lip, possibly regretting her confession. He wouldn't let her stop. He gently pressed his fingers into the sweet place where the corset ended and the hip began.

"But how could you know that?" he asked.

"I have an ancient gift. A talent. It's hard to describe, but I can tell where gold and silver are buried. I know it sounds crazy. I don't blame you if you don't believe me."

"So you tried to throw yourself into the grave to get buried gold?"

"Not exactly," she said. "The funeral was the first time I felt my gift. The Nytte. It's difficult to explain."

Then she spoke for a few minutes, spinning out some unfathomable foolishness about Old Norse Gods and powers that ran in her bloodline and this Nytte thing.

"You must promise you won't tell?" she said once she had finished.

James nodded absentmindedly. He had her secret, but what to make of it?

"James! You must promise!" Sissel said.

James looked down. He saw his own face distorted in the wide, shining pupils of her eyes. He suddenly felt bad. Very bad.

"I promise," he said.

The tension went out of her body, and she melted into his chest. He held her tight.

"Thank you," he said. "Thank you for trusting me, Sissel."

She should not feel safe. Not around him.

"This means . . . this means I can still call on you?" he asked.

Sissel nodded.

He saw her eyes flickering to his lips. She wanted to be kissed.

James knew it would seal things between them, at least in her mind it would.

He couldn't bear to do it. She was . . . all this stuff about gold . . . she was unhinged. He found his conscience would not allow him to kiss the girl.

Instead he pressed his lips to the back of her hand, then he stepped to the side and out of the embrace.

"I don't trust what I might do, if I kiss you," he lied.

He walked to the table and began packing up the remnants of their feast. He put the crackers, the biscuits, the candies into a bag.

"Yes," she said. "You won't tell, will you, James?"

James turned, made himself look earnest and adoring. "I swear I won't. Now, let's get you back to the hotel."

James walked her down the quiet street, arm in arm, back to the hotel. Sissel appeared nervous, anxious. He imagined she was regretting telling her secret.

She seemed to him now a silly young creature. Why had he found her so fetching? She was just a wisp of a thing, hardly a woman at all.

Now that she had succumbed to his charms the allure was gone, as it often happened. He felt bad about that. But he felt worse about her "secret." The delusion of a sick mind, it had to be. There was no such magic in the world.

He had thought her so cunning and smart not to trust him. It turned out she was mentally unsound.

As he walked home he wondered, Had she told McKray she could find gold? It would explain his sudden interest in her . . .

Peavy was waiting for him in the store, cleaning up the mess he'd left.

"Did it work?" he asked. "She finally spill for you?"

"Yeah," James said. "She sure did."

"Attaboy," Peavy said.

"You're never going to believe it," James said. "Never in a million years."

"What?" Peavy was smiling. He crossed his arms, ready for a good story. "What did she say?"

"She thinks she's got magical abilities."

Peavy laughed and swore. Then, "How so?"

"Sissel Hemstad believes she can feel where precious metals are buried in the ground."

He expected a great guffaw from Peavy, but the smile had fallen off his face. "What?" he said.

"Yes. That's what she told me. It all fits together. She must have lost her mind when her brother murdered those fellas back in

Norway. Then she came here and the fire happened and the shock of it pushed her over the edge of sanity. The doctor said she had suffered a great shock—"

But Peavy was gone, hustling out of the room.

"Where are you going?" James called.

"Hold on a sec!" Peavy shouted, his voice diminishing as he climbed the ladder to the attic above the back room.

He heard the big man's feet moving in their attic bedroom.

After a moment Peavy descended, a sheaf of papers in his hand.

"What's that?" James asked.

"The Baron's original letters."

"I never saw them."

"You don't see everything," Peavy snapped. He held up his hand.

"Here it is! Listen to this: 'Any unusual behavior should be reported, especially pertaining to the following circumstances: anomalous weather conditions, including snow, hail, thunder.' No, wait, that's not it."

His eyes scanned the pages of thin paper.

"Here: 'Alert me at once if any of the siblings display extraordinary strength, or ability to carve or build unusual wooden structures or tools—'"

"What on earth?"

"Just listen! 'Or show an ability to find, identify, or manipulate precious metals.'"

Peavy lowered the paper and looked at James, a half-cocked smile on his face.

"Good work, James," he said. "You've just made our Baron a happy fellow."

James felt, suddenly, very sick.

He offered Peavy a weak smile.

Peavy took down a bottle of whiskey and two tumblers from the shelf.

"Yes, yes, indeed!" he said, pouring them each a generous slug. "That's fine work. That's bonus-making work!"

CHAPTER THIRTY-FIVE

Sissel had hardly slept. She spent the night in a gradual state of dawning alarm.

At first, she had lain in bed remembering the touch of James's arms around her body; the memory of his strong hands on her, the warm scent of his neck, and the feel of his lips brushing against her ear had lit her whole body on fire.

But as the flames burned down, she thought of the story he had told her. His sister Clara. At school he'd mentioned growing up with cousins. Never a sister. The story left an odd taste in her mouth. Why wouldn't he have mentioned her?

Dread crept up upon her. Could he have invented the story just to gain her sympathy? No. That was inconceivable.

And why, after she had told him, did he not ask her to prove she could find metal? Wouldn't the next thing to do be to say, "Prove it, then." They had plenty of silver items in the store, maybe even some gold. She could have shown him.

But he hadn't asked.

She started to feel discomfited, anxious. He hadn't asked, she realized, because he had not believed her.

Around three she got up to pace in her room.

Why had she told him? She was a fool! He wasn't trustworthy. She knew he wasn't. What if he made it a joke? What if he told the boys at school? Or people in the store?

When Stieg found out he would be furious. As he should be! Why had she gone to James's arms? The heat of his body had melted her resolve. Or maybe it had been his confession, the feeling of closeness. She had wanted to reciprocate—her secret for his. Oh, she was a fool!

She harangued herself that way for hours. Finally, just as the sun dawned, she fell back to a miserable sleep.

NOW STIEG WAS knocking on her door.

"One moment," Sissel cried. Quickly she dressed in a freshly laundered white blouse and one of her gray skirts, sweeping her hair back into a loose bun. All the while she was thinking of James. What could she say to him to make him understand how crucial it was he not tell a soul?

Outside her window, down on the street, there seemed to be an unusual amount of foot traffic.

Stieg was irritated with her for being late.

"The next time you're late, I will go on without you," he told her.

"I'm sorry," Sissel said.

There was a lot of noise coming up from the lobby. Sissel and Stieg descended the stairs to find it overrun with strangers. Men, who, judging by their clothes, varied in prosperity from scrappy miners to savvy business investors, glutted the space, all eager to have a word with McKray.

It made Sissel's head ache.

Even Collier looked harassed, and the day only a few hours begun.

"Stay close," Stieg instructed. He pushed through the melee, only to be met, at the door, with two of McKray's miners carrying a crate through the door. The wooden crate was loaded with rock, visible through the slatted sides. A rough square of canvas was nailed over the top of the crate.

Conversation flared at the sight of the miners and the crate as the men speculated over the amount of gold McKray was finding.

Sissel turned as the men with the crate passed her. She sent her sense into the crate.

The noise immediately faded.

She felt through the box. Nothing. It was cold, dead stone. The brass buttons on a gentleman's vest standing near were louder.

It was a scam.

Suddenly she saw it all—McKray was running a great scam. There was no gold in his mines at all.

She thought of all the land he'd bought up. Cheap land. He would have bought theirs, if Stieg had not put him off.

Now the hotel lobby was overrun with men wanting a piece of McKray's vast land holdings.

The gold in his office . . . it wasn't even from around here. She knew this in her bones. He'd used it to salt one of his own, barren mines.

The door to McKray's office opened, and he stood there, the room in shadows behind him. He saw the people, the crate. There was an expression of haughty pride on his face. A tough, seasoned look. Then he saw Sissel and his face changed. His eyes softened.

He was a . . . a cheater. She knew she shouldn't be surprised, but she was. She was disappointed in him. Terribly let down. Tears pricked her eyes—McKray was a swindler.

She shut her Nytte as abruptly as slamming a door. McKray mouthed, *Wait!* but she turned and pushed her way through the men now swarming forward to try to get a word with him.

Stieg was waiting for her outside and said something she couldn't hear. She felt safe to say yes. She crossed the street to the boardinghouse.

By the time they had been seated at one of the long tables, her hearing was back. She sat, slumped at the table, listless. It was strange how hurt she felt, knowing McKray was out to cheat the farmers around town. He'd proven himself to be dishonest before—he'd tricked her at the dance—but somehow she'd come to think of him as trustworthy.

Mrs. Boyce's daughters began bringing out the platters of scrambled eggs and sausages.

"Did you sup with the Oswalds last night?" Stieg asked.

Sissel was distracted, still thinking through what she had just learned.

"Yes," she said, then, "No, I'm sorry. I wound up having a bite at the general store."

"Aha! Did James make a picnic for you?"

"Of a sort," she said.

"Have I been terribly lax as a chaperone? Is he behaving himself?" Stieg asked.

"Oh no. It was fine. But I'm not sure . . ."

A basket with biscuits came around. Sissel took one.

"Not sure of what?"

"I don't think he's the right sort," Sissel said. "To tell you the truth, I'd be happy for us all to go to Helena, if that's what you decide is best."

"Really? With all your friends here? What about Isaiah McKray?"

A fierce blush came over Sissel's cheeks and neck.

"Him," she said. "He's too old for me."

Stieg tsked at her unkindness. "I thought he was growing on you."

"No," she said. "He's . . . he's a ruthless sort. It's all business with him."

Sissel focused on spreading butter on a biscuit.

Stieg took a sip of coffee. He thought for a moment, then laughed. "What will Hanne say when she finds out how much you've changed since she went away! Goodness, you've discarded two suitors now, gained your health, gained quite a bit of strength all around, I'd say. I can't wait to see her face."

He winked at Sissel. She offered as convincing a smile as she could in return.

THE SCHOOL DAY dragged on and on. The smaller pupils were distracted by the unusual busyness of the street. Wagons were rolling in. There was a train of burros parading down the street, tied one after another.

Sissel had taken her oral examination on the Boston Tea Party. She'd only gotten one fact wrong—misstating the date of the Tea Act. Now Abigail was giving her report on the Stamp Act. Truthfully, no one was paying very much attention; it was already a dull subject and Abigail was not a gifted speaker. Stieg had had to rap on his desk several times to curtail whispering about the goings-on outside the window.

No one was whispering to Sissel, though.

Alice was studiously avoiding Sissel. She wouldn't even cast a glance her way. James was the opposite. Every time Sissel turned her head, he was looking at her. Not the playful, flirting looks she was used to from him, but sneaking, furtive glances. He seemed to be assessing her in a way that felt almost clinical.

They had greeted each other stiffly at the beginning of the day. She had hardly known what to say to him. It felt like they were strangers, somehow.

Sissel felt again the shame that had crept upon her in the night. What a fool she was to have trusted him with her secret!

Her only idea was that they must move. She must persuade Owen and Hanne and Knut that they should all accompany Stieg to Helena.

Howie was being examined on the Boston Massacre when three hard raps sounded on the door. Every head turned to the back of the classroom. The door swung open, and there stood Isaiah McKray, hat in hand.

"Begging your pardon," he said. "But I need to speak to young Miss Hemstad."

This caused a flurry of shocked glances and whispered exclamations, especially from the girls. McKray had the decency to look embarrassed. Stieg looked completely perplexed.

"I see," he said. "And this must happen right now?"

McKray took two steps into the room. He seemed too big for it.

"Now. It's terribly important. It's business."

Sissel saw Stieg's mind putting things together.

She saw her brother come to the realization, untrue, that Sissel had helped McKray find gold. She could almost detect the exact moment when Stieg was hit with shame for not figuring it out sooner. His eyes locked on Sissel's, the question writ plainly in them: Had she helped McKray find his gold?

Sissel couldn't answer that question with a glance—it was too complicated. She broke the connection, looked down at her hands.

Stieg took a steadying breath.

"This is most unusual," Stieg said. He stood up, then he sat down again. "I hardly know what to say. Sissel?"

"May I be excused, please?" she said. She kept her eyes lowered. It seemed best to act demure and proper.

"Yes," he said. "Fine."

Sissel rose. Alice took her hand abruptly and squeezed it, breaking her silence to whisper, "All right?"

Sissel smiled at her. She squeezed back and nodded.

James's expression was closed and hard to read. Anxiety? Suspicion?

"Howie," Stieg said. "Please tell us the number of British troops stationed in Boston in the weeks before the attack."

OUTSIDE, SISSEL STALKED away from the schoolhouse, toward the boulders at the edge of the yard, the same ones she'd sat on with James. McKray followed her.

Sissel spun on McKray.

"By coming and interrupting class this way you have told my brother everything, do you realize that?" she hissed.

"I'm sorry. I'm a clod," McKray said.

"You're a swindler, and I want nothing to do with you," she said.

"Partner with me," McKray said. "I'll give you a fifty-fifty split on everything I make. Mining, the hotel, all of it."

"What? Why?" Sissel sputtered.

"You figured out my game. I knew it this morning when I saw you at the hotel. And all morning I've thought of nothing else. That now you'll despise me. And I can't bear it."

Sissel was struck dumb.

"Be my business partner," he said. "I'll go by the letter of the law from now on, I swear it."

"You are scared I will expose you for a fraud," she said. "So you are offering me this arrangement to ensure my silence."

"Nope."

"Then you just want to harness my ability to find gold," she said.

"Listen here," McKray said. "You're the only person I've ever met who has seen the truth of me. Of who I really am. And that feels right. It feels right to have someone I can talk to without having to wrap my words in a bunch of puffery.

"And I see you, too, you know. I see how proud you are. And ambitious. I see how hard it must be, to be a female and to have ambition. All the limits our world puts on the fairer sex, and men pretend they are for your own good, but they're only to keep you all down.

"I see you, Sissel Hemstad. I want to help you."

He put a hand on her arm.

"Think of what we could do together."

"I can't trust you," she said.

"You can. I kept your family's secret."

"You're a swindler."

He blew out a great big breath.

"All my life I only cared about what one person thought of me. My father. This little thing I've pulled off, this little gold boom, it's right out of his playbook. If he were, here he'd slap me on the shoulder and congratulate me. Hell, the reason I did it is to impress him, if I'm honest.

"Now, I see how ugly it all is. And wrong. I'm seeing it that way because all of a sudden I care more about what you think of me than what my father does."

"Me?"

"You. Miss Sissel Hemstad, a sixteen-year-old girl who is stubborn and smart and . . ."

He brought himself up short.

"Look, I'm young enough to change my ways. Partner with me and I'll show you."

Sissel was exasperated, but she also was tempted. She knew he was being truthful with her. She felt it in her gut.

"Obviously, I would have to tell my brother," Sissel said. "I'd have to tell him everything. He will be furious, you understand that."

"I deserve it. And I can take it."

Sissel looked to McKray's eyes. They were hopeful.

"No," she said. "It's absurd."

"Don't say no," he said. "Say you'll think it over."

"Why would I?"

"Because I think you'd like to be my partner," he said.

"You're awfully forward," she said.

"Yes, we're alike in that way."

AFTER SCHOOL WAS dismissed Stieg exited the schoolhouse without waiting for her. James, also, did not have anything to say. He slipped away after sending her a slight wave in her direction.

Sissel wanted to speak to Alice and try to make up with her, but she had speak to Stieg first.

On the walk home, Stieg's strides kept lengthening, leaving Sissel to scurry to catch up. They came upon Mr. Campbell, who wanted to shake Stieg's hand and congratulate him on another school term come to an end. Stieg was amenable and polite, but Sissel could tell he was seething inside.

They reached the hotel, but Stieg looked at it and shook his head and continued charging down the street. Stieg was still carrying his school satchel. Sissel held the pail they used to carry their lunches.

Sissel wasn't sure if he was headed to the farm or if he just wanted to get out of town so his raised voice wouldn't be heard by the towns-folk. Yelling was imminent.

Only when they were a fair distance from town did she dare to speak.

"Can you walk slower?" Sissel asked. "Please?"

Stieg spun around as if she'd stung him.

"I told Hanne we'd be fine, you and me. I told her that we were close. That it would be good for you to have some independence. And you've . . . you've lied to me at every turn!"

"I'm sorry!"

"Tell me you are not the reason McKray struck gold!" he said.

"I'm not," she said.

Stieg's eyes went wide.

"You lie to me still?"

He spun away, hands on hips, too angry to speak.

"Stieg, you are right. I have lied to you, but not about that, because McKray hasn't struck gold."

"I credit myself as being an intelligent man, but, Sister, you have lost me."

"I will tell you the whole story," Sissel said. "I have been stupid and deceitful and you must know all of it."

And so she told him about sneaking out to practice her Nytte, and about running into McKray. Then she told him about Alice's combs, and how he had tricked her into revealing her Nytte.

They continued to walk as the story poured out. She talked about her ride with McKray, and how he had given her the wanted poster and asked for her help.

She told him about her afternoon with McKray when the newspapermen had ambushed them. And the twenty dollars she had earned. Then she told him of McKray's business proposal.

"He wants to give you half of his money?" Stieg said.

"Half of his business prospects. I don't know all the details."

"Wonderful. Excellent," Stieg said sarcastically. He rubbed his forehead and exhaled deeply. "Is that it? Is that absolutely everything?"

Sissel shook. Her body trembled. She hadn't said a word about James. She feared if she didn't tell him now, about how she had told James about her Nytte, that there would be a wall between her and her brother. One she might never be able to breach.

"No," she said. Tears came to her eyes. "I was stupid, Stieg. I did something so foolish . . . Oh, I am so ashamed!"

Stieg stepped forward. He placed his hands on her arms.

"What is it?" Stieg asked.

"I told James. About my powers."

"Oh, Sissel," he said.

"I am so sorry. He seemed so broken and sad."

"McKray figured it out on his own, but you told James yourself?" he said.

"It was a stupid thing to do," she said.

"No. I've been the stupid one. I was too trusting—" Sissel tried to break in, to apologize, but he cut her off with his hand. "Rolf was right. I have not used sufficient caution. I got comfortable and complacent.

"We must leave," Stieg said bitterly. "We have no choice but to leave. Too many here know about us. We must go where we know no one, and keep it that way."

"Are you sure?" Sissel said. "McKray . . . I think he's sincere. It could be such an opportunity."

"He's a swindler and a cheat! He tried to buy our land, Sissel. Our one bit of property in the world, just so he could sell it off to a bunch of gold-crazy prospectors!"

"But he offered us more than what we paid for it . . ."

Stieg didn't seem to hear her, just started walking back to town.

"We'll go after I dismiss school tomorrow. I couldn't live with myself if we left before I finished the term. It wouldn't be fair to the children; they've worked too hard."

"What about McKray?" Sissel asked.

"What about him? He tricked you and manipulated you. Now he wants to use you to find gold."

"I think he's sincere," Sissel said.

"He's tricked you three times, Sissel. Have some dignity."

Sissel drew back. It was unlike Stieg to be so cruel. His face was twisted in anger.

"What a fool I've been!" he said. "Thinking the freedom was doing you good—"

"It was! It did!"

"When you've been sneaking around with McKray doing God knows what!"

"Why do you feel that you must control me so?" she said. "It's my Nytte. Why can't I use it as I see fit?"

Stieg stopped in the middle of the dusty road and turned toward her.

"You got a Nytte, and without one thought for the safety of your brothers and sister, you started showing off for some man we hardly know!"

"I wasn't showing off!"

"Do you have any idea the sacrifices we have all made to keep you safe? To keep you alive? The Baron is still looking for us, Sissel. We know this. If he knew of your gift, he would send all the Berserkers he has after us. And you revealed your powers to two outsiders!"

"I'm sorry," she said. "I am."

Stieg nodded. "I'm sure you are."

They walked together. A farm they passed had a field of rippling wheat, nearly ripe. Soon the fields would be harvested, and all the schoolchildren would be needed at home to do their part.

"I am half of a mind to leave now," Stieg said. "We could pack up now and slip out. With all the commotion at the hotel, I don't know that anyone would notice."

Sissel's breath caught in her throat. She couldn't leave Alice without saying good-bye! And to leave McKray without an answer would be rude.

"But it seems more kind and fair to leave tomorrow after school," he said. "It would cause a commotion if I disappeared without ending the term properly."

Stieg walked ahead without casting Sissel a glance.

"We will tell everyone Owen has found work in Texas."

"Texas?"

"Yes. And then we'll move east, to a big city. We'll change our names. Try to disappear."

"What about Helena? Your job?"

"We can't stay in Montana, where so many people know us. So now you see—" Stieg cast her a glance. He must have seen how stricken Sissel was, how terrible she felt about the loss she had caused him, because his face softened.

"Now you see why Mr. McKray's offer is out of the question."

"Yes," she said.

"You and I will speak with Mr. McKray together. We'll turn him down once and for all."

Sissel said nothing, only trailed a few steps behind him as they made their way back to Carter.

CHAPTER THIRTY-SIX

James stood in a small copse of aspens a good fifty feet off the road. He was crouching there, for the Hemstads had changed direction and were now coming back. He had trailed Sissel and Stieg, keeping far enough away that he now had trouble making out their argument. It was either about him or about McKray's odd appearance at the school, or both. He should be concerned about Isaiah McKray turning up, but mostly he felt confused.

James had spent the day feeling foggy headed and disoriented. The whiskey he drank with Peavy the night before hadn't helped. Between them, they drained the bottle, then started a new one, and gotten a quarter of the way through it before James nodded off.

More troubling than the hangover was the whole idea of Sissel having power of some kind over metals. Peavy had hailed James as a hero repeatedly, talking about how happy the client would be. James argued late into the night that it was all the delusions of a fragile, hysterical girl, but Peavy didn't care about Sissel, or her health, or whether she had powers at all. What he cared about was pleasing the Baron and getting a bonus.

As the liquor had taken hold, Peavy started wondering if he'd make enough money to buy the store outright. Or maybe, he fantasized, the Baron would give it to him as a reward.

James felt it might be best to leave town. He had an uneasy feeling about the whole thing. Sissel had cooled on him—he could see that she regretted baring her soul to him. She wasn't about to get her heart broken if he left.

Let some other idiot take over guarding her. Someone who believed in the occult.

He wanted more whiskey, that's what he wanted. To liberate him from his thinking, which went round and round, and to ease the guilt that kept chafing his conscience.

In the end, it was all for the best that the Baron knew about Sissel's "magic." He was protecting them, wasn't he? Maybe he'd get her a good doctor.

Here they came now, passing him by. Neither looked to the left or the right. They continued on straight and steadfast, no idea they were observed.

He had a mind to jump out. To scare them.

Then he'd tell them, "Look! All along you've been carrying on while other men have been protecting you! We've been keeping you safe this whole time and you never knew!"

He said nothing, just squatted there in the bushes, feeling mostly like a coward.

He trailed them at the leisurely pace they set all the way back to town. They went into the hotel, where a large crowd was gathered on the porch.

After they were inside, James ducked into the store.

Peavy was in the front, selling overpriced gear to some newbie prospectors. Peavy gave James a salute and a wink. The store had gotten so busy with the land rush that Peavy had had to hire on two new boys to help behind the counter. One was Howie from school. James had put in a good word for him.

Howie was now weighing out sugar for Mrs. Denmead, who looked thoroughly irritated at the commotion.

"How was school, son?" Peavy asked as James came behind the counter.

"Fine," he said.

"Nothing interesting to report?"

James shook his head. "Nothing of note."

"Good," Peavy said. He was wrapping a hardtack in brown paper for a prospector with few teeth and little hair. "I need you here in the store. We've never been so busy."

James leaned in close to whisper, "What about the hotel?"

"Clements is on it," Peavy said.

Good, James thought. The less he had to do with the Hemstads, the better.

"I believe those men over there want several pounds of beans." Peavy pointed to three men arguing near the pickle barrel.

"I'll get right to it."

"Oh!" Peavy said, clapping his hands together. "We're making money today!"

CHAPTER THIRTY-SEVEN

Back at the hotel, a new order had been established. Those waiting to see Mr. McKray had been shooed out onto the porch. As she and Stieg pushed through the throng, Sissel saw scraps of paper in the hands of several of the waiting parties and wondered what they were.

In the lobby she had her answer. Collier had a stack of them on his desk. They were numbers.

Two men in travel-worn suits stood at the desk, talking to Collier, who looked far more in control than he had the day before.

"Mawkins, Noah, and Paul." Collier jotted into a ledger. "And what's your business?"

"What do you think we're here about?" one said crossly. "We've come to town to prospect. And found your McKray holds almost all the promising land available for sale. So we want to buy a piece from him."

"And we'll pay extra for a good one," the other fellow said in a low, conspiratorial tone. "Put that in your ledger."

"I shall indeed, gentlemen. Your number is forty-six. I wouldn't expect to talk to him before tomorrow."

"But in the meantime, we can take a room here? That how it works?" the first one sneered.

"Hardly. We haven't got a single room to let. But you are welcome to sleep in our stables, free of charge. Or on the front porch."

The two men took the number and walked out, muttering to each other.

Collier sighed and blotted the words he'd written in the ledger. He looked up, and finding Stieg and Sissel there, he smiled.

That was a surprise.

"Ah, familiar faces," Collier said.

"Good evening, Mr. Collier," Sissel replied.

She wondered how much he knew about his employer's feelings for her. Collier's manner had certainly changed toward them.

"It's been a long day of dealing with angry strangers," he said. "Mr. McKray can't sell the land fast enough to suit them."

"Yes, he's a shrewd businessman, to be sure," Stieg said coldly.

"This afternoon he started trying to tell the men that there's no gold to be found. That his mines haven't proved up the way he'd hoped. If anything, it made them want the land more!" Collier said. "They think he's protesting to cover up some huge deposit. Imagine! And some of these men! The roughest sort—"

"We'd like a word with Mr. McKray," Stieg cut in.

Collier straightened up. He'd been settling in to chat.

"Well, be my guest," he said, gesturing to the stack of numbered slips on his desk. "You can expect to speak to him in the morning."

"Don't be ridiculous," Stieg said. Sissel laid her hand on his arm.

"Mr. Collier, I'm sure that if you tell him my brother and I are here, he will want to see us."

She was right. Collier only opened the door to the office and spoke their names and McKray came to see them. His eyes lit up when he saw Sissel. It made her feel sorry for him; he wasn't going to get any good news.

"We'd like to speak to you in private," Stieg said.

"Please come in," McKray said, gesturing for them to enter his office.

If the lobby of the hotel was overbearingly feminine, McKray's office was masculine efficiency to an extreme.

The walls were paneled with oak, and a fireplace was set into the far wall of the room. Two leather armchairs stood in front of a massive desk loaded with neat stacks of papers. Behind the desk was a bookshelf with stacked volumes. Sissel saw Stieg's eyes flit to the books. Most seemed to be law books and ledgers along with a large dictionary and a thesaurus.

The only decoration in the room was a large map of the territory nailed to the wall. This had pins stuck into it and pale blue lines outlining parcels of land, with further subdivisions within them marked in green pencil.

The office was, Sissel realized, a fairly good expression of McKray's inner character. Sturdy, unfussy, and all about business.

It made her smile. She was fond of him, she realized, despite all his scheming.

"Please, sit," McKray said. They seated themselves, Sissel and Stieg in the armchairs and McKray behind the desk. "May I call for coffee and cake? Are you hungry?"

Sissel nodded yes, but Stieg said no.

"Sissel had told me a long story this afternoon, and I must say, McKray, you have abused her trust in a way I find most deplorable."

McKray nodded his head. "Yes, I agree."

"You agree?"

"If I could do it again, Mr. Hemstad, I would do it all differently, I would. I can't go back and do it over, but I can promise you that going forward, I would have only her best interests—"

Stieg shook his head. "There is no 'going forward.' My sister Hanne has asked us to join her and her fiancé. We are leaving tomorrow."

"I see," McKray said. He straightened a stack of papers that was already square. "So you've discussed my business proposal—"

"There are many reasons why I would not allow such a partnership, Mr. McKray. Sissel's age would be one—"

"I can wait until she comes of age."

"Her susceptibility to your particular brand of manipulation would be another—"

"She sees right through me. That's one of the things I most admire about her."

"But the greatest one would be that I don't trust you. And there's nothing you can say that would reverse my position on that."

McKray looked toward the window, clearly composing a retort.

"I suppose it wouldn't forward my case any if I pointed out that she's nearly an adult and should be allowed to make decisions for herself?"

Sissel felt a surge of pride in McKray at this. She spoke before her brother could.

"It doesn't mean much to him, but it does to me," she said.

"Mr. McKray, I agree with my brother. I can't help you with your mining business. I must turn you down, although, I will say, that I'm pleased you asked me. And I appreciate the way you offered."

Stieg stood. His neck was red.

"We should settle our bill before we go."

McKray waved it off. "Please, don't. I don't want your money."

Stieg placed six dollars down on the table. "This is for the past several weeks. Now we're paid up. Thank you for taking us in."

McKray got to his feet.

"I wish I could do the whole thing over," he said. "It truly pains me that we part this way."

"Come, Sissel," Stieg said. He took her by the arm and led her from the room.

SISSEL SLEPT POORLY, tossing and turning. She hated to leave town this way, running scared. To leave Alice, her only friend, without ever telling her the truth and making up. It didn't feel right at all.

Around midnight she had an idea. She'd wake early and go visit Alice before school started. Though she couldn't tell her friend why they were leaving, she could at least have a private moment with her and try to apologize for the distance that had come between them.

At dawn, she rose and put on the lovely tan dress Alice had given her.

Sissel had used some of the twenty dollars she'd earned from McKray to pay Bridget for all the laundering she had been doing for her. Now, thinking of it, she put a dollar in an envelope and wrote Bridget's name on the front—a little tip, and she knew Bridget needed the money. She left it on the floor of her empty armoire.

Sissel wrote a note to Stieg, saying she was going to visit Alice and that she would see him at school. Sissel looked at herself in the mirror. She tucked a few stray strands of hair into the bun she had made. She looked older, she thought, maybe because her eyes looked a bit sad.

"Onward," she whispered to her reflection.

Sissel stepped into the hallway, slipped the note for Stieg under his door, and made her way quietly down the hall.

The clock in the lobby told her it was five thirty. Early enough that few guests were around, but late enough for the hotel to be stirring. There was no one at the front desk, but she heard pots clanging in the kitchen. Since there were sleeping bodies out on the porch, she decided to go out through the kitchen. She nodded to the cook and her assistants, already busy making biscuits for breakfast.

Outside, the morning air was fresh and cool. The rising sun had painted the town in a wash of copper. It was so pretty, in the light, with the mountains as a backdrop that Sissel felt a terrible pang of homesickness for Carter, though they'd not yet left it.

She walked over to Elm Street. Around her, the town was waking up. She heard the kitchen sounds and morning discussions coming from some open windows. She saw movement through the open windows at the Oswalds' house and approached.

"Good morning," she called as she neared. "Anyone awake?"

"Why, Sissel, good morning, dear," called Mrs. Oswald softly through the window. She came to the door in her apron and waved Sissel in.

"My, my!" she said. "You're up with the roosters!"

"Is Alice awake?" Sissel asked.

"Yes, but she's not down yet. Go and help her, will you?"

Sissel climbed the stairs. She would miss the Oswalds' house, too. It was a lovely timber house with plenty of windows, each with cheery curtains that Mrs. Oswald changed with the seasons, a luxury afforded to them, of course, by owning the fabric store.

Sissel knocked on Alice's door.

"Yes, Mother, I'll be right down," came Alice's voice.

Sissel edged the door open. She affected a motherly scold, "If I have to call you one more time . . ."

Alice turned in surprise. She was braiding her hair at the vanity.

Sissel hoped Alice would be happy to see her, and she was rewarded with a big smile.

"You!" Alice said. "Oh, Sissel. I'm so glad to see you!"

She stood and gave Sissel a warm embrace.

"I'm so sorry—" they both said in near unison.

"No, I am the sorry one," Alice said. "You are allowed to have as many beaus as you please, and I should not be so nosy. And as I thought about it, I realized you're probably friends with the maid and were protecting her . . ."

"I should have told you about the combs," Sissel said. "You've been such a wonderful friend to me—"

"I lay here tossing and turning all night thinking you must hate me—"

"Never," Sissel interjected.

"—and wondering what on earth happened with McKray!"

Sissel laughed.

"Why did he interrupt school that way? What did he mean when he said he had business to discuss with you? How does James feel about it all?"

She was leaning into Sissel, her eyes lit up with excitement.

"Not," she said, "that you have to tell me . . . but I hope you will."

Sissel exhaled. She was going to lie to her friend one last time.

"McKray has been courting me," Sissel said. "And the reason he came to the school . . . was that we have to go away. And he was pleading with me not to go."

"You have to go?"

"I hoped it wasn't true, and so I didn't tell you. But we are leaving town," she told her friend. "Hanne and Owen want us to join them. Owen has found work in Texas."

"No! But when? How soon?"

"Today," Sissel said. "We leave this afternoon, after school."

"For how long? Surely you'll come back . . ."

"I'm not sure," Sissel said.

Tears suddenly filled Sissel's eyes to overflowing. Alice was so trusting and kind, and Sissel had fed her lie after lie.

"Oh, Sissel, I am so sorry. What about James and McKray?"

"Stieg says I'm still young. That I'll meet new beaus . . ."

Alice gathered Sissel into a hug, and Sissel allowed herself to cry without restraint.

"You've been such a lovely friend," Sissel said when the tears were done. "I don't know how to ever thank you for all you've done for me."

"Why, hush. You'll thank me by being my dearest friend for the rest of my life. We'll write and visit. We won't lose touch."

"Girls!" Mrs. Oswald called up. "Breakfast will be ready soon!"

Alice resumed braiding her hair, all the while planning for how they would stay friends. She was trying to cheer Sissel up, and Sissel was grateful for it.

"We'll leave our children with our husbands, whoever they turn out to be, and we'll travel to Helena to go to the opera house! Some summers we'll visit the mineral baths in Colorado. They're so healthy, no one could deny us a week or two taking the waters."

"Girls! You'll be late!" came the call from downstairs.

Alice took her hand.

"The last day of the summer term of school," Alice said. "And so much has happened."

"Yes," Sissel said.

As they went downstairs, the smell of corn flapjacks, maple syrup, and butter came wafting up.

"You'd better eat quickly," Mrs. Oswald said. "Wouldn't do to be late. Not today."

Sissel and Alice ate the good, warm breakfast and then made their way to school.

CHAPTER THIRTY-EIGHT

James woke to the sounds of business in the store. That meant he'd overslept considerably. It was past seven if the store was open.

An empty bottle of liquor clattered as he swung his feet to the floor. The sound made him wince. He swore and pulled his suspenders up from where they dangled at his waist.

He was going be late for the last day of school if he didn't hurry. He cussed while he fumbled his feet into his boots and grabbed his cleanest shirt from one of the pegs on the wall.

There was something off in the attic, he realized—it was tidy. Peavy had cleaned up, but not like he was moving out. His clothes were still in their places, and his carpetbag was still stowed on the high shelf that ran around the top of the room like a crown. It was tidy as if he were expecting company.

"Peavy?" James called. Oof. His own voice hurt his head. He

rubbed his temples. He needed to end his little affair with Old Fire Copper whiskey.

He felt vomit rising in his mouth and pulled over the trash bin.

Mostly Peavy used it to spit tobacco chaw into, and the sight and smell of the little brown heaps was enough to bring the bile up, but James saw a crumpled telegram on top.

He pulled out the telegram and read it. Bits of tobacco fell onto the floor as he straightened out the thin paper.

It read:

TAKE POSSESSION OF ITEM STOP KEEP SECURE AT ANY
COST STOP FORFEIT OTHER ITEMS IF NECESSARY STOP
CLIENT EN ROUTE STOP

James felt the blood drain out of his guts.

He blinked, trying to clear his bleary vision. He brought the telegram over to the window and read it again.

Sissel was the item. Client was the Baron Fjelstad.

They meant to take Sissel prisoner.

He closed his eyes. The room was swimming around him.

Forfeit other items meant kill the other Hemstads, if need be.

"This is your job," he said out loud to himself. "It's a part of your job."

But he folded the telegram and shoved it into the pocket of his pants. He put the trash bin back where he'd found it and quietly descended the ladder.

He grabbed his jacket and slipped out the back door. Let Peavy think he was sleeping it off—he couldn't let this happen to them. Not to Sissel. Not to any of the Hemstads.

JAMES ENTERED THE hotel just as the kitchen staff opened the double doors leading into the dining hall for breakfast. There were a dozen hotel patrons filing in. Neither Sissel nor Stieg was among them. He dodged through the customers, then took the stairs to the second floor two at a time.

He'd not been into Sissel's room, but he knew the number. Twenty-six. If she wasn't here, she might be eating at the boardinghouse. He drew the telegram out of his pocket. He'd give it to her—she wouldn't doubt the danger she was in if he gave it to her as proof.

"Sissel," he said, knocking on the door. "It's me, James."

The door gave way. It was unlocked.

James pushed through the door and nearly stumbled over a large trunk.

He heard a shuffling sound and turned. Something hit him on the side of the head, hard.

James fell, knees slamming on the corner of the trunk. His shoulder hit the floor first, then his head. He turned to look over his shoulder.

It was Clements who had hit him. Stupid, oafish Clements. He stood there grinning at James with his broken-toothed sneer.

The room was spinning, his head shrieking in agony.

"It's me, for God's sake—"

"I knew you'd turn," Peavy said as he stepped from the shadows. "I told Clements, 'Wait and see. He'll be coming through the door any second now.' Get him up," he ordered Clements.

"Peavy, stop," James said. "This is wrong!"

Clements pulled James over to Sissel's writing desk and dumped him in the fine chair.

They had several lengths of good hemp rope from the store. Clements tied him up with it. "Come on, Peavy," James said. "We're on the same side. Let's talk it over."

"Gag him," Peavy said. Clements stuffed a hand towel from the washstand into his mouth. James nearly choked.

"You little son of a bitch," Peavy said, shaking his head. "You came here to warn her."

Peavy crossed to the door and locked it.

"You are a sorry sort of a Pinkerton, I'll tell you. I only kept you on because the girl seemed to like you. I had just about given up when you got her to squeal. So there's that. But otherwise, good God. Sloppy surveillance, poor reporting, hesitation when it came time to act. Worst of all, you got a conscience.

"Well, never mind. It won't be long now. I hear Mr. Hemstad's letting school out early."

James tried to ask what they meant to do.

"Aw, Jamie, you lost the right to ask questions when you walked through that door. Clements, why don't you help him rest for a while?"

Clements came at James with one of his big hammy fists raised.

"No! Wait!" James tried to say. He reared back in the chair, but there was no escaping the heavy thud and the sick darkness that followed.

CHAPTER THIRTY-NINE

I t was only after Sissel and Alice settled into their seats, laughing, as Stieg gave one final shake of the bell, that Sissel realized James was not at school. Neither was Howie, but Alice whispered that Peavy had paid him double to open the store early for all the prospectors.

Sissel found it strange that James wasn't there. How odd that he would not come for the certificate ceremony. She felt she was to blame somehow. The awkward strangeness between them had kept him away.

All the younger students were dressed their best. Abigail and Minnie had taken special care with their outfits and hair. Sissel wished, for a moment, she'd curled her hair, but she let go of that thought. She hardly cared what the other older girls thought. They had whispered about her and glared at her all term long. Now she was leaving them behind. It was one thing to be glad of.

Stieg looked worn out, but proud of his students as he handed out the crisp, official certificates. Each student's name was written in Stieg's fine, elegant script, along with the levels they had completed, the name of the school, and the date.

Sissel was pleased with her marks. She had passed the ninth-grade levels in history, grammar, and composition and the tenth-grade levels for arithmetic and spelling.

After all the certificates were passed out, several of the younger students came forward with gifts for her brother. There were several apples and a new pencil, and one girl had brought in a small pound cake.

Stieg rose and addressed the class.

"Students, I am proud of our class and what we have accomplished. By fortifying your mind, you protect yourself against folly. Great feeling can cause great destruction—it must be tempered with restraint and wisdom.

"I see no reason why each and every one of you could not pass to the highest grade level and graduate with top marks. You have the stuff within you to be a class of great thinkers."

Sissel looked at the collection of children, dressed in Sunday clothes but some still missing buttons, ribbons. Only the older girls and boys wore shoes; the rest had bare feet swinging from the bench seats. She felt Stieg might be exaggerating, but the faces of the students were rapt with attention. He had them dreaming of an academic future.

"My charge to you is to continue with your fine work and do not let up until you have graduated grade twelve! With that, I dismiss school."

Huzzahs and hurrahs went up simultaneously. School was out.

ALICE INVITED THEM to come for lunch, but Stieg begged off—there was too much to do to get ready to go. She insisted they come to say good-bye on their way out of town. Stieg acquiesced and Alice hugged Sissel a temporary farewell.

"Listen," he said after Alice had gone. He handed her his teacher's satchel. "Go and arrange for our trunks to be brought down to the depot. I've got the use of two horses from the livery. I'm going to ride for Knut. The train comes through at five twenty p.m. We can make it, but only if you meet us there with all our things."

"All right," Sissel said.

Stieg pressed a ten-dollar bill into her hand.

"Where did you get this?" Sissel asked.

"Did you forget? I had the balance of my salary come due today."

"But I still have money," she said. "From . . . what McKray gave me."

"I forgot about that," Stieg said. "I'll keep it then. But listen, if McKray tries to speak with you, you must cut him off."

"I will," she said.

"You must!"

"I will!" It was enraging that her brother felt he must always control her. She knew how to behave.

"Very well. I'm sorry to be so strict." He spun to leave, then called over his shoulder, "Three tickets to Helena."

AS SISSEL PASSED the front desk, Collier hailed her.

"Miss Hemstad," he said. "I understand you will be checking out today."

"Yes," she said. "I'm sure you have people lined up to take the room."

"I just wanted to say, it was a pleasure having you at the hotel." He looked a bit stiff and uncomfortable giving this compliment. His mustache twitched a bit.

"Thank you, Mr. Collier," she said. "It's a lovely hotel."

He gave a little bow, turned, and began barking instructions to a porter carrying a crate of potatoes.

SISSEL DUG THE hotel room key out of her satchel and unlocked the door. She had so much to do! Finish packing, call a porter—

Something wasn't right about the light in her room. She registered something blocking the window. Then she was pulled roughly inside and a thick hand clamped over her mouth. She was so startled she nearly screamed.

James was there, tied to a chair, his head slumped forward.

Next to him was his father, Mr. Peavy.

When the door shut, James looked up. He had been beaten. His right eye was blackened, the skin around it swollen and maroon colored around the lid. He had also bled from the lip. There was a stain on his shirt collar.

Sissel made another sound of surprise, and an unseen man behind her pulled her into his body roughly. He had her arms pinned behind her with one arm while the other hand completely covered her mouth. She could barely breathe through her nose.

"Easy, Clements," Mr. Peavy said, and the grip on her mouth was loosened somewhat. Sissel struggled to calm herself so she could breathe.

James was trying to talk to Mr. Peavy though he had a towel stuck in his mouth. He was saying something that Mr. Peavy seemed to understand.

"I'm not going to hurt her, you idiot. My whole job is to keep her safe until the Baron gets here. It was your job, too, until you went and got soft."

Now a shock went through Sissel's body. The Baron? The Baron was coming?

Her eyes met James's.

"Mmm thorry," he pleaded through the gag.

"If you'd a done your job, you wouldn't be in this fix," Mr. Peavy said to James. He was looking at his son with an expression of derision.

All the pieces came into place in a terrible slam that hit her bodily—he wasn't James's father—she'd been betrayed.

James. Mr. Peavy. They were on the Baron's payroll somehow. Oh, she felt sick. Sick down to the bottom of her gut. She wanted to shout at him. To punch him, or kick him. Waves of shame and anger flooded her.

All those moments she'd wondered why James liked her. All those times she'd thought it was a bit too good to be true. She had been right!

Peavy was watching her, and he laughed.

"Yep," Peavy said. "You've been played, little girl. And frankly, you held out a lot longer than any of us expected against young James's charms. Most jobs, just takes a fella as good-looking as this one just a few days, maybe a week, to get a lady on her back and spilling secrets."

Here James shouted at Mr. Peavy and struggled against his bonds. Mr. Peavy backhanded him across the face. Blood from his nose flew out in a wide arc to spatter on the carpet.

James's head lolled forward again. He'd lost consciousness.

"Now, I'd like to talk to you a bit, Miss Hemstad," Peavy said.

He took his bowie knife from the sheath he wore on his belt. She'd seen him cut rope with that knife often enough in the shop, to tie a parcel or to open a box. Most merchants had a knife at hand.

Now he held the knife to the little cleft between James's ear and his skull.

"Clements will take his hand away from your mouth. If you scream or call out, I'll slide this little knife in here and end James's life. I won't feel too bad about it. In the end, he turned out to be a piss-poor detective.

"Shall we talk? Blink if you get me," Mr. Peavy said.

Sissel blinked.

The thug Clements took his hand away, and she drew in a shaky breath. A foul unwashed smell from the man's fingers was on her lips, and she wanted to spit.

"What do you want?" she asked.

"Oh ho!" Mr. Peavy laughed. "No questions for me first about how we did it or who we are or when the Baron's coming?"

Sissel took her time answering. She needed to think.

Peavy had a knife . . . Could she take it from him?

"You figured it out all on your own, have you?" he said.

"You three were hired by the Baron to take us prisoners," she said.

"Not exactly, sis. We were hired to protect you. Why do you think no one's come after your big brute of a brother? That's 'cause we've had our agents going to every small-town sheriff in a two-hundred-mile radius, finding those old wanted posters, and taking possession of them. Warrant like that, with a nice big payout, takes a good long while to go away. Didn't it ever seem a bit easy to you all?"

Sissel didn't answer. Tears began to pool at the corners of her eyes.

"You had such a nice little setup. Paid-for protection services! And you all were never the wiser."

He walked forward until he was standing close. The knife was in his fist.

"But then James finally got you to spill your secret. Now the Baron himself is coming to meet you. Of course, it'll take about a week. So in the meantime, you and me and a good number of my Pinkerton associates are going to hole up until he gets here."

Sissel took a long slow breath in, preparing.

"The Baron wants it done with as little bloodshed as possible. That's why we're having this nice, civil conversation."

Sissel threw open her Nytte and reached, as hard as she could, for the blade in Peavy's hand. It had a grip made of stag horn she couldn't control and a steel blade, the metal sickeningly cold and oily. It made her nearly gag just to touch it with her mind, but she gripped it hard.

Peavy's eyes went wide as she tried to pry the knife from his grip.

"What the hell?" he said.

Then his eyes flashed to her.

"Ha!" he said. "It's true!"

She pulled at the blade with her mind.

Peavy struggled with the knife. His arms jerked up and down as she tried to wrench it from him. She seized the brass lamp with her mind and pulled it to herself, smashing Peavy in the back on the way.

"Punch her!" Peavy shouted, his voice coming from far away.

"What?" She felt Clements's deep voice resonate behind her chest.

She desperately sought other metals in the room. The fittings on the bed, the brass rivets on the easy chair, she started to shake it all. If she made a loud sound someone would come—

Peavy's lips moved. "Hit the girl!"

Clements whacked her on the side of the head. The blow was awkward, coming as it did from behind and around, but the pain was intense. Her brain rattled in her skull. Black blotches spattered over her field of vision. Her legs gave out suddenly, and her Nytte was gone.

Sissel's body collapsed onto the carpet, but Clements hauled her up again.

Peavy put the knife under her throat.

He said something to her. He brushed a tendril of Sissel's hair off her forehead. His touch made her skin crawl.

He spoke again, waited for an answer. He grabbed her and shook her.

"I can't hear!" she cried. "I don't know what you're saying."

Peavy cussed. He didn't seem to believe her.

"Give me a few minutes and I'll be able to hear again," she said miserably.

Peavy turned from her and stood at the window for a moment.

Sissel used the moment to think. What could she do? Was there some way to leave a sign for Stieg?

CHAPTER FORTY

Seventy-eight miles away, Hanne gasped. She was punching down the dough for the evening's bread.

"What is it, sunshine?" Witri asked her. "You daydreaming about that ranch of yours?"

She had told Witri about Owen's sad news, and the providence it bore them. He made the appropriate offers of condolence, but he'd also been to the Double B, and he'd spent a good amount of time telling her about the well-appointed ranch house, the large barns, and the many, many acres of good pasture.

An image gripped her. Sissel! Sissel cuffed on the side of the head. The feeling of it possessed her. Pain. A terrible shock. Danger.

"Oh!" Hanne said. She stepped back from the table, and the dough clung to her hands, sliding to the ground.

"I'm sorry," she said. She bent and retrieved the dough. Witri reached over and plucked it from her hands. He brushed the dirt off.

"I'm so sorry," Hanne said.

"Oh, they won't notice," Witri said.

"No," she said. "I have to go."

"What?"

"Something's wrong," she said. "I can't explain."

Witri put a plump hand over her wrist.

"Take a breath, child."

"Something is wrong at home, Witri. I have to go."

She went up to the front of the chuck wagon, where the personal gear of the cowboys was stored, next to the jockey box. She climbed halfway up, tugging and pulling at her saddle for Jigsaw. It was the only saddle stored there, as all the other rigs were in constant use.

She hauled it out and lugged it toward the remuda, where Jigsaw was kept with the other horses.

"What do you mean, go?" Witri called after her. He hustled, trailing her. "I need your help here, missy."

"You got along fine without me before," she said, straining to carry the heavy rig.

"Hanne Bennett! You quit this playing! It ain't funny!"

She didn't stop.

"Now I ain't gonna pay you for just a couple weeks' work, you know," he called, hustling after her. "You gotta see the drive through before you get paid."

"Mr. Lester," she called to the horse master. "I need Jigsaw saddled."

Witri put a firm hand on her shoulder.

"Hanne Bennett, we've gotten to be friends, you and I. You know we have. Tell me what's going on or I won't sleep at night!"

There was genuine concern on his face.

Hanne felt another wave coming from Sissel. Hanne could feel

Sissel's heart pounding; her sister was afraid for her life. Hanne pressed her hands over her heart. Her breath caught in her throat.

She put her own hand on Witri's shoulder, mirroring him.

"Listen," she said. "I'll tell you the truth. When people I love are in danger, I can sense it. That's a secret, between the two of us. And right now my sister's in trouble. I have to go."

"Dang it," he said. "I believe you."

He kicked a clod of dirt.

"Swing back by the chuck wagon and I'll send you with supper."

He tramped away sullenly.

Lester came leading Jigsaw on his rope line.

Hanne's frantic hands fumbled with her saddle, but the seasoned horse man helped her. He had Jigsaw saddled quickly. He even cupped his hands to help her mount.

She raced the horse toward Owen.

"It's Sissel," she called as she rode up.

Daisy was wagging her tail, happy to see Hanne and Jigsaw.

"I have to go," she said. "Right now. You can stay. It's fine if you want to stay but I have to go."

"What did you feel?"

"She was struck," Hanne said. "And she was scared."

"Well, that could be a lot of things . . . ," Owen said.

Hanne wheeled Jigsaw around.

"Catch up if you want to come," she called over her shoulder. "Or I'll come back and find you when I'm sure she's all right."

She kicked Jigsaw, and the horse jumped to a gallop.

"I'm coming!" Owen shouted. She heard him kick his horse into a gallop. "But I have to trade my horse for Brandy . . . And I have to tell Tincher!"

"I can't wait!" she yelled. The sensation of danger was so strong she felt she could follow her sense of Sissel all the way back to Carter.

There was a whistling sound, and then a rope landed neatly around her shoulders, pinning her arms down. Owen had lassoed her! The shock of it made her lean back, and Jigsaw slowed her pace.

"Goddamn it, Hanne!" Owen cussed. "It's three-day ride to Carter. Fifteen minutes won't make a difference."

CHAPTER FORTY-ONE

Clements asked a question; Sissel felt it in the resonance of his chest behind her back.

Peavy began to answer. He talked on and on, and her hearing came back midway through. "They're on the way in number. I told them I could handle it, but with the client in transit they wanted lots of manpower here. Oh, you'll meet the big boys. Jasper O'Brien, out of Denver. Tyrone Baker, he's practically famous."

Sissel's expression must have registered she'd heard him because Peavy came close and peered into her eyes.

"So you really have magic powers! Now it all makes sense, why McKray was courting you, why the Baron wants you so bad."

Sissel shrugged.

"Try it again and I'll start carving up your beau, got it? Say, 'Yes, sir.'"

"Yes, sir."

"Listen to me, young miss, I've been a Pinkerton for thirty-four years. I've tracked and captured some terrible men in my life. Terrible men who did bloody, awful things I can't even mention in your company. It's made me a bit hard-hearted.

"But I don't need to be rough with you, or with your brother Stieg, who is currently on his way to get Knut. Or Hanne and Owen, now working the Bar S cattle drive somewhere around Auburn.

"No, I want you all to live long, healthy lives! I want to deliver you to the Baron in the best of health. Hell, I'll get a bonus if I do! Look at this."

He held out a telegram. Sissel read it.

"See, you're the item. And the other items are your sister and your brothers. *Forfeit*, in this application, means kill. You understand? This means my Pinkerton pals will kill them unless you do just as I say. If you understand say, 'Yes, sir.'"

"Yes, sir."

Sissel's skull was pounding, and her arms hurt from how tight Clements was holding them.

"Good."

Peavy crossed back over to James, who was still unconscious.

"Wake up." Peavy said. He jabbed James's shoulder with the tip of the knife. James jerked awake.

"Time to go, James," Peavy said loudly. "Now, here's what's going to happen. We four are going to walk out of here. Easy. Relaxed. Like we're all good friends. Anyone asks what happened to you, James, you say you got in a fistfight last night. You'll look ashamed. Sissel will look disapproving. I'll look like a steamed-off father. I'll explain we're taking you to the doctor to get your lip sewed up.

"There's a nice coach waiting outside. We'll all slip right in and be on our way. Sound good?"

Peavy slid his fingers under the rope holding James's gag and slit it with the knife.

"That sound good to you, James?"

"Yes, sir," he said, his voice sounding dry and constrained. James worked his jaw tenderly. "Not so sure I can walk."

"That's all right. I'll have my arm under you, James, looking right supportive. And if you try anything I'll stab you in the ribs. It'll all work great."

Peavy set to untying James.

Clements released Sissel, and she rubbed at her sore shoulders.

"Up we go," Peavy said, heaving James to his feet.

"Clements, you go on ahead. Go out the back door and around the front. Loiter on the porch like you got business with Mr. McKray. Nearly everyone does in town these days. Go on."

Clements edged out the door.

Peavy sighed as he looked at Sissel.

"Poor star-crossed lovers. I'm sorry it's got to end this way." He poked James with the knife. "Give the girl an apology."

James squinted at her through his one good eye. "I'm sorry," he said. "I tried to warn you. I came here to—"

"No chatter, Romeo," Peavy cut him off. "It's time for our little show. Sissel, you go first. And just think about your sister and your brother and your other brother, and how happy you are they have their eyes, their livers, and their kidneys, that kind of stuff."

It was so strange to walk down the hallway she had walked down so many times in a natural, normal state, only this time being kidnapped.

They came toward a wealthy couple who, seeing James in the hall, gasped and murmured.

"I know, I know," Peavy said in a genial tone. "My son looks worse than he feels! Gonna get him to the doctor."

They took their time down the stairs. James moaned at each step.

Collier was not at the front desk. It was one of the young porters, looking nervous to be holding down the post and trying to placate a ticked-off prospector. Sissel couldn't think of any way to signal them or to do much of anything, and then they were out in the street.

A large black passenger carriage stood at the ready, drawn by four horses. The shades were down.

A lean-faced man with gray hair and gray eyes stood next to the carriage. He held the door open and took Sissel by the arm.

"Miss," he said politely.

Sissel took one look back over her shoulder, lingering, hoping to see McKray or Bridget or someone she knew. Without a word, the man stepped close behind her, blocking the view of her from passersby. He put his hands on her waist and hoisted her easily into the carriage. Someone else grabbed her arms from inside and hauled her in. She strained in the seat, looking out the window.

James, coming out of the hotel, started to drag his feet. "Wait!" he said. "Help!"

Peavy seemed to rejigger his hold on the young man, as if to keep him from slipping, but Sissel saw the knife flash at James's hip.

James moaned, sagged to the side.

"All right, son, don't worry. I've got a stage right here." Peavy seemed terribly worried. "Make way, please."

Peavy half dragged James to the carriage door. Blood was trailing them from James's left leg.

"Come on, son," Peavy said.

The gray-eyed man helped Peavy hoist James into the carriage.

Sissel tried to touch him, to move to him, but there was a man holding her fast in the dim cabin. He was a lanky black man who had a hand over her mouth. He was so strong she could barely move at all.

"To the doctor," Peavy cried for the benefit of the men watching outside. The man with the gray eyes tapped on the roof.

The carriage lurched forward. James slid off the seat, so he was sitting on the floor of the coach. He gasped. Gasped again.

Sissel could see blood pooling on the floor of the carriage.

"Jesus!" Peavy swore.

"Making a mess of the carriage," the man with gray eyes said.

"Hello, O'Brien," Peavy said. He nodded to the man who held Sissel. "Baker."

Peavy kicked James in the side. "I didn't hire this son of a bitch. I got stuck with him, so don't blame me."

"Where will we pitch him?" Baker asked.

James's eyes were open, staring straight up.

Sissel realized he was dead. She began to scream—she could not stop herself. The horror of the boy she knew shifting around on the floor as the carriage jostled. She screamed and sobbed, biting the hand over her mouth.

"She's biting me," the man named Baker said calmly.

"Put her out," O'Brien said.

Then a cloth soaked with a foul-smelling chemical was pressed over her nose and mouth. She gagged, nearly retched.

Everything went calm and quiet.

CHAPTER FORTY-TWO

Sissel woke to a kind touch on her forehead. A cool cloth, dabbing her temple, the area bruised and sensitive.

Then it came rushing back—the carriage, Peavy, James yelling for help, James dead on the floor.

She was outside, on a hillside, lying on a cot. A wool blanket was tucked in around her, and there was a gag in her mouth, a piece of linen, slick with her saliva.

She struggled for a second, found her hands and ankles were bound.

"Shhh," a male voice said. "You're safe, little miss."

A man with a face out of a nightmare was smiling down at her, kneeling at her hip. A scar ran from the inside corner of his left eyebrow down through the cheek and to his mouth. It was a messy scar, puckered and white against his tan face.

A whimper escaped Sissel.

"There, there," he said. "I know I present a frightening facade, but

I promise you, I am the soul of gentleness. My name is Dr. Oakman. The Pinkertons hired me to make sure you are hale and healthy when the Baron arrives."

Sissel's eyes darted around, taking in the camp. The sun was just going down, the sparse woods and boulders around them tinted orange. There was already a campfire. Three men were seated around it. Two other men were cooking at the fire.

Several others busied themselves near a large wagon, loaded with supplies, distributing bedrolls. She heard the sounds of horses nearby.

How many of them were there? She counted eight she could see, plus the doctor.

Dr. Oakman moved his hand toward her face, and Sissel jerked away.

"There, there, little one, no need to fear."

He dabbed again at the bruise on her temple, from where Clements had socked her.

Sissel's heart was pounding in her rib cage. She was afraid, for certain.

"Now, I need to remove this gag, little miss. I want to give you a tonic to help you rest and heal. They made me put the gag on you, but I'm hoping to leave it off now. I know it's not comfortable."

With cold, slim fingers, he untied the rope and removed the cloth.

Slowly, through her nose, Sissel took a deep breath. As soon as he removed the cloth, she shouted, "Help!" Her voice came out shrill, raspy. "Help me!"

Several men laughed at the campfire.

"Shut it!" she heard someone rebuke them.

Dr. Oakman frowned at her.

"No!" he said, as if scolding a dog. "That's very bad!"

Peavy and O'Brien, the gray-eyed man from the carriage, came over.

O'Brien took her jaw in his hand and turned her face gently to the left and right.

"We weren't properly introduced. I'm Jasper O'Brien, and I'm in charge now." Sissel saw Peavy shift with irritation.

"No one can hear you, Miss Hemstad. We're miles and miles away from anyone. Don't waste your energy. How do you feel?"

He seemed smart and normal and responsible, and this troubled Sissel more than any of the rest of it.

"Please," she said. "Please, let me go."

"Does your head hurt overmuch?" he asked.

"I've done nothing wrong," she pleaded.

The man continued as if he hadn't heard, speaking to Dr. Oakman. "Does she have a concussion?"

Peavy interrupted, "Clements hardly touched her. Like I said, she was using her powers on me—"

"I've heard enough from you," O'Brien said.

"Mr. O'Brien, it was not an easy task, to get a girl out of a busy hotel in the daylight—"

"I am not talking to you, Mr. Peavy. You can present your excuses for your incompetence to Mr. Pinkerton yourself when we get back to Chicago. Now you'll excuse us, I wish to talk to the doctor about the health of this young girl!"

O'Brien turned back toward Sissel. Peavy stood glowering at O'Brien's back, then tramped back to the fire.

"I don't know this Baron Fjelstad," Sissel said. "He has no right to have me held, you realize that, don't you? This is a crime."

Mr. O'Brien nodded; there was an air of regret on his face, as if he didn't like the job himself.

"Make her sleep," he said to the doctor.

CHAPTER FORTY-THREE

Owen did Hanne the favor of not speaking for the first half-day of the journey. He understood her need to ride hard and fast.

But when they drew to a stream, he told her they needed to let the horses drink, and forced her to eat one of the ham biscuits Witri had packed for them.

"What did Tincher say?" she asked.

"Very little," Owen said. "He was disappointed, but if we can make it back quickly, he'll allow us to rejoin the drive."

"Good," Hanne said. "I'll feel so stupid if we've left for nothing."

But she didn't feel like it was nothing. Ever since Mandry had been shot, there had been a sense of something creeping up on her. Some slow, hidden danger, like a cancer spreading, deadly and persistent.

"What did you feel? Back at the camp?" he said.

"First she felt a terrible shock. She was afraid for her life. Then someone hit her," Hanne said. "And now . . . now there's a slippery feeling. It's hard to describe. She feels like she's floating."

"Is she in danger right now?"

"No," Hanne said, her shoulders slumping. "Not that I can feel."

Owen thought about that as he chewed on a mouthful of biscuit. Daisy sat at his feet, and he tossed her a chunk, which she caught neatly out of the air.

"Then we need to slow down." He saw Hanne's position shift, saw her prepare to argue with him. "Just a little. If we ride our horses lame we'll have to go on foot."

"I never should have left her!" Hanne burst out. "This is my fault!"

"Whoa, now. There's no saying what's happened. Maybe she had a bad shock and fainted. Maybe what you felt was someone, I don't know, slapping her back to her senses . . ."

Hanne nodded, but that did not feel right at all.

"And you know another thing to take into account—"

"Can we ride now?" she interrupted.

ALL THE REST of the ride, and through the breaks Owen made them take when it got too dark to ride safely or when the horses needed rest, Hanne listened for her sister. There was nothing.

Maybe Owen was correct. Maybe Sissel was safe.

But when they finally got to Carter after two and a half days of hard riding, Hanne knew all was not as they'd left it.

The town was glutted with strangers, for one thing. She recognized only a few of the faces she saw. Most were men, prospectors, by the look of it. She felt tension in the town itself, like it was humming.

They rode up to the Royal, and Hanne slid off her horse, throwing the reins to Owen. She knew he would see to the horses. She couldn't care less about the horses.

She took the steps in two bounds and strode into the lobby. There stood the fussy Mr. Collier at the counter. His face lit up with surprise seeing her. She opened her mouth to speak, but it was Stieg she heard.

"Sister!"

She turned.

Stieg was seated in a slim, ornate armchair. In a matching chair next to him sat Isaiah McKray. Knut was behind them, seated on the floor, leaning against the wall. His face pure misery. All their faces drawn and gray.

They'd been waiting for her.

"Where is she?" Hanne said.

"Come this way," McKray said. He gestured to a door behind the front desk.

"Where is she?" Hanne crossed to Stieg and grabbed him by both arms.

"Taken," Stieg said, low enough that no one could hear. "And we can't find where."

"Collier, have the kitchen make up coffee and sandwiches," Mr. McKray said, then to Hanne, "Please, do come into my office where we can speak in private."

"What does he know?" Hanne asked Stieg of McKray.

"He knows everything," Stieg told her.

Hanne scowled at them both. McKray looked determined and unflappable.

"Sissel trusted him," Stieg said. "And after the past few days, I do, too."

Hanne stalked into the office. She heard Owen come in and greet Stieg and Knut. They all entered the oak-paneled room behind her.

"Does Collier know, too?" Hanne said to Stieg.

"He knows only that Sissel has been kidnapped," Stieg said.

"But McKray knows everything else?" she said. She did not try to hide her anger.

"He knows more than you do, Sister. Stop glowering at us all and listen. There is much I need to tell you!"

Everyone sat down, but Hanne would not, could not.

Stieg had sat down in an armchair near McKray's desk. He looked comfortable in the office and Hanne realized her brother had spent a lot of time in there in the past few days.

Stieg leaned over, resting his elbows on his knees.

"Sissel has a Nytte," he said. "Shortly after you left, it developed. And you should know that her health immediately improved. She's much stronger now, Hanne, much—"

"What is the Nytte?" Hanne asked. "Is she a Shipwright?" That seemed the only reasonable guess.

"She's a Ransacker."

Hanne put her hand out to steady herself against the wood paneled wall.

"A Ransacker? But how can that be? Are you sure?"

"She can find metal, Hanne, and pull it to her—"

Hanne took this in, then burst out, "Why didn't you tell me? Why didn't you . . . send word? Or come for us?"

Stieg held his hands up.

"How were we to find you? And she wanted to surprise you, Hanne! She wanted to get strong and find gold and make up our fortunes— look, it doesn't matter why we didn't tell you, she's been taken."

"Who took her?"

"As best we can tell, it was Mr. Peavy," McKray said.

"From the general store?" Owen asked.

"That's the one."

"James's father?" Hanne said.

Stieg scrubbed his hand over his face.

"Several employees saw her leave the hotel with James and Peavy. James had been beaten badly. Peavy told onlookers he was taking him to the doctor, but they never arrived."

Hanne was clenching her teeth together, her hands in fists.

"McKray has been helping us to search for her. We've kept it quiet. Obviously we didn't want to involve the law."

"If I can weigh in, I think it's time to call the sheriff," McKray said.

"We can't," Hanne said.

She focused her gaze on Isaiah McKray. The sleeves to his shirt were rolled up, the collar rumpled. There were shadows under his eyes, a trace of beard on his jaw.

To his credit, McKray didn't flinch from her examination.

"That's what Stieg told me," McKray continued. "And I know about the former warrant on Knut as well."

"Stieg!" Hanne said.

"He found out on his own months ago. It turns out he can keep a secret," Stieg said.

"But the law doesn't need to know about the Knit-tah thing you all have," McKray interjected. "They don't need to know how you came here, any of that. Sissel's been kidnapped, and we know who did it. They'll put out a reward on Peavy. They'll hunt him down."

"No," Hanne said. "If we are trusting you, then you will trust us. I can find her myself."

Stieg let out a breath. "That's what I told him."

* * *

WHEN SISSEL WOKE it was midday. She was terribly thirsty, and hungry, and hot under the blanket.

The Pinkertons had set up a makeshift sun shelter above her. Two stout, sharpened sticks had been planted in the ground. A length of canvas was stretched between them, anchored to the ground behind her and stabilized by two thin ropes attached to heavy rocks in the front.

There was another such tent fashioned nearby. Dr. Oakman and two other men sat underneath it, playing cards. She did not see Peavy or O'Brien.

Sissel fought her thirst. The doctor might dose her with laudanum again if he knew she was awake. She needed to think and to plan.

She lay still and opened her senses to the metals in the camp. She did not know what she would do with them, but she wanted to know what was at hand.

First Sissel felt shiny, flimsy reverberations around her. It was tin, lots of it. Tin plates and utensils . . .

Then she touched on shotguns held by the men near the campfire. The vibration of long lengths of steel were augmented with gunmetal, a monstrous alloy of bright, flashy copper with sickening lead and green-tasting zinc. The guns were like eels, slippery and vicious. They'd bite her if they could.

Casting farther out, she found a large collection of guns, all stored together a distance up the mountain. She had to reach for them as if they were buried, through rock. They must have stored additional firearms in a cave.

She drew her sense back. For a moment she had to close her eyes and rest. Dizziness and nausea threatened to overtake her.

She was weak, she noted. She needed to eat.

Sissel cast her sense out again. Could it be that she'd find some nearby farm? Maybe she could get someone's attention somehow. Maybe send them a signal?

Sissel imagined herself a beacon, sending out a signal all around, searching, searching for metals to speak to.

She felt six more of those shotguns spaced evenly below the mountainside camp in a perfect half circle.

Sissel let the Nytte drop. Tears flooded her eyes. She didn't want to feel hopeless. She wanted to believe Hanne would find her and she would be rescued, but it was hard when faced with the certain knowledge of six shotguns pointed outward and herself in the center.

When her hearing came back, she gave into her thirst.

"Water," she croaked. "Please."

Dr. Oakman came over straightaway.

"My little one," he said. The puckered white scar running across his left cheek made his smile seem a sinister sneer.

He helped her to sit up.

"Bring some fresh water," he ordered the man in the tent. "And start the broth to warm."

One of the men playing cards got up quickly and moved to the supply wagon. He wore an apron and held a pipe clenched between his teeth—the cook, Sissel reasoned.

"You must be famished," the doctor said. "I have a special broth laid by. Pork and ginseng—reviving and strengthening. After such a sleep as you've had, you must take broth first or you'll be sick. Then I'll have the cook make you some toast and jam. If you keep that down, I'll have him scramble you some eggs. How does that sound?"

The doctor spoke to her with a forced and patronizing jollity, as if he were a nursemaid and she a pouty ten-year-old. Sissel could hardly bring herself to look at him.

The cook brought over a tin cup of water. Dr. Oakman held it up to her mouth. Sissel hunched forward eagerly.

She would have drained the cup, but he allowed her only a couple of mouthfuls.

"Now we wait a moment, then you can have more."

Sissel sat, looking at her bound wrists, avoiding the doctor's eyes and thinking of what to do. Could Hanne be in Carter by now? Rolf had once said that Berserkers could sense danger to their clan from leagues away. Certainly Hanne would have felt it when the brute Clements had struck her.

In fact, she thought, Hanne might be close enough to feel it if Sissel was hurt again.

The doctor didn't seem to like Sissel's silence. He tapped the binds at her wrists, pointing out that the ropes had been padded with strips of silk.

"I didn't want your wrists to become chafed," he said.

"Thank you," she said, her voice small and hoarse. "That was thoughtful."

"Some of these men are little more than butchers," he said. "And I travel with them, patching them up. Such is my lot! It's a rather nice change for me to have someone young and pretty to care for." He brought the tin cup back up to her lips.

She gulped as much water as he would let her have.

"Easy, easy," he chided.

"Can you tell me where we are?" she asked. She added a shade of fear to her voice. "Are we very far into the wilderness?"

"Oh gosh, I don't know myself," he said. "We're in the hills. Came north a bit. The roads twist all around, don't they? Me, I just came along with the wagon!" He smiled.

"What day is it? Is it Saturday?"

"Sunday!" he said, as if telling her the punch line to a joke. "You've had quite the sleep!"

Now the cook came with the cup of broth. Steam issued from the cup, and he was using his apron to shield his hand from the hot handle.

Sissel's pulse quickened. Here was a chance.

As the cook bent down to set the cup on a flat rock near Dr. Oakman's hip, she reached for the Nytte.

She gritted her teeth and batted the cup toward herself with the Nytte. The liquid splashed down onto her arms and shoulders. Some of it landed on the sleeve of her dress, but enough of the steaming-hot broth fell on her left arm and the back of her hand that she felt sharp, boiling pain.

HANNE WAS RUBBING Jigsaw down with a piece of gunny sack. As dignified a mount as he was, Jigsaw made ecstatic faces as she worked.

McKray and Owen were arguing with the livery master about which horse from his stock might be strong enough to bear Knut's considerable weight, when Hanne's head jerked up. Sissel had been burned!

Hanne grabbed Jigsaw's mane and swung up onto the horse, kicked him into a gallop.

"Wait!" Stieg called. But Hanne raced out of the stable, holding on to the horse's mane.

An old miner leading a mule and cart cussed at Hanne as she and her horse sprang out into the road.

"We've got to follow her!" she heard Owen shouting.

SISSEL BREATHED THROUGH gritted teeth. The burns stung as Dr. Oakman applied ointment and bandages. Low, angry red blisters had welted up on the back of her hand where the broth had touched her.

Dr. Oakman had cursed the cook to the devil and beyond. Oakman made a slit at the shoulder of Sissel's tan dress so he could treat the blistering skin underneath. He did not untie her wrists though, despite her assurances that she would not try anything.

Sissel scanned the woods outside the circle of the campsite for movement. She saw nothing.

The ointment the doctor applied seemed to be helping. She didn't want that. She needed the pain.

The cook brought another cup of the broth, walking very slowly. This broth was cooled to lukewarm. Sissel sipped it greedily and planned and waited.

The blisters throbbed, but she wondered if that steady kind of pain was the kind that would bring a Berserker on the run. She suspected not.

OWEN, STIEG, KNUT, and McKray caught up with Hanne about twenty minutes later. The trail had gone cold, and Hanne was off Jigsaw by then, pacing through the woods, looking for tracks. Daisy joined her, sniffing the ground, circling like she'd lost something in the brush.

Owen had brought Jigsaw's bridle and saddle. He didn't say a word to Hanne, just saddled Jigsaw and gave him some oats.

Hanne sat on the ground. She spat into the dirt and worked up a little paste of mud.

Using it as paint, she drew runes on her face.

Odin's rune, the *Othala*, to ask for protection, guidance, success. The *Fehu*, Freya's sign. Thor's rune for aggression.

She began to pray. Knut came and knelt behind her. He put one of his broad, beefy hands on her shoulder and began to echo her prayers in his deep voice.

McKray watched them from beside his horse.

Hanne cared not a whit what he thought.

"She's asking the Gods to help her," Stieg said. "Praying for control."

She was not praying for control, far from it. She was praying for power and vengeance.

THE LUNCHTIME MEAL had been prepared. The men came to eat in shifts. Sissel waited until she saw Peavy take his plate.

"Who's running the store, Mr. Peavy?" she called across the camp.

"Oh," Peavy said. "I expect Howie's got it all under control." He set his plate down on a rock and strode over to peer down at her.

"Aw, look at your pretty skin, all marred with blisters. I told them you'd pull some nasty trick, but they didn't believe me."

"Do they know about all the money you've been stealing from the store?" Sissel said loudly.

She didn't know it to be true, but the way Peavy twitched, she reckoned she'd struck a chord.

"Were you really keeping an eye on me and my family, because it seemed like you really enjoyed playing store."

"Shut it!" Peavy said. Baker and a couple of other men had wandered closer, clearly listening.

"And there's all the whiskey you drank—"

Peavy grabbed her by the shoulder and shook her. Not enough.

"He was the joke of the town!" Sissel called to the other men. "The great, fat joke—"

Peavy slapped her across the face. "I said shut it!"

"Peavy!" came O'Brien's voice roaring across the camp. "Get away from her! You talk to her again, or so much as look at her, you're going back to Chicago in a casket."

"She's lying!"

"She's a sixteen-year-old child trying to bait you, you buffoon."

Sissel's cheek stung. The inside of her mouth had been cut by her teeth. She spat out some blood.

She brought her two bound hands up to fish a hair from her mouth with her fingers. She pressed her pointer finger into her mouth, making the wound hurt.

Was it enough?

"Come, Hanne," Sissel prayed. "Find me."

CHAPTER FORTY-FOUR

Hanne scouted away from the others. She told them to follow, if they wanted to, but to keep back. She wanted nothing to do with them, did not even want to let their questions break her focus, not for a second.

All she wanted, now, was for her Berserker sense to possess her.

There!

She turned her head toward the sensation. Sissel was smacked. Her mouth cut and bleeding. It was not enough to show Hanne where to go.

The fleeting image was gone.

"Take me," Hanne moaned helplessly. To be on the edge of her Nytte this way, neither fully possessed by it, nor having it at rest, was anguishing. And with her sister in danger? Anguish in heart and body.

She wanted the monster Berserker to come possess her. She wanted swift, merciless action.

"Take me!" she shouted.

*　*　*

O'BRIEN WALKED AWAY from Sissel, still shouting at Peavy.

Sissel took a deep breath and threw herself forward off the cot. She smashed down onto the ground and drove her head against a large, flat stone.

Her head made a thwacking sound against the stone. It cut into her head. She jerked her head up again and brought it slamming down.

"Sir!" one of the men shouted, pointing. O'Brien turned around and launched himself at her. He prevented her from hitting her head a third time.

"Oakman!" he yelled. "Where's the damn doctor? Oakman!"

Blood and snot and tears were running down Sissel's face.

"I'm right here!" Oakman ran out of the woods, buttoning his pants. "For heaven's sake! What happened?"

"Oh, find me, Hanne. Find me," Sissel prayed.

HANNE RAN.

Finally, finally, the Nytte possessed her fully and she stopped thinking. Only ran. Up, up, through the trees.

Pine needles, dirt, thin trees, dark shadows. Sissel was up ahead.

There! A man with a long rifle.

Someone to kill, finally.

The man hid at the base of a large conifer. Two barrels aimed out from the crook of his arm. Eyes shaded by a flat-brimmed hat.

Hanne did not care to be quiet. She came running at him.

"Stop!" he shouted. Then he fired. A chunk of tree at her shoulder exploded. She ran on. Another shot. Pine bough shattered above her head. Three more steps.

She crashed onto him, snatching the gun from his hands. She pressed it onto his throat.

The man's hat had fallen off. His hair was the color of cinnamon. He struggled to heave her off him, his hands clutching the rifle as she crushed his throat with it.

Even before his coarse gasps stopped and his eyes went wide, then lifeless, Hanne was locating the next target.

"Pryor?" a voice called.

Her Nytte let her see—a big man, clothed in a green coat, aiming another rifle in her direction from a ways off.

Hanne crept over the dead man, pried the gun from his dead-claw grip. Perhaps she'd use it as a club.

Her lot were behind her; she could sense them vaguely. They were not in danger. Sissel was ahead, up the mountain.

The woods had gone all silent. The quiet of stalking and hunting. The birds held their song. Men held their breath.

AT THE SOUND of a shot, Sissel began to weep with thanks. She lay back.

It was only a matter of time now.

Oakman was measuring out a dose of laudanum, but at the sound of the shot chaos erupted in the camp. He dropped the bottle and it shattered.

HANNE COULD SEE every leaf in detail; every pine needle stood apart from its fellows. The second man was hiding behind a bush, his belly flat to the ground. His breathing was fast. He was trying to steady it.

She darted through the trees, her feet soft on the carpet of pine needles.

"Hanne!" came a distant shout. Owen.

She stilled herself, but the man caught sight of her.

He fired.

Now Hanne dashed for him. She ran straight at him. He fired again, and she dipped her shoulder. The bullet went screaming past to blow a hole in a bystanding tree.

The man was at a disadvantage, lying under that brush. His clever hiding spot meant he could not up and run. He backed frantically out on his hands and knees.

Hanne helped him. She grabbed him by the ankles and threw her weight backward, hauling him out.

He mule-kicked her in the face, landing the blow at her jaw. She tasted blood and smiled.

"Please," she said, her voice a low rumble, "let's fight."

The man scrambled to his feet. He was big boned and well muscled. A squashed nose from some previous fight. Tawny skin, dark hair. An ear like a mashed potato.

He drew a bowie knife from a sheath at his hip.

"I don't want to hurt you," he said.

"Shut up and fight."

Now the dance of darting and feigning. He swung, she dipped away. He passed the knife to his other hand. Wiped sweat on his pants.

He lunged at her and she slipped under his arm, elbowed him in the kidneys. He took the blow with only a grunt and swung again. The blade grazed her arm. A bright slash of red opened up.

Hanne retreated, clutching her arm. A tree was behind her, and she pressed her back to it.

The man thought he had an advantage. He came forward. As he swung, Hanne reached up and grabbed the tree trunk. She lifted her legs and double kicked him in the chest.

He staggered backward. The knife skittered out of his hand into the pine needles. Hanne launched herself from the tree, kicking him again. He hit the ground hard.

Hanne straddled his head. He reached for the knife, just out of reach.

Hanne pushed her cut forearm into the man's mouth. Pushing it down so he could not bite or breathe.

He choked on it. Eyes wide in horror. Her blood coating his lips and whiskers.

Hanne heard a noise in the wood. Aha! There was another sneaking up! Slipping from tree to tree. Now she had to finish this one.

She hammered on the sides of his skull. One, two, three and he was dead.

The sneaking-up man saw Hanne kill his comrade.

Wide-eyed, he backed away.

Then he shouted, "Fall back!"

He cupped a hand over his mouth and hollered, loud, "Fall back!"

SISSEL FELT MOISTURE on her face. Light rain.

Sissel could have laughed for happiness. Stieg! Rain meant Stieg, she was sure of it. With the rain came a billowing fog. Within moments, thick mist cloaked the entire camp. Oakman had left her side to locate another bottle of laudanum.

"Who called to fall back?" Hall demanded.

"I couldn't tell, sir," said another man.

The men cursed as the fog enveloped the camp. She heard the table clatter down as someone shinned his knee on it.

"Damn this mist!" one of them yelled.

"Runner, report in!" shouted Hall. "Baker, you stick with the girl. Take care of her."

Baker was the man who had restrained her in the carriage.

He strode over and nodded to her respectfully. "Miss."

Baker took a cloth from the doctor's kit. He started wrapping it around Sissel's bleeding head.

"I can do that!" Oakman said, returning, but Baker ignored him.

"Fall back!" O'Brien shouted.

Baker picked Sissel up, her hands and feet bound, and heaved her over his shoulder. He stormed through the campsite, heading uphill, likely toward wherever it was they had stashed their cache of guns.

Slung over his shoulder, Sissel could see nothing but the backs of the man's legs. The fog was so thick that as he moved an eddy of clear air swirled behind each leg.

Soon, she told herself. Her siblings would save her soon.

HANNE RAN DOWN the squealer. He didn't even try to fire, was just running for all he was worth toward the top of the hill.

Ah. It was no fun to kill a man fleeing.

Hanne picked up a rock and fired it at his head. He fell and lay twitching facedown on the ground.

She stalked over. The rock had struck the back of his skull, above the neck, and now that part was spurting blood. He was dead enough. There was a good knife tucked into his belt, and she took it.

Hanne looked up the mountain. She heard her brothers and Owen running up behind her.

"Oh, Hanne," Owen said.

"Come back to yourself, Sister," Stieg said. He was squinting against the daylight, a sign of a headache. "Say the words with me, '*Ásáheill, heill, Odin! Heill, Thor!*' Call them to you."

Stieg put a hand on her shoulder, and she leveled a look of incredulity at him that he should touch her. He drew it away. She could see he was scared of her, and that was right.

"I've created a fog," Stieg said. "We can steal her away if we are smart about it. No one else needs to die."

Hanne could not tolerate this standing and talking. She began to move up the hill.

"Hanne, you don't want this!" Owen called after her.

She ignored his soft words, and they floated right off, like all words do when the time for killing has begun.

BAKER WAS CLIMBING up the rocky trail, past glacial boulders, through shallow drifts of scree. His breathing was labored.

Sissel bumped and banged, her stomach flattened against his muscular shoulder, her face against the top rise of his backside. She hardly cared about that, just tried to keep her head from cracking into rocks. Her bound hands swung down, wrists blistered and chafing.

Behind them on the trail, the other Pinkertons were following. She heard them cursing the rocks and the fog and the gear they carried.

There was another round of gunfire.

"Hurry up!" someone called to someone else below them.

Baker reached some kind of plateau.

"Everyone coming?" a voice said from just above.

"Yes," Baker answered.

"I heard the shots."

He bent over and placed her on the rocky ground. They were at a small flat landing; the peak of the mountain rose above them, all sheer rock, with scree collected in some places. Baker put his hands on his hips and breathed deeply. "Thin air," he said.

A burly man in a black suit stood at the entrance to a large, jagged fissure in the rock. A cave.

This fit together with what Sissel had gathered with her Nytte. The guns she had felt had been behind stone.

"Get her in," the man in the black suit said. "Put her well to the back. I laid blankets there to keep her comfortable."

"Wait," Sissel said, trying to stall. "May I please use the bushes to . . . you know?"

"No," the man said. "Piss yourself for all we care. Get her in."

"No need to be rude, Shaw. She's just a girl," Baker said.

Baker picked Sissel up again, this time carrying her as a man would his bride.

Ducking his head, he stepped through the mouth of the cave.

A MAN WITH a white scar running down his face came stumbling out of the mist. He was looking over his shoulder as he ran and nearly collided with Hanne.

All she had to do was reach out and grab him.

"My sister?" Hanne said.

"Let me go," the man said. "We're under attack!"

Hanne slid the knife from the other dead man into this soon-to-be-dead man's belly.

"I know," she said.

INSIDE THE CAVE it was dim. Sissel's eyes fought the green mists of light blindness as they adjusted.

Baker must have had trouble seeing, too. He stopped, not wanting to place a foot wrong.

Shaw came up behind them. "Her pallet's in the back. You'll see." He lit a match and put it to the wick of a lantern, then lowered the glass globe.

The light spilled out. The space cleared overhead, rising steeply from the low mouth of the cave. The ground was studded with sharp rocks, not at all flat. Sissel could see some blankets placed at the back wall of the cave, under a low ledge of rock.

Two crates stood near the mouth. Sissel assumed they were full of guns. Next to one of the crates was a large machine of some kind, covered with a black cloth. It was on a tripod; she could see legs protruding under the cloth, angled out and mechanically adjusted to be flat on the uneven ground. A telescope, she figured, for spotting the enemy. These men didn't seem given to half measures. It figured they would bring expensive gear.

Shaw set the lantern onto a natural rock shelf on the wall. It sat slightly sideways.

Peavy pushed in behind Shaw. In his hand he carried a gunnysack, Sissel assumed, with supplies of food. In the other was a long rifle.

"Hope everyone makes it up," Shaw said to Peavy.

"Can't say I like this plan," Peavy answered.

O'Brien came in right behind him.

"You don't have to like it, Peavy, you just have to do it," O'Brien said. He blew out a tired breath.

"How is she?"

Sissel expected Baker to answer, but instead Shaw took hold of the black cloth covering the telescope and pulled.

It was not a telescope.

It was a gleaming Gatling gun, brass and black steel, ten barrels extending from the rounded hopper. Ten barrels aimed at the mouth of the cave, where her Hanne would come running.

HANNE TRAILED TWO big men as they climbed up through the crevices and nooks of the lower mountainside. The fog was thick around them.

"I'm just sayin' it's spooky. Fog, midday, July?" one of them said, a redheaded man. He was scared and trying to cover. He had two pistols holstered at his hip as well as a shotgun.

"Follow orders and move your tail," the other said. He was small and lithe. Moved with a feline grace. He'd be more satisfying to kill than the other.

The two men held shotguns awkwardly as they shinnied through the tight places between boulders, and they even had to set them aside at times when scrambling up.

Hanne walked lightly on the rough scree. Her footsteps were nearly silent. She came closer and closer. Their death was following them, now just the length of a horse away, and they clattered on, oblivious.

Suddenly Hanne was seized from behind.

She writhed. Kicked. Someone terrifically strong had her!

"Lower your weapons," Owen's voice shouted to the men ahead.

"You're surrounded," McKray said.

Stieg, Owen, McKray, they all stepped out from the mist, above, below, surrounding the two Pinkertons.

"Please, Hanne, don't fight," a sweet voice said in her ear.

She forced a breath through her nose. This boy was beloved to her. He was of her family, and she could not harm him. Nevertheless, she strained against his massive strength and let out a mangled howl of frustration.

"Hold her, Knut!" Stieg shouted. "Hanne, we need to ask them some questions. We need to know who they are and why they took Sissel."

"Put down your guns!" Owen shouted to the men again.

"Let's all be calm," the smarter one said. He bent down slowly and set his rifle onto a rock. The redheaded man made a show of lowering his rifle to the ground, but on the way up, he drew both his pistols. He aimed one at Owen and one at Stieg, arms open.

The rage burned so hard Hanne could hardly bear it. Her hands wanted to strangle, her feet to kick, her teeth to bite that man dead.

"Throw down your pistols or we will let her kill you," Stieg said.

The redhead snorted. "Let me tell you kids, I'm a very good shot."

"Oh, she'll kill you," McKray said. "I've never seen anything like it. Four of your company are already dead at her hand. One she choked to death with his own Winchester, one she felled with a rock, one she pounded on his head till he died, and the last one she killed with a knife."

"Lower your guns, Adam," the smarter one said.

"I can hit them both at the same time."

"If Knut lets her go, you'll be dead before the bullets leave the gun," Stieg said.

"I'm game to see that!" the redhead scoffed.

"Adam! Set down your fancy goddamn pistols. Now!"

The redhead spat on the ground to show what he thought of the order. He slowly put down his shining guns.

Hanne felt Knut take a deep breath of relief. He released his hold on her, thinking, perhaps, the danger was past.

She darted forward. In three steps she had the redhead by the hair. She forced his head backward until he fell onto his back, then she put her boot on the side of his skull.

"Easy, Hanne, easy!" said Owen. He rushed to her side.

"Ask what you want," she said. She added just enough pressure to make him gasp in pain. "He'll answer."

They learned the men were Pinkertons, professional detectives. Hired by the Baron Fjelstad, who was on his way, and that they had orders to protect Sissel at any cost to lives. Sissel was in a cave up above, with others guarding her.

Stieg directed Knut to hold on to the smart one, and Hanne was allowed to restrain the redhead, with a promise she would not kill him. Stieg, Owen, and McKray withdrew a few paces to discuss. They spoke in hushed tones—incredulous, fearful, angry. Pinkertons had kidnapped her? Peavy was one of them? What of James, then? And most of all they spoke of the Baron. The Baron was coming?

Talking, talking, talking. Like the chattering of starlings.

All Hanne had heard that was important was that Sissel was being held in a cave above them.

Finally, Owen and McKray came and bound the hands of the two men, using some rope Owen had brought from the horses. McKray hauled the redhead up, and the man spat again at his feet.

"I'd watch it if I were you," McKray said.

The redhead cussed and said such dirty curses that Owen shoved his bandanna in the man's mouth and tied it with more rope.

"Might as well gag the other one, too," McKray said. He used more rope and his own clean handkerchief to do so.

"Let's move," Owen said. He jabbed the redhead in the back with the barrel of his shotgun. Silenced and bound, the man started to climb, sending dirty looks over his shoulder from time to time.

FIVE PINKERTONS NOW crowded into the cave. Sissel sat at the back, on her pallet. The lamp sat nearby, throwing dancing shadows up the uneven rocky walls.

O'Brien had gone to the mouth of the cave and whistled three times.

They'd all listened.

No reply had come.

A few minutes later he whistled three times again. A signal, obviously.

Then he turned, grim faced. "Jesus Christ," he cursed. "We've lost six men?"

He turned to a young man. "You sure Smith was dead?"

"He was brained with a rock, sir. I saw the girl do it."

"What about the doctor?" O'Brien asked. "Oaktree?"

"Oakman, sir. He went running when the shooting started, sir."

"Goddamn it! All right. Shaw, set the gun," he said. "Men, make some space!" he told the Pinkertons crowded near the mouth of the cave. "You two help Shaw."

Several of the detectives helped move the massive gun and adjust the legs.

Now the Gatling gun stood in the center of the mouth of the cave, aiming out. Shaw was behind the gun, his fingers on the handles. Another man took the lid off one of the wooden cases, and Sissel saw hundreds of gleaming cartridges.

"Please," Sissel said. Her high voice cutting through the low mutterings of the men. "Let me talk to them. I'll get them to leave."

No one answered her.

"They are very young. Please!" Sissel cried. She rose from where she'd been sitting onto her knees. Held her bound hands in front of her, beseeching. "I beg you!"

"Quiet her," O'Brien said.

"Hanne!" she yelled, then Baker stuck a greasy cloth in her mouth and her cries were muffled.

"Damn this fog! Shoot at any sign of motion," O'Brien told the man behind the Gatling gun. "We keep the girl safe and alive at any cost."

"Yes, sir," Shaw said. He wiped his hands on his pants and gripped the handles again. It seemed to Sissel he was smiling.

OWEN AND MCKRAY forced the Pinkertons up the narrow path ahead of them.

Stieg used one hand to climb up the rocky trail. The other he kept pressed to his temples. He summoned all the fog he'd made and pushed it now ahead of them, issuing a slow, steady breath as best he could.

The fog was unnaturally dense and impenetrable. It was thick in Hanne's nose and throat.

They came up onto a ledge of rock, maybe ten feet across, and

Hanne saw it through the fog: the dark, jagged slash of the entrance to the cave. Sissel was there! Inside! So close now and all between them were bad men in need of dying.

Knut put a restraining hand on her shoulder.

"Steady, Hanne!" Stieg said.

Owen spoke to her. "We aim to trade these men for her. We'll get her back, I promise you."

Talk, talk, talk. Hanne grabbed her head. She felt like ripping it off.

SISSEL HAD TO save her siblings. She had to.

She cast inside, flinging her mind open to her Nytte. There was the giant gun: steel, brass, gunmetal. The alloyed metals clanged and clashed in her mind, ringing with sick triumph over her, so loud she felt her head would shake apart. She couldn't even touch the Gatling with her powers, much less control it or move it.

She let her Nytte drop and sagged down, slumped in a heap.

AS THEY APPROACHED the cave, the captured men began to call out urgently from behind their gags.

"We have your men," Stieg shouted. "We want to trade."

There was a pause; then a steady voice said, "Come get her."

Hanne moved forward, but Knut grabbed her by the arm.

"Wait!" he said.

Owen and McKray pushed the Pinkertons toward the cave's entrance. They dug their heels into the ground, struggling.

*　*　*

SISSEL DID NOT hear but felt the commotion. Baker stiffened beside her. All the Pinkertons shifted eagerly to see out the mouth of the cave. She saw Peavy leaning forward to watch.

Sissel crawled forward on her belly and got a clear line of sight through the legs of the men, through the legs of the tripod.

Two men with their hands tied were pushed out in front of the cave and mowed down, bullets shearing the air, discarded shells spurting from the Gatling gun like sparks from a blacksmith's forge.

The men reeled back, their bodies doing a sick jig from the bullets, and toppled to the ground. The mist around them was red with blood spray.

She saw Hall make a slashing motion with his hand to cut the fire, but it was too late. The men were dead.

HANNE TRIED TO break from Knut's restraining hand. His grip was like an iron band. "Sissel!" she shouted.

SISSEL THOUGHT OF her beautiful sister.

She could not allow Hanne to enter that jagged frame of sunlight and face the Gatling gun.

She cast her Nytte at the gun again. Though it sickened her, though it was like oil and acid flooding her mind, she cast her senses fully inside the wretched machine.

She identified brass! Brass she could pull. The small, lithe brass-cased bullets that sped through the steel barrels.

Sissel ground her teeth together and pulled those bullets hard enough to jerk the whole gun off its tripod.

The bullets ripped into the roof of the cave, firing through the neck of the man responsible for feeding the gun in a spray of blood. The Gatling gun ate the rest of the bullets in the chain, as the cave began to rain down rock.

The cave walls began to tremble, then the ground to heave.

A rock hit Peavy on the head and he fell.

Sissel saw Baker look up, confused.

He pushed her back, under the ledge of rock, then he threw himself down on top of her.

He's trying to save me, Sissel thought.

And the rocks continued to fall.

A TERRIBLE ENEMY was waiting inside the cave, a gun that spat out bullets faster than she could dodge them.

Hanne cast her eyes about. She needed a shield. Was there a rock she could carry in front of her?

Then there came a deep, low rumble from the cave.

"Look!" Owen cried.

A section of the rock wall high above began to shift and fall in on itself.

"No!" McKray shouted.

The rocks crumpled, as if sucked down by mud. Stieg, wonderstruck, let the mist fall all at once. A heavy white blanket settling on a bed.

Hanne broke from Knut's restraining arm and raced across the rocky ledge.

Dust and shale bellowed out of the cave. She was blinded. One man threw himself out, bumping into her. She pushed him away. She heard the cries of men inside snuffed out as the rocks crushed down. Sharp rocks skittered out the mouth of the cave. The cave was filled, fallen in on itself, and she could not enter. There was nowhere to go. She could not move forward. All was stone.

Hanne fell to her knees and howled.

CHAPTER FORTY-FIVE

Owen, Stieg, and McKray stared, shocked and grieved, at the rockfall where the mouth of the cave had been.

The survivor, a heavy-set man in a black suit, scooted back from the cave toward the edge. He crawled over the bodies of his shot-up companions and sneaked off over the ledge. No one thought to stop him.

Hanne lay where she had collapsed. She did not want to be consoled, or touched. Her Nytte had ebbed away, and she was herself again.

The hunger that came whenever she used her Nytte engulfed her, and she welcomed it.

All her worst nightmares had come to pass. She had become possessed by the Nytte again and slain men. But that was the least of it—she failed Sissel. Now Hanne only wanted to die so she could join her.

"Hanne must eat," she heard Stieg say.

"I'll go to the Pinkerton campsite and see what I can find," Owen said.

Hanne was curled up on her side. Tears coursed out of her eyes and ran down her face to the ground. Her body cried out for food. She clamped her arms around her stomach and shut her eyes.

Some time passed.

Daisy found her and licked at her face, wriggling with joy at being reunited. Hanne turned from her, pushed the dog away.

Owen came and put in front of her a loaf of brown bread and a leg of cured ham, almost whole, only a few slices shaved off the front of it. Her stomach rumbled and her mouth watered, and she turned her face from it.

Daisy lay down next to Hanne, tucking her body against Hanne's spine.

"I'm so sorry," Owen said. Kneeling beside her. "I don't even know what to say. But you have to eat, Hanne. Or you'll get sick . . ."

He took out his knife and began to hack off pieces of the ham, setting them on the ground near her. He also set his canteen near the bread.

"Please eat and drink, Hanne. Do that for me."

She heard love and tenderness in his voice.

It seemed impossible to find her way back to it. The Berserker had taken her too far over the edge. She didn't think she could navigate back to the mild Hanne or the Hanne the lover, or Hanne who had hope for the future.

She closed her eyes and would not speak. After a few moments Owen rose from her side and went back to the others.

There was no way Sissel could have survived the cave-in, they said. They were making plans to flee from the Baron. They were saying Hanne must eat and rest. They were saying, "Do we try to hide the bodies, or do we just run like hell?"

HANNE HEARD A THUMP. Then another thump.

"It's no use, Knut, you're wasting your strength," she heard Stieg say.

Then three thumps in rapid progress.

Hanne sat up.

Knut was clearing rocks from the mouth of the cave.

He was hurling them across the ledge, clearing room.

"She's gone, Knut."

Knut shook off Stieg's restraining hand and continued to move the rocks.

Hanne fumbled on the ground for the ham. She tore off a mouthful, and began to chew.

"McKray! You know there's no chance she could be alive in there. You're a mining man."

"It's a slim damn chance, that's for sure, but Knut has the right of it. We should dig."

McKray crossed to Knut and began to help.

Stieg and Owen stood back talking, then they, too, went to the mouth of the cave.

Hanne drank down some good, clean water.

She brought the bread with her and ate with one hand as she began to lift smaller rocks away with the other.

It was grisly business.

The first of the corpses were mangled so badly that both McKray and Stieg stepped away to vomit. Knut continued lifting out the rocks, without stopping, even the ones stained red with blood or black with bile. The second corpse they recognized—it was Mr. Peavy. Knut didn't pause when he saw who it was, just pulled the man's mangled body out and left it on the ground behind him.

It fell to McKray, Owen, and Stieg, to drag the body farther away as Knut continued moving in, prying out the rocks that glutted the cave. They forced Hanne to do the easier work, hauling rocks away from the mouth and dropping them down the side of the mountain, to keep room clear to work.

There seemed no hope at all, but after they cleared several feet of rock and boulder, they found a man alive! When Stieg took the man's arms to pull, he woke up and screamed with pain. Both legs broken, a terrible gurgling sound coming from his rib cage when he breathed, but alive.

He passed out before they got him outside.

It was decided, then, that McKray would ride to town for a doctor, and for a few men to help. He said he had some men he trusted whose silence could be bought about the nature of the cave-in, if it came to that.

He departed as quickly as he could along the treacherous ravine, winding his way back down the rocky trail to where they had left their horses tethered in the foothills.

Owen made another trip to the Pinkerton camp and came back with blankets, a tarp, lanterns, and more food. He draped the injured man with the blankets, then he piled the corpses onto the tarp and wrapped them up as best he could.

The light began to fail, but still Knut moved rock and Stieg and Owen dragged it out and Hanne pushed it over the side of the ledge. Night descended and they hauled rock.

The skin on the palms of Hanne's hands blistered and burst. Fatigue landed on her. She had eaten the rest of the bread and the ham when the spasms of hunger demanded it, but all she wanted to do was dig.

Stieg was working through a terrible headache. He was too weak to carry rocks for long, so he held the lantern for Knut.

They cleared the rockfall from the entrance to the cave. One great, slanted rock face of the two that had formed the cave was still largely intact. It was the other face that had sheared away. This seemed promising. The one stable wall might prevent any further collapse.

Some hours past midnight, McKray shouted that he was coming up and not to throw down any rocks on him.

He appeared, holding a lantern and leading Dr. Buell from town up the craggy ravine onto the ledge. He had six miners with him. Six! All of them geared up with picks and shovels and wearing their heavy canvas jackets and hats with candles.

He also had fussy Mr. Collier with him, the last person Hanne expected to see, hauling a sack with more supplies.

"Dear God in heaven!" the doctor exclaimed when he lifted a lamp and saw the corpses they had piled near the edge of the ledge.

"We must drag these away before all else!" Dr. Buell said.

"No," McKray said.

"The stink will draw animals, and flies will come!" the doctor protested.

"If there's any chance our sister is alive," Stieg said, "we need to work fast. We don't have time to spare for the dead."

The doctor, corrected, said no more about them. He and Collier began to tend to the wounded man, who was still unconscious. The miners surveyed the cave.

"Form two chains," one of them said. He spat out a mouthful of chewing tobacco. "Three here, three there. Just toss the rocks out. Fast as we can go."

Knut would not leave the front, so he became the first link in one chain. McKray wanted to be the other. The six miners arranged themselves into two lines behind the lead men. The rocks got handed out and back through the line. The last man on each line threw rocks down the ravine.

Owen and Hanne fell into each other near the wounded man, exhausted. They sank to the ground as the miners began moving the rock with a much improved speed. Stieg came to sit near them.

"I should have brought a stretcher," the doctor mumbled to Collier. They were taping the man's rib cage, Collier carefully shifting his weight up so the doctor could pass the tape underneath.

"I'll go for one whenever you say," replied Collier.

Hanne watched Collier dully. Then she got to her feet and joined one of the stone brigades.

Owen got up and joined the other.

A LINE OF yellow light appeared out in the distance. Sunrise. The dawn painted the bellies of some low clouds pink. As the light grew, Hanne saw the great Montana wilderness spread out before them. She had not realized how far up the mountain their chase had led them.

The rocks came back, endlessly.

Tears had started to flow down Hanne's face some time ago. The miner to her right told her to take a break but she would not. Owen begged her to rest but she didn't want to.

It was just that it had sunk in. Every rock was only bringing them closer to Sissel's crumpled body.

* * *

A SHRIEKING PAIN in Sissel's shoulder woke her, and she struggled to draw a breath. Her face was pressed into the shirtfront of a cold, heavy mass of man. She knew it must be Baker.

There was such tremendous weight pressing down on her chest she had to breathe shallowly. Her vision was filled with utter blackness and she heard nothing, not even her own thin breathing.

Her lips and nostrils and face were covered in a fine, choking grit. It made her cough, and the movement shot her whole body through with pain. Her shoulder and arm were crushed. The way she lay, her bound hands were wrenched to the side, under Baker's weight and the weight of the stone.

She fought not to black out again, but she could not hold out against the pain.

THE MINER TO her left loaded a chunk of granite into Hanne's arms, which were chalky white with rock dust except in patches where she was scraped and bleeding. There was pity in his eyes. His name, some-one had said, was Mario. An Italian, come to be a miner in Montana. Now helping them on a fool's mission, and without complaint.

Hanne gasped. Her body jerked as if hit by lightning. Sissel couldn't breathe. Sissel's shoulder was broken. Sissel was awake, under the body of a dead man.

"She's alive!" Hanne cried.

She dropped the rock in her hands and pushed her way through the chain of men.

"Move!" she cried. "She's alive!"

SISSEL BLINKED AWAKE, tried to remain still. She took small sips of air, keeping her lips closed to filter the grit. She mustn't cough.

Her heart was beating like mad. She wanted a drink of water. She wanted to be out from under Baker's dead body. She wanted to draw in a deep breath, and it was all folly.

Sissel knew she was bound to die there in the mountain.

HANNE MOVED PAST the miners, their candlelit hats showing her a space that grew narrower and narrower the farther they got into the cave.

She climbed over bigger rocks they had been unable to clear out, scraped her leg on a jagged edge of sandstone. She came to McKray, wearily pulling at the rocks, standing near Knut, who was nearly wedged in. Their hands and feet were bloody. There was a body caught up with the rocks. They were trying to free it.

Hanne pressed her hands to the mass of rocks to Knut's left.

"Here, here, here," Hanne said. She patted the rocks. "She's here."

"Come, boys," McKray shouted. "She's close! All hands up here."

Hanne dug furiously at the rocks. Her bleeding palms scraped against the rough rock, but she hardly felt them. Her fingernails tore away.

Sissel was panicking. Gasping for breath. Near. So near.

BAKER'S BODY MOVED. Like he was pressing down, trying to get up. Was he not dead? Was he now going to die on top of her?

She was scared. She was so terribly scared in the dark. She let herself weep.

Then, miraculously, some of the weight was eased. She could take a breath. Baker's body slid, just an inch, then it was pulled off her.

She screamed with the pain of it, but could not hear her voice. Light shone on her. So bright she had to squint. She could not bring her arms up to shield her face. She had to shut her eyes to that light.

Was this death?

Then a small shadow fell over her face.

It was a hand. The shadow of a hand.

Sissel opened her eyes and saw there, crouched above her, Hanne, holding a lamp and speaking to her.

CHAPTER FORTY-SIX

D r. Buell had told them not to move her, not an inch. Once they'd pulled the body of the man off, they saw Sissel's hands were bound, and wrenched violently to the side of her body. Her left arm lay at an angle that was all wrong. Her hands were swelling below the rope.

But Dr. Buell said she could not be moved, not yet. He instructed them to clear out the rock around the girl as much as possible but to leave her lying flat and still. He did pass up a pair of thick medical scissors so that Hanne could cut away the bonds binding her wrists. Hanne tried to work carefully, not to jar Sissel's body, but it was hard to maneuver the scissors between Sissel's body and the rock ledge she was pressed up underneath. Sissel's ragged jacket sleeves were in the way—Hanne had to snip the cloth away. Hanne recognized it as the tan dress Alice Oswald had given Sissel.

McKray and Stieg and Knut and the miners worked, but Hanne would not leave Sissel's side. Sissel had passed out, from pain or relief

Hanne did not know. The men cleared the rock, hollowing out an area around the rock shelf that had protected Sissel from the collapse. They carried out the body of the man who had shielded Sissel with respect, reverence, even.

Perhaps outside they were hooting and hollering and slapping one another on the back with joy. Hanne didn't move. She put her hand on her sister's chest, above her heart, and stayed there, kneeling on the hard cut rocks, praying. She imagined she could pour her strength into her sister's body.

The rock dust made Sissel look, in the dim lamplight, like a dried-up husk of a person, like a ghost. The wretched shape of her distended shoulder and arm made it all the more gruesome.

Someone passed her a canteen, and she tried to pour a bit of water into Sissel's mouth, but Sissel didn't wake, and Hanne only wetted the neck of Sissel's dress.

When there was enough rock cleared out for Dr. Buell to work, he came and tapped Hanne on the shoulder.

"You'll have to back out, Miss Hemstad, so I can examine the girl."

Hanne did so, reluctantly. But she hovered behind him. He had brought his black leather bag into the cave, and he opened it, removing several instruments as well as a syringe and a vial of clear liquid.

Then the doctor began to touch Sissel's limbs, delicately feeling for breaks. He reached over Sissel's body and laid a hand on her left shoulder, and Sissel woke. She cried out, withdrawing from his touch. Her eyes popped open, wild with pain. Hanne felt the pain, like a lightning strike.

"Hanne!" Sissel said.

"Sissel, you're alive. You're all right!"

"There, there," the doctor said. "Don't get too excited, Sissel. You mustn't move until we know if your back and neck are all right."

Sissel's eyes fluttered closed, but the doctor touched her shoulder.

"No! Don't sleep," he said. "Not yet."

Hanne released a breath. It came out a bit like a sob.

". . . thirsty," Sissel said.

Dr. Buell reached back to Hanne, and she passed him the canteen. He tilted a sip into Sissel's mouth. She sputtered, and asked for more.

The doctor then examined her as best he could, asking if her skull, neck, and spine felt all right.

"It's just my shoulder," Sissel said.

Tears began to course from the corners of Sissel's eyes, cutting paths through the grit.

"All right, don't fret. We'll get you out."

Dr. Buell turned away from Sissel and began to prepare the syringe, opening the vial and drawing the fluid into the barrel.

"What are you doing?" Sissel asked.

"I'm giving you morphine," Dr. Buell said. "I can't set your shoulder in here, and getting you out is going to hurt."

"No, don't," she said. "I don't want to sleep again. Hanne, don't let him. Hanne!"

Hanne felt Sissel's panic as if it were her own.

"It's all right," Hanne said, reaching to Sissel, touching her foot, her leg. "The doctor knows best."

"No!" Sissel shouted. "I will take the pain. Don't do it."

Dr. Byers paused. "It'll hurt."

"That's all right," Sissel said.

"What do you want to do?" he asked Hanne, turning his head to her.

"Don't ask her!" Sissel said. She coughed and blanched and kept on speaking. "It's my body and I say what happens to it."

"She's right," Hanne said. "Don't give her the drugs, not if she doesn't want them."

The doctor shook his head and put a cap on the needle, returning the syringe to his bag. "She'll be begging for it by the time we've got her out," he said.

But Sissel didn't beg for the morphine.

Hanne worked with the doctor and Mario, the smallest of the miners, best able to fit into the small space they had hollowed out. They loaded her onto a sturdy woolen blanket and carefully, slowly maneuvered backward, out of the claustrophobic tunnel. Sissel moaned and vomited several times. Hanne could see her clinging to consciousness, fighting to stay awake.

She felt Sissel's pain, but not shrilly—she was not in danger, just hurting.

When at last they got her outside and laid her on the ground, Stieg and Owen and Knut crowded around her, kneeling down on the ground or bending over her.

"Stieg!" Sissel croaked. "Knut!"

"You saved us," Stieg said, tears spilling down his face. "You destroyed that big gun somehow, didn't you?"

Knut had lowered his big head to Sissel's hip and was weeping into the grimy fabric of her skirt. McKray hung back, his hat in his hands. Behind him stood his miners and Collier.

"All right, give her space," the doctor groused. "I've got to set her shoulder"

Sissel's eyes took in her family members, the miners, the massive quantity of rock they had all moved, and, back against a boulder, the dead bodies bleeding out. They were only partially covered by the tarp, a Pinkerton's crushed leg sticking out from the gristly pile.

Knut moved, to position himself between Sissel and the sight of the bodies.

"Dear God, what did I do?" Sissel sobbed.

Her siblings tried to comfort her, shushing her, telling her she had saved them.

Isaiah McKray pushed through to her side. He dropped to his knees and took her hand. Sissel's hand in his looked tiny and fragile.

"They deserved it," he said. "You only did they forced you to do. You're alive. That's what's important. None of us dared to hope it."

"Yes, yes! She's alive, and I must set the shoulder so if you will all please step back!" Dr. Buell said. The strain of the night was showing on him. His eyes were red and his hair stringy, laced with rock dust.

Sissel would not let go of McKray's hand, so he was the one to help the doctor hold her down.

Hanne had thought she would do it. She had no intention of leaving her sister's side, but she could see Sissel had changed during their separation. This Sissel knew what she wanted.

ON THE ROCKY LEDGE, as the sun rose higher in the sky and the flies began to collect on the stiffening corpses of Russell Peavy and the other detectives, the group began to plan. The miners had set off with Collier and the doctor. Collier was to pay them all handsomely, once for their work, and once again for their silence.

Sissel was lying on a blanket and had another wrapped around her. They felt like the same blankets from the Pinkertons' camp, though it seemed like eons ago that she'd been bound in the cot.

Her siblings were standing off a few feet, looking out over the valley. Hanne was keeping a keen eye on the trails leading up to the cave.

"We should get on the train," Stieg said. "The Baron will be here any day. Bringing Nytteson! We can't fight them."

"I think you all need to make a decision quickly, that's for sure," McKray said. "This Baron could be in town now, waiting, or headed here at this very moment."

"With more Pinkertons," Owen contributed.

"We abandon our land, then," Stieg said. "Abandon our belongings and flee south. To Mexico?"

"I brought a good chunk of cash," McKray said. "Just in case . . . in case I could bribe the Pinkertons. I wish I could have . . . Anyway, the money's yours. There's enough for tickets and probably a little house somewhere down there."

"You offered to buy our land. Take it," Stieg said.

"No, I won't. I can sell it for you, if you like."

"Can Sissel travel? She's very weak," Hanne interrupted.

"Sissel's stronger than you remember—"

"I'm right here, actually," Sissel said. "And I don't want to go to Mexico."

She sat up. Her shoulder was tightly bound, but it screamed at her.

"Lie down!" Stieg said.

"Be careful," Hanne said at the same time.

"We must stay here and fight," Sissel said. "We can't run from the Baron anymore."

"What if he brings Nytteson?" Knut said.

"So what? We'll fight them."

"We appreciate your spirit, Sissel, but that's not an option," Stieg said. "He'll have more Pinkertons with him, or Nytteson, or both."

"We thought we were safe, all this time, all these years, and all along, we've been living under his shadow."

Sissel cast her eyes across the faces of her siblings.

"No," she said. "We will run no more."

Sissel saw Hanne look to Owen. Some question passed between them and was answered silently, then Hanne nodded.

"I have a place where we can go," Owen said. "We could make a stand there, if it came to that."

AFTER ONE LAST conversation about the regrettable necessity of leaving the dead men unburied, they began the descent, heading for the clearing where Hanne and the others had left their horses the day before.

Everyone was tired and hungry, and the descent steep—they moved slowly. Sissel tried to hide how exhausted she was, and how her shoulder pained her. Edging down the tight crevasses of stone was difficult, especially with only one good arm. At times the pain made stars swarm up before her eyes.

It occurred to her that gold might help her heal, and so she asked if anyone had any. McKray had a gold pocket watch, and he was happy for her to have it. Hanne slipped the watch carefully into the bandage, near Sissel's shoulder. The gold throbbed, warming the area like a hot water bottle.

It made her sleepy and a bit dizzy, so it was decided Knut would carry her. He picked her up carefully, cradling her in his arms.

"I missed you," she said to her brother.

"I missed you, too. I did not like to be at the Lilliedahls, though I did not want to complain. I don't want to be away from my family again."

"Me either," she said. The gold throbbed with warmth, acting almost like a sedative. She allowed herself to relax into Knut's strong arms and rest.

When they passed through the Pinkerton campsite, which was tossed and trampled, Owen, McKray, and Stieg gathered up any items they felt would be of use on the trail. They found several bed-rolls, a coffeepot, some coffee, and some food in a pantry box. All that was loaded into sacks.

When finally they reached the horses, they found them agitated and anxious. They'd not been properly watered or cared for in the horrific events of the night before.

Owen insisted they water the animals straightaway, so they led the horses through the sparse pine forest. It was cool, and the dim light was soothing after the bright, bouncing sunlight on the mountainside.

Knut set Sissel down on a boulder when they reached a grassy little pond in a field. The horses plunged knee deep into the water and drank heavily.

Stieg, Owen, and Hanne began to talk about the journey ahead. Sissel was going to call them to her when McKray came to her side.

"Miss Hemstad," he said, looking out over the little pond.

"Mr. McKray."

"I credit myself that before all this I grasped how . . . singular and unique you are among young ladies. But I couldn't have known how tough you are. What you've endured . . . it's flat-out astonishing."

Sissel studied him. His jacket was missing, his shirt sleeves rolled up and stained with sweat. His trousers were rumpled and torn. He'd been cut on the cheek, by rock, no doubt; the blood had dried where it ran.

His face was drawn and tired, but his hazel eyes shone with emotion.

"When I thought . . . when we all thought you were dead . . ."

He coughed. Shook his head. Fell back to silence.

"I am so thankful for the assistance you gave us, Mr. McKray," she said. "You are a good friend. A true friend. If it hadn't been for you, and the men you brought, I would be dead now."

He shook his head. Sissel looked away, allowing him privacy by which to wipe his eyes.

"Your brother told me that you all want me to go back to Carter," he said. "To keep an eye out for the Baron and to watch what happens at the store. To throw the law off you, when they ask questions . . . but I'd rather come with you, if there's going to be a fight. I'm a good shot and I'm strong—"

Sissel laid her slight, pale hand on top of one of McKray's.

"We will deal with the Baron."

"You know, if the Pinkertons have been spying on you for so long, he probably knows where Owen's family's ranch is. They may have someone watching it even now . . ."

"It's time for us to meet the Baron Fjelstad. If you can keep the town safe, and look in on the Oswalds, please, that would be a gift."

"I'll do it," he said. "And after . . . may I come to call? I'll do it right this time. I'll do everything right."

McKray moved his hand, revolving it so that Sissel's hand dropped into his. The physical warmth of his hand enveloped hers. She remembered how his touch made her feel—safe and grounded and whole.

"Yes," she told him, the word itself making her shy to speak aloud.

"Could I ask a favor of you, then?" he said.

She looked up and met his eyes.

"Would you call me Isaiah?"

"All right," she said. "Then, Isaiah, you must call me Sissel."

"I will, Sissel." He was smiling at her now, a grin that infected her with its happiness, bleak circumstances notwithstanding. "Sissel, I will."

"I should give you your watch back, before you go."

"I hope you won't," he said. "It's yours now. And a promise of more to come."

Sissel laughed. "More gold, you mean?"

"More gifts," he said. "In general."

A few minutes later, they parted ways; the Hemstads, Owen, and Daisy headed north, to the Double B Ranch; McKray headed south, to Carter.

CHAPTER FORTY-SEVEN

t was several days' ride to the Bennett ranch, far into North Montana Territory, and the time wore slowly. They were all alert and on edge as they rode through the forests and fields, but none so much as Hanne.

Though she knew her Nytte would signal her if any one of her party was in danger, she could not let down her guard. She insisted she ride at the back of the group, swinging Jigsaw around to scour the trail behind them with her eyes. Pinkertons might follow, or the Baron's group, or the law—who knew what charges they might face.

She had killed again. Three men? Four men? She could not remember.

She had washed the blood and sweat off her hands and arms, but there was still grime under her rock-torn fingernails. She studied her hands. How could such small, plain hands have wrought so much destruction?

As Hanne rode she found there was no guilt in her heart over the killing of those Pinkerton men. They had stolen her sister. If placed in the same position again, Hanne knew she would do the same. But she did despair that she'd been so unwilling to submit to the will of the Gods. Instead of praying for them to inhabit her and fill her with light and understanding, she had wanted only the Berserker to overtake her. She had wanted to slaughter and avenge.

She thought of this as she swept her eyes over the forests and valleys behind them. Would she pray to the Gods, when the time came to fight the Baron, and hope to be filled with light? Or would she welcome the Berserker? Would she even get to choose?

When it got too dark to ride, they would stop for the night. Owen would say if their position was such that they could afford a fire. Hanne hardly cared. She just wanted to make it to the ranch—to arrive to a place that was defensible. She wanted her sister to sleep on a good bed, and eat a warm meal.

The first night, Hanne had not been able to sleep. Everyone else had flung themselves down after a dinner of bread, cheese, and canned peaches, all lifted from the Pinkertons' camp. Despite Owen's repeated pleading that she lie down and rest, Hanne had prowled the circumference of the campsite, watching the forest, where the shadows cast by the rising moon seemed to creep up on them. Hanne didn't want to talk to him, or to her brothers.

Her shoulders and arms were sore from hauling rock, and the long scrape she'd got on her leg was beginning to scab over. Her weary body begged her to lie down, but she could not rest.

She was upset with Stieg, she realized, because she'd left him with Sissel and he'd failed to keep her safe. It wasn't fair, but Hanne knew that emotions were frequently unfair. She didn't want to talk to him, though. Not to Stieg, or to Knut, or to Owen, even. She just wanted to stay alert, and she wanted them all to be safe.

Eventually Owen got up and argued with her. He was going to take the watch and she must lie down.

"Hanne," Sissel said, interrupting their hushed discussion, "I'm cold. Can you come sleep with me?"

"I can't sleep," Hanne said. "I don't want to."

"Well, I can't sleep and I do want to, but I'm too cold," Sissel said. So Hanne went over to her little sister, huddled in her bedroll on the ground.

Sissel was lying on her good side, her bandaged shoulder facing up. Hanne drew close behind her, cradling her sister with her body, and flung her bedroll cover over them both. Hanne rested her forehead against the back of Sissel's head, burying her nose into Sissel's dirty hair.

Tears began to flow. Hanne tried not to sniffle.

"Don't cry, Sister," Sissel whispered. "I'm all right."

Hanne squeezed her eyes shut. Her whole body began to tremble.

"We're all right, Hanne," Sissel said. She turned her head. She couldn't move much because of her shoulder, but she leaned back into Hanne.

"I know. I'm sorry," Hanne said softly. Her tears were dropping into Sissel's hair. She wiped them away from her eyes, but she could not stop her body's shaking.

Daisy came over and licked at Hanne's face.

"Oh! Good girl, Daisy. Thank you," Hanne said, squirming to get a hand up to push Daisy off.

"Try to let go," Sissel said. "The fight is over. For now at least. Curl up to me and let's try to sleep."

Hanne did as she was told, and Daisy lay down on the other side of Hanne. She was sandwiched between the dog and her sister, and eventually she succumbed to the warmth and slept.

THEY WENT ON riding doggedly, stopping only when the horses needed rest. By the morning of the second day, their meager supplies had run out and for breakfast all they had was coffee. But Owen told them not to despair—they were almost to the ranch.

They had passed near to the town of Bullhook Bottoms, a bustling town much like their own Carter. Knut asked if they could go in and get some food, but Stieg snapped at him—no. Not when they were so close.

They had ridden along a well-traveled road, bordered by a cattle fence on one side, and now approached a wide gateway set in the fence, with an arch above. At the center were logs shaped into strange letters, a reversed *B* back-to-back with a proper one. Almost like a rune, Hanne thought.

"What does that stand for?" Knut asked.

"Double B," Owen said. "That's the brand for our ranch. All our beefs have it stamped on their flank."

The gate was designed to be opened from horseback.

Owen lifted a pull rope, and their group walked the tired horses through the gate. Daisy was the only one with any energy at all. She frisked in the long prairie grasses, impatient to get on to the house.

"What does it mean, Double B?" Knut asked as Owen wheeled Brandy around and shut the gate behind them.

"Well, just double B. That's the name of the ranch. But *B*'s for Bennett. So I guess you could say it's Bennett and Bennett."

Hanne knew how her betrothed's mind worked and imagined

Owen would now be thinking about the fact that he was now the one and only Bennett.

The road led over a small hill.

Owen urged Brandy onward. He was chewing the inside of his cheek, his expression dark and anxious.

She edged Jigsaw over to Brandy, and the two horses momentarily put their noses together and whickered, as if commiserating.

"Are you all right, Owen?" Hanne asked.

She wished she could reach out and hold his hand, but she was not a skilled enough horsewoman to come so close.

"It will be good to get a hot meal," he said. "I just hope there's food in the larder."

"We'll make do with whatever we find," Hanne said.

Owen nodded.

THE RANCH CAME into view as they came over the hill. Hanne hadn't understood the scale. Not at all.

The ranch sprawled out in the box canyon below. The house itself was massive, a two-story home with a stone foundation and pillars, and flat-hewn logs for the upper floor. A wide sitting porch surrounded the house.

A fair distance behind the house stood several outbuildings—one a large two-story barn, the other a low, elongated building that she supposed was a bunkhouse. An elaborate system of stalls and holding pens spread out from the barn, covering perhaps a half acre. Pasture fields spread outward into the valley, and there was a natural pond back a ways.

Windbreak trees stood in lines and semicircles at the edges of some of the pastures, a line of tall oaks edged the ranch house itself.

"Gods above," Stieg murmured, bringing his horse up beside Hanne and Owen.

"That's all yours?" Knut asked in amazement as he and Sissel came up.

"That's what the letter said," Owen replied. He shook his head.

"What is it?" Stieg said.

"It's empty," he said. "I've never seen it so empty."

He was talking about cattle, Hanne understood. It was true, only a few dozen animals could be seen, dotting the pastures beyond the barn.

"Well, let's go see what's what," Owen said, and he urged Brandy onward.

AS THEY CAME up to the house a skinny old woman in a loose gray work dress and a flapping apron came off the porch. She stood squinting with one hand held up to shield her eyes.

"Lucy!" Owen called.

She clapped her hands and rushed out into the yard, coming to grab the bridle of Owen's horse.

"Owen Bennett, thank God," she said. "They said I was a fool to stay on, but I was determined to wait!"

Owen dismounted and Lucy nearly flew into his arms. She hugged him tight.

"Oh Lord, Owie, they're all gone."

Hanne saw the old woman's face was shining with tears.

Knut helped Sissel to dismount. Hanne noted Sissel's face was alarmingly pale. She swayed on her feet. Hanne slid off Jigsaw and went to Sissel's side.

Lucy released Owen from the embrace and wiped her eyes with her apron.

"Forgive an old woman's tears. It's good to see you, boy, that's all, and who do you got with you?" Lucy continued. "And when's the last time you all ate? And good Lord above, is that Jigsaw?"

"I'll tell you everything, Lucy, I promise."

"And here's my Daisy dog!" Lucy said. She bent down, and Daisy licked all over her face. Lucy grabbed Daisy by the ruff and kissed her back.

"Let me introduce you to my fiancée, Hanne Hemstad, and her family."

"I'll be!" Lucy exclaimed. She wiped her face and hands on her apron as she stood up. "My Owie got himself a bride. I'll be!"

Hanne offered her hand, but the cook swept her into a bony hug.

"This is Stieg and Knut and Sissel," Owen said. "And we're starving."

"Then save the introductions!" Lucy exclaimed, giving them half a wave. "I'm gonna ring the bell for Daniel. You remember Daniel Harris, he's one of the hands your father hired on, rest his soul. He stayed on to help keep the place running. I been payin' him wages out of the grocery money. I didn't know if that's what you'd have wanted, but I was determined to keep things as best I could until you got here. Anyway, Owie, you get the horses put away and I'll get cooking."

She hustled off toward the house.

"I got a good ham!" she hollered over her shoulder. "Plenty of eggs!"

"That's Lucy," Owen said. He had a smile on his face. The first smile Hanne had seen there in days, it seemed.

"She's a good talker," Knut said.

"She's a good cook, too," Owen added.

Hanne turned to Sissel—she had the sense something was wrong with her—and Sissel took two steps and fainted into Hanne's arms.

OWEN LEFT THE horses at the front of the house, where they immediately began to crop the grass. He opened the large wooden front door and led the way for Knut, who was carrying Sissel.

Inside, the house was dim and cool, despite the bright sunshine outside. Heavy curtains were drawn against the heat of the sun.

Knut immediately bumped into a delicate table near the door. Hanne turned and steadied it. Another table flanked the entrance on the other side, each draped in a lace cloth and bearing a fancy glass-globed lamp.

Owen led them to the right, into a formal sitting room. Knut laid his sister down on an elegant rose-colored fainting couch, now serving its purpose.

"Lucy," Owen called. "We need some water!"

"I'll get it," Hanne said. She left the parlor and headed to the back of the house, down a hallway with floral wallpaper. Framed photographs hung on the wall, and Hanne caught glimpses of pale-headed children and prize steer as she hurried along.

From the back of the house came the sound of a dinner bell—a metal triangle being hit with a rod. That must be Lucy calling for the ranch hand.

At last Hanne came to the kitchen. It was large, with bare stone walls, and a door that led to the outside off to the left. There was a long table for cooking, and another one near the corner for informal meals, with six chairs around it.

A fireplace was set in the back wall, tall enough that Lucy could've stood in it if she'd wanted to. Pegs had been stuck in the mortar between the stones that made the chimney, and all sorts of pots and pans hung down. A six-lid woodstove stood nearby, its stovepipe running along the wall to feed directly into the chimney.

Hanne saw what she was looking for—running along the right-hand side of the room was a counter with a water pump above a sink basin. Shelves with everyday plates, glasses, bowls, and mugs lined the wall.

Lucy hustled in from outside, lugging a large ham hock. She set it on the worktable with a thud.

"I need some water," Hanne said.

"Dear Lord, you scared me!" Lucy said.

"My sister has fainted. I just want some water for her," Hanne said. She crossed to the pump.

"Poor thing," Lucy said. "You all been traveling hard. I can see it. And her injured. Well, I wish I had lemons for lemonade. That's a good reviver. But I got ginger root. I'll make her some sweet ginger tea."

Hanne pumped the handle up and down, and after only a few strokes, clean, cold water gushed out.

She took a glass and held it under the water. She gulped down some, then filled it again. She also took a flour sack towel from the counter and wet it.

"I fell behind in the baking," Lucy said. "We don't have bread— I'm ashamed of it. But I'll get a meal together soon enough. And I'll get that ginger tea going and coffee, of course."

"Thank you," Hanne said. "I'll come help in a moment."

"No need. No need! This here is my dominion, and I know what I'm doing!"

IN THE FRONT ROOM, Hanne came and sat next to Sissel on the couch. Stieg was seated on an elegant wingback chair, watching over Sissel.

Hanne dabbed at Sissel's forehead with the damp cloth.

"Owen and Knut went to water the horses," Stieg said.

The towel came away dirtied with grime from the trail.

"I think she's just exhausted," Stieg said.

"We all are," Hanne said. Her voice was tight. She hadn't been alone with Stieg since the awful events on the mountainside.

"You're angry with me," Stieg said.

"I'm tired and hungry. Let's not talk now."

His eyes were flashing. "You think I let Sissel be kidnapped—but you don't know any of it. You don't understand how willful she had grown. And secretive!"

"If we must discuss it," Hanne said, her voice cold, "then I don't want to do it now. I do not want to say anything I will regret."

"Very well." Stieg stood and stalked from the room without another word. She could see from the way he held his body that he was furious.

"It's not his fault," Sissel said softly.

Hanne turned to find her sister's eyes open. They shone with the muted light that came in at the edges of the brocade curtains.

"I was stubborn and foolish. Oh, Hanne, if only you knew all the mistakes I made, you wouldn't be mad at Stieg."

Hanne handed Sissel the glass of water. She took a long sip.

"I don't want to be mad at either of you," Hanne said. "I'm worried we have a fight ahead of us. That's what we need to focus on."

The house was quiet around them, save for the ticking of a grandfather clock in the hallway.

"Hanne," Sissel said. "James died because of me."

Hanne drew back. "James was a spy!"

"He was. Yes. But I still believe he was a good person."

"He wasn't," Hanne said.

"No," Sissel said. "He tried to warn me. Once he realized that the Pinkertons meant to kidnap me, he tried to tell me."

Hanne said nothing. She knew her lips were pressed tightly together. She knew she was frowning—she probably looked just like their mother at that moment, always disapproving.

Hanne heard the boys' voices from the porch. Owen was talking with a man who was saying, "Yes, sir," and "No, sir." He must be Daniel.

"You liked James," Sissel said.

"I liked him because he made your life bearable!" Hanne said.

"He died trying to protect me," Sissel said. "And that makes me terribly sad, because he was good. He was!"

Sissel covered her face with her good hand and wept. Hanne heard the boys come in. Owen poked his head into the room, but Hanne silently signaled to him that he shouldn't enter.

She listened to Owen lead her brothers toward the kitchen.

"You're overtired, Sissel. You need to rest. We all do," Hanne said. "Lucy is making a meal, and I'll see about a bath for you."

"I caused the cave to collapse, Hanne. I caused men to die. Mr. Peavy was there. I keep seeing his face. How do I live with that?"

"I'm not the person to ask—"

"You're the only person I can ask!"

Sissel sat up and reached her hand toward Hanne. Hanne took it into her own hands. As strong as her little sister had become, there was a deep need in Sissel's eyes. Need and pain. Hanne steadied herself so that she might respond with kindness.

"I have felt terrible guilt, Sissel. After I killed the gamblers, back home, I wanted to die. Ever since I became a Berserker, I have felt a dark, black shame."

Sissel squeezed Hanne's hand. Hanne's throat tightened with emotion.

"But then, once Rolf taught me to pray—to surrender, it changed. In Wolf Creek, I surrendered to the Gods, and when they filled me with their power, I saw . . ."

Hanne rubbed her lips, gazing toward the window. She stood and whisked open the heavy drapes. Light flooded the room, illuminating flurrying dust motes.

"You saw what?"

"We are all made of light, Sissel." Hanne turned to face her sister, raising her arms in the bright beams of sunlight. "We are all a part of the same great, glorious light, and the Gods, they are playful with human lives. They laugh at our misery and our shame, because we invented it."

"You saw the Gods? You saw them laughing?"

"I was the Gods, Sissel. I can't explain it, but I became one with all the world."

"I don't understand. How did all of that make you feel better about taking the lives of men?"

Hanne took a big breath and let it out slowly.

"It's hard to explain." she said. "All I know is that the Gods don't want you to feel ashamed."

"What do they want me to feel?"

Hanne held her hand into the light. The skin was dry, dirty. Fingernails ragged. Knuckles scabbed over.

She rotated her hand, watching the play of light and shadow.

"Alive. The Gods want you to feel alive."

AFTER EATING A hastily prepared meal of ham, eggs and cornmeal flapjacks, the Hemstads were offered baths. Sissel asked for one, but all Hanne wanted to do was sleep.

Lucy showed Hanne to a lovely bedroom, with a round braided rug and a rattan rocking chair. The wallpaper was a soft blue color, sprigged with bouquets of forget-me-nots. The bed was unmade, but there was a colorful quilt folded at the foot.

"Give me ten minutes and I'll get the bed made up proper," Lucy said.

Hanne sat down heavily on the mattress. Sleep was overtaking her hard.

"No need," Hanne said. "I'm only going to rest for a moment."

"Are you sure?" Lucy said. "Wouldn't take me long."

Hanne looked around the room, blinking. She felt tired, yes, but there was something else, something warm and limb-loosening, as if she were drunk.

She felt safe, she realized.

"Really, it's fine," Hanne said.

"Well then, I'll leave you be. Me and Daniel will keep watch. You go on and rest," Lucy said. She shut the door behind her.

Hanne sat on the bed, staring down stupidly at her boots. She had to unlace them before she could lie down. That was her last thought before falling into a bottomless blackout of a sleep.

WHEN HANNE AWOKE it was dawn. *How could that be?* she wondered. She heard chickens clucking outside, a rooster crowing.

She found she had slept in her clothes. Sometime in the night, she had drawn the quilt up. The mattress had dirt on it at the bottom from her boots.

She made her way down to the kitchen, where she was unsurprised to find Lucy already hard at work.

"Morning, Miss Hemstad," Lucy said. "I hope you slept good."

"Yes, I guess I was more tired than I thought," Hanne said. She felt awkward, standing there in her dirty, hard-traveled clothes.

"Are my brothers awake? Owen?"

"Owen's out on the porch, sitting watch."

Hanne started out.

"I got bathwater on," Lucy said. "Don't you want to freshen up, Miss Hemstad? I sorted through some old clothes what was stored in the attic and I think I found some for you."

"Thank you, Miss Lucy. That's very kind," Hanne said. She wasn't sure how to speak to Lucy. She certainly wasn't used to being waited on.

Hanne had been so tired when they'd arrived—she couldn't even remember if she'd been civil. And did any of that matter, with what was coming?

* * *

HANNE PUSHED OPEN the large oak door and stepped onto the front porch. The house faced south, and the reflected sunrise glowed softly on the mountains and hills to the west.

Owen was seated in one of the rocking chairs, with his shotgun across his knees. Hanne thought he was asleep, but at the sound of her footsteps, he looked around.

"Good morning," she said. "Have you been out here all night?"

"I spelled Daniel just a few hours ago. He's a fine hand. I'm glad he's been here to help Lucy around the place."

Owen stood and stretched. He looked handsome and clean in fresh, pressed clothes. They must have belonged to one of his brothers.

"I feel like I haven't seen you in a week," Hanne said.

"I'm not sure you did, though I was riding next to you the whole while."

Hanne looked up to read his expression.

"You had other things on your mind," he said gently. "Can I show you something?"

Hanne nodded yes and he took her hand. They stepped off the porch and walked out around the right side of the house, toward a rise in the ground crested with a couple of willow trees.

Hanne still couldn't believe the splendor of the ranch. Now, rested and back in her right mind, she was intimidated by both the vastness of it, and the promise.

Owen led her up to the trees, and Hanne saw this was where his family members had been buried.

Five simple wooden crosses stood over humped mounds of dry earth.

"Lucy tells me she ordered stone markers," Owen said. "They'll be coming from Helena. These three are for my brothers: Matthew,

Harvey and Paul. Lucy said Matthew only got back with the money and collapsed. Died the next morning."

"I'm so sorry," Hanne said.

He gestured to two graves set a bit apart, side by side. "That one is my father and there's my stepmother."

Hanne rested her head against Owen's forearm.

"I am so sorry, Owen. I can only imagine how awful it feels."

"I don't have time to be sad, really, not with what's likely headed our way. But I'll tell you—"

He turned his face to hers. Hanne gazed up into his warm, deep brown eyes.

"You feel like family to me, Hanne. And I'm glad for it."

Hanne wrapped her arms around him and held him close. She inhaled the smell of him, leather and spice and wood smoke and whatever it was that made him Owen Bennett.

"We should have married," Hanne said. "Long ago. Back when you first asked me."

"Shhh," Owen said. "We'll marry when all this is finished."

"Is that a promise?"

"That's a promise," Owen said. And he kissed her.

CHAPTER FORTY-EIGHT

Stieg stood at the window in the front parlor, peering through the heavy drapes. Sissel came to stand next to him.

"They're here, Gods protect us," Stieg said.

An hour earlier, Daniel had come riding from town, to announce that a Norwegian nobleman had gotten off the train in Bullhook Bottoms, accompanied by a large group of his countrymen. Owen thanked him for the information and gave him a month's wages, telling him not to return for a week. Daniel agreed rather quickly and departed, wishing them luck.

Lucy cursed his name and said he was a coward, but no one else resented Daniel's leaving. Sissel didn't hold it against him at all.

Two grand carriages borne by matched teams of Morgan horses came bouncing up the long drive. Each carriage was large, glossy, and new, one black with yellow wheels and the other mahogany brown, edged in red. A team of two drivers sat on each carriage.

"Just driving right up to the house," Owen said, gazing out the other parlor window. "So at least there's that."

"What do you mean?" Sissel asked.

"They didn't try to sneak up on us. Surround us."

"I don't think that's the Baron's style," Stieg said, eyeing the fancy rigs as they rolled up to the ranch house. Knut and Hanne gathered next to Owen at the other window. Sissel looked to her sister—did her Nytte warn her of danger? But Hanne did not seem any more agitated than the rest of them.

"How many people do you think he has brought?" Knut asked.

"We'll see soon enough," Hanne said. Daisy was pacing the room, growling low in her throat.

The drivers of the carriages jumped down, all of them hastening to lower the steps and open the doors.

"That your Baron?" Lucy asked, coming up from behind them. Sissel jumped a foot, her heart pounding. Lucy looked amused. "Didn't mean to startle you. This the fella we're expecting, though, ain't he?"

"Yes," Owen said. "It's him."

"Then I'll put some coffee on, should I?"

"It's not a social call," Sissel said. "We're not entertaining them."

"Maybe it's a good idea," Stieg said. "After all, it's the polite thing to do. And they might be hungry."

"Got it," Lucy said. "Anything else I can do?"

"Do me a favor and take Daisy with you?" Owen asked. "She's picking up on our nerves."

"Sure thing," Lucy said, and she called Daisy as she left the room.

"Look!" Knut said, pointing out the window.

Two muscular young men in fine suits had stepped out of the

mahogany carriage. They were the same build, the same height, and as they turned, Sissel saw they were twins. They joked with each other, smiling and chatting. Climbing out next was a tall, scowling minister, wearing the black robes and starched white neck cloth of the Lutheran church.

The minister looked up at the house, and Sissel had the impulse to hide behind the thick brocade fabric of the curtain. Stieg put his hand on her arm to steady her.

The door to the black carriage opened next. First a man as large as Knut emerged; he had an amiable look on his face and breathed a deep breath, gesturing, it seemed to Sissel, at the loveliness of the scenery. An Oar-Breaker, without doubt. Behind him a slender man in a trim, elegant suit stepped out. He wore a bowler hat and carried a brass-tipped cane. The way he carried himself conveyed alertness and intelligence, as well as privilege and power.

Sissel knew who he was, and she whispered it aloud: "The Baron."

More men were climbing out of the carriage. There were two Pinkertons in city clothes, and another three men who looked Norwegian, from their height and their blondness. One was tall and thin, like Stieg. He wore spectacles and carried a slim leather suit-case. They all seemed perfectly at ease.

"There's ten of them!" Knut said.

"Fourteen if you count the drivers," Owen said.

Fjelstad strode through the group, coming toward the house.

Sissel stepped back from the window; they all did. There was a flurry of straightening clothes and tidying hair.

Everyone except Knut was dressed in clothes from the attic. Hanne was wearing one of Mrs. Bennett's more demure gowns, a cream-colored velvet with gold buttons up the front. Owen wore a dark, charcoal suit from one of his brother's closets. He looked dashing. Together, he and Hanne looked like a young, wealthy couple.

Sissel liked her own dress less—a heavy, peach-colored gown years out of style. It was one of Mrs. Bennett's dresses from when she'd first married. It better fit Sissel's slight frame than any of the others. The material was thick: at least that was something, if there was to be a fight. Sissel's shoulder felt better, so much so that she refused to bandage it again. She didn't want the Baron to see a single weakness.

"They don't look mean," Knut said. "They look very friendly."

"Make no mistake about it," Sissel said. "That man is our enemy."

"Yes," Stieg said. "Only let's present ourselves as calm and reasonable so we can better learn his plans and how to make him leave us alone once and for all."

Sissel nodded. Hanne put a hand on Sissel's shoulder. Hanne's hand was very cold.

There was a rap on the door.

Hanne and Sissel took seats in the parlor, as they'd planned. Stieg came to stand behind Sissel, and Knut stood next to the wall.

Owen made to answer it, but Lucy swept in from the kitchen.

"You're the master of the house," she hissed at Owen. "Go stand by the fireplace."

Owen crossed to the hearth and Lucy waited until he was settled before opening the door.

"Good morning, sir," Lucy said. "Shall I take your hat and cane?"

"Why, thank you," came the voice of the Baron. It was a refined and melodious voice, hardly a trace of a Scandinavian accent.

Fjelstad turned to his left and saw them there, the Hemstads and Owen Bennett, all arranged and set out like a tableau.

He raised his arms.

"My family!" he said. "How I have looked forward to this day. Rolf has told me so much about you all."

He stepped into the parlor, coming straight for Stieg.

"You must be Stieg." Fjelstad extended his hand. Stieg shook it stiffly, surprised by this aggressive friendliness.

"This will be Hanne," Fjelstad said, gesturing. "Well met, Nyttesdotter! Hail, Freya! What joy it gives to behold you! And you must be Hanne's fiancé, Owen Bennett. Congratulations, young man." Fjelstad pumped Owen's hand.

The Baron spun then, grinning over toward Knut. "I see brother Knut. Yes! The Oar-Breaker! Hello!" He shook Knut's hand. "You are all as Rolf described!"

Fjelstad now let his gaze rest on Sissel. She met his eyes coolly.

"And you must be Sissel. By all the Gods of the Æsir, I am humbled and honored to meet you, young lady."

At this Fjelstad knelt in front of her chair. The Baron Fjelstad knelt at Sissel's feet! Sissel raised her eyes to her siblings, she was so shocked at this behavior. She saw that two of the Baron's men—the minister and the tall man with the spectacles—were standing in the doorway, taking in this strange scene.

"I am at your service, young Sissel Amundsdotter. Nyttesdotter. Ransacker."

The Baron was peering up into her face, examining her features as if to memorize them. Sissel tried to keep her face still.

She saw the Baron's eyes dart to her hands, which were folded in her lap, as if he wished to take one and kiss it.

She did not offer her hand to him.

"You've shocked them, Fjelstad," said the minister, his voice as coarse as gravel under a wheel.

"We are indeed taken aback to be addressed so informally," Stieg said, finally regaining his tongue. "We hardly think of you, sir, as a friend, much less family, after your recent actions against us."

"Ah yes, there is so much to be explained. I must beg your pardon a million times, for I've gone about everything wrong. But if you will allow me to explain, I will prove to you all that I've never meant any of you harm. Quite the opposite! My mission in life is to preserve and uphold the Nytteson. These men, whom I've brought all the way from our beloved mother country, will attest to this if only you'll listen."

"There is one man we might listen to," Hanne said. "And you have not brought him. Where is Rolf Tjossem?"

"He is ill. I regret to say that I had to leave him behind. But he wrote a letter for you. Let's begin with his letter."

The Baron held his hand out toward his men at the door. The man with the spectacles came into the room, removing a leather document holder from his jacket. He extracted a sealed letter and handed it to the Baron, who gave it to Hanne.

Hanne slid her finger under the wax seal and scanned the letter.

"'I fear my days are few, my dear friends,'" Hanne read aloud. "'I have made the decision to unburden my soul to the Baron, for I have come to believe that he truly has your best interests at heart. I have told him everything about our time together and our travails at Wolf Creek. It is my greatest wish that you will take shelter at the Baron's estates at Gamlehaugen. If the Gods are merciful, perhaps you will arrive in time to see me again. I know I expressed doubts to you in the past, but I have come to see clearly that we all must come together now.' And it goes on . . ."

Hanne handed the letter to Stieg, who read over it.

"It's in his hand," Stieg said. "Though it's shaky."

"He had a terrible fever," Fjelstad said. "If he had told me about his friendship with you sooner, I would have insisted he return here."

"Instead you had us spied upon," Hanne said. "You had a spy pretend to be Sissel's suitor!"

"Yes, I must apologize for that. What a bungling mess! It can all be explained. Must be explained!" Fjelstad said. "Call the Pinkertons in," he told his men.

Now there was an awkward moment as the Baron stood there while the Pinkertons were summoned.

"Is there a chair?" Fjelstad asked. "May we sit? It's been a long journey."

There was a bustle as the chairs in the corner were brought forward and several more from the dining room were brought in. Lucy popped her head in. She caught Sissel's eye and asked silently if she could bring coffee. Sissel shrugged yes. It seemed to be turning into a social event, after all.

"Let me introduce your brothers," Fjelstad said as the furniture was being arranged. "This is Pastor Jensen, and this is Björn: He's a Swede but he's a Nytteson so we like him, anyway."

Björn smiled at what was clearly a well-broken-in joke between them.

"Out the window, here, you'll see the big fellow Harald, and the twins, Arne and Johan. I'm honored to present them to you, for they are your brothers," Fjelstad said.

"I know well who my brothers are," Stieg said. "I have two and only two. Knut and Owen."

"I hope in time we can convince you that you have a much larger family," the Baron said.

The Baron and his men sat on the chairs that Owen and Knut had brought in. The Pinkertons came in from the porch, removing their hats. The Baron gestured for them to sit as well. Sissel saw their expressions were grave.

"My name is Alvin Phillips," the taller of the two began. "On behalf of the entire agency, I apologize to you. Things got completely out of hand up there in the hills. We're having a hard time piecing together what happened, so you all probably know more about it than we do."

"Your men kidnapped my sister and tried to kill us when we came for her," Hanne said simply.

"Well, it wasn't supposed to go like that," Phillips said. "We were hired in the spring of 1884, with the express goal of keeping the four of you safe. The Baron was concerned that there might be attacks on you due to the previous warrants out on Knut."

"Russell Peavy killed one of your own men when he tried to save Sissel," Stieg said. "His name was James."

Phillips ran a hand through his coarse black hair.

"You all met Peavy," he said. "He was an unpredictable man. We don't know why he killed James Collins."

Sissel heard this name—James Collins. That was James's real name. Whatever bitterness she had felt toward James seemed to disappear like smoke in a fog.

She was horrified to feel tears pricking at the corners of her eyes. She forced them to go away. She caught the minister looking at her and made her face go cold.

"It didn't need to happen," Phillips was saying. "Everything should have gone clean and easy. We never wanted any of you to be hurt. It was our godforsaken job to protect you."

"Did you have a man following us?" Owen asked suddenly. "On the cattle trail?"

"Yes, two men were watching the drive," Phillips said. "As I understand it, they took out a man who was planning to harm your wife."

"Mandry," Hanne said. "They shot Mandry."

"Your men started a stampede that nearly killed Hanne and me!" Owen said.

"Yes, they bungled everything!" the Baron exclaimed. "And I was told they were the very best."

"We are the best," the other Pinkerton said, low and angry. "But we can't do our job if we don't have all the facts. Like, say, magic powers. That's something we need to know about—"

"Todd!" Phillips said in a silencing tone. "It's no excuse. Lives have been lost. A big mess has been made, and we bear responsibility for it."

"They're going to clean everything up," the Baron said. "No one will ever trace any wrongdoing back to you all."

Stieg walked away from his place, rubbing his mouth.

Lucy came in with a silver tray. The scent of coffee accompanied her.

"Thought you might like some refreshments," she said. She set down the tray, which was loaded with a pot of coffee, some sugar in a bowl, a pitcher of cream, and some china cups.

"Lovely," the Baron said. "Americans and their coffee! So delightful. Thank you."

Lucy went away and came back with a wooden cutting board. On it was a loaf of bread, a wedge of cheese, and a carving knife. Knut went over and sawed off a piece of bread and then one of cheese. He returned to his place, happily chewing, while Lucy poured coffee for the Baron and his men.

The Baron poured a dollop of cream in his cup and stirred it with a spoon. He took a sip.

For a moment there was only silence. They heard Lucy go out the front door, bringing another tray to the men waiting outside. Their happy words of thanks came through the windows. They did seem to be a genial bunch, Sissel admitted to herself.

"You want us to believe that you've only been trying to protect us this whole time and everything you've done was for our own good?" Stieg said.

"Oh, I do!" the Baron said. "I desperately want that, Stieg. For it is the truth. I wanted you all to stay here, safe, in America. And then my plan was always to come, myself, and invite you all to come to Gamlehaugen. To me, we are family. I want to teach you all about the Nytte, the ancient texts; I want you to meet your brothers. They've come such a long way to meet you."

"They're not our brothers," Stieg said. "I said it before."

"We see it differently," Björn said suddenly. His English was just as crisp and clear as that of the Baron. "And I hope you will come to see it our way. You see, Stieg, I am a Storm-Rend, like you. There is only one other that we know of, in the whole world. He's out there—Johan Jäåsund, one of the twins." Björn gestured out the window, and Sissel saw Stieg's eyes flit outside.

"We share blood, we share history and we share a set of skills that hardly anyone in the world can comprehend," Björn said. Stieg began to speak, but Björn held his hand up. "But what makes us kin is that we truly care for one another and have chosen to live together, under the Baron's auspices. If only you will listen to the Baron Fjelstad and believe him, you could join our family, too."

Sissel looked around at her siblings. There was strain on Stieg's face and anxiety etched on Hanne's features.

"That's not all of it," Fjelstad said. "I want to be truthful with you." He looked over them all and sighed. "I would have come to meet you all sooner, I should have, but there is tremendous political unrest in Europe right now. We've learned of a secret alliance among Germany, Austria-Hungary, and Italy. There may come a time when the Nytteson are needed to protect our mother country.

"These are things that Rolf and I argue about often. He wants to keep the Nytte a secret, and study it, and use it to praise the Gods. But I feel that we may soon need to use our power. That is why I've gone to such lengths to try to keep you safe, and why I've come all this way to speak to you, now."

"This is all very difficult to believe," Stieg said.

"I don't believe it," Hanne said outright.

"I don't blame you," the Baron said. "You all must have expected me to be a terrible, ruthless man. But I'm not that way. I'm here to ask for your forgiveness and your help. But I know it will take time.

"I'll take my men and go to the town. We'll be staying in the hotel. All I ask is that you give me the chance to earn your trust."

"Impossible," Hanne said, rising. Sissel saw her sister's cheeks were flushed and her hands in fists. "Your men kidnapped my sister! They took her up into a cave and they shot at us. They would have killed me and my brothers!"

"That was all a misunderstanding."

"No," Sissel said, rising. "I saw the telegram. It said to secure the item at any cost. To forfeit other items."

"I never sent that! I would never say that. I live to protect you! I consider you all family to me. Will you please hear me out? Meet the others, they'll tell you," Fjelstad said. "Please! Join us for dinner tomorrow in town—"

"You should go," Knut said. His deep voice and the certainty in it surprised them all.

"No, no! You must allow us to convince you. It's so important!"

"You've said your piece. We listened. Now we're done," Owen said. "We are asking you to leave."

The tension in the room was thick and getting thicker.

The Baron rose to his feet now, and the minister and others joined him. Sissel noted the stance of the minister and the way he held his hands—ready for a fight. Was the intimidating Lutheran pastor actually a Berserker? The Baron's bodyguard?

"You are young," the Baron said. His face and neck were flushed. "You must listen to reason!"

"No!" Sissel said. Recklessly, she opened her Nytte and reached for the knife on the cutting board. Though the blade was steel, the handle was silver. She took hold of it and slashed the knife through the air toward the Baron.

Sissel brought it to a stop right in front of Fjelstad's face, the point poised directly in front of his left eye.

"Sissel!" Hanne shouted.

She saw the minister go tense as power flooded through him. Yes, a Berserker, Sissel thought.

"We are done listening to your slick lies," Sissel said. "You will leave, and take your men with you."

The Baron was frozen, his mouth open.

"You have no idea what I can do to you and your men," she said. "If you value your life, you will go."

Sissel pulled the knife back toward herself, catching it neatly in her hand.

Hey Nytte had closed her hearing, so she could not hear what, if anything, the Baron said.

Fjelstad rose, shaking his head. He looked disappointed and saddened by her actions. Sissel felt that even this, this posture of weariness, was a lie.

HER SIBLINGS WERE arguing when her hearing returned some minutes later. Stieg was pacing, and Owen sat in one of the chairs, his head cradled in his hands. Knut was seated near the cheese plate, polishing off the rest of the food.

Hanne stood at the window, looking out.

"But there is truth in what he told us," Stieg said. "Tensions are rising in Europe. I've been reading about it in the papers."

"Yes, but you can't really be entertaining the thought of going with him to Norway," Hanne said.

"What about the letter from Rolf? I'm convinced by it. And what I would give to see Rolf again!"

Sissel saw a true need in her brother's eyes. She realized suddenly how much her brother missed the company of other learned minds.

"I don't think we should trust him entirely, but the Baron's story does make sense," Stieg continued. "The Pinkertons could have misinterpreted his requests and . . . the events on the mountainside were not entirely their fault."

Hanne glared at Stieg. "They were my fault, were they?"

"I saw the telegram," Sissel said. Her siblings looked at her, realizing she could hear them again. "The Baron wanted me and was willing to sacrifice your lives."

"Oh, Sissel, why did you show him your power?" Hanne said, turning from the window. "I fear it will just make him want you all the more."

"He can't be trusted," Sissel said. "I know it."

"I've read and reread Rolf's letter," Stieg said. "It's his handwriting, and it sounds like all his other letters. I think it's genuine and he wants us to trust the Baron."

Sissel rose and took the letter from Stieg.

"He's not what I expected, that's for sure," Owen said. "He's got a lot of charm."

"Charming men can be evil, too," Hanne said.

"But it may be . . . ," Stieg said. "It might be that he is not evil, just overambitious. Overprotective and controlling. I remember how torn Rolf was about him—he so wanted to believe the Baron was a good man."

"You find yourself wanting the same thing now?" Sissel said.

"It would be such an opportunity if we could go to Gamlehaugen," Stieg said honestly. "To study the ancient texts themselves."

"You know, if he goes back to Norway now," Owen said. "Then maybe he can be trusted. I mean, if he leaves us alone, then that proves he has good intentions toward you all."

"Until we know the Baron's intentions, I'm going to keep watch," Owen said.

"That seems wise," Stieg said. "I can help."

"Me too," said Knut.

"I'm going to change clothes and help Lucy with lunch, if she'll let me," Hanne said. She went to move past Owen and he grabbed her hand. She leaned in and gave him a kiss on the cheek.

"May I take Rolf's letter and study it?" Sissel asked. "I feel there's something here."

No one objected. They broke up the meeting, retiring to change into work clothes and get on with the day.

CHAPTER FORTY-NINE

Lucy was rolling pie crusts when Hanne came into the kitchen. Hanne had changed out of the fancy dress into some good, simple everyday clothes of Mrs. Bennett's that Lucy had provided. The shirt was a light chambray and the skirt simple dun-colored wool.

"Miss Hemstad," she said, giving a little curtsy. "I take it the meeting went all right?"

"Stop for a moment, please," Hanne said. Lucy looked anxious. She grabbed her apron and started wringing her hands on it. "I don't want to break with what's proper, but could you just call me Hanne? I'm not a very fancy person, and I don't think I'll like being called Miss Hemstad very much."

A great grin broke over Lucy's face. Hanne smiled in return.

"Well, sure, I can call you Hanne!"

"And I'll call you Lucy."

Lucy nodded her head effusively.

"As for the meeting, it was . . . intense. A little confusing. But it appears that the Baron has left. We hope he's gone for good."

"All that worrying for nothing!" Lucy said. "I'm glad. You all had enough trouble, from what Owen tells me."

"What needs to be done?" Hanne said, looking around the kitchen. "I've no desire to sit around idle while you do all the work."

Lucy looked around the kitchen, too.

"All's good in here. How are you at pulling weeds?"

"I'm very good at pulling weeds," Hanne said.

THE KITCHEN GARDEN was triple the size of the one they'd had back in Carter, but not even half as productive. It had clearly been neglected during the long illness and demise of the Bennett family. Three rows of cabbages were growing well but a wide swath of potato plants looked withered and drooping. They should have been harvested already, Hanne thought. The potatoes would be good for nothing but seed.

A tangle of sugar snap peas grew over a brace. The peas looked old and tough. There were some toppled tomato plants, the fruits rotting on the ground. But Hanne saw a few green tomatoes on the plants, and so she decided to start there. She'd cut off the dead growth, brace the plants, and weed around them.

Hanne found some milkweed plants and dug them up, with the intention of replanting them elsewhere. She knew that butterflies laid their eggs in the milkweed plants, and they were considered good luck. She was digging around the roots of a tall plant when a terrible jagged image made her gasp.

Daisy. Her foot caught in a trap. Oh, the pain of it!

Hanne jumped up.

She looked around—there! The little wood off beyond the hilltop where the Bennetts were buried. That's where Daisy was with her leg in a trap!

Hanne walked, then ran, racing up the hill, past the graves, and into the woods. It was mostly pines, and the needles made no sound underfoot.

She felt sharp, blood-red pain coming from the dog's foot.

Where was she?

Hanne saw a flash of white and black through the woods and moved to it without thought.

There she was! Daisy was caught in a metal trap, and the foot was badly injured. The dog was whimpering and made a howl of pain as Hanne tried to open the trap, but she was licking Hanne's face, too, licking her face and hands, so thankful for being found.

Suddenly Hanne felt two thick arms wrap around her rib cage and crush her, lifting her off the ground and into the air.

Hanne fought, kicked, thrashed, but she could not break free.

"Release the dog," said a voice.

A man stepped out from behind a tree and pressed a lever on the trap. The jaws opened wide and Daisy scrambled free.

Hanne fought the man who held her, but it was like being held by a granite statue—she could not budge him.

Within a few moments, with Daisy now safe and free, her Berserker energy ebbed away and reason returned. She realized it was the Baron's Oar-Breaker who held her, and the Baron himself appeared from behind a tree.

"Hanne," said the Baron, "please forgive me. You must forgive me. We only want to talk."

"Owen!" Hanne shouted. "I'm in the woods. Help!"

The Oar-Breaker, Harald, put his beefy hand over her mouth, and she bit it.

"Ow!" he yelled. He gripped her tighter. He crushed her to him, and the air went out of her lungs. Stars swarmed up in her vision.

"Don't bite me again," Harald said in her ear; then he let up a bit so she could breathe.

The Baron came closer.

"Please don't make me gag you," the Baron said. "I just want to talk to you. I only want to speak, truly."

Hanne closed her eyes and tried to stop her shaking breath. She cast a prayer up to the Gods. *Help me, Freya,* she prayed silently. *Be with me. Be with me.*

"I will listen," she said. "Set me down."

Harald set her on her feet, but kept his arms around her.

"Your sister, Sissel," the Baron said. "She's young and impetuous. I didn't know what she might do if I tried to speak to you all again. Please forgive me for this terrible trick."

Hanne glared at the Baron. She was in no position to argue, so she said nothing.

"Hanne, everything I said is true, but there's more. I didn't want to burden you all with it, all at once, but I need your help.

"There is growing unrest under King Oscar. Many feel that the enforced union with Sweden is not to be borne. They seek to replace him with Norwegian nobility. They seek a way to kindle the pride of the Norwegian people. We feel it is time to take back our country."

"You are going to overthrow the crown?" Hanne asked. "Is that your plan?"

"We have the backing of many important men in parliament and the church and among the landowners," the Baron said. In the dark forest, his eyes gleamed bright.

"And you all are in support of this?" she asked the Baron's men.

"I believe King Oscar will fail us if it comes to war," Björn said evenly. "And I believe war is coming."

"The Church is overrun with libertines," Pastor Jensen added darkly. "And we cannot rely on the King. There is only one man I trust to lead Norway back to strength." He nodded toward the Baron.

"Oh," Hanne said. The Baron looked proud. "So the Nytteson will serve as your private army and hand you the crown."

"No one would dare fight against us, not after they've seen what we can do," one of the twins said.

"Imagine the awe of the people when they find out about the powers of the Nytteson," the Baron said.

"It will restore national pride," Björn added.

"All will witness the power of the Old Gods and we, united with the Church, will lead Europe to peace and prosperity," the Baron said.

"You men believe this is the will of the Gods?" Hanne asked, looking around. The twins and Pastor Jensen nodded, but Björn did not quite meet her eye.

"And you, sir," she addressed the Baron. "You believe this is the will of the Gods?"

"Yes!" the Baron said. "With my whole heart I believe it is meant to be."

Hanne composed her face to look like she was considering these arguments. What she thought of was how to get away and how to warn her family.

"Then I owe it to my siblings to bring them this information," she said. "My brother, Stieg, he especially would want to know. Let me go. I will convince them to meet with you."

Hanne avoided looking at the Baron's face. She tried to keep her face solemn and neutral. She was not a good liar; she knew this.

When Hanne brought her eyes up, she found the Baron looking at her with a disappointed, sad half smile on his face.

"No," he said. He sighed. "You don't believe me, and so . . . I can't let you go. Pastor Jensen, bring the jacket."

"Wait," Hanne said. She began to struggle. Harald's arms clamped down hard.

The minister came forward with a leather garment that was scarcely recognizable as a jacket at all. It had two long, long sleeves that tapered to points and ended with a buckle, and it didn't seem to open in the front but in the back.

"This won't be easy, lads," the Baron said. "Do your best," and then the Nytteson converged upon her.

Hanne lashed out. She writhed, trying to bite, but there were too many hands on her. She kicked, got one in the head. Elbowed another in the eye.

The men cursed but they swarmed her, and Hanne found her arms shoved into the sleeves. The sleeves were then strapped across her chest, and she was flipped onto her front, facedown in the pine needles. They buckled the sleeves around her back.

She kicked and screamed, and one of them forced a gag into her mouth and fastened it around her head.

The Berserker raged but could not free herself.

CHAPTER FIFTY

Stieg was right, it was Rolf's handwriting.

The wording sounded like him, too. A bit formal, perhaps, but Sissel was certain Rolf was the author.

Nevertheless, there was something wrong. Sissel wished she had Rolf's other letters on hand, but they were back in Carter, at the hotel, along with all their belongings.

Sissel stood and brought the letter to the window. She looked out at the fat clouds drifting past in the sky and let her mind drift like the clouds. Their shadows floated across the empty pasturelands of the Double B Ranch.

Hanne and Owen and Knut would all be happy here, but Sissel was worried about Stieg. He wanted to trust the Baron because he wanted so badly to study at Gamlehaugen with Rolf.

She couldn't let that happen.

If only she could find proof of the Baron's true nature . . .

She studied the letter again. Rolf's hand had been shaky when he'd penned it. Possibly a sign of duress. Several pen strokes had been too light—Rolf had had to go over them twice.

Sissel peered more closely at the paper. *I have made the decision to unburden my soul to the Baron, for I have come to believe that he truly has your best interests at heart . . .* There, on the second *I* in the sentence—it was darker than the rest of the letters.

She scanned the page, looking for other anomalies.

The *W* from *Wolf Creek* had clearly been gone over twice. Were the letters significant? Was he spelling out a message? There were only four darkened letters, and they spelled *I-W-T-X*. There was no significant word with those letters in English or Norwegian. She tried to think of the old Norse words he'd taught them, but she couldn't remember anything with those letters.

Sissel observed that not the entire *T* had been gone over, only the right arm and the stem.

When she peered at the *I* more closely, she saw it had two small marks at the bottom, as if the tall, straight letter had two feet coming down.

A chill ran down the back of her neck.

"Runes," she breathed aloud.

They were runes on the letter. Rolf had sent them a message!

The *W* was *Ehwaz*, but upside down. Right side up, she knew it was the symbol of a horse, and meant transportation and also communication, trust. Inverted this way, it was a perversion of what the rune stood for—so it conveyed an impasse, lies, betrayal.

Sissel found she was pacing.

The *I* was not an *I*, but an inverted *Algiz*—hidden danger, warning.

The half *T* was really *Laguz* facing the wrong way—perversity, madness.

When she studied the *X*, she did not immediately recognize the figure.

Sissel racked her memory. She cast her mind back to long winter afternoons by the fire that she and her siblings had spent with Rolf, learning the runes and all their different meanings. She remembered his patience, and how he'd drawn them for her on the hearth, his fingertip cutting a path in the dust from the charcoal.

Was it *Nauthiz*? Need or distress?

No.

She realized what it was, and she rushed for the door. It was *Gebo*.

Gift. Marriage. Wife.

"Stieg!" Sissel shouted. She went racing down the stairs just as Owen came rushing out of the back hallway. He held Daisy in his arms and Sissel saw one of the dog's legs had been bandaged.

"Have you seen Hanne?" he asked.

"No," Sissel said. "But I need to speak to all of you right away!"

"Hanne!" Owen shouted up the stairs. His voice was tinged with desperation. "Are you up there?"

Stieg came from the study.

"What's wrong?"

"Hanne's missing," Owen said. He went out onto the front porch. "Hanne!"

Sissel clutched at Stieg's arm. "Stieg, there are runes in the letter. Rolf was communicating with us."

"What?" Stieg said. Sissel showed him the *Algiz*. It was the easiest to identify.

Knut and Lucy came out from the back hallway.

"What's going on?" Lucy said.

"*Algiz*. Inverted . . . ," Stieg said. He dropped his arm. "We're in danger. Terrible danger."

Owen slipped inside, backward. He shut the door. His face was grim.

"Pinkertons riding up out front," Owen said. "A lot of them."

DAISY WOULDN'T STOP BARKING.

"Daisy, enough!" Owen said.

The dog fell back to pacing. Sissel saw she was still limping, favoring her bandaged paw.

Ten Pinkertons on horseback were approaching the house, each carrying a rifle, but that wasn't the big concern—they had three of the vile Gatling guns at the rear of the procession. Each was mounted on a special cart, with a driver at the front and drawn by two horses.

Last came the Baron's rented carriages.

"Where's Hanne?" Owen said. "Who saw her last?"

They were gathered around the windows in the front parlor, looking through the gaps between the heavy drapes.

"She was out in the garden, weeding the garden," Lucy said.

"They must have her," Stieg said. Owen looked to him. "I think they tricked her with Daisy. Otherwise, she'd be here. She'd feel the threat."

"Oh God, if they hurt her—" Owen said. Sissel noticed he was holding his rifle so tightly his knuckles were white.

"We will have to fight to get her back," Stieg said. He drew away from the window to look from Sissel to Owen. Stieg looked pale and afraid. "How many guns do we have?"

"Plenty," Lucy said. "They're stored in the attic. Knut, would you help me get them down?"

Lucy took Knut by the arm and led him away.

"Lucy, would you take Daisy?" Owen said. "Lock her in the pantry until it's over."

"Come, girl," Lucy said.

Daisy gave Owen a look Sissel would have swore said, *Don't make me leave you.*

"Go!" Owen commanded, and she slunk off, limping, behind Lucy and Knut.

The sound of horses nearing grew closer. Sissel looked out the window. Two of the wagons with the Gatling guns had broken out of the procession and were circling around to flank the house.

The rest of the group stopped about a hundred yards away.

"They're surrounding us," Sissel said.

"Can you control those guns?" Stieg said.

"Only when they're firing," Sissel said. "The bullet casings are brass and I can move them. But I can't push the gunmetal or the steel."

A knock on the door made Stieg, Owen, and Sissel all jump.

They looked to one another—then turned to the door.

CHAPTER FIFTY-ONE

They opened the door to find Björn there. He was trying to look calm, but perspiration had made his hair wet at the temples. He held his hands clasped together. Sissel suspected it was because they were shaking.

Owen surged forward and grabbed Björn by the front of the shirt.

"Give her back!" he shouted, then cursed the Baron and Björn and all the Nytteson.

"What can the Baron mean by this?" Stieg demanded.

"He wants to t-talk, that's all!" Björn stammered. "Please! He's a good man!"

Sissel pushed through the men.

"I know what he wants," Sissel said. "I'll go talk to him."

"What?" Stieg cried. "No!"

But Sissel was already past them all, striding off the porch and toward the Baron's retinue.

"Sissel!" shouted Stieg.

"I know what he wants," Sissel shouted back. "Stay there and stay safe. I will get Hanne."

Sissel heard Björn promise to return her to them safely and then hurry after her. She did not turn to give her brother a last look, but set her eyes on the Baron across the field and marched to him.

Sissel drew in a big breath of fresh air. Her skirts brushed the grasses as she walked. She felt strangely peaceful, for she knew she was doing the right thing. She would save the lives of her sister and her brothers, and Owen and Lucy as well. It was so easy, actually, now that she knew why he was here.

She walked past the Gatling gun they had aimed at the front of the house, and past the Pinkertons, who felt called by decency to tip their hats to her, as if they hadn't come there to possibly slaughter her and her siblings. Björn trailed behind her, almost scurrying to match her confident stride.

The two grand carriages stood next to each other, and the Baron and his men waited in a space made between them.

The Baron plastered a smile onto his face as she approached.

"I cannot tell you how glad I am to see you!"

"Where is Hanne?"

The Baron gestured to the black carriage.

"She's safe inside. I am truly ashamed of how drastic these measures are, but I will stop at nothing to help mother Norway. I must ask you, beg you, to come with me to Gamlehaugen as my guest to see Rolf and to learn of what we are trying to accomplish."

Sissel studied him as he lied to her.

"I ask only that you give me one month!" he said, smiling. "One month of your time. I will show you the splendors of my estate there, and you will attend classes that will help you hone your gift.

Rolf will teach you himself! Imagine his joy at being reunited with you—"

"I know what you want," Sissel said. "I know why you are here."

"I have told you why we are here," he said.

"No," Sissel said. "You have said many things. Some of them are true. Some are lies. I can't tell them apart, but I know what it is you really want."

"And what's that?"

"You want a Nyttesdotter bride."

The Baron's eyes widened. For a moment, the composure slid off his face and she saw him startled. Startled by the truth of it.

"You came here to try to get me or my sister to marry you. You want a Nyttesdotter bride. You carry the Nytte in your blood, but you don't have a gift yourself. And that's what you want most of all— Nytteson children."

The Baron sputtered. He cast a quick glance at his men. Sissel saw shock flash over Björn's face as he gauged the Baron's reaction. Björn hadn't known.

"Is it true?" Björn asked. "Do you have the Nytte in your family, sir?"

"Yes. Yes . . . Come," Fjelstad said to Sissel. "Let's go for a walk."

"No," Sissel said. "There's no need. Set my sister free, leave my siblings alone forever, and I will marry you."

Sissel watched his face as he studied her in return. The Baron was in his late thirties by her estimate. She noticed as his eyes flicked over her youthful figure. She swallowed, trying to quell the disgust she felt.

"You will?" Fjelstad said.

"Sir, with all due respect," Björn said. He was clearly uncomfortable. "She's only sixteen."

"Of my own free will," Sissel said, keeping her eyes locked with the Baron's. He smiled.

"Why . . . Miss Hemstad! Sissel! You have no idea what it will mean for the people of Norway—"

Sissel held up her hand to stop him.

"My only care is the safety of my family," she said.

"I would need you to demonstrate your Nytte to the people, from time to time," Fjelstad said, bargaining now plainly.

Sissel nodded her head. "As long as my family is safe."

"And of course, if anything happens to me, like, say, a knife in the eye, or a knife in the throat, or a knife in back, the Pinkertons will come back in force. But, assuming that you and I get along well, I will leave your brothers and sister here, in this valley, in peace forever. They may come visit us, as they please. Stieg would love the library!"

Björn stepped up to the Baron. He kept his voice low, but Sissel could hear anger in it.

"Baron Fjelstad, I must beg you to reconsider. We need all the Hemstads with us if we are to defeat the king—"

"But, Björn, think about it. We may not need force, not when we have a queen such as Sissel to offer the people. And the Nytteson heirs to the throne."

Sissel looked at the other Nytteson. They seemed unsettled with the change in plans. Harald's brows were knit.

"We need them all, sir," Björn said.

"And what better way to get them to come to our side than to join together with their family marriage?" the Baron said. "They will come visit Sissel. They will see what we are planning, the righteousness of our claim. They will be convinced."

"Yes," Sissel said. "My brother Stieg wants to come to Gamlehaugen and study with Rolf."

"He can come with us!" Fjelstad said.

"But right now, you must tell the Pinkertons to stand down," Sissel said. "Release my sister, and I will take her to the house and tell my brothers the news."

"See how smart my bride is!" the Baron crowed. "A natural peacemaker. But . . . I cannot let you go back with your sister to the house. She will be too protective. She will attack. You know it's true.

"No, you and I will depart, and once we are on the train to Chicago, then I will have the men let her go."

"I won't go with you until I see her freed," Sissel said.

The minister stepped up to the Baron and whispered something in his ear.

The Baron smiled. "Say, that's a good idea. Pastor Jensen says he can marry us right now, right here."

Sissel was surprised but she saw the logic in it—if they were truly married, then her siblings would be forced to accept it, and the Baron would have to uphold his end of the bargain.

"Very well," she said.

The Baron took Sissel's hand and clutched it. His hand was sticky and clammy. She looked at her husband-to-be, his thinning blond hair slicked back with pomade. The expression in his keen gray-blue eyes made her think of a hungry dog eyeing a chop.

A raven landed in the grass a few yards off. Sissel saw it cocking its head at them, studying them with its black, beady eye.

"Look," one of the twins said in a voice hushed with awe. "Odin, he comes to see the wedding!"

She turned to face Pastor Jensen, and he began to speak. "Do you, Sven Erikson Fjelstad, take this woman, Sissel, daughter of Amund, now named Hemstad, to be your lawfully wedded wife until death do you part?"

"I do," the Baron said.

"And, Sissel Amundsdotter Hemstad, do you take this man, Sven Erikson Fjelstad, to be your lawfully wedded husband for as long as you both shall live?"

"I do," she said, but as brave as she tried to make her voice, it came out only a whisper, filled with dread.

"Louder, please, so the Gods can hear," Pastor Jensen said.

"I do," Sissel said.

"Then in the sight of the Old Gods, and in the name of Jesus Christ, I pronounce you man and wife."

A cheer went up from the Baron's Nytteson. Björn was the first to congratulate her. He shook her hand gently, a compassionate expression on his face.

"Congratulations," he said. "I believe you will find—"

One of the twins interrupted, spinning her away. "Sister!" he said, and he kissed her on the cheek.

"Hurrah!" Harald cried. "We have our queen!"

"Hail to the queen!" they began to shout. The raven took flight and settled on the seat of the Gatling gun's cart.

Sissel turned to the Baron. "Enough," she said. "Let my sister go and let's be gone."

"You're right, my dear. Of course." The Baron turned to Björn and Harald. "You two, bring Hanne out of the carriage. And give her the good news. She's free to go, and Sissel and I are man and wife."

CHAPTER FIFTY-TWO

The air in the carriage was stifling, and Hanne had to inhale slowly, through her nose, because the gag made it difficult to breathe.

She was sweating heavily in the leather straitjacket. To not be able to use her arms, to be incapacitated and helpless was terrifying. It was only through constant prayer that she had been able to quell waves of rising panic.

After an indeterminable stretch of time, she felt two men board the carriage. The vehicle listed severely to the side, so she knew one of them was the Oar-Breaker before she even opened her eyes.

"I bring good news, Sister," said Björn. He sat on a large steamer trunk that occupied a good deal of space on the other side of the carriage. "We are truly family now. For your sister, Sissel, has married the Baron. And you are to be set free."

Hanne tried to speak, but the gag prevented it. She wanted to call him a liar, to spit in his face.

"It's true. Pastor Jensen has married them. You are safe, so don't fight us!"

Harald sat behind her on the fine leather seat of the carriage. He jerked and pulled at the buckles on her jacket. Then Björn took hold of the front of the straitjacket and began to peel it off her. As soon as she regained the use of her arms, she writhed and scrambled to shuck the terrible garment. She reached up and tore off the gag from her mouth.

"You lie!" Hanne spat. "I don't believe you!"

"Come," Björn said. "You'll see. You're safe, and we are leaving."

He opened the door to the carriage, and the sunlight blinded her.

It was hard to walk; her legs had cramped up during the long wait. But she stumbled to the door and was helped down by one of the twins.

"Back off, men. Give her space," the Baron said.

There was Sissel. Hanne rushed forward into her arms. Sissel looked frightened and so small, surrounded by all the men.

"Are you all right?" Hanne said.

"What did they do to you?" Sissel cried. She was touching Hanne's face. Hanne knew there must be an impression from the gag left on her cheeks. "Did they hurt you?"

"Say it's not true," Hanne said. "You've not traded your life for mine."

"Not her life, Sister," the Baron said. "She has made me a very happy and proud man by marrying me."

"Never," Hanne said.

"Yes," the Baron said. "Pastor Jensen has done the honors."

Sissel spoke, just barely audible. "They have three Gatling guns, Hanne. We were surrounded. It was the only way."

Hanne looked from Sissel to the Baron, who was smiling proudly, to the faces of the Nytteson around him.

"No," Hanne said. "No!"

She reached for the Baron, to throttle him, but she was lifted off her feet by a gust of wind. The twin, the Storm-Rend, was using his Nytte on her. The wind whisked at her clothes. She spun in the whirlwind head over heels and was lofted in the air, thrown back toward the house. Her bun came undone and her long hair whipped everywhere.

As she approached the house, the wind became more gentle and she was deposited on the porch, almost tenderly. Her long blond tresses fell gently to her shoulders.

"Hanne! What happened?" Stieg cried. He was on the porch, as was Owen. Owen knelt and swept her into his arms.

"Are you all right?" he said.

Hanne brushed her hands down over her skirt, smoothing it.

"Get ready to fight," she said.

CHAPTER FIFTY-THREE

"Set her down!" Sissel screamed.

One twin was laughing as the other blew Hanne across the sky. He had his lips pursed and was blowing out little puffs. His eyes were locked on Hanne.

"Set her down gently, Johan," Björn said. It was hard to make out the house clearly from where they stood, but it seemed to Sissel that Johan had, indeed, put Hanne down lightly.

"Come," Fjelstad said. "We'll go, and the Pinkertons will follow."

"You won't hurt my family?" Sissel pleaded.

She had felt powerful, but that was gone. Now they were all at the Baron's mercy.

"Baron, look!" one of them said.

There were streams of something rising from the ground around the house. Whipping tendrils of dust and dirt, Sissel realized. The rising dust began to diffuse into the air, then to whirl around the house, cloaking it in shifting sheets.

"It's Stieg," Johan said. "He's doing that!

"Prepare for attack!" Fjelstad shouted. He grabbed Sissel and forced her toward the carriage.

"Don't hurt them!" she screamed. "You promised!"

"Get her in the carriage," Fjelstad commanded, pushing her into the arms of Harald, the Oar-Breaker.

"In the trunk, sir?" he asked.

Sissel looked to the Baron.

"It's for your safety, my dear," he said, and planted a kiss on her forehead.

Harald lifted Sissel and slung her over his shoulder.

"Put her in the trunk? What do you mean?" she heard Björn protest.

Gunfire rang out. Three shots in rapid succession.

"Don't let them use the Gatling guns!" Sissel screamed.

Sissel opened her mind to her Nytte as Harald carried her into the carriage.

What could she use to save her family?

It was so dark inside Sissel couldn't see, but she kept reaching out with her senses. The Gatling guns, three of them, made her sick to touch them. What else was there to use?

AS SOON AS the dust was flying, Hanne crept forward toward the nearest Gatling gun.

Owen, Lucy, and Knut were positioned through the house with shotguns and plenty of ammunition. Stieg was sitting in the side parlor, fully concentrating on holding his whirling dust storm around the house.

Hanne tried to keep low, thankful that her dun-colored skirts were a similar color to the dirt in the air. Her Nytte had not fully taken hold of her yet, but she knew that as soon as the first bullet fired, it would consume her.

"Gods to me, Gods to me," she repeated in her head. "For Rolf, for Sissel, for Stieg, for Knut, for Owen, for Daisy, for me."

"I can't see anything," she heard a man say.

"It's in my mouth," another said, cussing.

"Hold your fire," came the command from farther away.

"But something's moving," yelled a man quite close by. "There's someone out there!"

Then the first bullet fired and the Nytte fully possessed her.

It was not the clean white presence of the Gods she had felt before. There was too much anger in her, perhaps. This was the bloodlust-filled Berserker, and Hanne welcomed her.

She could feel the two men at the gun. They were ten paces to her left, and their hearts were beating like rabbits'.

Hanne got low to the ground and moved in fast.

"Look!" one of them said. She had the heel of her palm up his nose before he could say another word. He fell as she turned to the other. She took hold of his head and smashed it into the crank of the terrible gun. The handle gauged a hole in his skull. She pulled his head off the crank and the dead man's body slid to the ground.

A call came to open fire. From the back of the house, she heard rapid gunfire from the second of these monstrous machines. Then at the front of the house, from the third, but before she could deal with the other guns, she had to disable this one.

Hanne put her hands on the long, round cylinder of the giant gun and tried to pry it off. It was attached too strongly to the cart. All she could do was rotate the head in the setting, the way it was meant to be moved.

She let out a growl of frustration.

"Open fire!" a voice said, coming closer. "Henry! Jake! Fire it up!"

She tore the chain of bullets away from the head of the gun. That much she could do. There was a whole crate of the bullets linked together this way. Hanne lifted the crate.

"Goddamn it! Open fire," the man shouted. He came out of the swirling dust storm looking irritated.

Hanne lifted the crate of bullets and threw it down on him.

He fell, bleeding heavily from a gash on his head. She leaped onto him to finish him, but he was already dead. Then a hand grabbed Hanne's shoulder and spun her around.

It was the minister.

"Hello, pretty," he said. He drove his fist into her face.

INSIDE THE CARRIAGE, Harald kept Sissel pinned to his chest with one arm while he opened a large steamer trunk. A vibration blasted out at her from the trunk like light from a lighthouse.

Lead was shrill and toxic. Sissel clasped her hands over her ears. It was flowing into her head and poisoning her.

"I'm sorry, Sister," Harald said. "But you'll be safe in here."

The trunk was upholstered, lavishly, in velvet, but lined, underneath, in lead.

He deposited her into it.

"Don't!" she cried. "Please!"

She brought her arms up to stop the lid, but he batted them away and closed it.

HANNE REELED BACK from the minister's punch. She'd never been hit so hard before. No one had ever been fast enough to touch her before.

She leaped at him, and he met her in the air. He pulled her to him, trying to choke her. She got her knee up between them and used it to push him away. As he fell, she lashed out and scratched him down the face.

"Only a girl would do that," the minister growled. He dived forward, hooking his arm around her neck, dragging her to the ground. He was on top of her for one moment; then Hanne head-butted him.

He fell off to the side. Hanne tried to chop him in the throat, but he was already rolling out of reach.

"You're fast," he said. "But there's lots I could teach you."

Hanne kept low to the ground, looking for a weapon.

Bullets pounded the stone foundation of the house from the back and the side. She needed to see to those guns, not fight this old man.

He swung, and she ducked the punch. There, she sighted a shotgun one of the dead Pinkertons had dropped. She backed toward it.

"No, you don't," the minister said. He jumped forward, and Hanne reached behind her to grab it when a terrible pain tore through her consciousness. Stieg! He'd been shot.

The minister struck her across the temple with his fist. The blow spun her body around. Hanne fell to her knees. She dived for the rifle, but he snatched the gun away.

She had to go. She could feel the agony her brother was in. She had to help him.

Hanne got to her feet and tried to run.

The minister grabbed her by the skirt and threw her to the ground.

She tried to mule-kick him, but he caught her leg, and there was a sickening *crack!* that reverberated through Hanne's body. She scrambled, but she couldn't get to her feet.

The leg wouldn't hold her weight.

She crawled in the dirt toward Stieg. The dirt settled around her like snow. Her brother had let the dust storm fall.

"The first lesson you have to learn," the minister said to her, bending close to her ear, "is not to love."

SISSEL SNAPPED HER mind shut to her Nytte. She reeled from the lead, swallowing bile.

Sissel got her feet up against the lid and pushed with all her might. It didn't budge.

There was light coming into the trunk, a small amount of it. Sissel saw there were some airholes drilled into the trunk and covered with thin slats.

She pressed her ear to one of the holes and heard the sound of the Gatling guns firing.

She closed her eyes and tried to think. The Baron had made this trunk for her in Norway, she realized.

He had always meant to take her home, willing or not.

This was the kind of a man he was.

She pounded her hands against the lid and screamed.

HANNE TRIED TO CRAWL, but each time she raised her chest off the ground, the minister stepped on her, pushing her back into the dirt. Her leg dragged behind her.

"The first female Berserker in a hundred years," he said, leaning close and speaking loud so she could hear. "And I beat you without breaking a sweat. Though you did draw blood, I'll give you that."

Hanne turned and looked at him over her shoulder. His dark robes were covered in dirt, and his face bled where she had scratched him.

New pain came coursing through her—Owen. Her beloved. His shoulder.

Owen was bleeding, falling down, sliding onto the floor.

The minister grabbed Hanne by the hair and yanked her head back. He put his foot under her shoulder and flipped her onto her back. The pain from her leg made the world go dark for a moment.

"Are you broken enough?" the minister said. "Can I take you to the Baron? Or do I have to kill you like I did your old friend Rolf Tjossem?"

SISSEL BRACED HER feet against the lid and heaved again, pushing with all her might, screaming and shouting.

"Odin!" she called in desperation. "Help me! Freya!"

Sissel pressed her hands to her eyes. She remembered what Hanne had said about Wolf Creek—opening her heart to the Gods. Surrendering to them. The divine possession.

"I am lost," she said. "I surrender. I surrender, you sick bastards!" Her voice was hoarse and scared.

The gunfire droned on outside, a steady terror.

Sissel lay back, hopeless, and opened her Nytte. This time to die.

Let the Baron come and open his trunk and find her dead inside it.

The lead washed over her, blinding her, filling her eyes and ears and mouth, encasing her, embalming her. She felt her pulse slow; her heart fought to throb against the deadening lead.

"*Heill, Æsir*, help me, Gods," she whispered, and she let go.

Booming into her came a source of light.

Sissel was flooded with power.

She gazed in amazement at her hands. They glowed, as if light ran in her veins.

She placed them lightly on the lid of the trunk, thought of freedom, and the trunk exploded outward.

Sissel thought of standing and found her body being drawn through the air. She watched the pieces of the trunk moving in slow motion as she passed them.

She pushed open the door of the carriage. It flew away from her hand.

The Baron stood just steps away with a few of his men. The Pinkertons, she saw, were attacking the house.

She could hear nothing, but Sissel felt bullets streaming toward the house, from one gun in the front of the house, and one gun on the side. The bullets were cased in brass, and she found it easy to locate each one midflight. It made her smile.

First she reached to the gun on the side and located the stream of bullets. She pushed, hard, and the bullets became jammed into the barrels. The gun exploded.

Men died, and a tremendous, rich grief possessed her for a fraction of a second and then was gone. The lives of men were precious beyond measure—and yet so easily spent. The Gods communicated this truth to her. They were with her. Were her. Had always been.

The Baron turned and saw her standing at the door of the carriage.

He held his hand up to shield himself from the light radiating from her.

He shouted to his men, but she could not hear.

Sissel looked at him, her head cocked to the side. She could see what he was made of—he was made of layers, which were transparent and the Gods helped her read them all at once. His musculature and his veins and organs, but also his desires, his emotions, the anatomy of his soul.

He was a desperate man, filled with envy.

His men were coming at her. She wanted to look at them. To see what kind of men they were, but before she dealt with them, she needed to stop the rest of the bullets, and the men attacking her family.

She reached for the bullets streaming from the remaining Gatling gun and redirected them, sending them to targets. She shot out one knee of each Pinkerton. The bullets went just where she placed them. Dead center of the kneecap. The Pinkertons fell, one by one.

The men fell in agony and the gun stopped firing.

Sissel saw, close to the house, that the black-robed minister was standing over her sister. He had hurt her badly. He held a shotgun in his hand and was turning, now, to look and see why the last gun had stopped firing.

Using her Nytte, Sissel plucked the rifle from his hands and brained him with the wooden stock. He fell. Again, she felt the pulse of grief for his life, then she was at peace.

She turned back to the Nytteson converging on her. They were squinting at her, trying to shield their eyes from her light.

"My brothers," she said. "Do not fight me."

She reached for the brass and steel of their buttons and zippers and belt buckles and hoisted them into the air. She left them up there, suspended.

The Baron fell to his knees in supplication.

"Please," he said. "I only ever wanted . . . I only ever wanted to give glory to the Gods."

A raven landed on Sissel's shoulder.

She looked it in the eye, and then they both turned their heads to the Baron at the same time.

"The Gods say this raven brings their justice," Sissel told the Baron.

The raven tucked its wings and flew at the Baron, transforming into an arrowhead of black obsidian. It buried itself in his heart and flew out the other side of him.

The Baron collapsed backward, mouth round, empty eyes staring up at the sky.

Sissel set her Nytteson brethren back down to the ground gently, and released them.

THE SHOOTING HAD stopped and the minister had fallen, felled with a great crack to the head. Hanne hadn't seen and didn't care how he had died. She crawled to the house. Toward her family.

With every move, her Nytte ebbed away until she was herself again. Pain swept up on her in waves as her powers retreated.

"Stieg," she called. "Owen!" Her voice was a rasp.

Knut burst out of the house.

"Hanne!" he cried. He ran forward and lifted her. She nearly fainted with the searing agony of her leg.

The parlor was shot to pieces. Splintered furniture and shattered glass were everywhere. Owen sat against the door to the back hallway. He had a kitchen towel pressed against his shoulder.

"Owen," she said.

"I'm all right," he said. "Go to your brother." He pointed with his good hand.

Knut brought her through the parlor to the sitting room beyond. Stieg was propped in the corner, bleeding from the neck. Lucy had a piece of fabric of some kind pressed on his wound, but the blood was seeping out. There was blood on her hands and all over Stieg's clothing and the floor.

Knut set Hanne down beside him.

"Stieg," she wept.

Her brother lifted a hand and let it fall. He was trying to speak, but making no sound.

SISSEL WISHED HERSELF inside the house. She took a step and was there instantly, passing through the bullet-chipped stone walls and into the sitting room.

Hanne wept beside their brother Stieg, whose lifeblood was draining through a wound at his neck. Knut was there, too, standing, kneading his large hands and not knowing what to do. And the woman Lucy, who radiated her own goodness.

Sissel was dazzled by the sight of her siblings, how beautiful they were, but she also saw the blood flowing out of her brother's neck, and the veins and organs slowing down.

The raven came and landed on the ledge of the broken window, perching lightly on a shard of broken glass. He spoke to her with one glance—the Gods couldn't help, but she was welcome to try.

Sissel closed her eyes and focused on Stieg. She reached for the iron in her brother's blood.

* * *

LIGHT FILLED THE ROOM, so bright Hanne thought for a moment she was dying, but it was fading now, and she could make out the glowing figure of her sister, Sissel.

Sissel was standing over Stieg, her hands extended toward him.

As Hanne watched, the glow left Sissel's body, starting with her feet and head and then shrinking, until only her hands were illuminated.

Then the glow was gone, snuffed out, and Sissel stood there in the room. As soon as the light left her hands, her sister's body began to shake with effort.

"*Heill, Odin*," Hanne said. "Thank you. Thank you."

SISSEL KNEW THE Gods were leaving her. She felt their glorious all-knowing strength abating, draining away.

The raven departed, winging off into the darkening evening.

Sissel focused on working her Nytte on her brother's blood. She pulled the molecules back toward his heart. Then she shifted focus and tried to make the ones at the wound coagulate.

She knew Hanne and Knut were talking to her, trying to reach her, but she stayed centered on the blood. The little bits of iron, they were so small, she had to concentrate with everything she had.

There was a pop in her ears. Sissel felt a trickle of blood flow down her neck.

Finally, she felt Stieg's wound had closed enough. Only clear plasma leaked from the terrible wound.

Stieg opened his eyes and looked at her.

"Sister," he said, but she could not hear him. There was no sound at all.

Owen had then come into the room. He hugged Hanne. Knut embraced Sissel. Daisy went licking at faces and hands. They all needed to touch one another and express their love. Sissel didn't want to tell them about her ears. She waited until she had hugged each of them and then she edged out of the room.

The colors of the outside were so bright she had to shade her eyes. The tawny gold of the prairie grass, the green of the trees, the silver-gray of the trunks of the pines—it was all so beautiful she could have wept, but she walked on.

She reached up and smeared away the blood on her neck, two trickles from the rupture of her eardrums.

There, near the rented carriages, the Nytteson were gathered around the body of the Baron. She felt an unexpected tenderness for Björn, Harald, and the twins, Arne and Johan. Arne saw her coming and nudged the others. She didn't know how they would greet her—they had a right to be furious or vengeful, but she didn't think they would be. The twins were quick to anger. She knew this about them because she'd seen inside them, if only for an instant. They were young and impetuous, but they were decent men. Björn and Harald she knew and loved, somehow.

Sissel walked to them calmly, bearing herself as straight and tall as she could.

Björn turned to her. Tears were running down his face.

His mouth shaped the words, *I'm sorry, I'm sorry.*

He fell to his knees, and the other three did the same. Harald held the hem of her dress. *Forgive me, Sister,* he said.

Sissel put her hand on the great Oar-Breaker's head.

It always felt strange to speak when she could not hear her own voice, but she did so. "Come inside. You and my siblings must make peace, right now. We all must swear to never harm one another."

They were nodding, agreeing, rising to their feet, when Sissel caught sight of one of the injured Pinkertons struggling away from the house.

"And we must call a doctor for the Pinkertons," she added.

CHAPTER FIFTY-FOUR

Sissel sat on the porch shrouded in silence, dressed in black. She had taken to wearing a widow's blacks in the two months since the terrible shoot-out.

In the days after the fight, Björn had told her that she was entitled to the Baron's estate. Counting himself and Sissel there had been five witnesses to the marriage—he felt certain it would hold up in the Norwegian courts. But she didn't want anything of the Baron's, not his wealth, his title, or his lands. All she wanted was to wear black.

It suited her mood.

Her hearing was gone and would never return. Two doctors had come to examine her. The eardrums had not simply ruptured but had been lacerated. *Shredded* was the word one of the doctors used.

The Nytte was still there. Sissel could sense metals through vibrations in her head and chest, but she could no longer hear them singing. Anyway, she didn't want to work with her Nytte. She had only opened her mind to it once, to see if it was there.

She just wanted to sit on the porch and feel sorry for herself.

Sissel knew she was behaving poorly. A truly good girl would be more accepting, she thought. Good girls were meek and hid their suffering, instead of sitting out in plain sight and brooding every day.

But it was difficult not to brood, because no one could talk her out of it—they couldn't talk to her at all. Her brothers and sister tried to communicate with her by writing, but writing slowed everything down on a slate. It was dreadful. She preferred not to communicate at all.

Instead, Sissel sat on the porch and watched as Owen and Knut brought the ranch to life around her, as Stieg wrote long letters to Björn in Norway, and as Hanne planned her wedding.

The wedding was to take place back in Carter. Hanne had all sorts of lovely correspondence to show Sissel. She had asked the Oswalds to decorate the church. Reverend Neville would officiate. The Royal would host the reception.

At Hanne's insistence, Sissel would read the lengthy dispatches Mr. Collier sent to Hanne and try to hide the grief she felt in her heart at the memory of the Royal, and the longing she had for it.

McKray had visited several times. On his last trip, he brought a doctor from his father's mines in Colorado. Apparently so many men went deaf working in the mines that McKray Sr. had hired on a hearing specialist on staff. The specialist had examined her ears on the front porch. He had shaken his head. McKray had grown red in the face, asking the man question after question that Sissel couldn't hear. The man just kept shaking his head.

After that, Sissel asked McKray to go.

McKray wrote that he loved her. Scribbled it on the slate.

She told him it didn't matter. That she wouldn't be his wife, not when they couldn't communicate properly. She told him she was going to be an old maid, and haunt the front porch of the Double B. She knew her voice was rising, knew she was shouting, because she felt the vibration of feet running as Hanne and Lucy came out onto the porch to see what was wrong. McKray tried to take her hands, but she tore them from his grip.

"If you care for me at all, you will leave and not return!" she shouted.

He left in a huff.

Maybe it was for him she wore black, she thought. Sitting on the porch, she found herself thinking of him often. She liked to remember how his hand had felt in hers when they danced together at the Ladies' Aid Society dance. It made her feel better to cry over McKray than it did about her lost hearing. She worried if she cried about her deafness, she might fall into a hole unescapably deep.

Things could have been much worse, Stieg had written to her one afternoon. *We might all be in jail now*, he'd said.

It was true, they'd been lucky.

The Hemstads had not called the sheriff after the Pinkertons' attack. Neither side had wanted the law involved.

A few days later, after his men had been bandaged up by the town's doctor and put on a train for Chicago, William Pinkerton came to apologize to the Hemstads and asked them not to press charges. He sat in the same room that the Baron had sat in, pleading his case. They'd had to sit on chairs from the kitchen, because all the fine furniture had been shot to pieces.

Pinkerton offered them a settlement of five thousand dollars not to speak to the press about the incident. Stieg accepted. After they all signed the contract, William Pinkerton assured the Hemstads they'd never hear from him or the agency again.

The Nytteson had left six weeks ago, after spending several weeks helping repair some of the damage caused by the shoot-out and getting to know their new brethren. It had been difficult to convince her siblings, at the beginning, that Björn, Harald and the twins were worth trusting, but Sissel told them truthfully that she'd seen into the young men's hearts. They were good men who had been led astray. She reminded her siblings that they had all seen how charismatic the Baron was—a man with that kind of charm and sincere passion could incite sensible men to immoral acts. Sissel spoke at length, and she won out. It helped that she couldn't hear her siblings protest.

In those first days after the fight, once the wariness wore off, there had been a lot of talk. Björn and the others showed a clear need to talk about the Baron, and how he had hid so many parts of his terrible plan from them. Fjelstad had told them each different things about their mission in America. They learned that only Harald had understood the true purpose of the terrible lead-lined trunk. The rest had been told it contained photography equipment. Harald apologized to Sissel, Stieg scratching his words on the slate as quickly as he could. Sissel told Harald she'd already forgiven him, and he gathered her up in his enormous arms for a hug.

The saddest information that came out as they untangled the lies the Baron had fed them was that Rolf was not sick but dead. When Hanne revealed what Pastor Jensen had said—that he had killed Rolf—there were tears all around. Owen brought up a bottle of old Scotch whiskey from the basement, and they all toasted Rolf Tjossem.

After this, they all seemed truly bonded as friends. Every dinner turned into a long storytelling session. Arne and Johan told stories of all the mischief they'd made for their mother before they came to work for the Baron and had everyone laughing. Stieg tried to write it down for Sissel, but it was hard to follow. When Björn talked about his life another evening, Sissel saw tears reflected in the eyes of more than one person around the table. Again, the written description didn't convey the emotion of his tale.

The night after that, Hanne began to tell the tale of why they had left their home in Øystese. Stieg joined in the narration, still trying to write down what was being said. Sissel told Stieg to stop writing. She'd just watch as her siblings told the story. Watched as Owen joined in, telling them about how he came to join up with the Hemstads. Watched as Björn, Arne, Johan, and Harald exclaimed about the story and asked questions and shook their heads in wonder.

It was around that time Sissel had asked the dressmaker in Bullhook Bottoms to make her a black dress.

Brooding about being left out, forever left out, Sissel noticed something no one else seemed to—there was something between Stieg and Björn. She saw her brother light up when Björn came into the room, and saw the way Björn smiled for Stieg. Björn would say something that was undoubtedly clever, then flash his eyes to Stieg's face to measure his response. There was love between them, more than a brotherly love. They kept it hidden, but she could see it plainly.

Sissel noted how Stieg steadied himself when Björn let them all know that he had to return to Gamlehaugen to oversee the dissolution of the Baron's estate. Björn had much to do, because the Baron had made provisions in his will for Björn to inherit the contents of the library, along with an enormous sum of money to ensure the continued protection of the Nytteson.

Stieg and Björn kept up a steady correspondence in the weeks since he and the others had returned to Norway.

Just this morning, Stieg told her, by writing on her slate, that Björn had invited him to come to Norway to help him organize the library. Perhaps even to oversee the training and instruction of the next generation of Nytteson.

"I like Björn very much," Sissel said, trying to keep her voice low. "I feel you two are perfect companions." This was as close to saying it outright as she could, but she wanted him to know that she at last understood something important about the way his heart worked, and that he had her blessing.

Stieg held her hand but would not meet her eye. After a long moment he squeezed her hand to acknowledge what she'd said and went off by himself in the direction of town, perhaps to mail a letter.

That had been several hours ago, before lunch. Now dust was coming up the long drive to the ranch house. Sissel thought that perhaps Stieg had gotten someone to give him a ride home.

But it wasn't any wagon she recognized. It was a handsome black carriage, drawn by a team of matched chestnut Morgans.

As it got closer she felt footsteps approaching from within the house. It was Lucy. She stood next to Sissel, wiping her hands on her apron. Hanne came around from the back of the house, where she'd been working in the garden. Since it was October now, she was pulling the last cabbages and carrots, and preparing the beds for the winter.

Hanne looked to Sissel and gestured to the carriage, asking if her sister knew anything about it.

"I haven't a clue," Sissel said.

The rig drew right up to the house.

The driver stepped down and tilted his cap to them.

Sissel's eyes flitted over to Hanne—if there was any danger within, her sister would move fast.

The driver opened the door and out came Isaiah McKray.

Sissel felt her heart leap—she was so happy to see him—and she felt angry at the same time.

He held up a hand to stop the barrage of protests he knew to expect. Then he reached back inside and offered his hand to a lady within.

An elegant lady in a slate-gray traveling dress stepped down. Sissel was struck by the sudden fear that he'd found another girl to marry and had brought this lady here to introduce them. But that couldn't be. McKray wasn't cruel, and this lady, Sissel now saw, was considerably older than either of them.

Her hair was dark brown and her skin was a lighter brown, a beautiful copper color. She had a white, crocheted wrap draped gracefully around her shoulders and held a little book in her hands. She pleasantly shook Hanne's hand, and Lucy's, introducing herself with words that were probably lovely and Sissel could not hear.

Sissel just stood there with her hands on her hips glaring at McKray—what kind of nonsense was he up to?

"If this is another doctor," Sissel said to him, "I'll ask you to please turn back. I have no interest in being prodded and fussed over again!"

The woman handed McKray her shawl and the little book and began to move her hands. She moved them in a very definite pattern, not like a dance, but practical and exact.

Sissel watched the woman, turned to gauge Hanne's response, and McKray's. The woman put her hand out and tapped Sissel on the hand.

Her mouth very clearly shaped the word, *Watch!*

The woman moved her hands around for another moment and then took the book back from McKray. She opened the front cover and took out a little note.

Then she handed the note and the book to Sissel.

Hello, Sissel. Here is what I just said to you: My name is Rosa Early. I have come from the California School for the Deaf to teach you and your family sign language. This will enable you to communicate fully with them. Mr. McKray sent for me and has paid for me to stay here for the length of time it will take to fully instruct you and your family.

Sissel took a step back and collapsed into her rocking chair. Tears flooded her vision.

McKray came to kneel in front of her. She realized he'd shaved off his beard. He took her hands and held them to his chest. He was saying something, but she didn't need to know the words to feel the sentiment.

She laid her hand on his smooth cheek. His skin was pale where the beard had been. McKray's hazel eyes were pleading with her, and she knew this offer was a lifeline. He wanted her to join him in the world again.

"All right," she said.

A grin spread across his face. She saw him say, "*Really?*"

"I'll try."

CHAPTER FIFTY-FIVE

They had overdone it. Hanne knew it was true. She wished that she could somehow take back some of the extravagance, but it was too late for that. The guests were entering the church at this moment. They would be gasping and exclaiming over the beautiful decorations the Oswalds had installed right at this very moment.

Since it was October and there were no flowers to be had, they'd used streamers made of a gauzy white crepe de chine and ribbons, yards and yards of grosgrain ribbons in three complementary shades of yellow and gold.

Downstairs, in the restaurant of the Royal Hotel, there were waiters polishing the silverware, checking the place settings. It was going to be a big party. They had invited more than fifty people for the reception—nearly everyone they knew in town, plus Lucy and Mr. Witri and Owen's old cowboy friend Mr. Hoakes, who had brought his new bride.

The day before, Hanne had counted ten cases of champagne being delivered, along with a crate of oranges, and too many baskets of produce to count. Collier had presided over the arrangements like a quartermaster. He'd hired on extra staff; after the luncheon was served, the waiters were going to clear away the tables for dancing! It couldn't be a proper Norwegian wedding without dancing.

Hanne turned to Sissel, who was helping her dress.

"Is this all too fancy?" she asked Sissel in sign language. "Too much?"

Sissel smiled. "No," she said. Miss Early insisted that Sissel speak and sign at the same time, just like her siblings. "You deserve a beautiful wedding, my sister."

Hanne peered into the mirror. She smoothed her hands down the skirt of her *bunad*.

McKray had sent the Hemstads' beloved trunk by wagon right after the shoot-out. In it was the traditional Norwegian costume that Hanne had sewn, embroidered, and beaded for herself over the course of many long winters when she was a girl. First, there were the voluminous white petticoats, embroidered at the bottom. The skirts that went over them were black, with rows of red and gold braid at the bottom. A white shirt with full sleeves and a crisp, high neck was to be worn under a tight-fitting vest. It was the vest that Hanne had poured her attentions into, month after month by the fireside back in Norway. Two panels patterned with diamonds ran up the sides, framing a V-shaped panel right in front, which was worked with starflowers and square Norse crosses in gleaming white and gold floss. The finishing garment was a crisp white apron edged with more embroidery.

This splendid getup, back home in Norway, would be topped with the bridal crown, a tall, majestic antique that belonged to the town's church. The bride's hair was always worn loose, brushed out and gleaming, with the crown set atop her head. Here in America, there was no such crown to be found.

Hanne wouldn't let herself be sad about that—she had every other thing she wished—most important a loving and devoted fiancé waiting at the church.

There was even a fiddler waiting to play her to the church. A nervous young man dressed in his Sunday best could be heard tuning his instrument outside the window right now. The only thing she worried about was that her head might look too plain.

"Should I put my hair up?" she asked Sissel in sign language. "Is it too strange down this way?"

Hanne's mouth felt dry. Her heart was pounding.

"Wait," Sissel said. She slipped out the door, going to her own room next door and came back holding a crown!

She handed it to Hanne. It was ingeniously made—not of metal, but of gold metallic lace.

"I made it with Alice," Sissel said.

Hanne turned the delicate crown in her hands. They had built the crown onto a circle of copper wire, standing the lace up on its edge and reinforcing it with wire. It was nothing like the tall crowns from home, but it was lovely and special. A crown made just for her.

"Sissel, thank you. It's beautiful."

Sissel took the crown from Hanne and placed it carefully on Hanne's head, securing it with several hair pins. Sissel arranged Hanne's thick blond hair so that it fell in waves over her shoulders and down her back.

"You're perfect. Now it's time to go," Sissel said.

Hanne clutched at her sister's hands. Suddenly she felt shy and nervous. Why had she insisted on wearing her *bunad*? Alice had offered to make her a lovely American dress.

"It's too much," Hanne said. "The dress. Oh, I wish I had an American dress!"

She was horrified to find tears pricking the corners of her eyes.

"Breathe, Sister. Take a breath," Sissel said. She smiled at Hanne.

Hanne was struck by how efficient and grown-up Sissel looked. She had matured years in these past few months.

"Do you think the Gods would want to see you wed in some silly, lacy American dress?" Sissel joked. "No, today you are in your best Norwegian clothes, telling everyone who sees you where you are from and who you are."

Sissel gently turned Hanne and directed her to look in the mirror hanging above the washbasin.

"Look how radiant and beautiful you are, Hanne Amundsdotter 'Hemstad.' You make us all proud today. And . . ." Here Sissel's eyes began to match Hanne's with glimmering unspent tears. She whispered the rest: "If our mother and father could see you, they would be bursting with pride."

KNUT AND STIEG were waiting downstairs.

"Oh, Hanne! Look at you!" Knut cried. He and Stieg both wore matching charcoal-colored suits that Alice and her mother had sewn.

Stieg seemed to have no words. He nodded and gulped, fighting tears himself.

After today, things would change. Stieg was going to Norway in a few weeks to join Björn. The two young men had plans to found a small boarding school for Nytteson with the money that the Baron had left to Björn.

Hanne and Owen had invited Knut to live with them at the ranch, and he accepted their offer. He had plans to farm some of the former pasturelands, and Owen was happy for him to do so. Owen wasn't going to raise cattle, but work on training cow dogs, as he'd always wanted to do.

As for Sissel, Hanne wasn't sure what her sister wanted to do, but judging by the long visits that Isaiah McKray had been making to the ranch, she felt confident Sissel would be married within the year.

Hanne liked to watch them walking together. Sissel seemed completely relaxed and herself around him. McKray's sign language was the best of all of them. He could make Sissel laugh, and the sound of her giggling was a golden, glittering gift to her siblings. Hanne imagined she and McKray would live here, in Carter. Close enough to visit, but far enough away for Sissel to have as big a life as she wanted.

Stieg took Hanne's right arm, and Knut took her left. Sissel walked ahead with the fiddler, who set a lively pace. He was a good Norwegian boy and knew all the traditional wedding songs—the Telemark bridal march and "The Miller Boy's Wedding March" and "Spring Dance Song."

THE SCANT PEOPLE in town who hadn't been invited to the wedding— some prospectors who still lingered in town, and several families passing through—came into the street to clap and cheer for them as they went by. Hanne watched Sissel marching ahead, laughing and clapping out of time with music she couldn't hear.

A raven was perched on the eaves of the church building. Hanne saw it and stopped for a moment. Stieg saw it as well. "*Heill, Odin*," he said quietly. "The All-Father comes to see you wed, Sister."

Hanne murmured, "*Heill, Odin*," and bowed her head.

There was a small gaggle of Stieg's former students waiting outside the church. They cried out joyfully, seeing the procession, and the raven took wing.

In what felt like a very short time, the procession reached the church.

The fiddler began to play the wedding march, and slowly walked up the stairs and into the church. The children rushed around him to get inside.

Hanne felt her body trembling. Stieg patted her hand on his arm reassuringly. They all stepped into the small foyer.

Inside, the church was beautifully decorated with the looping garlands of fabric and ribbon and filled with people—their friends—standing, craning their necks to see her. There were the Oswalds and there was Mr. Collier, seated, improbably, next to Lucy, who was grinning her lopsided smile.

Sissel took one last look at her sister over her shoulder. She gave Hanne a wink, then straightened her shoulders and walked down the aisle, with no trace of a limp. Isaiah McKray was standing in the first row, waiting for her.

Everyone rose as Hanne and her brothers stepped into view. Between the three of them—Stieg, Hanne, and Knut—they were too wide to fit down the aisle. There was a laugh as they sought to adjust themselves; Hanne was glad for the laugh because it broke her own nervousness for a moment. Stieg and Knut ended up stepping just behind her so that Hanne stood alone at the top of the aisle.

She looked up and saw Owen Bennett waiting at the end of the aisle for her, standing in a fine black suit, next to Reverend Neville. His face was turned to her with such hope and delight, she thought her heart might burst with the joy of it.

ACKNOWLEDGMENTS

I have many people to thank, but before I move into gratitude, I first want to mention that I've taken liberties with the geography and history in this book regarding the small town of Carter, MT. I'd like to speak directly to the residents of Carter, MT. By the US Census, I see there were 58 of you as of 2010. I've made your town a bit bigger, relocated it somewhat and played with its timeline. I hope you'll forgive me for these liberties. To make it up to you, email me proof of residency and I will send you a copy of *Ransacker* for free. Now, on to the festivities!

I am indebted to my agent, Susanna Einstein, for her endless confidence in me and in this book. I'll never forget the way she stood with me as I wrote draft after draft of this darling novel. Thank you, Susanna.

The support and enthusiasm of my manager, Eddie Gamarra, was also invaluable during the writing process. I'm so excited to be storming Hollywood with you, Eddie. I am terrifically fortunate to be working with you and everyone at Gotham Group.

I have a secret weapon and her name is Kristin Bair. Thank you, Kristin, for your tireless reading and your excellent notes. Both Sissel and I would have been truly lost without you.

I have another secret weapon (every author/mom needs at *least* two) and it's my brother, Sam. Brothers, your friendship and advocacy sustain me and make my work possible. And while I'm on the topic of making my work possible, I'm forever thankful to my parents, Geraldine and Kit Laybourne, for their unfaltering and exuberant support.

I've had a wonderful run with Feiwel & Friends and this seems like the perfect time to express my gratitude.

Jean Feiwel, thank you for believing me and taking so many great risks with me.

Liz Szabla, I'm truly grateful for your vision and for helping me keep the faith. I've loved getting to work so closely with you.

Holly West, many, many thanks for the care and attention you gave me and my first books.

Alison Verost, thanks for your advocacy and for the many cocktails we've shared on the road!

Molly Ellis, you wonderful lady, you've been such a joy to work with all these years. Thank you.

Greg Ruth, thank you for another perfect illustration. When I see Hanne and Sissel in my mind, I see them as you've drawn them.

Liz Dresner, thanks so much for your work designing the cover and the interior.

Anne Heausler, you've made each of my books better in a thousand ways. My gratitude always!

Morgan Rath, it's been such a pleasure to get to know you. Many thanks for all your work to get the word out about *Berserker* and *Ransacker*.

And my endless gratitude to everyone else at Macmillan who helped to produce, market, and promote this book and all my others. You guys love books and it shows!

Thank you to my rock-star assistant, Melissa Jolly, at AuthorRX and to Caitlin O'Brient Bauer and the team at Royal Digital Studios for my awesome new website. I also want to thank Sandy Hodgman at Hodgman Literary and Susan Graham at Einstein Literary Management for their fine work on my behalf. I'm also thankful to Lauren Festa, who was instrumental in promoting *Berserker* and ran a truly fierce street team. She even bought a Viking helmet!

I love belonging to the YA community and I want to take a moment to speak to my author friends—thank you for your companionship and your counsel. This wouldn't be nearly as much fun without you. Anna Banks, Leigh Bardugo, Libba Bray, Jessica Brody, Ava Delaira, Adam Gidwitz, Mallory Kass, David Levithan, Marie Lu, Alex London, Jennifer Mathieu, Gretchen McNeil, Danielle Paige, Mary Pearson, Mitali Perkins, William Ritter, Leila Sales, Tamara Ireland Stone, R.L. Stine, Greg Cope White, Kiersten White, and Jeff Zentner. You all inspire me to be a better writer and I love hearing your stories.

I'm thankful to Ed Manning and David Conway for writing with me once a week for, oh, the last three years. Thanks also to those who've joined our group along the way-Donna Miele, Stacey Hascoe, Larry Grossenbacher, Seth Gable, and Katherine Gates.

Ellie and Rex, I'm so proud of you guys I can't even say.

Greg, you're every romantic lead I've ever written rolled into one and I couldn't have written any one of them without your love and support. Thank you.

Lastly, I want to thank all the readers, librarians, teachers and booksellers who have connected with me over the years. Your enthusiasm in getting the word out about my books means so much to me. I am honored you choose to spend your time with me in the pages of my books.